A DETECTIVE CHIEF INSPEC

WE PLAY WITH DEATH

NEW YORK TIMES #1 BESTSELLER **TONY LEE** WRITING AS

JACK GATLAND

Hooded Man MEDIA
INSPIRATION • PRODUCTION • PUBLICATION

Published by Hooded Man Media.
Cover photo by Paul Thomas Gooney

First Edition: August 2025

PRAISE FOR JACK GATLAND

'Fast-paced and action packed, Jack Gatland's thrillers always deliver a punch.'

'This is one of those books that will keep you up past your bedtime, as each chapter lures you into reading just one more.'

'This book was excellent! A great plot which kept you guessing until the end.'

'Couldn't put it down, fast paced with twists and turns.'

'The story was captivating, good plot, twists you never saw and really likeable characters. Can't wait for the next one!'

'Totally addictive. Thoroughly recommend.'

'Moves at a fast pace and carries you along with it.'

'Just couldn't put this book down, from the first page to the last one it kept you wondering what would happen next.'

Also by Jack Gatland

DI DECLAN WALSH BOOKS

LETTER FROM THE DEAD

MURDER OF ANGELS

HUNTER HUNTED

WHISPER FOR THE REAPER

TO HUNT A MAGPIE

A RITUAL FOR THE DYING

KILLING THE MUSIC

A DINNER TO DIE FOR

BEHIND THE WIRE

HEAVY IS THE CROWN

STALKING THE RIPPER

A QUIVER OF SORROWS

MURDER BY MISTLETOE

BENEATH THE BODIES

KILL YOUR DARLINGS

KISSING A KILLER

PRETEND TO BE DEAD

HARVEST FOR THE REAPER

CROOKED WAS HIS CANE

A POCKET FULL OF POSIES

CHEATING MY DESTINY

STAND AND DELIVER

WE PLAY WITH DEATH

HIS DEAD MAN'S HAND

TOM MARLOWE BOOKS

SLEEPING SOLDIERS

TARGET LOCKED

COVERT ACTION

COUNTER ATTACK

STEALTH STRIKE

BROAD SWORD

ROGUE SIGNAL

SNIPER ALLEY

SHADOW THREAT

SENTRY POINT

ELLIE RECKLESS BOOKS

PAINT THE DEAD

STEAL THE GOLD

HUNT THE PREY

FIND THE LADY

BURN THE DEBT

TAKE THE KING

LIAM HARPER BOOKS

FINAL STRIKE

BLOOD RIDGE

TRACK SHIFT

CARLYLE & SILVER BOOKS

SILVER AND THE SUNDAY CYPHER

DAMIAN LUCAS BOOKS

THE LIONHEART CURSE

STANDALONE BOOKS

THE BOARDROOM

As Tony Lee

STANDALONE

TWELVE TASKS

THE PLAYING CARD WAR

KNAVE OF SPADES

QUEEN OF BLADES

CHARMING

LAST PRINCE STANDING

For Mum, who inspired me to write.

For Tracy, who inspires me to write.

And to Dennis Carr, taken too soon.

CONTENTS

PROLOGUE

IT DIDN'T MATTER WHAT THE ROYAL MARINES THOUGHT OF Sean Acker; what mattered was what Sean thought of the Marines – as he hugged the edge of the alleyway, weapon in his hand, waiting for his target to approach.

All his life, Sean had been a staunch advocate of the Marines. He'd even joined when he was sixteen years old but, after six weeks in basic training, he'd been dismissed. There was talk about attitude issues, or the fact that he'd had a stand-up row with his commanding officer on more than one occasion... that he didn't have the right mental attitude to be a Royal Marine.

But Sean knew the truth. He was simply half an inch too short. That's what it said on the papers.

Sean was angry that he couldn't fulfil his dreams of being a Royal Marine for the rest of his life. He'd always wanted to be a career officer, but other than managing to stretch himself by an inch, there was nothing Sean could do.

He could cope with a physical disability like his height stopping him from being a Royal Marine; the bullshit about his attitude was something completely different. He knew Erik at work had been saying that. Erik was a prick, and would also learn very quickly, very soon, about the level of skill that the Royal Marines had taught Sean Acker. He may have only been with them for six weeks but the training he had accepted from them lasted his life.

He was still very much a Royal Marine, even if the Royal Marines didn't think he was.

He attended the rugby games in full attire. He had attended weddings in uniform, although not his original one – that'd been taken when he was told to hand it back before the end of training – although it was incredibly easy to buy a replacement off the internet these days, and even his Facebook profile – indeed, all of his social media profiles – had the Royal Marines logo. Anything connected to them was instantly repeated, processed and then pasted onto his media followings. He was a member and group admin of several Royal Marine online groups and forums, and arranged meetups regularly with ex-Royal Marines, although he wasn't surprised to see they observed him with mild amusement.

He knew it wasn't because he was kicked out early. No, they respected him too much for that; they told him this when he bought them all rounds of drinks. He knew it was because he wasn't able to serve, and he'd never shot a gun in combat.

Well, maybe he hadn't, but it didn't mean he hadn't been in combat.

He'd been fighting for his life every year since University.

Sean Acker had gone to college immediately after being discharged. He'd ended up working on a business degree at Oxford, his "service" helping him through interviews and a nameless scholarship – likely the Royal Marines – helping financially. However, he ended up dropping out in his second year because of stress, not the bullshit "issues with lecturers" that had been claimed after he left, the university trying to cover their own arses. After deciding what to do with his life, he took, and excelled in, a variety of different roles, always leaving when he realised he wasn't being appreciated, before working in finance. It was a "get rich quick" idea as everyone in the City seemed to do well, but twenty years on from Oxford, Sean hadn't really progressed as far as he thought he would in that time – probably again because of his height. Finance seemed to be filled with good-looking tall men who based your work levels on your appearance. Sean never gave a shit about his appearance; he was a ginger – that was all that mattered to his friends down at the gym, so why should it matter to his employers? The friends at the gym also respected him for being an ex-Royal Marine, always asking him to repeat the stories to new arrivals. He'd thought his employers, knowing he was an ex-Royal Marine, would give him respect at work, but he was wrong.

Those City wankers didn't care.

They didn't give him *anything*.

I'll teach them about respect, he thought to himself as he shifted the pistol in his hand.

He'd been given information that Daryl would come this way tonight. Daryl didn't realise that Sean was after him, which was his mistake. He should have seen this coming, there was a lot of payback involved here, and that arrogant little prick was about to gain a big surprise.

Sean cricked his neck as he considered what he was doing right now, looking down at the weapon in his hand. To some it was nothing more than a childish game – something that had been played every year for twenty years now. But to Sean it was his life. Out of the nineteen previous occurrences, he'd won *fourteen* of them. He would have said it was his Royal Marine training that had helped him, but the fact of the matter was that Sean Acker was good at his job, and his job right now was to take out Daryl Collins.

THE GAME HAD BEEN CREATED WHILE THEY WERE AT OXFORD. Gary and Alex had been the people who had the original idea – taking some college game they'd found online involving water pistols and assassins and adapting it for their group. The plan was very simple. There were twelve players at any time, and every month the specially invited players would go to *war*.

Each one was given a playing card. Over the years they'd stayed the same, but a couple of years ago after an incident, they'd changed up the cards, taking new identities, as if this would wash away the pain.

Sean had kept *his* card, though. All his time playing, he'd been the King of Spades. They bloody well wanted him to take a new one, the Queen of Hearts in the next match – which was Gary's idea as a joke. Gary didn't think it was as funny after Sean had punched him in the face, a moment of personal delight for Sean that had enabled him to keep his original identity.

Sean wasn't a queen. Ex-Royal Marines weren't queens.

Sean was definitely a king.

The players would meet in a bar where two brand-new packs of cards would have the relevant playing cards removed, shuffled together, then dealt onto a table face down. Back in the first ten years of the game these would then be placed in envelopes, posted second-class, and arriving a couple of days later at each player's house. Now, however, once a year these were placed by the game masters into a randomiser that would spit out emails after three days had passed, giving two random cards to each player.

These cards, these *players* were your target – your job in the game was to take them out, and then once you had done so, you would take the two cards that *they* had – or more, depending on whether they'd killed other players before you killed them. The more cards you had, the more targets you had, but you also had more chance to remove the two people who had your card in their pack.

There had been games over the last two decades when, by the time they reached the last three or four players, each assassin had their own cards, which made it a bit useless. But there were other rules that could be called up at this point – "wild card assassins" thrown back in to make the game interesting, given a player and an offer.

Kill the player, gain their place.

Sean had never needed this. All Sean cared about was that he took out the people on his target list.

There were complicated ways to do that as well. You were only allowed three water-based weapons, and rain wasn't one of them. Most players had a standard pistol-sized water pistol – often in the shape of a "Glock" water pistol – for main encounters, as well as a super soaker-sized rifle for when they knew multiple people would be going for them, and a small personal item, often of their own choice or design, as a last chance weapon to escape a hit if they had nothing else. Maybe it was a tiny water pistol, the kind you'd gain from a Christmas cracker. Rachel used a water bomb, which was stupid, because if it burst while in her possession she effectively blew herself up, the dumb bitch. Or in Sean's case, it was a doctored 50ml syringe without the needle attached, strapped to the inside of his watch, which, if he found himself attacked, could squirt out like Spider-Man's web, catching the assassin unaware. These all had to be registered at the start of the game. There were no changes allowed.

The rules were simple as well. Originally, there had only been one; anything went – but eventually it was amended to "except if it was at a place of work or learning, and your home". This meant you couldn't wander into someone's job and shoot them in the face in the middle of a boardroom meeting. This rule had turned up after Justin Kelly had decided to go and collect his bounty on Diane Williams a decade earlier by walking into her place of work and trying to shoot her with a water pistol, forgetting that she *worked in a bank.*

After he'd been held down and secured, the police had come, the bank had been closed down and he'd been eventually released with the caution of "don't be a dopey bastard". Meanwhile Diane had been fired. Which was unfair, everyone could see it wasn't her fault – but she got her own back by taking Justin out, shooting him between the legs in the game the year after, when he was on a date, and then letting the poor girl who'd agreed to dinner with him know she'd "just seen him piss himself in the back corridor", before he could get back to the table.

Because *dinners* were still fair game.

Also, there had been several occasions where a player had

claimed he or she hadn't been struck by the water and therefore *wasn't* dead. Bloody Belinda and Chris almost killed an entire year's game playing because of this, so after that, all kills had to be filmed. Often it was someone holding a phone as they shot at you, but most preferred to film with the "off" hand.

Sean preferred a bodycam. After all, if it was good enough for the Royal Marines, it was good enough for him. He'd even convinced Dirk he needed one – "See the death in HD 1080 glory".

And now, with his bodycam primed and his fake plastic water pistol Glock in his hand – but not just any old water pistol, his was a specially created carbon-fibre mould around a basic setup to make it look as close to the real thing as possible, including weight – Sean Acker waited for his target. He knew it was going to be Daryl or Belinda. They were the only two who would have travelled this route, and luckily for Sean, he had both of their cards. Whoever turned up first would be taken out, although he really hoped it was Daryl, the cocky prick.

There were footsteps walking down the alley now, more a slightly overgrown pathway beside a series of buildings that led to the car park and garages behind. Somewhere to the side was Stationers' Hall, which was where swanky City people did whatever you did in Livery Companies – Sean had never been asked to join one; he was too cool.

In the distance, he could hear the bells of St Paul's. There was a part of his mind that knew that if he'd been noticed by the police, he'd have a lot of explaining to do – just like Justin had. But bar situations out of his control, no one had ever caught Sean Acker unaware. He'd been trained by the Royal Marines, after all – even if it had only been for six weeks.

He'd also worked with Royal Marine trainers personally and on his own time, and at his own cost. He was as good and as trained as any of the best, no matter what they thought of his height, or as some people claimed, his attitude.

Someone was coming.

He gripped his pistol, realising his palm was wet. It wasn't nerves or sweat – he was absolutely sure of that. It had to be a leak in the plastic.

Bollocks. There'd better be enough water inside.

Usually he could tell, the plastic on a normal toy gun being see-through, but the casing was solid black, so it didn't show in darkness. It'd be good enough though, and he'd check it once he'd killed whoever was coming round the corner, before taking their cards.

He hoped they'd have Gary's card. He wanted that prick more than anything. Another rule you had in the game was you couldn't just go off books and kill whoever you wanted. That had happened a few times when they first started playing, and eighteen years ago, a long, drawn-out game of strategy had turned into a massacre on a Sunday afternoon in a park, with everybody bringing their biggest weapons.

It'd been *awesome*. But Gary, always bloody Gary, wasn't happy and complained.

The steps were heavy. It was a man. Daryl, perhaps? Maybe not. There was also a chance it wasn't a player, at which point, Sean would simply say he was waiting to prank his nephew – point out the fact his "gun" had an obvious orange end to the barrel and allow whoever it was to be on their way.

When the figure sounded no more than ten feet away, and knowing the range was enough for his water pistol, Sean spun around the corner, facing his nemesis.

It wasn't Belinda. It wasn't Daryl – but it was a player.

'Oh, for God's sake,' Sean muttered, lowering the gun. If he'd thought about it clearly, he would have realised there was every chance that *he* could have been the target here – that they might have had his playing card and had worked out he'd be waiting here for his own targets. If they'd gone for him, and he'd killed them first, he could have claimed their cards in self-defence, but Sean Acker was too angry to think of that.

'Didn't you listen to the rules?' he snapped. 'When approaching another player you're supposed to—'

But he didn't get a chance to consider this, as before he could continue his tirade his opponent raised their own pistol. And this, strangely, wasn't colourful, and didn't have an orange tip –instead there seemed to be some kind of suppressor, a *silencer* at the end. It was black and heavy-looking and, as it fired with a strangely echoing *phut* and the bullet ripped through the tactical webbing on Sean's chest, penetrating deep into his chest, his eyes widened in realisation that this *wasn't* a water pistol.

He sagged to his knees, unable to speak as the blood filled his mouth, spitting it out as he stared in confusion. His opponent – or rather, his *killer* – placed their gun away, pulling out a second, similar-looking weapon. This, however, was a more familiar looking blue water pistol.

The hand came up; the gun directly aimed at Sean's face.

He managed one gurgled word.

'Why?'

But he didn't get an answer. As the water pistol squirted him, soaking his hair and face, he'd already slumped to the side, the life now out of his eyes.

The killer placed the water pistol away, leaning down,

and with their latex-gloved hands reached into Sean's pockets, pulling out the two playing cards. Then, sticking them in their own pocket, they pulled out the King of Spades. It wasn't the same as the others – this was a custom deck, black, silver and gold, and as they unclipped Sean's bodycam, squirrelling that away into a pocket, they pulled out a small metal spike. It was around double the size of a cocktail skewer, but it looked more solid than one of those.

With this in hand, they placed the playing card onto Sean's lifeless chest, picking up a half-brick and slamming the spike through the card, pinning it to his body, before rising, checking around and walking back the way they came, leaving Sean Acker's body lying on the floor.

The Royal Marines would never know, would never fire a salute at his funeral.

After all, he'd only lasted six weeks before being removed.

1

BURLINGTON BERTIE

THE RAIN HAMMERED AGAINST THE WINDOWS OF ST. Benedict's homeless shelter, drowning out the morning traffic, as DCI Declan Walsh stood in the entrance, shaking water from his overcoat. Twenty minutes earlier, he'd been sitting in his office at Temple Inn, staring blankly at a report on burglaries in Covent Garden, so the call from Shaun Donnal had been a welcome, if surprising, escape, even if it meant braving the biblical downpour that had settled over London that morning like an unwanted relative.

St. Benedict's was already in full swing despite the early hour – volunteers dishing out breakfast, caseworkers huddled with clients in corners, and the low murmur of too many broken lives packed into too small a space.

Declan spotted Shaun across the crowded hall. The former MP – once tipped as a future Home Secretary before the whole *Victoria Devington* affair knocked him off his trajectory – was deep in conversation with an elderly man. His balding, salt-and-pepper hair was now cropped, his glasses new and no longer the black-rimmed NHS ones Declan had once seen him wearing. He looked every inch a counsellor, the role he'd been training for when Declan had last seen him, no longer one of the visitors.

'Shaun,' Declan called, raising a hand.

Shaun looked up, his face splitting into a tired smile. He patted the elderly man on the shoulder and made his way over to Declan.

'Declan,' he said, extending his hand. 'Didn't think you'd brave the flood.'

'Needed an excuse to dodge paperwork,' Declan replied, shaking the offered hand. 'Though I'm not sure what you think I can do for your lot. Last time I checked, City Police don't handle housing benefits or anything.'

'Still a copper through and through,' Shaun said with a half-laugh. 'Come on. Let's grab a coffee.'

SHAUN'S OFFICE WAS BARELY LARGER THAN A BROOM CUPBOARD, with filing cabinets that looked ready to topple and a desk buried under paperwork, leaflets, and mugs with tea stains from last week. A faded photo of Shaun with then-Prime Minister Tony Blair – from his Westminster days – hung crookedly on the wall.

'Black, right?' Shaun asked, already pouring from a thermos.

'Thanks,' Declan said, taking the chipped mug. He stayed standing – the only visitor's chair was stacked with folders that looked like a game of Jenga waiting to happen. 'You doing okay?'

Shaun paused, considering the question.

'Can't complain,' he eventually replied. 'Beats sleeping on the streets, wondering when you'll be found out.'

Declan nodded, taking a moment to sip the coffee. Shaun had hidden off the grid for years after losing the 2015 election, believing he was a killer, and one step from capture. Only now was he finally regaining his life.

'Family?'

'Sally talks to me, we meet up once a month, but it's civil, you know?' Shaun said, screwing the Thermos lid back on. 'Feels more like a care worker session with me as the target than father-and-daughter bonding. But baby steps, and all that.'

He took a sip of the coffee, wincing.

'Christ, that's not good. Sorry.'

'It's fine,' Declan forced a smile, even though he'd thought the same when he sipped at his. 'So, what's this about?'

Shaun perched on the edge of his desk.

'Wanted to say thanks, first off. That word you put in with Baker's office paid off. Home Office approved our funding request – full amount, no questions asked. We've hired two more caseworkers and we're looking at a satellite location in Vauxhall.'

Declan nodded, surprised. He'd mentioned Shaun's shelter to the Prime Minister, Charles Baker six months back, but as ever, Baker had seemed more interested in his main course than homeless statistics. Of course, that could have been because he was asking on behalf of Shaun, and there were still confusing relationships involved there.

'Hey, is it true Baker's going?' Shaun looked up, his eyes a little more intense than they were a moment earlier. 'They're voting him out?'

'There's a vote likely,' Declan nodded. 'Won't affect us—'

'Of course it will,' Shaun chided. 'You're the Charles Baker golden boy. What will you become when the wannabe-Nazi Tamara Banks takes over?'

'We keep out of politics.'

'Tell that to your Detective Inspector,' Shaun replied cautiously. 'Word in Westminster is Tamara's telling everyone Anjli's her version of you and Charles.'

Declan winced a little at this. Tamara had made contact with Anjli a few weeks back, but Anjli, aware of what it was, had avoided it.

'Well, regardless of that, I'm glad something worked out,' he said. 'But I'm guessing that's not why you dragged me across town in this weather.'

'No.' Shaun's face turned serious, voice dropping automatically though the office was empty. 'We've got a new resident. Been with us about two months. At first, I didn't think much of it – just another face needing shelter. But recently she keeps talking about your father.'

Declan's eyebrows lifted.

'My father? He's been dead for years.'

'I know. That's what caught my attention,' Shaun sipped his coffee. 'She's in her seventies, calls herself "Burlington Bertie".'

'Burlington Bertie?' Declan couldn't hide his amusement. 'Like the music hall song?'

'That's the one. Dresses in men's clothes including a little cravat, spats and a monocle when she feels like it. Which is fine, I don't judge people, but she's got early-stage dementia, so she drifts in and out ...'

Shaun dropped his voice further.

'Look, Declan, She claims she was an informant for Patrick Walsh. Says she knows something about a group called the "Garden Collective".'

Declan frowned, searching his memory.

'Garden Collective? Never heard of it.'

'I looked into them. Activist group from the late eighties and nineties who targeted historical buildings and development projects – claimed they were preserving London's architectural heritage and green spaces. The kind who'd chain themselves to bulldozers one day and sabotage construction sites the next.' Shaun ran a hand through his hair. 'Normally I wouldn't bother you with this. Half our residents have stories. But Bertie… she knows details about your father. Stuff that wasn't in the papers.'

Declan felt that familiar tightness in his shoulders. His father's ghost had a way of haunting him just when he thought he'd finally buried everything.

'What sort of details?'

'She knew things about him, mentioned the team he had in Tottenham by name, definitely showing a familiarity I hadn't expected,' Shaun replied. 'And she mentioned that someone's been accessing information about the Garden Collective at the Reform Club, claiming to be doing research on behalf of the Walsh family.'

Declan's interest sharpened.

'The Reform Club? What would information about my father's cases be doing there?'

'Apparently, according to the rolls, your father was a member,' Shaun said. 'Didn't you know?'

Declan shook his head.

'I knew he belonged to the National Liberal Club, but he never mentioned the Reform Club.'

'Might have been political,' Shaun suggested. 'Lots of police brass were members back then, along with politicians, judges, journalists. It was a place where information could be exchanged off the record. Even I was a member, until I... well ...'

He smiled weakly, the comment not needing to be finished.

'Some senior officers kept copies of sensitive files in the private archives there – technically against regulations, but common practice. Especially for cases with political implications.'

'I'd like to talk to her,' Declan said.

Shaun nodded, looking relieved.

'I thought you might. She's usually in the day room around this time. Fair warning though – her lucidity comes and goes. Some days she's sharp as a tack, others she's lost in the past.'

They made their way through the shelter, past crowded tables and overworked volunteers. The day room was quieter, with a television murmuring in one corner and a few residents reading donated paperbacks or simply staring into space.

'There she is,' Shaun said quietly, nodding towards a slight figure seated by the window.

Burlington Bertie was nothing like Declan had expected. She was tiny, barely five feet tall, with a shock of white hair cut short in a man's style that might have been fashionable in the 1960s. Despite the shelter's warmth, she wore a threadbare tweed jacket several sizes too large, and a man's shirt and tie. Her face was a map of wrinkles, deep creases carved by decades of London weather and hard living. But her eyes – pale-blue and surprisingly clear – fixed on Declan the moment he stepped into the room.

'Walsh Junior,' she announced, her voice carrying across the room. 'About bloody time.'

Several heads turned towards them, and Shaun sighed.

'She's having one of her clearer days, it seems.'

Declan approached her table, noting the neat pile of playing cards stacked in front of her. She appeared to be in the middle of a game of Patience.

'Mrs …' Declan began.

'Just Bertie,' she interrupted. 'Never married, never saw the point. Not that I didn't enjoy men's company. You look like him, you know. Same eyes. Same way of standing – like you're ready to run after someone at any moment.'

Declan pulled up a chair opposite her.

'Shaun tells me you knew my father.'

'Knew him?' Bertie snorted. 'I saved his bloody career more than once. I was his eyes and ears when he couldn't get into places. Police detective sticks out like a sore thumb in certain circles. But old Burlington Bertie? Nobody notices old Burlington Bertie.'

'You weren't always old,' Declan observed.

A cackle of laughter burst from her.

'Sharp, too. Just like your dad.' She leant forward, lowering her voice conspiratorially. 'I wasn't always Bertie either. Had another name back then. Another life. But that was before the Garden.'

'The Garden Collective,' Declan prompted.

Something flickered across Bertie's face – a shadow of fear, quickly masked.

'Not here,' she said, glancing around the room. 'Too many ears. Some of them aren't attached to friends.'

Declan exchanged a look with Shaun. Paranoia wasn't uncommon among the homeless, especially those with mental health issues. But there was something in Bertie's manner that gave him pause.

'Why don't we take a walk?' Declan suggested. 'Get some fresh air.'

Bertie's eyes narrowed suspiciously, but then she nodded, gathering her playing cards. She slipped them into her jacket pocket and stood up, suddenly seeming taller, straighter.

'There's a small garden out back,' Shaun said. 'Should be empty this time of day.'

'Mainly because it's pissing down,' Bertie muttered. 'That's good. We can find shelter and talk there. Crazies don't come out in the rain.'

Declan bit back an answer to that.

The rain had eased to a light drizzle by the time they stepped outside. The garden was a modest affair – a few benches, some raised beds with spring vegetables, and a small patch of lawn. But it was, as Shaun had predicted, deserted.

Bertie walked ahead of them, her gait surprisingly spry for someone her age. She selected a bench partially sheltered by an overhanging tree and sat down, patting the wet space beside her for Declan to sit.

'You've come because of the records,' she said without preamble.

'What records?' Declan asked, taking a seat beside her.

Bertie leant closer.

'Your father kept certain case files at the Reform Club. His "insurance policy", he called them. Someone's been asking about them. I heard they went there last week, claiming to be doing research on behalf of the Walsh family. Looking for anything about the Garden Collective.'

'Are you sure it was the Reform Club? Dad never mentioned keeping files anywhere.'

'Of course he didn't,' Bertie said with a dismissive wave of her hand. 'That was the point. He called it his dead drop – somewhere even his own department couldn't access if things went sideways. The Garden Collective case had too many connections to powerful people. Property developers, councillors, MPs with investment interests.'

She tapped the side of her nose.

'Always good to have insurance.'

'My father always kept copies of his cases,' Declan argued. 'He had them in a secret room. I found it and I found them, and I can tell you; there's nothing about—'

'Of course not!' Bertie snapped irritably. 'This wasn't his case! It was a favour for Anthony.'

'Anthony?'

'Farringdon. Security man. Has one of those memories – remembers everything he ever sees. He'd remember your father. Patrick used him sometimes, when he needed someone with that kind of memory.'

Declan leant back on the bench, watching Bertie. He knew Anthony Farringdon well and was very aware of the relationship he'd had with Declan's father.

But this was new.

For a start, surely Declan, as next of kin, would have been informed of this when Patrick died?

What if he had, and Declan never realised?

'So, Farringdon has the files?'

'No! Keep up! Christ, I'd hoped you'd be as good as your old man, but the apple really did fall far from the tree,' Bertie sighed. 'Anthony asked for Paddy to look into it. Tom Keating was the case sergeant.'

Declan didn't miss the familiar name – only Danny Martin had ever called Patrick Walsh "Paddy".

'Tom Keating was at Tottenham North?'

'That's right. Not any more though. Retired about fifteen years back. Not well in the head – what do they call it now? Dementia. Nasty thing.' Bertie tapped her own temple. 'We all lose bits and pieces as we get older, but poor Tom's losing whole chapters.'

Bertie shuffled on the bench, almost as if she was moving too close to her own mental state and deciding to step back from it.

'Tom's carer is the sister of an old friend of mine. Said some bloke came round last week, asking specifically about Paddy's unofficial investigation into the Garden Collective. Had ID that convinced old Tom they were legitimate. Young, apparently, but if we're looking at Ruth, my friend, anyone under fifty is "young". He was asking about the Reform Club files, asking how to gain them.'

Declan frowned. There was a slim possibility this was legitimate – perhaps some architectural historian researching preservation movements or another police officer looking into cold cases, but his instincts told him otherwise. And if Tom Keating had been suffering from dementia, it wouldn't take much to convince him of anything these days.

'Monroe might remember,' Declan mused aloud. 'He worked with Dad and Tom back then.'

'That Scottish fellow?' Bertie wrinkled her nose. 'Met him years later. Never trusted him. Too smooth by half.'

'But why would anyone be interested in a defunct activist group from forty-odd years ago?' Shaun asked, caught up in the story.

Bertie's eyes took on a faraway look.

'Because some of them aren't defunct. When the people died, some of them just went underground. Changed their names, their faces—'

'People died?'

Bertie ignored the question, just continuing on as if nothing had been said.

'Got respectable jobs, became the very developers and planners they once fought against.'

Her gaze sharpened again, focusing on Declan.

'But they never changed what they believed. And they never forgave the people who betrayed them.'

'Who betrayed them?'

'Informants. People who talked to the police, who spoke up at court,' she tapped her chest. 'People like me. And others.'

'Bertie, are you saying you were a member of this Garden Collective?' Shaun asked.

Bertie snorted.

'Course not. I was working for your dad by then,' she said to Declan. 'Passing information. There was a big operation planned – something to do with the old Shadwell Bell Foundry. They were going to occupy it, sabotage the developers, expose corrupt council officials. Your father was trying to stop it. Needed to identify the key players.'

Declan was trying to place this in the timeline of his father's career. From what he knew, this must have been before Monroe joined his father's team, especially as Bertie "met him years later".

'So this would have been in the early nineties?' he asked.

'Thereabouts. I'm not good with dates any more.' Bertie's hands fluttered nervously over her playing cards as she started laying them out again on the bench. 'It was after they'd tried to destroy that old brewery in Spitalfields. Before the big property boom really took off. Your father was working out of Tottenham North then. This was before that Scottish fellow joined him.'

'Monroe,' Declan supplied, frowning.

'That's the one. Never trusted him.' Bertie shook her head. 'Too smooth by half.'

Declan glanced quietly at Shaun, noting that he too had picked up on the comment about Monroe being duplicated.

Bertie was starting to repeat things, and that wasn't a good sign.

'And you think that day has come?' Declan asked gently.

Bertie's eyes darted around the garden as if checking for eavesdroppers.

'I know it has. Three of the old informants have died in the past year. "Natural causes," they said. Heart attacks, strokes. But it's them. They're finishing what they started.'

The skin on the back of Declan's neck prickled. He'd heard enough conspiracy theories in his career to recognise the patterns – the vague "they", the connections seen between unrelated events, the sense of being watched. But he'd also learned not to dismiss such theories outright.

Sometimes, very occasionally, the paranoid were actually onto something.

'Do you have names? Of the informants who died, or the people you suspect?'

Bertie shook her head.

'Too dangerous. Walls have ears.'

'Bertie,' Shaun said gently, 'you're safe here. No one's listening.'

'Who told you someone was looking into my father's records?'

'A woman came by and explained what was going on ...'

For a moment, she seemed about to say more. Then her expression changed, becoming confused, almost childlike.

'I'm cold,' she blurted. 'Is it time for tea?'

Declan recognised the shift immediately – her lucidity slipping away as quickly as it had appeared. Shaun caught his eye and gave a small, sad nod of confirmation.

'Let's get you back inside,' Shaun said, helping Bertie to her feet. 'I believe they're serving tea in ten minutes.'

'Poor Linda,' Bertie muttered suddenly, staring at one of the bushes. 'She knew about the supports, tried to get them out. But they wouldn't listen.'

'Who's Linda?' Declan asked gently.

Bertie looked up, confused.

'Linda? Do I know a Linda? Teatime soon, did you say?'

As they walked back towards the shelter, Declan looked at Shaun.

'How often does this happen?' he asked quietly.

'The clarity comes and goes. Sometimes she's lucid for hours, sometimes just minutes. The doctors think it'll get worse over time.'

'And how did she end up here? She must have had a life before.'

'She did,' Shaun confirmed. 'Worked here and there, mainly cash in hand for various companies around the City for decades. Had a small council flat in Whitechapel. But she was evicted six months ago – kept causing disturbances, accusing neighbours of spying on her, found walking down the street in her pyjamas one day at five in the morning. Social services got involved, but she fell through the cracks. We're trying to get her placed somewhere more suitable, but there's a waiting list.'

They reached the dayroom, where Bertie immediately settled back at her table by the window, arranging her playing cards in some pattern that made sense only to her.

'Can she even play in that state?' Declan muttered, half to himself.

'Honestly, I don't think she cares,' Shaun said. 'It's not even a full deck of cards.'

Declan raised an eyebrow at the comment, and Shaun, realising what he said vigorously shook his head.

'I don't mean her, I mean the actual deck,' he continued. 'It's missing a Queen. She probably lost it somewhere, but it buggers up a game of Patience.'

He straightened, sighing.

'I'm not sure how much of what she told you is real,' Shaun said. 'But she's been genuinely afraid these past few weeks. And, for what it's worth, I did some digging after she first mentioned the Garden Collective. They were real. Caused enough trouble that Special Branch had a file on them. Several members were arrested after a protest in Shadwell turned violent in ninety-two – three people died in the riot that followed, mainly because the whole bloody floor collapsed on them. They were suspected in dozens of cases of sabotage and vandalism at construction sites across London.'

'I believe you,' Declan said. 'And there might be something to her story about my father. The Reform Club connection is new to me, but it makes a certain kind of sense. Dad always did have contingency plans.'

'So, what will you do?'

Declan shrugged.

'Make some inquiries. I'll need to go visit Anthony Farringdon, see if he can help me access whatever files my father kept at the Reform Club. And I'll talk to Monroe, though it sounds like the Garden Collective case was before his time with Dad.'

His phone vibrated in his pocket. He pulled it out, glancing at the screen. It was a text from Anjli.

> Call me ASAP. Body found near Stationers' Hall.

'I need to go,' Declan said, already moving towards the exit. 'Work. But I'd like to talk to Bertie again. Will you call me if she has another lucid spell?'

'Of course,' Shaun said, following him. 'Is everything alright?'

'Probably not,' Declan replied grimly, typing a response to Anjli. 'But that's rather the nature of my job. I'll be in touch.'

As he hurried out into the rain, Declan cast one last glance back at Burlington Bertie through the window. She was staring at her playing cards with intense concentration, her lips moving in silent conversation.

He hailed a black cab that was passing, thankfully with its light on.

'Stationers' Hall,' he said as he slid into the back seat. 'Quickly as you can.'

The cab pulled away from the kerb, windscreen wipers slapping against the intensifying rain. As London flashed by in a grey blur, Declan's mind was already shifting gears, compartmentalising the Bertie situation to focus on what lay ahead, as a dead body meant his conversation with Bertie would have to wait. And as the cab navigated through London's congested streets, the rain drummed harder on the roof, drowning out everything but his thoughts about his long-dead father, and even more secrets he seemed to have kept.

2

KING OF SPADES

THE RAIN WAS RELENTLESS, HAMMERING AGAINST THE BLUE AND white police tape that fluttered in the downpour. Declan ducked under the cordon as PC Esme Cooper, currently arguing with a journalist who wanted to pass through, waved Declan under, water streaming from his collar despite his best efforts to stay dry during the short walk from the cab.

The crime scene buzzed with activity despite the weather. A couple of SOCOs in their white PPE suits moved methodically, racing against time as the evidence needed collecting before the rain washed it all away.

The actual crime scene was in a narrow service alleyway beside Stationers' Hall, a Tudor-era building that housed one of London's ancient livery companies. Additional tarpaulins had been stretched overhead, creating a makeshift roof to protect the scene from the worst of the rain, but water still dripped through in places, collecting in small puddles on the cobblestones.

Anjli stood with her back to him, sheltered under the

tarpaulin, her dark hair tied back, notebook in hand. She turned as he approached, her expression grim.

'About time,' she said. 'Doctor Marcos is just finishing her preliminary.'

The aforementioned Doctor Marcos crouched beside the body; her customary grey PPE suit already spattered with water and grime. She looked up at Declan's approach, her wild curls escaping from beneath her hood.

'Declan,' she nodded. 'Looks like you've managed to outrun the storm.'

'Not by much,' he replied, pulling on a pair of blue latex gloves and crouching down beside her to examine the victim. 'What have we got?'

The body lay sprawled on its back, arms splayed outward, partially sheltered from the rain by the building's overhang. The victim was a man in his late thirties, maybe early forties, with closely cropped ginger hair and a ruddy complexion. What instantly stood out to Declan, though, was that he wore what appeared to be tactical webbing over a dark polo shirt and combat trousers with numerous pockets. A single playing card – the King of Spades – was pinned to his chest with a metal spike that resembled an oversized cocktail skewer. The card looked different, *special* however, with silver and gold ink on top of black cardstock. Declan also noticed his hair appeared bedraggled although no longer damp, despite the partial shelter.

'Rain caught him before you got the tarpaulins up?' he asked, gesturing to the hair.

Doctor Marcos shook her head.

'No, the rain only started after the body was found,' she said. 'The overhang was erected after the first forensics appeared, and they kept most of the rain off him. The first on scene claimed when she found him, he was bone dry – except for the head.'

'Dodgy guttering?' Declan looked around.

'No idea,' Doctor Marcos stretched her back, aching from time spent crouched over. 'Body was found around five am this morning. By the time we got called, well ...'

Declan nodded. Even though this was in the City of London, the chances were Bishopsgate would have gotten the call first – which explained the larger than usual amount of white-clad forensic SOCOs wandering around.

They probably saw the card and the spike and decided it was one for us, he thought to himself. *Why bother with what could be a troubling and difficult-to-solve case, after all, when the Last Chance Saloon loved this sort of shit.*

'The tarpaulin was up by then, which was good, but even without it, the eave above this alcove kept him relatively dry where he was sheltered,' Doctor Marcos continued. Someone deliberately wet him, but it was some time ago.'

'Do we know who he is?'

'Sean Acker, forty-one years old according to his wallet,' Anjli now spoke. 'Cause of death—'

'Ahem.'

Anjli smiled.

'I'll let Doctor Marcos tell you,' she said, stepping back while making sure she stayed dry.

Declan turned his attention back to Doctor Marcos, who rose before talking, probably tired of crouching.

'Cause of death is a single gunshot wound to the chest. Entry wound here—' she pointed to a dark hole in the centre of the man's chest, '—with no exit wound, suggesting the bullet is still inside. From the trauma pattern, I'd estimate a medium-calibre handgun, fired at close range.'

'Time of death?'

'Around eight last night, based on liver temp and rigour. The rain makes it harder to be precise, but it also feels strange that nobody walked down here between then and five a.m.'

'They may have, but didn't see the body in the alcove, as he's wearing black clothing, as if he wanted to hide,' Anjli suggested. 'Or, they saw it but didn't call it in, maybe they thought it was a homeless person or something.'

'Yeah, that's possible. We'll know more after the post-mortem.'

Declan glanced at a black plastic object lying about a metre from the body, sealed in an evidence bag.

'Is that a gun?'

Anjli picked up the bag, holding it so Declan could see the contents.

'Looks like a toy Glock, 3D printed black to resemble an actual weapon, but with the end left orange. Full of water, hasn't been fired.'

'So, it wasn't this that soaked his face and hair,' Declan observed.

'No,' Doctor Marcos confirmed. 'As I said, his face and hair show signs of having been deliberately soaked with water, but hours ago. What I can tell you is that the killer made a point of it – soaking just those areas while the rest of Mister Acker here stayed relatively dry under the overhang.'

'So, someone shot him, soaked him with water, then pinned a playing card to his chest?' Declan frowned.

'Not quite,' Doctor Marcos replied. 'The sequence appears to be that they shot him, pinned the card, and *then* soaked him with water. The card and his clothing underneath it are relatively dry compared to the surrounding areas, but we can see water damage on the card, so we can tell that the chances are the water was applied after the card was in place, soaking the card in the process and, in the hours that followed, it's dried stiff.'

Declan looked around the alleyway.

'Any cameras?'

'Nothing directly covering this spot,' Anjli replied. 'We've got uniforms checking nearby buildings, but this appears to be a deliberate blind spot.'

'Shell casings?'

'None found so far. The shooter either picked it up or used a revolver.'

'Professional hit?'

Doctor Marcos shook her head.

'I wouldn't say so. The staging's too elaborate for a typical contract killing.'

Declan didn't want to ask how Doctor Marcos knew this. Unaware of his thought, Doctor Marcos continued.

'This was personal or symbolic. The card, the water pistol – they mean something.'

As he rose from the body, Declan noticed something on the victim's wrist.

'What's that?'

Doctor Marcos gently turned the arm to reveal what looked like a homemade device strapped to the inside of his wrist – a small plastic syringe without a needle, secured with electrical tape.

'It's an interesting contraption,' she said. 'It appears to be a modified syringe, positioned so he could squeeze it with a flex of his wrist. It contains water, like the pistol.'

'Some kind of last-ditch water weapon?' Anjli suggested.

'Possibly,' Doctor Marcos nodded. 'The level of preparation is... well, let's face it, it's a little peculiar.'

Declan surveyed the body again, noting the tactical clothing.

'He's dressed like he was on some kind of operation. Military background?'

'Not according to his ID,' Anjli replied, checking her notes. 'Works in finance, near Liverpool Street. Address in Bermondsey.'

'The tactical gear seems excessive for a night out in the City,' Declan mused. 'Anything else of interest?'

Doctor Marcos pointed to the victim's chest rig.

'Bodycam mount. Empty. Been removed.'

'So, our killer wanted to make sure we couldn't see what happened,' Declan said, standing up. 'But left us plenty of other clues. The card, the water pistol, the strange wrist contraption ...'

'And this,' Doctor Marcos added, holding up a second small evidence bag, this one containing two playing cards – a Jack of Hearts and an Ace of Diamonds. 'Found in his inside pocket. Different deck from the King of Spades.'

Declan took the bag, examining the cards.

'These look to be like the more regular playing cards we see everywhere. Well-handled. Significance of these and the black card?'

'Unknown at this point,' Doctor Marcos replied. 'But, along with the King of Spades pinned to his chest, it's an unusual collection.'

'Three cards, three targets?' Anjli suggested.

'Speculation,' Declan cautioned, 'but you could be right. It's definitely worth considering.'

He turned to survey the scene again, trying to reconstruct

the sequence of events. The alleyway was narrow but not completely isolated – a shortcut between the main road and a car park behind the buildings. Not the kind of place someone would linger without raising suspicion, especially in the evening.

'He didn't just happen to be here,' Declan said finally. 'He came for a purpose, dressed for some kind of action. The possibly stolen bodycam suggests he expected something to happen and wanted to record it.'

'Maybe he was hunting someone,' Anjli suggested. 'The tactical gear, the water weapons... it's like he was playing at being a soldier.'

'Or playing at being an assassin,' Declan added. 'But why water weapons? And why would his killer soak him after shooting him?'

His gaze fell on the King of Spades again, stark black against the victim's chest.

'Let's get him to our morgue,' he said. 'Anjli, get Cooper and De'Geer to organise a team to search his flat. I want to know everything about Sean Acker – his job, his social circle, his hobbies. Anything that might explain why he was dressed like a commando with water weapons in an alleyway.'

Doctor Marcos nodded, signalling to the likely Bishopsgate team to prepare the body for transport.

'I'll start the post-mortem as soon as we get him back. Should have something for you this afternoon.'

As the team moved in to finish processing the scene, Declan stepped back, turning over the bizarre details in his mind. *A man shot dead but staged with water weapons and playing cards.* It wasn't a standard killing – it was a message. But who was it for and what was it saying?

His phone buzzed in his pocket; a text from Billy.

> Ran victim through databases. Sean Acker, 41, works for Harding & Cross Investment. Clean record. Sending his full address details to Anjli now.

Declan showed the message to Anjli.

'Doesn't tell us much,' she mused. 'But maybe his apartment will. You sure you don't want me there?'

'I thought De'Geer would be here,' Declan frowned as he looked around.

'Dentist, not in until later,' Anjli smiled. 'Can you imagine his face when he realises he missed this?'

'Let's hope he's not angry. Last thing we want is an angry Viking,' Declan glanced back at the body being zipped into a black bag. 'Go with Esme to the apartment, see if you can find anything. I'm going to see what else Billy can find on our victim's digital footprint. Something tells me there's more to this than a military fantasy gone wrong.'

As he turned to leave, his eye caught the playing card again – the King of Spades –now being carefully placed into a separate evidence baggie by a gloved technician. The rain had finally stopped, but Declan couldn't shake the feeling that this was just the beginning of the storm.

The offices of the Last Chance Saloon, formally known as the Temple Inn Command Unit, were housed in a narrow Georgian building tucked away in the Inns of Court off Fleet Street. By the time Declan arrived upstairs in the main office, Billy Fitzwarren was already entrenched behind three monitors in his "spaceship" style desk setup, his pale-blond hair standing up at odd angles in what Declan recognised as his "deep research" mode as he spun in his gamer's chair from screen to screen. Billy's immaculate bespoke three-piece suit – today a subtle navy pinstripe – stood in stark contrast to his chaotic workspace, littered with empty coffee cups and scribbled notes.

He glanced up as Declan approached, his fingers still tapping away at the keyboard.

'I've been digging into Sean Acker's digital life,' he said without preamble. 'And it's a weird kind of fantasy world.'

'How so?'

Billy swivelled one of his monitors towards Declan.

'Facebook, Instagram, LinkedIn, Twitter – all of them list him as "Ex-Royal Marine." He's admin of three different Royal Marines support groups online and regularly posts about "his time in the service".'

'But he washed out after six weeks of basic,' Declan said, leaning closer and reading the profile Billy had displayed on screen.

'Exactly. Never even made it through training, but online he's practically the hero of Helmand Province.' Billy clicked through several social media posts showing Sean Acker in various military-style poses, always in tactical gear similar to what he'd been wearing when found dead.

'Interesting,' Declan mused. 'But plenty of people embellish their backgrounds. You, for example, don't tell people you're like fifteenth in line for the throne or something. Doesn't usually get them killed.'

'True, but there's more,' Billy continued, ignoring the jibe as he pulled up another screen. 'His emails and calendar entries show something called "Game Time" marked every November for the past several years, regular as clockwork.'

'Game Time? Sports fan?'

'Nothing in his social media suggests he followed any teams particularly. But I did find something interesting in his emails,' Billy continued, pulling up a message on his screen. 'Look at this, sent a week ago.'

'Are you supposed to have access to his emails yet?' Declan asked carefully.

'Not my fault that he had a rubbish password,' Billy replied casually as he nodded to the screen. It was a group chat message addressed to a dozen recipients, their addresses masked by nicknames rather than real names. The subject line read "FINAL ROUND," and the message was brief:

> Game Day confirmed for Friday. All players should have received their new targets by now. Remember, three weapons max, all registered before the event starts, as usual. No excuses for missed kills this time.

'Game day? So this is what, some kind of sport?' Declan asked, leaning closer.

'From what I can gather, it's more activity than sport,' Billy replied. 'There are dozens of emails in his inbox – I mean it's horrifying he leaves them all in there without labels or folders, but good for us – like this going back years. They call it "The Game", "Killer Cards" or sometimes "Royal Court". Looks like some sort of adult tag game with water pistols.'

'Killer Cards,' Declan repeated, thinking of the King of Spades pinned to Acker's chest. 'Any names of the actual participants?'

'Not yet. Looks like it was a blind recipient list. I'm waiting for Monroe to confirm if I can continue reading.'

'If it's some kind of paintball style game, that would

explain the tactical gear and the water pistol,' Declan nodded. 'And maybe the playing cards too – could be how they identify targets. But then why would someone shoot him for real? Unless the game turned deadly, or someone used the game as cover for murder.'

'Aye, laddie. If everyone's running around "assassinating" each other with water pistols, it provides the perfect opportunity to commit an actual killing and make it look related.'

Declan looked up as Detective Superintendent Alex Monroe appeared in the doorway to his office. The tall, white-haired Scotsman leaned against the frame, a mug of coffee steaming in his hand.

'Bullman said you were at a murder scene this morning. Playing cards and water pistols?'

'Word travels fast,' Declan replied. 'Just getting Billy up to speed.'

'Aye, I had to stop the wee laddie from breaking a dozen data protection rules. Anything I should know?' Monroe stepped into the main office. 'Or should I wait until Rosanna's played "Doctors" for a bit?'

'Possibly,' Declan hesitated, then decided to mention his earlier conversation. 'But not something to do with this. Before the call came in, I was speaking with an elderly woman at St. Benedict's shelter. Shaun Donnal tipped me the nod.'

'Shaun Donnal?' Monroe's eyebrows rose. 'I thought he'd disappeared off the face of the earth after that business with Victoria Devington, and then the murders with all the Father Christmas hats?'

'He's running outreach programmes for the homeless now. Seems to be doing good work.'

Monroe pursed his lips.

'As long as he's stopped stabbing people with screwdrivers, he can do whatever he wants,' he said. 'So, okay laddie, you went to see Shaun, and he aimed you at some woman. Why?'

'Calls herself Burlington Bertie. Like the old music hall song. She claims she knew my father, said she was an informant for him years ago. Mentioned something about a group called the Garden Collective.'

Monroe frowned.

'The Garden Collective? That's a name I haven't heard in a long time. Activist group from the early nineties. Your father worked a case connected to them back in Tottenham, before I joined his team.'

'Bertie said Dad kept files at the Reform Club. That mean anything to you?'

Monroe's face remained carefully neutral, and Declan immediately knew the old Scot was hiding something.

'Your father had his methods. Kept certain sensitive information away from the others. I mean, we all know that, we saw his hidden rooms and his backup files. But why's this woman bringing it up now?'

'She claims someone's been accessing those files, using the Walsh family name to get to them ...' Declan paused. 'She also mentioned you, said she never trusted you. Called you "too smooth by half".'

Monroe snorted.

'Well, that's specific, and does sound like me. But it could be anyone claiming to know your father. Half of London's criminal elements have a story about Patrick Walsh. Christ, even Johnny Lucas has a book's worth.'

'This one seemed different,' Declan said. 'She knew

details. And she mentioned she had another name back then, before she became Burlington Bertie.'

'Did she give it?'

'No.'

'Convenient. What did she look like?' Monroe asked, his tone more serious.

'Tiny woman, about five feet. White hair cut in a man's style. Wears men's clothes – tweed jacket, shirt and tie. Early seventies, I'd guess. Has some form of early dementia.'

Monroe's eyes narrowed slightly.

'Doesn't immediately ring a bell, but there were a few female informants your father used regularly. I'll ask around, see if anyone remembers someone matching that description. Keep me informed if anything develops on either front,' he said, turning back to his office. 'And Declan... be careful with old stories. Sometimes they're best left buried.'

After Monroe left, Billy looked up at Declan.

'Want me to look into this Garden Collective?'

'Let's focus on the murder for now,' Declan replied. 'But maybe run a background check on Burlington Bertie when you have time. See if her story checks out.'

'Will do,' Billy nodded. 'Although I could do with more than a music hall song. Should have more for you on the other case by the time Anjli gets back from Acker's flat.'

Declan stood, stretching his back.

'I'm going to check in with—'

He paused as Billy's phone rang – not because of the noise, but because he saw Billy's horrified expression.

'You okay?' he asked.

Billy held up the phone, staring at it as if it was about to attack.

'It's my father calling,' he whispered. 'He hasn't called since, well ...'

'Since the family disowned you?' Declan nodded. 'You should answer it.'

And, as Billy tentatively answered the phone, Declan headed out of the office. He knew Anjli would take another hour or so before she found anything, and Doctor Marcos was unlikely to have anything before lunchtime.

Maybe it was time to go have a chat with Anthony Farringdon.

3

MEMORY MAN, AGAIN

The rain lashed against Declan's window as his taxi pulled up outside the National Liberal Club at the junction of Whitehall Place and Whitehall Court. He dashed from the car to the shelter of the entrance, raindrops smacking against the white-brick neo-gothic facade like tiny bullets.

Inside, the familiar scent of beeswax polish and old leather greeted him. He paused briefly before the grand staircase, taking in the rotunda with its ornate marble banister and magnificent glass ceiling. The portraits of distinguished members seemed to stare down at him from their positions around the walls – generations of politicians, judges, and military men, all captured in stern Victorian poses.

The porter at the enquiries desk spotted him immediately.

'Detective Chief Inspector Walsh?' he asked, pretty sure he recognised Declan, but still unsure. At a nod, he continued. 'Mister Farringdon's waiting for you. Mentioned you might be in a hurry.'

Not needing an escort to show him the way, Declan

climbed the grand spiral staircase, nodding to a few familiar faces as he passed – at least one of them was an MP whose life he saved at a State Dinner.

The Churchill Room lay beyond a set of heavy oak doors, its high ceiling and red marble pillars lending it an atmosphere of faded grandeur. Between the pillars, windows with heavy green drapes looked out over rain-soaked London, beside glass-fronted mahogany trophy cabinets standing alongside busts of former prime ministers and military heroes, silent witnesses to centuries of whispered confidences and political machinations.

Anthony Farringdon sat in his usual armchair, *The Guardian* folded on the table beside him. At seventy-something, he still had the ruler-straight back of the military man he'd once been, his white hair neatly parted, his regimental blazer immaculate. His hands, resting lightly on the armrests, were marked with liver spots now, but Declan knew they remained as steady as they'd been when Farringdon oversaw security for both Downing Street and Westminster during three premierships.

'Declan, my dear boy,' he said, rising to shake hands. 'Bloody awful weather. You're drenched.'

'Worth it for the pleasure of your company, Anthony.'

Farringdon snorted.

'Bollocks. You're after something, as usual. Sit down before you drip on the Axminster. Tea? Something stronger?'

'Tea, please.'

With a flick of his hand Farringdon signalled a steward who, primed for the request, nodded and disappeared. Neither man spoke until the tea arrived and the steward retreated beyond earshot. The china was delicate, hand-painted with the club's emblem, the silver teapot reflecting the muted light from the rain-darkened windows.

'Now then,' Farringdon said, dropping a sugar cube into his cup. 'What's brought you out in this deluge? Not a social call, I'd wager, not with that look about you.'

'It's not. Does the name Burlington Bertie mean anything to you?'

Farringdon's teacup froze halfway to his lips, his eyes narrowing slightly. For a brief moment, the polished exterior cracked, revealing something sharper beneath – the intelligence officer he'd once been, before the club memberships and retirement dinners.

'Small woman?'

'Maybe. She's turned up at St. Benedict's shelter, claiming to know my father.'

'Well, well,' Farringdon murmured, replacing his cup in its saucer with exaggerated care. 'Emmy Clarke. There's a ghost from the past.'

'Emmy Clarke?'

'Emily. That's what we knew her as. One of your father's best sources back in the day. Sharp as a tack and twice as dangerous when crossed. Used "Burlington Bertie" as a kind of call sign, because of the song.'

'Song?' Declan replied. 'I know it's a music hall thing, but I don't know the lyrics.'

'It's a music hall song based *on* a music hall song,' Farringdon smiled. 'The original was penned in 1900, by Harry B. Norris. However there was a parody done fifteen years later called "Burlington Bertie from Bow".'

'Of course you'd know this,' Declan smiled.

'Curse of a photographic memory,' Farringdon explained. 'Anyway, as the latter goes, *"I'm Burlington Bertie, I rise at ten-*

thirty and saunter along like a toff; I walk down the Strand with my gloves on my hand, then I walk down again with them off. I'm all airs and graces, correct easy paces, without food so long, I've forgot where my face is – I'm Bert, Bert, I haven't a shirt, but my people are well off you know. Nearly everyone knows me from Smith to Lord Rosebr'y, I'm Burlington Bertie from Bow". The whole point was that Bertie was someone who could move through all worlds, while belonging to none, a story based on an older story.'

He sipped his tea, eyes distant with recollection.

'Fearless little thing. Could slip into places others couldn't – board meetings, private clubs, property developers' offices. Gathered intelligence that seemed impossible to obtain, used contacts and favours nobody realised she was owed.'

'What happened to her?'

'Vanished, must be thirty years ago now. After the Bell Foundry business.' Farringdon's eyes refocused on Declan. 'She was always worried about being cast aside. Again, with the song – *"So strict are my people, they're William the Conqueror's strain – if they ever knew I'd been talking to you, why they'd never look at me again."* What's she want after all these years?'

'She's got early dementia. Comes and goes. When she's lucid, she talks about an organisation called the Garden Collective. Claims someone's been accessing Dad's old files using our family name.'

'Christ,' Farringdon set his cup down with a sharp clink. 'That lot again. Nasty bunch of eco-warriors who thought saving old buildings justified pretty much anything. Started off with the usual – protests, sit-ins, bit of chaining themselves to bulldozers. Ended with people dead.'

'She mentioned an incident at the Shadwell Bell Foundry.'

'Bloody disaster, that was,' Farringdon's voice dropped, his usual polish giving way to something harder. 'Was only a foundry in name by then but was still history people wanted to build over. Three dead, dozens injured. Place collapsed during an occupation.'

'Accident?'

'That's what the papers said. Your father knew better. Someone had taken a saw to the support beams the night before.'

'The developers?'

'That's what everyone thought at first. Trying to discredit the protestors. Patrick dug deeper and found it was an inside job. Splinter group within the Collective wanted martyrs for the cause – you know, happy for everyone to die if it made a splash - and there were rumours they had worked with the developer himself. Sick bastards.'

Declan felt a chill that had nothing to do with his damp clothes.

'Were they caught?'

'Four charged, but only one convicted. Others vanished – new names, new lives. Not because they were hiding from the law, but more to distance themselves from a rather disreputable past. Word was your father had a list.'

Farringdon glanced around the room before continuing.

'The Collective fell apart after the Foundry incident. Too much blood on their hands. And the fact their leadership was behind bars. So much for martyrs being a rallying call.'

'And Dad was investigating them?'

'Not officially.' Farringdon offered a thin smile. 'He'd been warned off. Too many connections to people who mattered—'

'How so?'

'They were all sons and daughters of wealthy party donors, or important people. You know the type,' Farringdon sniffed. 'Tarquin doesn't like what Daddy does, so he protests. But only when he's on summer break from Eton or Harrow.'

Declan understood very well, as Anthony Farringdon continued.

'But Patrick never could leave a bone unburied.'

'So, he went off-book?'

'Completely. We bumped into each other during a security review at the Commons. This was maybe six months, a year before the disaster. Some of the Collective had threatened an MP backing a development bill. Patrick was hunting their leadership on his own time. I slipped him what I could – nothing that would get me shot, mind, but useful bits and pieces.'

'And these files Bertie mentioned?'

'Your dad kept certain materials at the Reform Club.'

'Why not here?'

'Because people knew he was a member here. The Reform Club? Not so much. Security through obscurity, we called it. Somewhere the higher-ups wouldn't think to look if things got sticky, especially with your father speaking out against John Major at the time.' Farringdon's eyes narrowed. 'If someone's accessing them using your name, that's bloody concerning.'

A steward approached their table, offering to refresh their tea. Farringdon nodded, and they waited in silence until fresh tea had been poured and the man had retreated once more.

'The thing about the Garden Collective,' Farringdon

continued, voice lowered, 'is that it wasn't just tree-huggers and architecture enthusiasts. As I said, they had connections to some serious people – politicians, civil servants, academics... people who've since risen to positions of considerable influence.'

'After being involved in something that killed three people?'

'The beauty of large movements, dear boy, is plausible deniability. *"Oh, that was a rogue element. I was just supporting historic preservation."*' Farringdon's impression of gentrified outrage was pitch-perfect. 'Easy enough to distance oneself, especially with the right connections.'

'What would someone be after in those files, after all this time?'

'Names, most likely. You've seen how your dad documented everything meticulously, keeping copies, all of that – he would have had who was truly involved, who provided funding, who looked the other way when things turned ugly,' Farringdon added some milk to his fresh tea. 'Or perhaps something specific about Bell Foundry. Rumours persisted that evidence was buried to protect certain interests.'

'Buried by whom?'

'Now there's the question.' Farringdon sipped at his tea. 'Your father had theories. Never shared them, not fully. But it upset him. Said it went high up. I have my own suspicions, but ...'

'But you only deal in facts.'

A flash of memory hit Declan – his father at the kitchen table late one night, whisky glass in hand, muttering about *"the ones you never see"*. He'd been working on something unofficial, Declan realised now, but at the time Declan hadn't been older than twelve, spending more time reading his *Magpies* novels than listening to his parents.

'I was at my father's house after he died,' Declan said. 'Went through his papers, even the ones he kept hidden. Never found anything about a Garden Collective.'

'He wouldn't have kept anything sensitive at home. Too vulnerable. The Reform was his insurance policy before he was promoted – secure, discreet, and legally protected by clubland confidentiality. Perfect place to stash documents that might otherwise disappear. And thirty-odd years later, he'd probably forgotten he even had them there.'

Farringdon set his cup down.

'If someone's trying to access those files now, they're looking to clean up old loose ends.'

Declan absorbed this, turning his cup on its saucer.

'Bertie mentioned something else – former informants dying suspiciously. Natural causes on paper, but she thinks they were murdered.'

'Emmy always did have a nose for trouble.' Farringdon leant forward slightly. 'Normally I'd say it's the dementia talking, but if anyone would spot a pattern like that, it'd be her. She had contacts everywhere – housing estates, town halls, business clubs.'

'Could you look into it? You've still got friends in interesting places.'

'For you? Of course. Give me the names if she provides them. But if Emmy Clarke has dementia, the Reform Club files might be the only proof that what she talks about is real.'

'Thanks, as ever,' Declan smiled, finishing his tea, and preparing to stand. As he did so, however, a thought seemed to strike Farringdon. His eyes narrowed as he studied Declan across the table.

'How's young Fitzwarren taking the news?'

Declan frowned.

'What news?'

'Ah.' Farringdon's expression shifted. 'I assumed he'd have mentioned it. It's all over the clubs this morning – Viscount Fitzwarren's stepping down. And, since young William's the only son ...'

'Billy would inherit the title,' Declan finished, stunned. 'You're certain?'

This made sense now – the unexpected phone call from his father before Declan left. From the sounds of things, Billy was the last to be informed about this.

'Three separate sources confirmed it over breakfast. Announcement probably due next week.' Farringdon lowered his voice to a murmur. 'They're putting out health reasons, but the truth's far juicier.'

'Go on.'

'Seems the old Viscount's been caught with his trousers down – quite literally – with a certain judge's wife. Photos exist, apparently.' Farringdon's lip curled slightly. 'By abdicating now, he's forcing Billy to deal with the mess. The old boy knows his son will find some way to bury the scandal rather than take the title. Using one's child as a human shield, especially when you've treated them like rubbish for years – utterly shabby.'

'Christ.' Declan rubbed his jaw. 'What would it mean for him?'

'Rather significant change of circumstances. He'd become "The Viscount Fitzwarren" – properly a lord. No seat in the Lords since the '99 reforms, but still a hereditary peer,' Farringdon leant back in his chair. 'Not exactly compatible with being a detective sergeant in the City Police, I'd imagine.'

'No law against it, though?'

'Not specifically, no. But highly unusual. Bound to create whispers, complications,' Farringdon's eyebrows lifted. 'He'd be officially ...'

He paused, considering it.

'*Detective Sergeant The Lord William Fitzwarren, Viscount Fitzwarren*, or something like that. Bit of a mouthful in briefings. And then there's the estate. The Fitzwarrens still hold considerable land in Gloucestershire. Tenant farms, charitable obligations. Not something one manages on a police officer's salary, even with old money. His father stepping back means he takes that on, even if he doesn't play well with his family.'

'Billy's never really spoken of any of this,' Declan mused. 'I mean, I know he's well off, his family's rich and all that ...'

'I suspect he's spent his entire adult life running from it.' Farringdon's voice softened slightly. 'Ancient families cast long shadows, Declan. I've seen men go to extraordinary lengths to escape their heritage, only to have it thrust upon them in the end. And sometimes, the heritage isn't financial.'

'True,' Declan replied, unsure if this was some kind of warning to him personally.

'Anyway,' Farringdon continued. 'Might explain any... eccentricities in the coming weeks. These transitions can be rather destabilising, especially for someone who's built an identity apart from his bloodline.'

As Declan rose to leave, Farringdon gripped his shoulder briefly.

'Give Billy my regards. And perhaps consider this – having a viscount on your team might prove surprisingly useful for certain cases. The aristocracy still has its own language, after all.'

'I'll keep that in mind.' Declan buttoned his coat, preparing to face the rain again. 'And I appreciate the insight on the Garden Collective. I'll let you know what comes of it.'

'Do,' Farringdon said, his expression grave. 'I find myself… concerned.'

As he emerged out onto the steps leading to the club entrance, Declan made a dash for a passing taxi, coat held over his head in a futile attempt to stay dry. By the time he slid into the back seat, his shoes were soaked through and water dripped from his hair.

Outside, the rain drummed against the cab, creating a cocoon of white noise that seemed to isolate him from the world. Through the streaming windows, London appeared distorted, buildings and people smeared into impressionistic blurs of grey and black. The perfect backdrop for the thoughts swirling through his mind.

Two entirely separate puzzles now demanded his attention. There was Bertie – or was it Emmy – with her fractured memories of the Garden Collective; worth following up, clearly, but not immediately pressing. If Farringdon's assessment was correct, these were old ghosts stirring, dangerous perhaps, but not requiring instant action.

Then there was his current murder investigation waiting back at Temple Inn. Though he hadn't discussed the details with Farringdon, the case weighed heavily on his mind, particularly the unusual elements that suggested they weren't dealing with a typical homicide.

And now this bombshell about Billy.

If Farringdon was right – and he usually was – the team dynamics at the Last Chance Saloon were about to shift dramatically. Declan had watched Billy fight for respect on his merits alone, never trading on his family name. What would this unwanted title do to all that hard work?

More concerning was the timing. In the middle of a murder investigation, having a team member distracted by personal drama was far from ideal. Billy was their tech specialist, their digital bloodhound. They needed him focused, not dealing with his father's scandalous indiscretions.

Although that was a little hypocritical, considering the case had a personal connection to Declan anyway.

Declan sat back in the seat as the taxi threaded its way towards Temple Inn. First stop would be the office to check on the investigation, but it looked like he'd also need a quiet word with his detective sergeant. Family complications had a knack for erupting at the worst possible times – Declan knew that from bitter experience.

And if Billy was about to become Viscount bloody Fitzwarren because of his father's grubby indiscretions, they had rather a lot to discuss.

4

BRIEFING

'LADIES AND GENTLEMEN, GATHER AROUND FOR OUR LATEST foray into the darkest recesses of human insanity,' Monroe began, spreading his hands wide as he surveyed the team. 'It appears we've been gifted with yet another borderline theatrical murder to solve.'

Behind him, the large plasma screen flickered to life as Billy Fitzwarren connected his laptop, displaying the crime scene photos in high definition. The stark image of Sean Acker's body with the King of Spades pinned to his chest dominated the screen, casting an eerie blue glow across the walls of the glass-walled briefing room.

The early afternoon briefing had been hastily convened once Doctor Marcos had something to announce. The rain had finally eased, leaving the City of London glistening in weak November sunshine that filtered through the grimy windows. A smell of damp wool and coffee permeated the air – what felt to Declan to be the signature of detectives who'd been out in foul weather.

Monroe stood commanding attention from the front

despite outranking Declan, who as DCI should usually host these briefings but he'd made an agreement with Monroe before they were both promoted. Declan sat to the right with Anjli beside him; Doctor Marcos occupied her usual spot at the back, scribbling notes in nearly illegible handwriting while Sergeant De'Geer and PC Cooper sat nearby, notebooks poised. Billy Fitzwarren hunched to the left, his fingers working his keyboard as he controlled the images on screen. Detective Chief Superintendent Bullman completed the scene, leaning against the doorframe with her arms folded and expression dubious, although this could have been because she hadn't intended to be here today, and "lucked in" – her own words – on the case.

'For those who haven't been fully briefed,' Monroe continued, jabbing a finger towards the screen, 'we're dealing with the murder of one Sean Acker, forty-one years old, shot through the chest at close range and then artfully decorated with a playing card – the King of Spades, to be precise – pinned to his body with what appears to be a glorified cocktail stick.'

'Skewer,' Doctor Marcos interrupted from the back without looking up from her notes. 'Metal skewer, likely custom-made. Double the length of a standard cocktail skewer but similar diameter. Not something you'd pick up at Sainsbury's.'

'I stand corrected, Rosanna,' Monroe replied with a theatrical bow. 'A custom metal skewer. Which only adds to the rather deliberate staging of our victim.'

'The card was custom as well,' Billy added, clicking to enlarge the image. The plasma screen now showed a close-up of the King of Spades, its black background and silver ink details clearly visible. 'Not your standard Bicycle deck.'

'Aye, that too,' Monroe nodded, turning back to the room. 'Declan, care to share what you found at the scene? For those who weren't there.'

Declan leant forwards, elbows on the table.

'The victim was dressed in tactical gear suggesting he was engaged in some kind of operation. However, this was discredited by the fact he carried a water pistol designed to look like a real gun and had a homemade water weapon attached to his wrist. It was implied by Doctor Marcos that his hair and face were soaked with water, applied after death.'

'It wasn't implied at all, it was confirmed because I am a shining star of the forensic world and a goddamned genius,' Doctor Marcos cut in, tapping her pen against her clipboard. 'The water was applied after the card was pinned, because the card showed signs of water damage, and not from the rain. Whoever did this was making a statement.'

'So, we have a man pretending to be a soldier, killed while carrying water weapons, then decorated with a playing card before being squirted with what looks to be another water pistol,' Monroe summarised. 'What did the autopsy tell us?'

Doctor Marcos rose from her chair.

'Cause of death was a single gunshot wound to the chest, medium calibre, likely 9mm. However there were scratches on the cartridge casing that suggests it was fired through a suppressor, or as we know it better, a silencer.'

'That'd explain why nobody heard the gunshot,' Monroe mused.

'Death between seven and nine last night. No defensive wounds, suggesting he either knew his killer or was taken completely by surprise. Toxicology tests showed traces of alcohol but nothing excessive. Just a bloke out for a wander in combat gear toting water pistols. As you do.'

'And what about this game?' Bullman asked from her position by the door. 'I understand there's something about a game?'

'Billy?' Monroe gestured towards the detective sergeant, before adopting an exaggerated, obsequious bow. 'Or should I say, *would your lordship care to grace us with your findings?*'

On the plasma screen, the image of the crime scene remained, casting Sean Acker's death in cold, clinical light. Billy's jaw tightened visibly, his eyes fixed on his laptop, the flush creeping up his neck betraying his discomfort as Monroe's joke landed with precision.

'Really?' Billy muttered, not looking up. 'Is that how it's going to be now?'

'Just having a wee bit of fun, laddie,' Monroe said with a grin. 'Not every day one of my detective sergeants becomes nobility.'

'It's not official yet,' Billy replied stiffly, his fingers tapping keys with more force than necessary. 'And I'd appreciate if we could focus on the case rather than my family situation.'

Declan caught Anjli's eye. It was clear Billy was still processing the news about his father stepping down as Viscount; having it broadcast to the entire team wasn't helping.

'Agreed,' Declan said firmly. 'The case takes priority.'

'Of course, of course,' Monroe agreed with a theatrical sigh. 'Though I must say, a viscount on the team might come in handy for those high society cases. Imagine the doors that'll swing open – the Garrick Club, the Carlton, all those places where toffs plot the downfall of working men like me.'

'The game, Monroe,' Bullman prompted, shooting him a warning look. 'We all know how much you love the upper class. I think Lord Carmody's still smarting from your last conversation. And we've run out of blue woad to paint your face with.'

'Lassie, you can *never* run out of blue woad,' Monroe winked.

Ignoring the comment, Billy straightened in his chair and tapped a few keys, and the screen behind Monroe shifted from the crime scene to a series of screenshots – emails and calendar entries displayed in neat rows. The team's attention moved to the new images as Billy found his professional footing again.

'Sean Acker was part of a group that called themselves "The Royal Court",' Billy explained, his voice steadying as he focused on the case. 'Twelve people who've been playing a modified version of an assassination game called "Killer" for nearly twenty years. Started when they were at Oxford together in the early 2000s.'

He clicked to display another screen showing a message with multiple recipients identified only by nicknames.

'The game works like this – each player receives a playing card identity, so in Sean's case, the King of Spades, and two target cards. When a player "kills" a target using water weapons, they collect that target's cards, expanding their list of targets. The last person standing wins.'

'So, Sean Acker was playing a pretend assassination game with water pistols when someone decided to use real bullets instead?' Cooper asked from the back.

'Looks that way,' Billy nodded as he glanced over at Anjli. 'I've pulled up the photos from your cloud folder.'

'Perfect,' Anjli said, standing to move closer to the screen. 'I uploaded everything from the apartment as soon as I got back.'

Billy clicked through to a new set of images, and now the

plasma screen filled with photos from Sean Acker's apartment. They showed groups of young people, male and female in various settings over the years, often brandishing water pistols and wearing exaggerated spy gear. In one photo dated *2018*, a visibly younger Sean Acker stood triumphantly holding a water rifle, his face split with a grin.

'As you can see,' Anjli explained, gesturing to the screen, 'they've been playing annually for twenty years, but this year was different. Notes in his calendar labelled it the "Final Round" – likely meant to be their last game.'

'Perfect cover for murder,' Monroe mused, pacing alongside the screen. 'Everyone's running around "assassinating" each other with water pistols. Nobody questions someone stalking the targets or carrying weapons.'

'Exactly,' Anjli agreed. 'And there's more. From what I can work out, three years ago, the game evolved. Two of the players – Alex Chen and Gary Webb – introduced "forfeits" for eliminated players. Started small but got more serious over time.'

'How serious?' Declan asked.

'I just saw notes about it,' Anjli glanced back at Billy now, the question out of her wheelhouse. 'Sean working out how bad his forfeits would be if he lost, that sort of thing.'

'From what I can piece together from encrypted messages on Sean's WhatsApp, they escalated from embarrassing social media posts to actual interference in careers and relationships. Real-world consequences.' Billy clicked through several screenshots on the plasma screen – messages between players discussing "forfeits" and consequences. 'The tone of the exchanges grows noticeably more tense in the more recent messages, with occasional references to disagreements about how far the game should go.'

'Or someone's using the game as cover for a more personal vendetta,' Anjli added.

'Morten, what did you find in his background?' Monroe asked.

De'Geer rose, his seven-foot Viking frame dwarfing the more diminutive Cooper beside him as he flipped open his notebook.

'Sean Acker was obsessed with being an ex-Royal Marine, but in reality, he washed out after only six weeks of basic training. According to former colleagues at Harding & Cross Investment, he constantly brought it up, wore military-style watches, and kept a rucksack with tactical webbing under his desk. Even dressed like a soldier at events.'

Monroe watched De'Geer's face.

'You don't approve?' he asked. 'You are our resident cosplayer, after all.'

'I dress like characters,' De'Geer argued. 'Little John, or Viking re-enacting. But I always know I'm playing someone, Guv. The impression I get here from Acker was he didn't believe this was a character. He believed this *was* him.'

'Neighbours described him as "intense" and "difficult",' Cooper, rising beside De'Geer added. 'He had frequent arguments with his building management about security issues. Several mentioned his tendency to exaggerate stories and achievements.'

'The playing cards found in his pocket,' Declan said, turning to Anjli. 'The Jack of Hearts and Ace of Diamonds. Those were his targets?'

Anjli nodded. 'We also discovered a notebook in his apartment with surveillance notes on two people – their work schedules, regular haunts, gym routines. No names, just "JH" and "AD".'

'Most likely his next intended victims,' Billy confirmed. 'Based on the game rules I've pieced together.'

'His apartment had a closet full of tactical gear,' Anjli read from her notes. 'Night-vision goggles, replica weapons – not these plastic guns filled with water, but exact airsoft duplicates – even camouflage face paint. He was taking this very seriously.'

'So, who are these players?' Bullman asked, pushing away from the doorframe and approaching the screen. 'Are they all potential targets now?'

Billy returned to his laptop.

'Based on email chains and social media, I've compiled a list.'

He tapped a key, and the plasma screen displayed a grid of social media profile pictures with names beneath them.

'There's Nathan Hargreaves, investment banker. I've actually met him a couple of times through Rufus Harrington, before he died. Silver spoon through and through. Alex Chen and Gary Webb, the ones who "evolved" the game with harsher forfeits – they both work in IT. Rachel Peterson, marketing executive. Diane Taylor, financial analyst. Daryl Collins and Belinda Morris, both in finance. Justin Kelly who works at a tech startup. There's also Victoria Lang, who apparently left the game a few years ago, and a few others I'm still tracking down.'

Monroe studied the faces on screen.

'Quite the collection of City types. Any obvious connections beyond the game?'

'Oxford,' Billy replied. 'All attended between 2002 and 2005. Most were part of the same societies or clubs. They started the game in what looks to be their first year and kept it going yearly after graduation, twenty years ago.'

'It's impressive they maintained it for twenty years,' Doctor Marcos commented. 'Most people can't keep a dinner club going for six months.'

'Alright then, laddies and lasses, assignments,' Monroe said, shifting to action mode. 'Anjli, take Cooper and see Nathan Hargreaves, purely as he's first on Billy's list. Billy, keep digging into the digital communications, see if you can identify strained relationships or serious forfeits that might create motive. Declan and I will speak with Chen and Webb, the game "architects". De'Geer, check out Acker's gym, any other social things he might have in his diary – if he was regularly boasting about his military background to anyone who listened, we might get a sense of who might have had reason to dislike him.'

As the team began gathering their things, Declan raised a hand.

'One other thing.'

The room quieted, everyone looking expectantly at him.

'This morning before the call came in about Acker, I was at St. Benedict's shelter speaking with a woman who calls herself Burlington Bertie,' he continued.

'St. Benedict's?' Bullman perked up. 'Shaun Donnal's place? How is he doing these days?'

'He's doing well,' Declan nodded. 'Running the outreach programme now. But about this Bertie woman—'

'And this connects to our murder how?' Bullman asked, getting back to business.

'It probably doesn't,' Declan admitted. 'She claims to have been an informant for my father years ago, working on a case involving an activist group called the Garden Collective. She mentioned that someone's been accessing files my father kept at the Reform Club, using our family name to gain access. I spoke with Anthony Farringdon, who confirmed parts of her story. The Garden Collective was a real group my father investigated unofficially in the early nineties.'

'The Reform Club?' Billy looked up. 'My family has memberships there. I could make some inquiries if you need access.'

'That might be helpful,' Declan nodded. 'Bertie claims former informants from that case have been dying over the past year – natural causes on paper, but suspicious timing. Given her dementia, it could be nothing. But I'd like to look into it.'

Monroe considered this.

'Fine. But keep it on the back burner. The Acker murder takes priority.'

'Of course,' Declan nodded. 'Oh, I know you said you didn't recall anyone named Bertie, but Farringdon said she was called Emmy Clarke.'

Monroe paused, his eyes narrowing.

'Right then,' he said, turning back to the room and clapping his hands together. 'Let's set about catching a killer who thinks murder is just a game. And Billy?'

Billy looked up, his expression carefully neutral.

'We'll chat about your impending lordship later.'

He winked to show he was joking.

Mostly.

'Wonderful,' Billy replied dryly. 'Looking forward to it.'

As the team dispersed, Anjli fell into step beside Declan.

'Garden Collective. You think there's something there?'

'Not sure,' Declan admitted. 'But when someone uses my family name to access my father's secret files, I get curious.'

'Fair enough,' Anjli nodded. 'I'll help if you need backup.'

'Appreciate it,' Declan said. 'I'm not sure Monroe's any

help there, judging on how he acted just then. But, for now, let's focus on this game. It's pretty bloody obvious we're most likely looking at a player who decided to change the rules in the most permanent way possible.'

Behind them, Billy sat staring at his laptop screen, though he was clearly seeing nothing. On the plasma display, the faces of the remaining players in "The Royal Court" continued to stare out at the empty room, but his mind was elsewhere.

Detective Sergeant The Viscount Fitzwarren.

Even after Declan's private briefing earlier, the reality of it still felt like a bad joke. His father's unexpected call this morning, the hastily arranged dinner tonight – all of it still seemed unreal compared to the concrete facts of the murder case before him.

Monroe paused at the door, looking back.

'Coming, Billy?'

'Right behind you,' Billy replied, closing the laptop and picking it up, before following Monroe out of the briefing room, passing Declan and Anjli as he did so.

Outside, the weak and momentary sunshine had already given way to new clouds rolling in from the west. Another storm was coming, and Declan couldn't shake the feeling that Sean Acker's murder was just the opening move in a much deadlier game.

RACHEL PETERSON CHECKED HER PHONE AGAIN AS THE LUNCH crowd around her thinned out. The cafe near her office was quietening down now, most of the City workers having returned to their desks for the afternoon. She stirred her coffee absently, scrolling through the group chat that had been unusually quiet since yesterday.

A message from Daryl popped up.

Has anyone heard from Sean? He's not answering my texts.

She frowned. Sean was usually annoyingly responsive, especially during game time. The King of Spades took the annual tradition more seriously than most of them. Rachel typed a quick response.

No, nothing here either.

This done, she set her phone down.

The "Final Round" had started on Friday. After twenty years, they were ending the tradition that had kept them connected since university. But something felt different this time; the game had changed over the past few years – what started as harmless fun with water pistols had developed into something with real-world consequences. Some of Alex and Gary's "forfeits" had gone too far, and a few of the players had really let them know last year, so much so that by the end Alex was sporting a black eye, and Gary had a split lip. And of course there was the issue about Nathan and his medication. Rachel needed to speak to him tonight, if they were all meeting. She'd found something that could seriously help him.

If he *wanted* bloody help, of course.

She adjusted the small water pistol concealed in her handbag. The *Queen of Clubs* playing card nestled in her wallet – her identity for the game. The rules were clear: three water weapons maximum and she'd chosen carefully this year. The tiny pistol for close encounters, water balloons for ambushes, and a modified spray bottle that looked like perfume for emergencies.

Her phone buzzed again. Another message from Daryl.

> Just heard from Nathan. Meeting tonight, 8pm at the usual place. Important update about the game. Everyone needs to attend.

Rachel frowned. *Unusual to change plans mid-game.* As she gathered her things to return to work, she didn't notice the figure watching her from across the street, observing her movements. She slipped her phone into her pocket and headed back to her office, mentally planning what time she'd need to leave to make the meeting.

The watcher remained still, waiting for the right moment. The Queen of Clubs had just become a *priority target.*

5

THE BANKER

THE LOBBY OF *CARRINGTON-HOWE INVESTMENT BANK* LOOKED like it had been designed by someone who thought "subtle" meant using actual gold instead of gold leaf. Thirty-foot ceilings with light fixtures like crystal octopuses, marble floors so polished you could check your reflection, and a reception desk the size of a small yacht.

Anjli Kapoor had interviewed *murderers* who showed less ostentation.

'Think they polish the floor with the tears of small business owners?' Cooper asked under her breath as they approached the reception desk, warrant cards already out.

'That's just for the brass handrails,' Anjli replied. 'The floors get the premium stuff – pensioners' dreams.'

The receptionist – impossibly groomed, impossibly blonde – looked up with practised politeness. 'Good afternoon. How may I help you?'

'DI Kapoor and PC Cooper. We're here to see Nathan Hargreaves.'

The smile remained fixed as she reached for the phone.

'Do you have an appointment?'

'We have a murder. That trumps appointment,' Anjli said, her tone making it clear this wasn't a negotiable point.

The receptionist's smile flickered for only a millisecond.

'Of course. I'll need to call up to Mister Hargreaves' office. If you could wait a moment ...'

The call was brief and discreet, and after a moment the receptionist looked back up at Anjli.

'Someone will escort you shortly. Please take a seat.'

Instead, they stood, watching the choreographed bustle of the financial world in motion – traders striding purposefully, clients being guided through with deferential nods, security guards scanning with calm professional suspicion. Seven minutes later, a woman emerged from the elevators; she was mid-twenties, with a sharp-cut bob, sharper-cut suit, and that irritating particular air of determined efficiency that came with being a PA to someone important.

Or at least to someone she thought was important, anyway.

'Detectives? I'm Melanie Ellis, Mr. Hargreaves' assistant,' she explained. 'He's just finishing a call. Follow me, please.'

The elevator ride was silent except for the muted classical music playing overhead. No one commented on the irony of Vivaldi's "Spring" while more November rain streaked the glass walls of the building, although Anjli assumed a "muzak" version of *Guns and Roses* classic anthem would have been even worse.

Melanie swiped her badge at a gleaming glass door etched with "Structured Products & Derivatives" and led them onto the trading floor.

Even after years on the force, Anjli found these spaces jarring – the strange tension of controlled chaos, dozens of screens flickering with numbers, graphs climbing and falling like fevers, hushed voices delivering millions into different hands. The smell of expensive coffee, computer equipment, and anxiety. They approached a glass-walled office at the far end of the floor; inside, a man leant against the edge of an imposing desk, scrolling through his phone with one hand, a Montblanc pen spinning absently between the fingers of the other. In his dark-blue, three-piece suit with subtle window-pane check, Nathan Hargreaves looked every inch the successful banker – just past forty but moving with the confidence of someone who'd navigated boardrooms for decades.

He glanced up as they entered, setting his phone down and moving forward to greet them.

'DI Kapoor, PC Cooper,' he said, offering his hand. 'Nathan Hargreaves. Please, have a seat.'

His handshake was firm, professional, exactly calibrated, and Anjli got the overwhelming impression this was a man who collected handshakes in the same way Christian Bale collected business cards in *American Psycho*. As they settled into the chairs opposite his desk, Nathan facing them, Anjli noted the touches that personalised the otherwise corporate space – a vintage *Patek Philippe* desk clock, a framed college rowing team photo, and a sleek MacBook, the latest model, beside the standard-issue banking terminals.

'Can I offer you anything? Coffee? Water?'

When they declined, he nodded to Melanie, who withdrew, closing the door behind her.

'You're here about Sean,' he said, his expression shifting from professional to concerned. Not dramatic, just the subtle recalibration of someone who knew how to modulate their emotions.

I'll need to remember that, Anjli thought to herself as she watched him. *They're always harder to read.*

'I take it you've heard?' Anjli asked. The name hadn't been released to the press yet, but these things always had a habit of leaking.

'Got a message from a friend at Bishopsgate police an hour back,' Nathan replied. 'I've been trying to reach him since last night. I missed our weekly squash game, but he didn't berate me for it which isn't – *wasn't* – like him. I still can't believe it.'

Anjli observed his face as he leaned back in his chair slightly.

'I know it's a little macabre, but I don't know the details. I was considering contacting Billy – he still works with you, right? I was going to drop him a line, see if I could arrange a little drink, find out the "tea" and all that. But, as you're here, can I ask how?'

'He was murdered,' Cooper said, notebook open on her knee. 'Shot once in the chest.'

Nathan's hand went to his own chest unconsciously.

'My God. Who would—'

He paused, processing.

'When did it happen?'

'We believe between seven and nine last night.'

He shook his head, genuine shock evident on his face.

'My friend said the case was passed on to you, but I wasn't sure why?'

'We handle complex cases.'

Nathan's expression shifted again, this time to something closer to wariness.

'And why is Sean's death considered complex?'

'Because whoever killed him left a calling card,' Anjli said. 'A playing card, to be precise. The King of Spades, pinned to his chest.'

Nathan went completely still. Only his eyes moved, widening slightly before his gaze dropped to his desk.

'The King of Spades,' he repeated quietly. 'That's Sean's card.'

'That's what we'd like to talk to you about, Mister Hargreaves,' Anjli continued. 'The Royal Court.'

Nathan met her gaze, his momentary shock now controlled behind a carefully neutral expression.

'How do you know about that?'

'We found playing cards on Sean's body, and evidence of some kind of game on his devices.' She leant forward slightly. 'We understand you're one of the players.'

For a moment, Nathan seemed to debate his options. Then his shoulders relaxed marginally.

'Yes, I'm part of the group. Have been since university.'

He reached for a glass of water on his desk, lifting it but not drinking.

'I can't believe someone would use our game as... as some sort of murder signature. It's sick.'

'Tell us about the game,' Cooper prompted. 'How it works, who's involved. We've got an idea based on social media posts, but nothing confirmed.'

Nathan set the glass down, composing himself.

'It started at Oxford. A few of us were at a party in our first year, and someone brought up this old game called "Killer" where you hunt targets with water pistols. We decided to adapt it using playing cards as identities,' his voice steadied as he continued, finding comfort in the factual recounting. 'It was just so we could blow off some steam, you see. Exams that year were an absolute bitch. If we didn't do something, we'd go crazy.'

'I'm sure this is a common issue,' Anjli deadpanned. 'But

in my experience people don't usually reach for water pistols.'

'Well, perhaps we're made of sterner stock,' Nathan snapped back, but his expression immediately returned to the composed nature as he continued. 'It was just a bit of fun. Everyone gets a playing card as their identity, plus two target cards. By the time we had it planned, there were twelve of us. You "kill" your targets with water weapons, take their target cards, and so on. Last person standing wins.'

'And it's been going for twenty years?' Anjli asked.

'Yes, annual tradition, but the twenty started after Oxford. We used to play it on campus during the terms. It was a way to stay connected after graduation. Different careers, different cities sometimes, but for one month each year, we'd all be playing together again.'

A brief, genuine smile crossed his face.

'Running through the City with concealed water pistols, stalking each other through department stores, coffee shops... it sounds ridiculous when I say it out loud, but it meant something to us.'

'Who else is in this "Royal Court"?'

'Apart from Sean?' Nathan paused, collecting his thoughts. 'There's Alex Chen – runs a tech startup. Gary Webb's a corporate lawyer who's partnered up with Alex. Rachel Peterson in pharmaceutical marketing. Diane Taylor's a financial analyst. Daryl Collins and Belinda Morris both work in finance—'

'A lot of you work in finance, it seems.'

'We were all in the same year, half the same courses, so we gravitated together,' Nathan shrugged. 'Victoria was very good at "matchmaking", shall we say. Anyway, it wasn't just finance bros, Justin Kelly's in tech – runs his own startup, probably purely to spite Alex, Christopher Wilson is in IT, and Oliver Drake, who joined last year is an analyst. There was also Victoria Lang, who I mentioned a second ago – she's a psychologist, but she left the game a while back.'

Cooper made notes, her pen moving silently across the page.

'That's eleven plus you.'

'Twelve total, yes. That's how many we need for the format to work properly. We use only the face cards and aces – Jack, Queen, King, Ace from each suit. Four cards spare in case we're thrown back in as a wildcard. Don't get me going on that – those rules are an entire bag of worms.'

'Which card are you?' Anjli asked.

'Jack of Diamonds.'

'And your targets?'

'Queen of Clubs and Ace of Hearts. Rachel and Oliver.'

'The new guy,' Anjli noted. 'How did Oliver join the group?'

'We had a spot open. One of the players... Daniel... he passed away. It was sudden.'

'And you just replaced him?'

'We felt we were honouring his memory,' Nathan's voice had taken a warning tone.

'But you didn't replace Victoria?'

'We hoped she'd come back, you know? That she needed a break. Daniel... well, that was a different situation.'

'Must be hard having a new face when you've spent almost two decades as the same team.'

'He wasn't a new face. He works downstairs.' Nathan shrugged.

'So he does work in finance, then.'

'I suppose.'

'And you suggested him?'

'No, Belinda recommended him when we needed a replacement. Pushed quite hard for him, actually. Almost like she already had him picked out before Daniel was even gone.'

'How did she meet him?'

'Christmas party a couple of years back. A few of the London guys came along. You know, free drink, all that. I think Belinda and Oliver met there. After that, no idea.'

'You mentioned Oliver Drake replaced someone named Daniel,' Cooper looked up from her notes. 'Who was that?'

A shadow crossed Nathan's face.

'Daniel Foster. He... he died early last year. Almost two years back. Suicide.'

The word hung in the air between them. Nathan seemed to retreat inward for a moment before continuing.

'After Daniel died, we needed a replacement player, as Victoria had also stepped down. Well, more stormed off in a hissy fit.'

'But you hoped she'd come back.'

'She did the same a few years ago – bitched after a game, left, but was back by the following November,' Nathan shrugged. 'We assumed she was waiting for an apology or something. Oliver was a colleague, Belinda liked him, seemed a good fit. We assigned him the Ace of Hearts,' Nathan explained as he reached for his water again, this time taking a sip. 'Daniel's death and Victoria's spat were part of why this was meant to be our final year. The game had lost its shine for some of us.'

Anjli noted how his right hand tightened almost imperceptibly on the glass.

'Did Daniel's suicide have anything to do with the game?'

Nathan set the glass down carefully.

'Not directly, no. Daniel had struggled with depression for years.'

He hesitated, but then, as if making an internal decision, he continued.

'There had been some changes to the game three years back. New rules about forfeits for eliminated players. We'd been slacking, pissing about a bit, and they thought this would focus us again. Daniel got hit with a particularly harsh one that affected his job. He died before he did it.'

As he reached for his water again, his sleeve pulled back slightly, revealing what looked like a surgical scar on his wrist. Anjli caught his gaze shifting to her, noticing the observation.

'Carpal tunnel,' he said, adjusting his cuff. 'Too many years of typing. The surgeon assured me it wouldn't affect my squirt gun abilities, so silver linings and all that.'

A folder on his desk shifted slightly as he moved his arm, revealing the edge of a silver blister pack of tablets, some text on them. Cooper's eyes flicked to it, then back to her notebook.

'Where were you last night between seven and nine?' Anjli asked.

If Nathan was bothered by the directness of the question, he didn't show it.

'Here, unfortunately. Singapore markets went haywire, and we had an emergency response meeting with our Asia desk before they opened again. About twenty of us were in the conference room from two in the afternoon until nearly midnight,' he gestured to the glass-walled meeting room visible across the trading floor. 'Building security logs and CCTV will confirm it. I'd told Sean I couldn't make squash.

That's probably why he decided to go hunting, but he never answered me back.'

'We'll need that footage,' Cooper said.

'Of course. Melanie can arrange it.'

'Let's go back to these forfeits,' Anjli added. 'You mentioned they became more serious?'

Nathan seemed to choose his words with deliberate care.

'There was a shift from harmless pranks to things that could affect someone's real life. The game began bleeding into reality in ways that weren't... healthy.'

'Who controlled these forfeits?'

'Alex and Gary designed them, kept them private between themselves and the eliminated player.'

Anjli made a mental note to pass this to Declan before he spoke to Chen and Webb.

'Given what's happened to Sean, do you think other players might be in danger?'

'If someone's using the game as cover for murder ...' Nathan's expression darkened; he trailed off, then straightened. 'We had already planned to meet tonight, after hearing Sean wasn't responding to anyone. I should tell the others what's happened.'

'Where and when?' Cooper asked.

'The Bell Tavern near Liverpool Street. Eight o'clock. We have some tables reserved at the back.' He hesitated. 'Should we cancel?'

'No,' Anjli decided. 'But we'd appreciate officers being present. Discreetly.'

'I understand,' Nathan nodded as he reached for a business card and wrote something on the back. 'My personal mobile. In case you need to reach me directly.'

As they stood to leave, Nathan's phone chimed with a

message. He glanced at it, a momentary tightness around his eyes before he slipped the phone into his pocket.

'Sorry, more Singapore issues. I'll have Melanie arrange for the security footage to be sent over.' He extended his hand again. 'Please keep me informed about the investigation. Sean was... complicated, but he was one of us.'

WHEN THE GLASS DOOR CLOSED BEHIND THEM, COOPER WAITED until they were out of earshot before speaking.

'So, how much of that man we just met was fake?' she asked.

'Hidden medication. Surgical scar he explained away. Convenient alibi,' Anjli responded.

'Prescription medicine,' Cooper added. 'I caught the name – *Lamotrigine*. Not sure what it is exactly, but I'll bet my badge it's not a painkiller.'

'And yet he seemed genuinely shocked when he heard,' Anjli noted. 'Either he's innocent, or he's very good.'

'What about this meeting tonight?'

'Could be legitimate concern. Could be a chance to get stories straight.' Anjli considered the options. 'Either way, we need to be there.'

'And Daniel Foster's suicide?'

'Definitely needs looking into. If there's a connection between his death and Sean's murder, it might give us our killer.'

They rode the elevator down in thoughtful silence. Outside, the rain had intensified, sheets of water cascading down the glass side of the building.

'What next?' Cooper asked as they stepped onto the pavement, the glass alcove keeping them dry for the moment.

'You attend the meeting tonight – you're less recognisable. I'll track down Victoria Lang, the psychologist who left the game. If anyone has perspective on the group dynamics without a stake in the current situation, it might be her.'

As they headed towards Temple Inn, neither noticed the figure watching from a parked black Audi across the street.

Inside, a hand reached for a phone, quickly typing a message.

Police just left. Meeting tonight still on – 8pm.

And with that, they drove off.

BACK IN HIS OFFICE, NATHAN HARGREAVES STOOD AT THE window, watching the tiny figures of Anjli and Cooper cross the street, running as if they could dodge raindrops.

The composed, professional banker was gone. In his place stood someone coiled tight with tension, evident in the rigid set of his shoulders and the muscle working in his jaw.

When they disappeared from view, he turned to his desk. Trembling, he moved the folder concealing his medication and popped two Lamotrigine from the blister pack, swallowed them dry before checking his phone again, re-reading the message that had come through during the interview.

We need to talk before tonight. Same place,
6 p.m.

No signature, but he knew who it was from. His thumb

hovered over the screen momentarily before he typed a single word in response.

Confirmed.

Nathan slipped the phone into his pocket and straightened his tie, the mask of the investment banker sliding back into place. After a moment more to compose himself, he pressed the intercom button.

'Melanie, please arrange for yesterday's security files to be sent to the police promptly,' he said, his voice betraying nothing of his inner turmoil. 'And clear my schedule after five. Something's come up.'

6

GYM-NASTICS

MORTEN DE'GEER HAD NEVER LIKED THE SMELL OF GYMS – that peculiar mixture of disinfectant, sweat, and desperation that seemed to permeate every fitness centre he'd ever visited. *Royal Marine Fitness* near Liverpool Street was no exception, though it added its own particular bouquet of protein powder and testosterone to the mix.

As his towering seven-foot frame pushed through the double doors, the familiar sounds of clanking weights, pounding treadmills, and grunting exercise enthusiasts washed over him, lessening as people took in his appearance; even in a gym full of well-built men, De'Geer's muscular Viking bulk drew stares.

A woman with impressive biceps gave him a curious once-over as he approached the reception desk. He decided to ignore her.

'Are you joining today?' asked the receptionist, a young Indian man who, despite his athletic build, still had to look up to meet De'Geer's gaze.

De'Geer paused, looking down at his police uniform and fluorescent jacket.

'Do you think I'm here to join?'

'We get a lot of police,' the receptionist shrugged. 'They often come straight from work.'

Accepting this, De'Geer flashed his warrant card, his massive hand making it look oddly small.

'Sergeant De'Geer. I'm here about Sean Acker.'

At the name, the receptionist's expression shifted from customer service smile to genuine concern.

'Sean? Is everything okay?'

'I'm afraid not. Can I speak to the manager?'

The receptionist picked up the phone and after a short conversation down it, where De'Geer just made out the words "police", "built like a brick shithouse" and "no *you* tell him you're busy", he was led by the young man to a small office towards the back of the gym, his large frame making the visitor's chair seem comically inadequate.

Across from him sat a man who introduced himself as Terry Winters, the owner. Unlike many gym proprietors De'Geer had met, Winters didn't have the polished look of a fitness influencer; instead, he had the weathered appearance of someone who'd spent decades in actual gymnasiums and boxing rings rather than Instagram-ready fitness studios.

'Raj said you were asking about Sean Acker,' Winters said, leaning back in his chair. 'Bit of a character, that one.'

'How so?'

'Always banging on about being an ex-Marine. Had all the gear, none of the experience. All talk, no walk, you get me?' Winters shook his head. 'I served eight years in the Royal Marines myself, so I knew he was full of it straight away. I asked around, got the scoop. Six weeks basic, that's all he did before washing out, but to hear him talk, you'd think he'd been with the Special Boat Service.'

'Did anyone confront him about it?' De'Geer asked. 'I'm guessing you get a lot of serving men and women here?'

'A few times,' Winters nodded. 'But it was pointless. Guy's dumb as a stump. Went in one ear, out the other. Some blokes here find it amusing. Others avoid him. He isn't a bad sort, just... desperate to be something he wasn't.'

De'Geer made a note of this.

'Did he have any close friends here? Anyone he confided in?'

'What do you mean "did"? He hasn't cancelled his membership...'

Winters paused.

'Oh. Shit.'

'Sorry,' De'Geer replied. 'We can't go into it as yet, but he passed last night we believe. Your answers will help.'

Winters considered this.

'Okay. Close friends. Not many, to be honest. Rubbed most people the wrong way. Though, come to think of it, he was always in deep conversation with one of our trainers, Craig Neeson. Those two were thick as thieves. Always whispering in corners.'

'How can I find this Craig?'

'He's on the floor now if you want to talk to him.'

'I'll do that,' De'Geer said, rising to his full height, causing Winters to blink upwards. 'Anyone else?'

'Not that I noticed. Sean kept to himself mostly, when he wasn't trying to impress the new members with his "war stories".' Winters also stood, looking considerably smaller beside De'Geer's Nordic frame. 'Come on, I'll show you where Craig usually works. Should I tell people?'

'That's up to you,' De'Geer shrugged. 'But I'd suggest doing it after I speak to Craig.'

THE MAIN WORKOUT AREA WAS CROWDED WITH AFTER-WORK fitness enthusiasts, as Winters led De'Geer through rows of machines, nodding towards a wiry, tattooed man supervising a client's squat form.

'That's Craig there,' Winters pointed. 'I'll leave you to it.'

De'Geer thanked him and moved across the gym floor, his size creating a natural pathway as exercisers instinctively made room for his approach, like a "Gym-Bro Moses" parting the Red Sea. He positioned himself within Craig's line of sight, waiting for the trainer to finish with his client. When Craig finally looked up, his eyes widened slightly; first at De'Geer's imposing presence, then with a flicker of something else – recognition, perhaps. Not of De'Geer personally, but of what he represented.

Authority.

Questions.

Trouble.

'Be right back,' Craig muttered to his client, before addressing De'Geer with forced casualness. 'Help you, mate?'

'I'd like to talk about Sean Acker,' De'Geer kept his voice low.

The change was instantaneous. Craig's face went blank, his eyes darting to the exit behind De'Geer, and without warning, he bolted – shoving past a startled gym-goer and sprinting towards the back of the gym.

'Police! Stop!' De'Geer called out, immediately giving chase. Despite his massive frame, De'Geer moved with surprising agility, dodging between exercise machines as Craig knocked a rack of dumbbells into his path. The weights clattered across the floor, causing several people to jump aside with alarmed expressions.

Craig vaulted over a bench press, knocking the bar from its rack; De'Geer sidestepped it, his long legs eating up the distance between them. The trainer swerved around a group of women on yoga mats, turning and punting a Pilates ball back towards his pursuer like it was a penalty kick.

The ball bounced harmlessly off De'Geer's thigh as he maintained the chase.

'You're only making things worse, Craig!'

The fleeing man crashed through a door marked "Changing Rooms", nearly bowling over an old man in a towel. De'Geer followed, apologising as he passed, cursing as steam billowed from the attached sauna, momentarily obscuring his vision. When it cleared, Craig was already pushing through the fire exit at the far end. De'Geer cut across a row of lockers, causing a young man to press himself against the wall in surprise.

The fire exit led to a narrow alley behind the gym, and De'Geer burst through the door just in time to see Craig scrambling over a chain-link fence at the end. Cursing once more under his breath, the sergeant broke into a sprint.

Craig dropped down on the other side, glancing back in panic – just long enough to see De'Geer launch himself at the fence. The seven-foot officer cleared the top with a powerful vault that would have impressed his Viking ancestors, landing with a heavy thud that seemed to shake the alley. The trainer turned to run again but found himself in a dead end – a small service area blocked by locked gates on all sides.

He spun around, back against the wall, chest heaving.

'It's not what you think,' he gasped as De'Geer approached, barely winded. 'Whatever you think it is.'

De'Geer reached out a massive hand and gripped Craig's shoulder, effectively ending any further flight plans.

'All this because I asked about Sean Acker?'

'Sean?' Craig frowned, genuine confusion crossing his face. 'Wait, this is about him, not me? What's he done now?'

'He's been murdered.'

The colour drained from Craig's face.

'Murder—? I thought this was about—' He cut himself off, eyes widening. 'Wait, Sean's *dead?*'

De'Geer studied him closely. The shock appeared genuine.

'Why did you think I was chasing you?'

'Jesus Christ,' Craig sagged against the wall, no longer resisting. 'I didn't... I had nothing to do with that.'

'Yet you ran when I mentioned his name.'

Craig gave a hollow laugh.

'Yeah, well, I thought you were here about our... business arrangement.'

'Which was?'

The trainer glanced nervously at De'Geer's grip on his shoulder, then sighed.

'Sean and I had an understanding. He wanted to be taken seriously. I helped him look the part.'

'How, exactly?'

'Look, he wasn't the only one,' Craig said defensively. 'Half the City boys who come through that gym want short-cuts. I just provide... assistance.'

'Steroids?'

'Among other things. Supplements. Pre-workout. Some

grey-area nootropics stuff that's not strictly illegal but wouldn't look good for a financial professional,' Craig shifted uncomfortably. 'Sean was more intense about it than most. Said he needed to be at his peak for "the game".'

De'Geer could guess what "game" Sean Acker had been talking about. But Craig, now captured, didn't want to stop talking.

'He never went into details. Some kind of elaborate thing he played with his university mates. Sounded childish to me, but he took it deadly serious,' Craig shook his head. 'Last few weeks, he'd become proper paranoid about it. Said someone was "playing by different rules" and he needed to be ready.'

'Ready for what?'

'Surveillance, he called it. Wanted stuff to help him stay alert for extended periods. You know. Proper "keep awake" shit,' Craig reached slowly into his pocket. 'I was supposed to give him this yesterday, but he never showed.'

De'Geer took the small, unmarked package, examining it. 'What's in it?'

'Nothing lethal, I swear. Just some tablets to keep him sharp. Like I said, it's a grey area,' Craig looked genuinely troubled now. 'Who'd want to kill Sean? He was annoying, sure, but harmless.'

'That's what I'm trying to find out,' De'Geer replied, pocketing the package. 'You'll need to come in and make a statement.'

As De'Geer led the subdued trainer back towards the gym, he pulled out his phone and dialled Declan's number. If this tattooed scroat's story was true, then the case had just developed an interesting new angle – one that confirmed Sean Acker had been genuinely afraid of something, or *someone*, in the days before his death.

NATHAN HARGREAVES CHECKED HIS WATCH FOR THE THIRD TIME in five minutes. The antique Rolex had been his father's, a graduation gift he'd received despite disappointing the old man by choosing finance over politics. The watch's gold case caught the fading light as he adjusted his cuff.

Six-twenty. They were late.

He stood beneath the partial shelter of an old stone archway near the entrance to St. Dunstan-in-the-East Church Garden, barely five minutes' walk from his office. The secluded meeting point offered privacy, multiple exits, and crucially, no surveillance cameras. The rain was picking up again after a couple of hours of grey skies, drops gathering on the ancient stone before trickling down like tears.

His phone buzzed with an incoming text. He checked it, grimacing as he did so.

Delayed. Keep waiting.

No name, no Caller ID, but none was needed. Nathan replaced the phone in his pocket and paced the small pathway between the ancient walls. His hand trembled slightly as he reached for his medication, discreetly slipping a tablet under his tongue. The anxiety that had been building since the police interview that afternoon refused to subside. Detective Inspector Kapoor had been too perceptive, asking all the right questions about the game and its evolution.

It was only a matter of time before they discovered the rest.

And now this meeting. Risky, but necessary if he wanted to contain the situation before it spiralled further out of control. Sean's death had changed everything. If the police started digging too deeply ...

Nathan swallowed hard, forcing the thought away.

One problem at a time.

RACHEL PETERSON HURRIED THROUGH THE RAIN, HER HEELS clicking on the wet pavement as she approached the office building near Monument Station. The text had been specific – the empty Harrington Finance satellite office on Lombard Street, six sharp. Not their usual meeting place, but given the circumstances, security made sense.

The message had come from a number she didn't recognise, but mentioned details only someone in the game would know.

> Urgent meeting about Sean and next steps. St. Dunstan's entrance too exposed with current situation. Use back office entrance instead. 6 p.m.

Initially, she'd hesitated. The timing felt odd – just hours before their scheduled group meeting at the *Bell Tavern*. But Sean's silence, followed by rumours of police asking questions, had convinced her this couldn't wait.

Rachel checked the small water pistol concealed in her handbag – a habit formed over twenty years of playing. The Queen of Clubs, her game identity, felt suddenly heavier in her wallet. Twenty years of tradition, friendship, and increasingly complicated entanglements, all bound up in a playing card.

If this was someone trying to take her out, they were going to seriously regret it.

The building's back-office service entrance was exactly where the follow-up text had described – an unmarked metal door down a narrow alley beside the main building.

> Security desk on front entrance will have questions. Use service door – keycode 5281. Take South Stairs to 4th floor, wait there. Building systems down for maintenance, so move quickly.

Rachel punched in the code, her unease growing when the door opened with a metallic click. The service corridor beyond was dimly lit with emergency lighting, the regular systems apparently offline as mentioned in the text. She hesitated at the threshold, then stepped inside.

She guessed that if this was a setup, then someone might wait to ambush her in the stairwell, so instead she took an alternative way up. The service elevator hummed quietly as it climbed, and Rachel checked her reflection on its brushed metal surface, tucking a strand of hair behind her ear.

Outside, thunder rolled across London's skyline.

Once out of the elevator, the fourth floor corridor was dimly lit, emergency lights casting long shadows. The fire exit to the south stairwell stood at the far end, and Rachel hesitated, unease prickling the back of her neck. She pulled out her phone, checking for any update or clarification.

Nothing.

With a deep breath, she pushed open the door.

The stairs beyond were dark, illuminated only by the city lights filtering through rain-streaked windows.

'Hello?' she called. 'Anyone here?'

Her voice echoed in the empty space. She took a few steps forward; keys clutched in her hand as an improvised weapon.

Maybe she'd gotten the time wrong. Or the location.

As she turned to leave, lightning flickered through the window, briefly illuminating the space. In that instant, Rachel glimpsed a figure standing in the corner – motionless, watching.

Her heart hammered against her ribs.

'Who's there?'

A voice came from the darkness.

'The Queen of Clubs. Right on time.'

Bollocks. It's a bloody card game setup. Rachel reached for her bag, for the water pistol inside.

'This isn't funny. What's going on?'

'The game has developed,' the voice replied. 'Didn't you get the memo?'

Wait. Hold on.

Rachel's shoulders relaxed slightly as recognition dawned.

'Oh, for God's sake,' she sighed, lowering her bag and turning back to the door, intending to leave. 'Is this really necessary? All this cloak and dagger nonsense when we could've just gone for a coffee—'

She felt movement behind her, and before she could turn a hand clamped over her mouth, and she felt another arm reach around her before a sharp pain hit her chest. Rachel looked down; a knife hilt stuck out from between her ribs, and fresh blood soaked her blouse, warm and wet.

It was then that her legs went.

The attacker caught her weight, lowering her to the floor, and the knife pulled free with a horrible sucking sound, the gloved hands wiping the blade on her jacket, then reaching for something else – a strange looking black, gold and silver playing card and a thin metal spike.

'Why?' The question came out as barely a breath when the hand shifted.

The attacker pressed the Queen of Clubs to her chest, and before she could protest one hand slammed back over her mouth, hard enough to crack her head against the floor, while the other hand shoved the spike through the card, and into the knife wound.

Rachel fought against the hand covering her mouth. A muffled noise escaped her, and tears tracked down her face.

'The rules changed,' the attacker said simply. 'Some games aren't meant to be played.'

Her vision going dark, Rachel felt water splash her face – one last sick joke on the game they'd played for two decades, before her body went still.

THE RAIN HAD INTENSIFIED, DRUMMING AGAINST THE STONE walls and ancient arches as Nathan finally gave up waiting. He'd been there over an hour, getting progressively more soaked as the rain found its way through the partial shelter of the ruins.

As he walked away through the downpour, he glanced back at the shadowy garden, its moss-covered stones now gleaming wet in the dim streetlight.

Another dead end. Another wasted opportunity to get ahead of whatever was coming.

His phone remained silent as he navigated through London's rain-slicked streets, finally hailing a passing black cab.

No explanations.

No further instructions.

Just the growing certainty that whatever control he thought he had over the situation was rapidly slipping away. Time was running out.

And somewhere in London, the game continued, the players unaware someone was screwing with the rules.

7

BELL TAVERN

Stars glittered above London, sharp and clear in the chilly November night; a brief, clear sky, and a respite from the constant rain. Esme Cooper hunched deeper into her jacket as she kept watch outside *The Bell Tavern*, a Victorian-era pub nestled among the glass-and-steel monoliths of the financial district. Through steamed windows she could see City workers packed shoulder to shoulder, Wednesday night in full swing. She checked her watch – seven-fifty p.m.

Right then. Time to—

She paused as she spotted Declan and Monroe approaching from Liverpool Street, Declan's collar turned up against the chill, Monroe's white hair catching the streetlights.

'Sir,' she nodded as they reached her. 'And Guv. Didn't expect you both here.'

'Alex and Gary have been giving us the runaround all day,' Declan said, breath clouding in the cold air. '"Technical difficulties" and "meetings being moved". We decided to join you and cut through the crap.'

'Aye,' Monroe agreed. 'Technical difficulties my arse. Pair of them watched us arrive at their office then disappeared out the back door like schoolboys ducking detention.'

'Three scheduled interviews, three no-shows,' Declan added. 'We've wasted enough time.'

'So much for surveillance, then?' Esme asked, straightening her civilian clothes – dark jeans and a simple jumper chosen to blend with the evening crowd.

'Any sign of them yet?' Declan asked, nodding towards the pub.

'Daryl Collins arrived twenty minutes ago with two others. No sign of Chen, Webb, or Hargreaves,' Esme reported. 'They've got two tables pushed together at the back.'

'No private room?' Monroe asked.

'Just the tables.'

'Makes our job easier,' Declan replied. 'Let's see what our wannabe assassins have to say for themselves.'

INSIDE, THE PUB WAS A WALL OF NOISE AND HEAT – LAUGHTER competing with music, the sour-sweet smell of beer and warm bodies after hours of office confinement. Football played silently on a screen above the bar, ignored by most in favour of shouted conversations and the ritualistic end-of-day unwinding.

Declan scanned the crowded room, quickly locating the tables at the back. Daryl Collins held court with a pint in hand, while two men Declan recognised from the case photos as Justin Kelly and Chris Wilson listened to whatever he was saying with varied expressions of interest.

Declan looked back at Cooper.

'Three of us might overwhelm them. Hang back, watch the door. Just another night at the pub until I say otherwise.'

They wound their way through the crowd, squeezing past groups of City workers bellowing orders at the bar. Daryl Collins glanced up as they approached, his sentence trailing off mid-anecdote, and his eyes narrowing slightly.

'Gentlemen,' Declan said. 'Mind if we join you?'

'Depends who's asking,' Daryl replied, a wariness creeping into his expression.

'DCI Walsh, City of London Police,' Declan said, showing his warrant card. 'This is Detective Superintendent Monroe.'

'And you're here because ...?' Justin Kelly asked, setting his pint down with exaggerated care. A sallow-faced man with thinning hair and nervous hands, he looked like someone who spent too many hours in front of computer screens.

'Sean Acker,' Monroe replied, pulling out a chair uninvited. 'Thought we might have a wee chat.'

Chris Wilson shifted uncomfortably, his tall frame hunched as if trying to occupy less space. His hand tightened around his glass.

'We were going to talk about Sean, anyway. Unofficial wake, you might say.'

'Then consider us mourners,' Monroe gave a bitter smile. 'Though we tend to ask more questions than your average funeral-goer.'

The pub door opened, admitting both a blast of cold air and Nathan Hargreaves. His gaze swept the room, pausing when he spotted the new additions to the reserved table. If he was surprised to actually see police there, he masked it quickly, unwinding a cashmere scarf as he approached, his charcoal overcoat and tailored suit marking him out among the more casual evening crowd. Declan had read Anjli's notes on her meeting, but she hadn't mentioned he had the carefully maintained appearance of someone who included regular gym sessions in his calendar alongside board meetings.

'Meet Walsh and Monroe,' Daryl half-muttered. 'They're police.'

Nathan glanced back at the bar and Cooper.

'I thought I saw PC Cooper there,' he said with a smile. 'DI Kapoor suggested someone would be visiting the pub. I didn't realise it was the entire office.'

'You knew?'

'I was going to tell you,' Nathan muttered. 'I was... delayed.'

Monroe leant back on the chair as he turned to face Nathan.

'You know laddie, you're looking remarkably composed, considering a friend of yours was murdered yesterday,' he said.

'Grief takes many forms,' Nathan replied evenly, hanging his coat on the back of a chair. 'Some of us process it by seeking justice.'

'Convenient,' Declan remarked. 'That's why we're here too.'

Before Nathan could reply to this though, Daryl's phone buzzed on the table. He checked it, frowning.

'Still nothing from Rachel.'

'She'll be along,' Justin said, draining the last of his pint. 'Her boss is probably being a prick again. Diane's got this thing on tonight so can't make it – I said I'd catch her up – but nothing yet from Dirk, either.'

'She would've texted,' Daryl insisted. 'Not like her to go dark, especially with what happened to Sean.'

Nathan sighed, looking back at the bar.

'Another round?' he asked the table, receiving nods. 'And you, officers?'

'Nothing, thanks,' Declan replied. 'We're working.'

'Of course,' Nathan said, wandering off to the bar to get a round in. Before Declan could follow up on Rachel's absence, the pub door swung open again, and Alex Chen and Gary Webb entered, deep in conversation that ceased abruptly as they spotted the detectives.

A wordless glance passed between them before they approached the table. Alex Chen looked every inch the tech entrepreneur – expensive casual clothes that tried too hard to appear relaxed, the latest smartwatch on his wrist. Beside him, Gary Webb embodied corporate law in his tailored suit, his glasses perched precisely on his nose.

'Detectives,' Gary said stiffly. 'Didn't realise you'd be dropping by.'

'Didn't you?' Monroe asked, eyebrows rising. 'Funny, I'm sure we told you in the meeting. No, wait, we never *had* that meeting now, did we?'

'Sorry. Back-to-back meetings,' Alex offered quickly, removing his jacket. 'End of quarter rush.'

'How convenient,' Declan said. 'Everyone in the City suddenly demanding your attention on the day we investigate your friend's murder, and a rush on an "end of quarter" that's not due for another month.'

'We're not avoiding you,' Gary insisted. 'It's just been a hectic day.'

'Three rescheduled interviews suggest otherwise,'

Monroe countered. 'You know, to the avoiding, not the hectic day part. But no worries, we're all here now.'

Nathan arrived with a handful of drinks, momentarily breaking the tension. When he left to get the rest, Declan leant forward, elbows on the table.

'So, chaps. Let's talk about The Royal Court.'

The shift in atmosphere was immediate. Chris Wilson suddenly found the woodgrain of the table fascinating. Justin Kelly straightened slightly, knuckles whitening around his fresh pint of real ale. Daryl Collins looked between Alex and the now returning Nathan as if waiting for someone to take the lead.

'It's just a name,' Alex said with a dismissive smile that didn't reach his eyes. 'Silly university thing that stuck.'

'Silly university thing involving water pistols, playing cards, and assassination games,' Declan countered. 'Over twenty years running.'

'We've had a wee look at Sean's place,' Monroe added. 'Man kept meticulous records. Had his King of Spades card framed on the wall, which isn't weird at all, next to photographs of all of you. Plus a collection of water weapons that would impress a six-year-old.'

Nathan cleared his throat.

'As I told DI Kapoor today, it's just a game we play. A tradition that's kept us connected over the years.'

'A tradition that evolved,' Monroe said, eyes fixed on Alex and Gary. 'With forfeits for losers. Your innovation, wasn't it?'

Alex ran a finger around the rim of his gin and tonic.

'The forfeits were voted on. Everyone agreed to the rule changes.'

'Unanimously?' Declan asked.

'Near enough,' Gary replied, adjusting his glasses. 'It just made the game more engaging as we got older. Raised the stakes.'

'Sean Acker was found with a bullet in his chest and his King of Spades card pinned to his body,' Declan said flatly. 'That engaging enough for you? Stakes raised enough, yet?'

Silence fell over the table. Justin Kelly, halfway through lifting his pint, set it down again untouched.

'None of us would hurt Sean,' Nathan finally said, his voice low. 'He was annoying sometimes, took the game too seriously with all his military cosplay, but he was one of us. The game was just that – a game.'

However, at this, Justin snorted.

'Tell that to Daniel.'

The name dropped like a stone into still water, and Declan could almost see the ripples of tension spreading visibly. Gary shot Justin a look of pure venom. Alex Chen suddenly became very interested in someone by the bar.

'Daniel Foster?' Declan asked, watching their reactions. 'The one who committed suicide two years ago?'

'There's no connection,' Gary said sharply. 'Daniel had depression. It was tragic but it had nothing to do with the game.'

'Bullshit,' Justin muttered into his pint.

'Something to add, Mister Kelly?' Monroe prompted.

'Leave it, Justin,' Chris Wilson murmured, eyes darting nervously.

'Why should I?' Justin challenged. 'Sean's dead, Daniel's dead, half the players haven't turned up, and we're all sitting here pretending everything's normal.'

'Nobody's pretending anything,' Nathan said, his tone carrying a warning. 'We're cooperating with the police.'

'Are we?' Justin asked, glancing around the table. 'Then

why don't we tell them about the forfeits? About what they did to Daniel?'

'The forfeits were part of the game,' Alex insisted, leaning forward. 'Everyone knew the rules. Everyone agreed.'

'We agreed to embarrassing dares,' Justin countered. 'Not *psychological warfare*.'

'That's enough,' Gary snapped.

'The forfeits weren't random,' Justin continued, ignoring him as he turned to Declan. 'They targeted vulnerabilities. Things that could actually hurt people.'

'You don't know what you're talking about,' Alex hissed.

'Don't I?' Justin challenged. 'Daniel got the worst of it. His forfeit would have destroyed him. Professionally. Personally. Everything.'

'And what exactly was this forfeit?' Declan asked quietly.

A tense silence fell as Nathan shifted in his chair while Gary and Alex exchanged glances. Before Justin could answer though, the pub door swung open again. Belinda Morris, one of the three women players of the game entered with Oliver Drake.

'What's going on?' she asked, reaching their table and taking in the scene.

'Police,' Nathan supplied. 'Asking about Sean.'

'Christ,' Belinda muttered, checking her watch. 'I left Emma's concert for this. First chair violin and I'm missing the finale.'

'Sean's dead,' Justin muttered. 'Or haven't you read the chat?'

Belinda's head snapped up.

'Is this a new rule we're adding?' she asked. 'When someone's taken out of the game they get a wake? Nobody told me this ...'

It was around now she finally realised that Declan and Monroe were the police Nathan had mentioned, punctuated by both men showing their warrant cards.

'Oh. Shit.'

As she slumped into a chair, Declan took in her appearance. She was expensively put together – designer handbag, carefully maintained highlights, the polished appearance of someone who'd built a successful career alongside family life. Beside her, Oliver Drake looked distinctly out of place – around ten years younger than the others, with the awkward demeanour of someone who'd been invited to a party where he knew nobody.

'Oliver, grab us drinks, would you?' Belinda almost whispered. 'Gin and tonic, double.'

Oliver nodded, clearly relieved to escape whatever tension he'd walked into.

'Replacement for Daniel Foster?' Monroe asked as the young man headed for the bar. 'The Ace of Hearts?'

Belinda's perfectly shaped eyebrows rose.

'You've done your homework.'

'We make it a point to understand the games people play,' Declan replied. 'Especially when they end with murder.'

'Look, I can tell you none of us killed Sean,' Belinda insisted, setting her handbag down with unnecessary force. 'We've been playing for twenty years without incident.'

'Except Daniel,' Justin said.

'Daniel killed himself,' Alex snapped. 'Stop trying to make it something it wasn't.'

'Did he?' Declan asked. 'Or did someone make it look that way?'

A heavy silence settled. Nathan broke it, his voice carefully measured.

'What exactly are you suggesting, Detective?'

Daryl's phone buzzed again. He checked it, frowning.

'Rachel's still not answering,' he tossed the phone aside.

'I've left three messages myself,' Belinda added, accepting her drink from a returning Oliver. 'It's not like her.'

'When did you last speak with her?' Declan asked.

'Yesterday,' Belinda replied. 'We had lunch near her office. She seemed ...'

She trailed off.

'Seemed what?'

'On edge,' Belinda admitted reluctantly. 'Said she felt like she was being watched. Obviously this was before whatever happened to Sean, so I just thought she was a bit paranoid.'

'Did she report this feeling to anyone? Police?'

'No,' Belinda shook her head.

'What kind of work does Rachel do?' Monroe asked.

'Marketing executive,' Alex supplied. 'Pharmaceutical advertising. Lot of pressure this time of year with the new drug launches.'

Nathan's phone vibrated on the table. He glanced at it, then stood abruptly.

'Excuse me a moment.'

Declan watched him step away to take the call, noting the sudden tension in Nathan's shoulders, the way his free hand clenched at his side as he moved to a quieter corner, his back to the room as he spoke.

'What card is Rachel, again?' Declan asked casually.

'Queen of Clubs,' Oliver supplied, earning sharp looks from around the table. 'What? It's on the game roster Gary sent when I joined. And they probably have it.'

'Gary keeps everyone's cards?' Declan asked, looking at the man in question.

'I keep on track of current assignments,' Gary shrugged. 'Makes it easier to track the game.'

'He's the Dungeon Master, so to speak,' Oliver added.

'Dungeon Master?' Monroe repeated. 'You mean like the game with the dice and the wee plastic figures?'

'Sorry,' Oliver said, looking embarrassed. 'I meant he's the organiser. Keeps everything running.'

'Is that unusual?' Declan asked the table. 'For one person to have that much control?'

'It wasn't always Gary,' Chris Wilson spoke up for the first time in several minutes. 'Used to be Daniel.'

'Until?' Monroe prompted.

Chris glanced at Alex and Gary, then back to his drink.

'Until it wasn't.'

'So, how are you finding the game, Oliver?' Declan asked casually, changing the subject. 'Being the new boy and all that.'

Before Oliver could answer, Belinda interjected.

'He's a natural. Picked it up faster than most of us did back in the day.'

Oliver smiled, a quick glance passing between them.

'I had good coaching. And last year was my first one, I only killed one person.'

He reddened.

'I mean—'

'I know what you mean,' Declan noted the smirking side-glance from Daryl to Chris, and decided to look into that later as before he could say anything else, Nathan returned to the table, his face carefully neutral but noticeably paler than before.

'Everything all right, Mister Hargreaves?' Monroe asked.

'Work call,' Nathan replied smoothly. 'The joys of global markets. Never stops, does it?'

Across the pub, Cooper had been watching the door. Now she made her way towards Declan, expression grim. She bent close to his ear.

'Guv, can I have a word?'

Motioning to Monroe to continue, Declan followed Cooper to a quieter corner.

'De'Geer just called,' she murmured. 'There's been another murder. Rachel Peterson. Found in the stairwell of an office building near Monument. Security guard found her during rounds.'

Declan's jaw tightened.

'Cause of death?'

'Knife to the chest,' Cooper replied. 'And sir, there's a playing card – Queen of Clubs, pinned to her body. Same as Acker, Morten reckons.'

Declan looked back to the others at the table, frowning.

Was one of these the killer? And if not, who else was missing right now?

Victoria Lang's Belgravia kitchen was spotless – all gleaming surfaces and expensive appliances barely used. She moved through it with the efficiency of someone performing a familiar ritual, filling the kettle for Anjli's tea.

'Milk?' she asked, reaching for bone china cups that looked like family heirlooms.

'Please,' Anjli replied, notebook open on her knee. 'Thank you for seeing me on such short notice.'

'I expected someone from the police after hearing about

Sean today,' Victoria said, bringing the tea tray to the living room. 'Though I admit, I'm surprised it took this long.'

'Missed you at work,' Anjli explained. 'It's been a day.'

'I'll bet,' Victoria smiled as she set the tray down.

The living room, like the kitchen, spoke of someone who really wanted to give it a sheen of careful curation – tasteful art on the walls, elegant furniture arranged just so. A wall of psychology texts lined one bookshelf, framed credentials on another. No clutter, no mess – everything in its proper place.

'You left the group, I understand?' Anjli asked.

'Two years ago,' Victoria confirmed, settling into an armchair. 'When the game changed.'

'Changed how?'

'It was meant to be fun,' Victoria replied, pouring tea. 'A way to stay connected after university. But three years back Alex and Gary got bored and started introducing these "forfeits" for eliminated players.'

'What kind of forfeits?'

'They started small – embarrassing social media posts, silly dares. Then they grew into something darker.'

'Darker how?'

Victoria set her cup down carefully.

'I'm a psychologist. I recognise manipulation when I see it. The forfeits became tools for control, designed to target vulnerabilities.'

'Is that why you left?'

'I tried to warn the others first,' Victoria said. 'When they wouldn't listen, I left. Professional ethics aside, I couldn't watch what it was doing to people. To the group dynamic.'

'And what about Sean? How did he fit into this dynamic?'

'Sean was ...' Victoria paused, choosing her words carefully. 'Desperate for respect. The Royal Marine thing, the tactical gear – it was all about creating an identity he thought others would value.'

'You knew him well?'

'We dated briefly at university,' Victoria acknowledged. 'Remained friends after. He could be intense, but underneath all the military posturing, Sean was harmless. Just someone trying to belong.'

Anjli glanced at the photographs arranged on the mantelpiece – Victoria with an older couple, presumably her parents; Victoria accepting an award; Victoria with a group of young adults at graduation.

'No pictures of the Royal Court,' she observed.

'I put those away years ago,' Victoria replied. 'Not all memories are worth keeping on display. I just keep the graduation photo up. No stupid water pistols there.'

'When did you last speak with Sean?'

Victoria took a sip of tea before answering.

'Tuesday night, actually. Around seven.'

'What did he want?' Anjli noted this down; it was an hour or so before he was murdered.

'He seemed agitated,' Victoria frowned slightly. 'Said he'd been doing research. Something about Daniel.'

'Daniel Foster?'

Victoria nodded. 'Sean had a theory about Daniel's suicide. He didn't believe it was suicide at all.'

Anjli leant forward.

'Did he tell you his theory?'

'Not in detail, not over the phone. He wanted to meet.' Victoria's gaze drifted to the window. 'We arranged for a breakfast this morning. He never showed up.'

'Because he was killed last night,' Anjli said quietly.

'Exactly.'

'Did he mention anyone who might want to harm him?'

'He didn't trust Alex and Gary,' Victoria replied. 'But then, neither did I.'

'Anyone else?'

Victoria seemed to consider her words carefully.

'There was something else he mentioned. He'd been researching an old activist group – the Garden Collective.'

'The Garden Collective?' Anjli kept her expression neutral, despite the sudden leap of interest.

If Victoria noticed Anjli's reaction, she didn't show it.

'An activist group from the early nineties. I don't know much about it, but Sean mentioned it was connected to Nathan's father somehow.'

'How?'

'I don't know the details,' Victoria admitted. 'Only that Sean thought it was significant.'

'Tell me about Daniel. What was his forfeit?'

Victoria's expression clouded.

'Daniel was gay but deeply closeted at work. He was up for QC - well, KC now, at a very traditional chambers. The forfeit designed for him would have exposed everything.'

'Exposed how?'

'Daniel had been in a relationship with someone in the group,' Victoria said carefully. 'The forfeit would have sent evidence of this relationship to every partner at his chambers.'

'That's more than a forfeit,' Anjli remarked. 'That's blackmail.'

'The line had blurred,' Victoria agreed. 'Which is precisely why I left.'

'One last question,' Anjli said. 'Do you still have your Royal Court card?'

Victoria rose and crossed to a desk drawer. She unlocked it and removed a playing card, placing it on the coffee table. The Queen of Hearts looked up at them from its black background, silver ink catching the light.

'I kept it as a reminder,' Victoria said. 'One that reminds me that games have consequences when the wrong people are playing.'

Anjli picked it up.

'This is different to the deck used.'

'Yes,' Victoria nodded. 'We used a special deck for the tenth anniversary. Daryl knows a printer so sorted us a pack each.'

Anjli took a photo, passing it back.

'Anything else kept?' she asked. 'Water pistols, anything like that?'

Victoria Lang paused, as if planning the perfect phrase.

'I'm afraid I'm a bit of a minimalist,' she said. 'If it doesn't bring me joy, I dispose of it.'

She looked down at the card.

'And apart from this, the game no longer brings me joy,' she said. 'Not since Daniel died.'

'Remember when he ambushed Gary outside that investor dinner?' Justin laughed. 'Scaled the bloody wall outside and waited on the balcony for two hours.'

'Soaked my Armani,' Gary confirmed, almost smiling at the memory. 'Though I got him back the next—'

He paused as Declan returned.

'I've just received some news,' Declan said, and the table

fell silent, all eyes turning to him. Monroe read his expression immediately.

'What is it?' he asked, though his tone suggested he already knew.

'Rachel Peterson has been found dead,' Declan said simply. 'Murdered, with the Queen of Clubs pinned to her chest.'

He knew it wasn't professional to give such information out, but Declan knew the killer could be here – there was a chance he'd get a reaction he could use. As it was, the wave of reactions was immediate and varied – Belinda's hand flew to her mouth, a small sound escaping. Daryl swore violently, shoving back from the table. Oliver froze, wide-eyed.

'No,' Chris Wilson whispered. 'Not Rachel too.'

Alex and Gary exchanged a look of naked alarm. Nathan alone remained composed, though a muscle jumped in his jaw.

'This gathering is now part of an active murder investigation,' Declan announced, rising to his feet. 'No one leaves London without informing us, and we'll need contact details for people who aren't here; I believe that's Dirk VanMeerten, Diane Taylor—'

'You think one of us did this?' Belinda asked, her voice rising. 'That's insane. We were friends for twenty years!'

'That's exactly the line of inquiry we'll be pursuing,' Declan replied. 'Two murders in two days, both victims from your group, both killed with methods matching your game.'

As shock rippled through the group, Declan met Monroe's eyes across the table. They needed no words to convey what both were thinking: somewhere in this circle of old friends sat a killer, methodically working through their old playmates, one playing card at a time.

After Anjli left, Victoria remained at her window, watching taillights stream along the street below. The city at night, so full of hidden corners and secrets.

Her phone buzzed. Unknown number.

Police involved now.

She stared at the message, her reflection in the window giving nothing away. After a moment, she deleted it and moved to her laptop.

The password screens gave way to files – old newspaper clippings, photographs, scanned notes in her neat handwriting. A photograph showed the Royal Court in university days, young and carefree; Sean with his arm around Daniel's shoulders.

Victoria touched the screen briefly, then closed the laptop.

So, the police were in the game now. How long before the game fell apart?

But then, Victoria knew better than most how quickly games could spiral out of control.

8

THE CARDED COLLECTIVE

By the time Declan arrived at the crime scene, Doctor Marcos was already there, custom PPE suit on, examining the body as other forensics officers worked around her, keeping out of her way in the process.

The fourth-floor emergency stairwell of the Harrington Finance building swam in the harsh glare of portable LED panels, and shadows crowded the concrete corners like waiting predators. Rachel Peterson lay sprawled on the stair-well floor; her expensive suit soaked with water at the chest and face; another signature element matching Sean Acker's murder. A metal spike had been driven through the playing card and into her chest and the Queen of Clubs – black back-ground with silver detailing, just like Sean Acker's King of Spades – was attached to the body, speckled with dried blood.

'Time of death?' Declan asked, snapping on blue latex gloves as he approached.

'Between six and seven this evening,' Doctor Marcos replied, glancing up before returning to the body. 'Single stab wound to the chest. Security guard found her while doing his rounds about half an hour after. Saw the stairs door was open, checked through it.'

'So someone wanted it found then.'

'Most likely. Clean entry, maximum damage. Whoever did this knew exactly where to stick the knife.'

'Different weapon from Acker,' Declan noted, crouching beside the body.

'But same theatrical bollocks,' Doctor Marcos countered, nodding towards the water-soaked hair and face. 'Kill them, pin a card on them, then splash them with water like some demented baptism. Ritualistic, not practical.'

'The pin looks like it went in deep,' Declan said. 'How much force—'

'Not as much as you'd expect,' Doctor Marcos replied. 'One end has a flattened "nail" part, so can be pushed. That said, it'd leave a mark on a hand if you tried doing it without something hard between. They used the stab wound here. We think they used a brick with Sean Acker. Literally hammered the bastard in.'

Declan scanned the scene, a slight frown crossing his face as he spied Billy Fitzwarren crouching by a small control panel near the door, his fingers deep in exposed wiring.

That didn't feel right – Billy typically stayed at Temple Inn, behind his digital fortress.

'Billy?'

The detective sergeant glanced up, blond fringe falling across his forehead. His tailored three-piece suit looked obscenely out of place among the blood and industrial concrete.

'CCTV's been properly buggered with,' he reported, voice clipped in the way it got when he was angry but refusing to show it. 'Forty-minute loop over the estimated time of death. Not amateur hour, this.'

'Bit of a surprise finding you here,' Declan said, moving closer. 'Thought you'd be mainlining coffee and database searches back at base.'

Something dark crossed Billy's face; there, then gone.

'Rufus Harrington owned this building,' he said flatly, turning back to the panel. 'Before the Red Reaper's vortex got to him, anyway.'

Ah. Declan nodded. *Made sense now.* Rufus had been Billy's friend, murdered because of his connection to Billy and The Last Chance Saloon. That the DS would feel drawn here wasn't professional, but human.

'Last time I was in this pile of concrete and glass,' Billy continued, not looking up, 'Rufus tried to poach me for his cybersecurity team over takeout wagyu beef tartare in his office. Told me my family would approve of the "suitable employment".'

'He spent half the time I knew him trying to drag you into respectability,' Declan said carefully, unsure how to respond to this; he was aware that if Billy had taken Rufus's offer, Billy would have left the unit before the Red Reaper case, and there was every chance Rufus would still be alive right now.

'And now I'm about to be forced into the aristocracy anyway,' Billy muttered. 'Irony's a vicious little bitch, isn't she?'

He paused as De'Geer's frame filled the stairwell entrance, his Viking head nearly brushing the ceiling, wearing a PPE coverall that only just fit.

'Got something, Guv,' he rumbled, holding out a tablet. 'Someone used a maintenance code at five forty-five. Service corridor camera caught this before going dark.'

Declan studied the grainy image – a figure in maintenance coveralls, face hidden by the peak of a cap and what looked like a disposable face mask.

Convenient.

'Hiding from a virus or from us?' Declan muttered.

'Knew where every camera was,' De'Geer said. 'This is all we've got. Thirty seconds of footage, then nothing until six-thirty p.m.'

'Height?'

'Average. Five-eight to five-ten. Build suggests male, but I'd not bet on it.'

Billy had moved to the victim's handbag, laid out on an evidence sheet like a museum exhibit.

'Phone's still here,' he noted, pointing with a pen. 'Screen active.'

Hearing this, Doctor Marcos wandered over, sealed the phone and handed it to Billy.

'See if there's anything about why she was here,' she suggested.

Billy pulled on fresh gloves before extracting the phone, using a stylus to tap on the screen.

'Last text came at five-thirty from an unknown number,' he announced. 'Says: "Urgent meeting about Sean and next steps. St. Dunstan's entrance too exposed with current situation. Use back office entrance instead. 6 p.m." Well, that's about as subtle as a brick through a window, isn't it?'

'She was lured like a tourist towards a shell game,' Declan said.

'There's more,' Billy continued, frowning at the screen. 'Three missed calls from Dirk VanMeerten's phone early yesterday. Text from him says: "Need to talk about game. Not safe. Call me." Cryptic much?'

'VanMeerten wasn't at the pub tonight,' Declan said, turning back to Doctor Marcos. 'Anything else of interest?'

'The liquid used is peculiar,' she replied, stripping off her gloves with a sharp snap. 'Not normal tap water. There's a distinct mineral profile – almost oily to the touch. I've taken samples,' she held up an evidence bag containing a deflated scrap of rubber. 'Found this under her. Remnants of a water balloon, most likely.'

'Consistent with their daft assassination game,' Declan noted as he turned back to Billy. 'Any other communication with the players?'

Billy scrolled through the phone, his face lit by the blue-white glow of the screen.

'Several texts with Nathan. Nothing suspicious. Oh hello, what's this?'

He tapped the screen, eyebrows lifting.

'Last week, she sent a message to Gary, saying she'd lost the list again.'

'Again?'

'Guessing she was known for being forgetful,' Billy shrugged. 'Gary was patronising about it but sent her a link to a spreadsheet. Game roster, looks like.'

'Can you open it?'

Billy tapped and swiped.

'Full list of players and their cards for this "final round". Sean Acker, King of Spades, Rachel Peterson, Queen of Clubs, Belinda Morris, Ace of Diamonds... they're all on here. I'll forward them to my system, go back and check.'

'You might as well check now,' Doctor Marcos said as she straightened. 'There's nothing more here for the moment, and I won't have anything until tomorrow.'

Declan nodded, looking around the stairwell, before returning his attention to De'Geer.

'Dirk VanMeerten,' he said. 'Get someone to check on him. And also Diane Taylor.'

He looked at Billy.

'Your offer to access the Reform Club. Can we do that tonight?'

Billy checked his watch.

'The reading room closes at ten, but with my family name, they'll make an exception.'

'Good,' Declan nodded. 'Doctor Marcos, anything else we need here?'

'I'll have preliminary findings for you by morning. Cause of death is straightforward enough; a single stab wound to the heart. The water and the card are ritualistic elements, not functional to the killing.'

'I'll be at the Reform Club with Billy,' Declan said to De'Geer. 'Text me when you've got eyes on VanMeerten.'

As they prepared to leave, Billy paused at the doorway, looking back at the scene. The harsh lighting cut shadows across his face, ageing him ten years in an instant.

'What?' Declan asked.

'Rufus used to say security was about people, not systems,' Billy whispered. 'The older I get, the more I think the arrogant sod was right, at least.'

THE REFORM CLUB HULKED AGAINST THE NOVEMBER SKY LIKE an architectural relic of empire, its Portland stone illuminated by spotlights that carved deep shadows into its classical pretensions. Despite the late hour, a doorman stood beneath the portico in a greatcoat, back straight as if the building itself demanded better posture.

He snapped to attention when he saw Billy.

'Master Fitzwarren,' he said, dipping his head with the perfect degree of deference. 'Unexpected pleasure, sir.'

'Evening, Howard,' Billy replied with the casual nonchalance of the truly privileged, despite the tension visible in his shoulders. 'This is DCI Walsh. Needs access to the archives.'

'At this hour, sir?' Howard asked, though he was already unbolting the door.

'Urgent business,' Billy said, as if that explained everything.

Howard nodded once.

'I'll fetch Mister Pemberton straightaway, sir.'

The entrance hall whispered of wealth and power, the daytime buzz of members replaced by an expectant nighttime hush, broken only by the gentle ticking of a grandfather clock worth more than most people's homes. As Declan and Billy walked, their footsteps echoed off the marble floor.

'How often do you darken their doorstep?' Declan asked quietly.

'Only when unavoidable,' Billy replied. 'My father practically lives here. Uses it as his London office. One more reason to stay away.'

They didn't get halfway across the hall before being intercepted by a grey-haired man in a perfectly tailored suit that still managed to look like a uniform.

'Master William,' he greeted Billy with a slight bow. 'A pleasure to see you, sir. Unusual hour for a visit. Your father was here just today, as it happens.'

Billy went rigid.

'My father?'

'Indeed, sir. Spent several hours in the reading room,' the steward cleared his throat delicately. 'He mentioned he was awaiting your response to some family matter.'

Declan watched Billy's jaw tighten, a tendon pulsing in his neck. When Billy spoke, however, his voice was light, almost bored.

'Did he indeed?' Only someone who knew him well would recognise the edge beneath the casual drawl. 'Mister Pemberton, we need to see the archive collections. Specifically files kept by a member named Patrick Walsh.'

Pemberton's eyebrows lifted fractionally at Walsh's name.

'The Chief Superintendent of the Metropolitan Police? Yes, I recall him. Fine gentleman. Unorthodox hours, but impeccable manners.'

'You remember him?' Declan asked, surprised.

Pemberton drew himself up a fraction taller.

'Thirty-seven years as night steward, Chief Inspector. I remember every member who visits.' A small smile tugged at his lips. 'Particularly those who tip generously at Christmas. I was sorry to hear of his passing. I believe you caught his killer?'

Declan paused – he hadn't expected to have a conversation about the Red Reaper.

'I did.'

'And I believe you also *ended* him?'

This stopped Declan in his tracks.

'Karl Schnitter fell from the roof,' he said. 'It was either his decision or an accident. I didn't do anything.'

'Of course, sir.'

'The files – are they still here?' Declan pressed, deciding he really wanted to change the subject.

Realising he'd crossed a line, the steward licked his lips.

'Naturally. Club policy forbids disposal of members' private deposits without explicit written instruction. This way, gentlemen.'

They followed Pemberton through corridors, passing portraits of dead men whose policies still shaped the living. Eventually, they reached a room that belonged in a Dickens novel; oak panelling, leather chairs, green-shaded reading lamps, and walls lined with books nobody ever read.

'Archives are through there,' Pemberton indicated a door at the far end. 'Private deposits in the secure room beyond. I'll need to accompany you to the door, of course. Club rules.'

'Can I ask why I wasn't informed of this?' Declan asked. 'As next of kin, surely this should have been passed on?'

'Usually it would, sir, but your father gave specific instructions not to pass anything on unless actively requested. As you are now, sir.'

Behind door number two lurked a room far less grand and far more practical – metal filing cabinets, microfiche readers that belonged in a museum, and computer terminals that had been cutting-edge during the Blair administration. Pemberton settled at one terminal, fingers moving over the keyboard with unexpected dexterity.

'Patrick Walsh... Walsh... ah, here we are. Cabinet F, Section 4.'

'Your archive,' Declan asked. 'How detailed is it?'

'Well, we keep private papers private, but many members keep their notation files here. I believe the trendy term for this is "second brain" or something along those lines,' Pemberton smiled.

'So you can search?' Declan asked. 'Could I request a favour? Could you check for anything my father may have put in the archive related to something called the Garden Collective?'

Pemberton nodded as he typed again.

'Yes, we have that name cross-referenced in several members' collections. Nothing by your father on the public record, but Lord Hargreaves has quite an extensive file on the subject.'

'Lord Hargreaves?' Declan repeated, glancing at Billy. 'Any relation to Nathan Hargreaves, our City financier?'

'Harold Hargreaves, third Baron Stretford,' Pemberton supplied with the easy familiarity of someone who'd memorised Burke's Peerage. 'His son Nathan had a membership application withdrawn some years back. Pharmaceuticals, I believe.'

He coughed delicately.

'Nothing proven, you understand, but the membership committee has certain standards. The Hargreaves family itself has been with the club since 1890.'

'Let's start with my father's files,' Declan said.

Pemberton unlocked Cabinet F with a brass key and extracted several acid-free archival boxes, placing them on a reading table beneath a pendant lamp that cast a pool of warm light in the otherwise dim room.

'I'll be just outside should you require anything further,' he said, withdrawing with the soundless grace of the professionally invisible.

The top box contained folders of meticulously organised notes in Patrick Walsh's distinctive handwriting; case files, witness statements, photographs of protest sites. Declan knew his father's organisational system the way he knew his own face in the mirror – he'd gone through enough of them over the last couple of years.

'Kept everything, didn't he?' he muttered, lifting a folder marked "Shadwell Bell Foundry Incident – Casualties" in red ink.

'Proper old-school detective work,' Billy remarked, rifling through another file. 'No digital footprint to follow. Look at this – surveillance photos of Garden Collective meetings. Dates, times, locations. All handwritten.'

Declan spread several photographs across the table; angry young people with placards outside construction sites and historic buildings. The faces were clear, the righteous fury of youth captured in black and white.

'Old-school surveillance,' he said. 'Dad must've had someone on the inside feeding him information.'

'Burlington Bertie?' Billy suggested, sliding a photo closer. 'She'd be the right age.'

'Possible.' Declan pulled out a folder labelled "Connected Interests" in his father's handwriting. Inside were newspaper clippings about property developments, planning applications, acquisitions. Several had a handwritten note attached.

Hargreaves Investment Trust – controlling interest.

'Nathan's old man was heavily invested in the very buildings the Collective was fighting to save, it seems,' Billy commented as he looked at it.

'Here's something interesting,' Declan said, extracting a thin manila folder from the box's bottom. Inside was a single sheet of paper with a list of names under the heading "Protected Persons – DO NOT PURSUE" in angry red capitals. Several names were crossed out, but three remained clearly legible:

Harold Hargreaves
George VanMeerten
Jonathan Foster

'VanMeerten,' Declan read. 'Dirk's father?'

'And Foster – any relation to Daniel?' Billy wondered. 'If they're on a "hands off" list in your father's files ...'

'Then someone upstairs was providing cover,' Declan finished grimly. He flipped the page over. On the back, his father had scrawled.

Authorisation from AC Willis – political considerations takes precedence. Case formally closed 12/05/92.

'AC Willis?' Billy asked.

'Assistant Commissioner, I reckon,' Declan confirmed. 'Dad was ordered to drop it.'

Billy had moved to another box, this one stuffed with yellowing newspaper reports about the Shadwell Bell Foundry incident.

'Three dead, dozen injured. Support beams deliberately weakened,' he said as he held up a grainy photo showing rubble, emergency services, and shocked bystanders. 'Proper carnage. Claimed it was water damage from an underground river, but then it was pointed out that underground rivers aren't that well versed in using saws on wooden beams.'

'Farringdon told me someone took a saw to the main supports the night before,' Declan said. 'Initially they blamed the developers but turned out to be radical elements within the Collective itself.'

'Creating martyrs for the cause,' Billy said with distaste.

'Charming tactics. Won't that look lovely on the recruitment brochures?'

Declan continued through another folder of his father's notes.

'Name that keeps recurring – Elizabeth Gardner. Significant player in the Collective by all accounts,' he said, scanning his father's notes. 'Multiple references to her leadership role.'

'Any connection to our current players?'

'Not that I can see,' Declan replied, shuffling through more papers. 'There are several Gardners mentioned, might have been a family affair.'

His phone vibrated; a text from De'Geer:

> Diane Taylor found – was at theatre last night. Checking for CCTV. No answer at VanMeerten's house. Uniforms on scene.

'We need to wrap this up,' Declan said, showing Billy the message.

'One more thing,' Billy said, extracting a final folder from the box. Marked "Informants," it was thicker than the others. 'List of people who testified against Garden Collective members when it all went pear-shaped.'

'Anyone we recognise?'

'VanMeerten, George,' Billy read. 'Appears multiple times. Gave evidence against key members. And look at this, a note about a Linda Gardner. Injured in the Bell Foundry collapse.'

Declan leant over to study the document.

'Connection to Elizabeth?'

'Daughter? Sister?' Billy suggested. 'The dates would work.'

Declan froze.

'Bertie spoke about a "Linda",' he said, thinking back. 'When she started losing the thread. Said "she knew about the supports, tried to get them out. But they wouldn't listen".'

'Sounds possible,' Billy nodded. 'I'd have to check more into them.'

He started flicking through the notes.

'Here's something. "Linda died in 1994 from complications of the Bell Foundry collapse". And there's a handwritten note from your father.'

Declan leant closer to read Patrick's neat script.

L.G. – structural engineer, found critically injured near damaged supports. Witness statements suggest she was evacuating others when collapse occurred. Sabotage or heroism?

'Your father wasn't sure if she caused it or tried to prevent it,' Billy observed.

'Seems like he suspected she was trying to help,' Declan replied, studying the note. 'But the notes link her to Elizabeth Gardner and the Collective.'

The pieces were arranging themselves like a jigsaw with half the edge missing. Something connected these decades-old events to the current murders, but the picture remained maddeningly incomplete.

At a knock from Declan to announce he was finished, the door opened silently, Pemberton materialising like Dracula.

'Finding everything satisfactory, gentlemen?'

'Yes, thank you,' Declan replied. 'These files are extremely helpful.'

'I should mention,' Pemberton said, 'there was another inquiry about these specific files recently.'

'Oh?' Declan looked up sharply.

'A woman claiming to be your sister,' Pemberton explained. 'Said she was doing research on behalf of the Walsh family.'

Declan froze. This was what Burlington Bertie had hinted at, although she'd said they were working on behalf of the Walsh family, not that they *were* the family.

'My sister?'

'Yes, sir,' Pemberton frowned slightly. 'I don't recall the name she gave, but the steward on duty had to turn her away. Club policy requires proper identification for accessing private deposits, and she didn't have any photo ID with her.'

Billy glanced at Declan, whose face had gone still.

'I don't have a sister, Mister Pemberton.'

A moment of silence fell as the night steward processed this information.

'I see,' he said finally. 'Most concerning. This would have been about five weeks ago. Unfortunately, our security recordings are only kept for thirty days.'

'Can you describe her?' Declan asked, his voice carefully neutral.

'All I can do is give what I was told. Middle-aged. Dark hair with some grey. Well-spoken. Professional manner. Beyond that, I'm afraid I couldn't say much more. According to the stewards, she was rather... unremarkable.'

'That's often the point,' Billy muttered. 'You get found if you stand out.'

'We need to go,' Declan said, urgency propelling him towards the door. 'Can we take copies of these documents?'

'You can do what you want,' Pemberton nodded. 'As Patrick's next of kin, they're yours to take.'

'We need to follow up with Dirk VanMeerten,' Declan said, checking his watch. 'Let's take these back to the office.'

'I'll run his details through the system,' Billy said, already typing on his phone. 'See if there are any reports.'

'And we need to talk to Burlington Bertie again,' Declan added. 'She didn't call me out of the blue after all these years without good reason.'

'Will there be anything else, gentlemen?' Pemberton asked.

'That's all for tonight,' Declan said, gathering the files. 'Thank you for your assistance.'

OUTSIDE, THE NOVEMBER AIR HIT LIKE A SLAP, AND DECLAN pulled his coat tighter against the chill as they called for a cab.

'Woman claiming to be your non-existent sister,' Billy commented. 'That's ballsy.'

'And using my family name to access files about a group connected to recent murders,' Declan added. 'Not a coincidence.'

'Nothing about this case is coincidental,' Billy replied. 'And it looks like someone's playing by rules set thirty years ago.'

9

NEW EVIDENCE

'LADIES AND GENTLEMEN, WELCOME TO OUR SECOND ACT IN what's shaping up to be a properly theatrical season of murder,' Monroe announced, spreading his arms wide as he surveyed the team gathered in the glass-walled briefing room. 'Two down, and God knows how many more of these water-sports enthusiasts are marked for the chop.'

'Guv, I'm not sure you mean that in the way it sounds,' De'Geer said.

'I mean everything I say,' Monroe gave a knowing nod. 'And with these Oxford graduates, with their cliquey little games, everything's on the table. Let's just hope it's not a *glass* one.'

The morning light filtering through Temple Inn's windows cast everything in shades of grey, matching the mood that had settled over the Last Chance Saloon team. Coffee cups outnumbered team members two to one – nobody had slept particularly well after the previous night's discoveries.

Monroe stood at the front of the room, his white hair

catching the light as he gestured towards the large plasma screen. Declan sat to the right with Anjli beside him, both looking like they'd spent the night wrestling with implications rather than sleeping. Doctor Marcos occupied her usual spot at the back, scribbling notes in her nearly illegible handwriting, while Sergeant De'Geer and PC Cooper sat nearby with notebooks poised. Billy Fitzwarren hunched over his laptop to the left, his fingers working the keyboard as he controlled the images on screen, and Detective Chief Superintendent Bullman completed the scene, leaning against the doorframe with her arms folded and expression sceptical.

'For those keeping score at home,' Monroe continued, as Billy clicked to display the stark crime-scene photos, 'we now have two members of this stupid bloody game dead within forty-eight hours. Both killed with proper weapons, both decorated with their respective playing cards like some demented greeting card service.'

The screen showed two photos – Sean Acker's body with the King of Spades pinned to his chest, alongside Rachel Peterson's corpse in the stairwell with the Queen of Clubs similarly displayed.

'Both part of a game with connections to the Garden Collective,' Declan added. 'An activist group from the early nineties that my father investigated.'

Monroe nodded to Billy, who clicked to display scanned documents from Patrick Walsh's Reform Club files.

'Aye, and here's where Patrick's meticulous record-keeping pays dividends,' Monroe said, his voice carrying genuine respect for his former partner. 'The man kept extensive files on a group of environmental terrorists who thought sabotaging buildings was an acceptable form of historic preservation.'

'The Shadwell Bell Foundry incident,' Billy supplied, looking up from his laptop.

'Inside job, apparently,' Monroe nodded. 'According to these files, and a wee chat Declan here had with Anthony Farringdon, Patrick suspected it from the start, but he was warned off by the higher-ups.'

'Weren't you part of the Tottenham North unit in 1992, Guv?' De'Geer asked.

'A bit of column A, and a wee bit of column B,' Monroe replied. 'I was fresh down from Glasgow as a brand new detective constable, keeping to myself and more concerned with settling my own scores with the Wright Brothers than paying attention to Patrick's off-the-books investigations. Wish I'd been more observant now.'

There was a moment of silence to this before Anjli raised her pen.

'Historical connections aside, have we found more on the connection to our current victims?'

'Harold Hargreaves – Nathan's father – was heavily invested in the properties the Collective was fighting to save,' Billy replied, pulling up filed documents from the time. 'From what I can work out, first from official records and then from then-DS Patrick Walsh's notes, George VanMeerten provided testimony against Collective members when cases went to trial.'

'Both names appear on my father's "Protected Persons" list,' Declan added.

Billy nodded to the screen as it displayed Patrick Walsh's handwritten note.

'Political considerations, it says. Someone upstairs was providing cover for certain individuals.'

Bullman pushed away from the doorframe.

'So, we're looking at children settling their parents' scores?'

'Maybe,' Monroe agreed. 'Though it's taken them thirty-odd years to get round to it.'

Cooper raised her hand slightly.

'Lassie, you don't need to ...' Monroe sighed. 'Spit it out.'

'What about Daniel Foster's suicide? Is there a connection there?'

'Jonathan Foster appears on the protected persons list,' Declan confirmed. 'The timing would fit for him being Daniel's father.'

'He is,' Billy confirmed. 'According to records, anyway.'

'What else do we have on Daniel?' Monroe asked.

'Victoria Lang said yesterday that Daniel was gay but deeply closeted at work,' Anjli spoke up now. 'He was up for KC at a very traditional chambers, and the forfeit designed for him would have destroyed his career, by exposing his sexuality *to* his very traditional chambers.'

'Daniel had been in a relationship with someone in the group,' Cooper added. 'The forfeit would have sent evidence of this relationship to everyone in his chambers. But it never happened, as he died before it could be done.'

Another moment of silence settled over the room as the implications sank in.

'Do we know who he was having a relationship with?' Declan asked. 'Could be relevant.'

'Could be motive if they were closeted too,' Anjli added. 'Daniel being outed meant they were being outed too. Silencing him would keep their secret.'

'So, we might have three murders, not two,' Monroe mused. 'Daniel Foster a couple of years ago, then Sean and

Rachel this week. Someone's been very patient indeed. Anything from the body?'

Doctor Marcos cleared her throat as she rose now.

'I've completed Rachel Peterson's post-mortem. Single stab wound to the chest, between the fourth and fifth ribs, angled upwards towards the heart. Clean entry, maximum damage. Death would have been quick.'

'Professional?' Monroe asked.

'Someone with anatomical knowledge, possibly. The precision suggests either medical training or previous experience, but it's a knife, Alex. You push the pointy end in, and if there's no defence, it can look as professional as anyone else.'

'No defence?'

'Doesn't look that way,' Doctor Marcos consulted her iPad. 'No hesitation marks, no defensive wounds. The victim was taken completely by surprise.'

'And then soaked?'

'Same as last time, the water applied afterwards,' Doctor Marcos nodded. 'It's unusual, though. Different mineral profile from standard London tap water, which has a very specific mineral signature from the Thames treatment works – high chlorine, added fluoride. What we found on Rachel Peterson doesn't match tap water at all, we're checking Sean's report to compare. I'm running tests to identify the source, but it suggests the killer brought their own supply.'

'Ritual importance,' Declan observed. 'They're not just killing these people – they're making a statement about the game itself, perhaps.'

Billy's phone buzzed on the table. He glanced at it, his jaw tightening visibly before he declined the call and returned to his laptop.

'Popular this morning?' Monroe asked, eyebrows raised.

'Persistent,' Billy replied curtly, though his fingers were typing with more force than strictly necessary.

Monroe obviously decided it was better not to ask.

'Diane Taylor?'

'Went to Chelmsford to see a play,' Cooper read from her notes. 'We have her on CCTV at the theatre, and also at a Wagamamas an hour before.'

'Dirk VanMeerten?'

'Still uncontactable, Guv.'

'Right then, assignments for today. Declan, you and I are going to corner Alex Chen and Gary Webb. They've been dodging us, they said bugger all in the pub, and I'm bloody tired of technical difficulties and rescheduled meetings.'

'About time,' Declan agreed.

'Cooper, bring Victoria Lang in for a formal interview – Anjli and Bullman can run it – if that's okay? And send a uniform to get a statement from Diane Taylor. If she starts to flag as a possible suspect we can bring her in, but currently she's in the "unlikely" list.'

Bullman nodded.

'More than happy to,' she said.

'Good,' Monroe replied, looking back at the room. 'I've got a wee niggle about Lang. She was too helpful yesterday – psychologists don't usually volunteer information unless they're managing the conversation.'

'Interview room?'

'Aye, let her stew in custody suite atmosphere for a bit. Nothing like institutional lighting to encourage honesty.'

Billy's phone buzzed again. This time he answered it with visible irritation.

'What do you want?' he snapped, then his voice dropped

as he noticed the room's attention. 'I told you; I'm working... no, this isn't something I can just—'

He paused, listening, his face going pale.

'How much exactly are we talking about?'

The room fell silent as Billy's end of the conversation became increasingly tense. Monroe raised an eyebrow but said nothing.

'That's not my problem to solve,' Billy said finally, his voice tight with controlled anger. 'You made your choices; you live with the consequences... no, I won't... find another bloody way.'

He ended the call and immediately switched his phone to silent, shoving it into his jacket pocket with enough force to suggest he'd rather throw it through the nearest window.

'Family drama,' he muttered before anyone could ask. 'Apparently stepping down from responsibilities comes with its own set of complications.'

Monroe's expression sharpened with interest, likely another anti-establishment joke brewing, but Declan cut him off before he could pursue it.

'Billy, I need you digging deeper into the Garden Collective connections. Cross-reference the family names in my father's files – particularly the Gardners.'

'Already started,' Billy said, clearly grateful for the change of subject. 'Elizabeth Gardner appears multiple times, as does Linda.'

'What about the mysterious woman who tried to access the Reform Club files?' De'Geer asked.

'I spoke with the Reform Club this morning, got a little more information.' Billy's fingers fluttered across the keyboard as he pulled up visitor logs. 'Sarah Walsh, she called herself. Claimed to be Declan's sister doing genealogy research. But she made a crucial mistake – told them she was Patrick Walsh's daughter, and anyone who actually knew Patrick Walsh would know he only had one child.'

'Amateur hour, then?' Monroe suggested.

'Or arrogance,' Billy replied. 'Someone who assumed the club staff wouldn't know personal details about members' families. Patrick barely attended anything at the club, preferred the National Liberal, and even then that was in his later days. He was a Detective Sergeant back then. Surprising he was even a member, if I'm being honest.'

Declan nodded.

'If I have a sister,' he smiled darkly, 'she'd better not want backdated Christmas and birthday presents.'

'De'Geer, Cooper – I still want you tracking down Dirk VanMeerten,' Monroe said. 'He wasn't at the pub last night, he's not answering his phone, and his father testified against Garden Collective members. Either he's hiding, or he's already dead.'

'We've checked his house, his workplace, and asked neighbours,' De'Geer rumbled. 'Nothing since Tuesday. No trace of a scuffle, though. We could request CCTV from building management, trace his movements.'

'Do it. If he's hiding, he can't stay invisible forever. If he's dead ...'

'We'll find the body eventually, Guv,' De'Geer finished grimly.

Bullman checked her watch. 'I need updates every four hours. "Two dead City professionals" is drawing attention from Guildhall. David – I mean Commander Bradbury is asking pointed questions about our progress.'

'Political pressure?' Monroe asked, ignoring the familial

slip there. It was known in the room that Sophie Bullman and David Bradbury were a couple, albeit secretly.

'The kind that ends careers if we don't solve this quickly,' Bullman confirmed. 'Plus there's been some chatter about bringing in additional resources if we can't wrap this up soon.'

'Additional resources?' Declan's tone suggested he found this prospect less than appealing.

'Scotland Yard's Murder Investigation Team. Apparently they're "concerned about the complexity of the case".'

'Aye, they're concerned about the media attention when this hits the papers,' Monroe snorted. 'Two City professionals killed with playing cards pinned to their chests? The tabloids will have a field day.'

'All the more reason to solve it ourselves,' Declan said firmly. 'Before it becomes a circus. But surely it's not at the point of a chase up? It's been a couple of days.'

'Which means someone up in the higher levels of power is looking to push something through,' Monroe suggested. 'We should find out who, and why.'

As the team began gathering their things, Billy's phone vibrated again through his pocket. He ignored it, but the tension in his shoulders betrayed his frustration.

'Billy,' Declan said quietly, 'if your family situation is affecting your ability to focus—'

'It's not,' Billy cut him off, then softened his tone slightly. 'It's just... bloody complicated. My father's created a situation where doing nothing has consequences, but doing what he wants has worse ones.'

'This connected to the scandal?' Monroe asked, his usual theatrical manner replaced by genuine concern.

'Among other things,' Billy said vaguely. 'Let's just say that inheriting responsibility isn't as straightforward as it sounds, especially when the previous holder has been... creative with their obligations.'

'Need time off to sort it?' Declan offered.

'No,' Billy said firmly. 'Work's the only thing keeping me sane right now. Besides, you need the technical analysis on the Garden Collective connections.'

'Fair enough. But if you change your mind—'

'I won't.'

As Monroe and Declan prepared to leave for their interview with Chen and Webb, Anjli approached Declan's desk.

'Quick word before you go?' she asked quietly.

They stepped away from the others, towards the window overlooking Temple Inn.

'I've been getting messages,' Anjli said, keeping her voice low. 'From Tamara Banks' office. That pinstripe weasel who interrupted our dinner. They want to arrange a meeting.'

Declan's expression darkened.

'What kind of meeting?'

'They're being vague, but it's about "future career opportunities" and "mutual cooperation". Standard political recruitment language.'

'Christ.' Declan ran a hand through his hair. 'I forgot to tell you.'

'Tell me what?'

Declan glanced around to ensure they weren't overheard.

'Shaun Donnal mentioned it when I saw him. Said Banks has been telling people she "owns" you – that you're her version of me, in my relationship with Charles Baker.'

Anjli's jaw tightened.

'Her version of *what*, exactly?'

'Political asset. Someone she can rely on to handle sensitive cases discreetly, without awkward questions or unwanted publicity.'

'And what did you tell Donnal?'

'Nothing, as the comment was passing and the conversation continued,' Declan replied. 'But Banks isn't someone who takes no for an answer easily. If she's decided you're useful to her political ambitions ...'

'She'll keep pushing until I agree to meet.'

'Probably. The question is whether you want to keep kicking that can down the street.'

Anjli considered this, watching the window.

'What would you do?'

'Honestly? I'd meet with her, listen to what she has to say, then politely decline. Better to know what you're refusing than to keep dodging blind.'

'And if she doesn't accept the refusal?'

'Then we cross that bridge when we come to it. But politicians respect directness, even when they don't like the answer.'

Before Anjli could respond, Declan's phone buzzed. He checked it, frowning at the number.

'Text from Shaun Donnal,' he announced. 'Burlington Bertie's coherent again and is asking for me specifically. Says she's remembered something important about "the woman who looked familiar".'

Monroe looked up from gathering his coat.

'If she's lucid, we need to take advantage of it. Those moments don't last long, and it could confirm if these bloody things are connected.'

'Agreed. Change of plans – I'm going to St. Benedict's. Guv, take Anjli with you to Chen and Webb.'

'What about Victoria Lang?' Anjli asked.

'Get the uniforms to take their time bringing her in,' Monroe decided. 'That way you're around when she arrives. Or Bullman can slum it with the real detectives and do some proper work on her own.'

The wink belayed the humour, but it was an honest statement – Bullman was more than capable of doing the interview alone.

'And if Bertie's remembered something significant?' Anjli asked as Declan gathered his coat.

'Then maybe we finally get ahead of this killer instead of constantly chasing their moves,' Declan replied, heading for the exit.

As he left, his phone buzzed again with another message from Shaun:

> Bertie's getting agitated. Keeps talking about "Elizabeth's daughter" and someone who "doesn't belong in the photograph". Whatever that means. Better hurry.

Declan quickened his pace towards the exit. Burlington Bertie might be losing her mind to dementia, but her memories of the Garden Collective era could be the key to stopping a killer who'd been planning revenge for three decades.

The question was whether her clarity would last long enough to make the difference.

10

FRAGMENTS AND ARCHITECTS

The rain had buggered off by the time Declan reached St. Benedict's, and he pushed through the shelter's doors to find Shaun Donnal hovering by the reception desk, clutching a mug of tea like it was his last friend in the world.

'She's in the garden,' Shaun said without preamble. 'Been pacing for an hour, muttering about faces and promises. Sharpest I've seen her since yesterday, but she's wound up like a clockwork toy.'

'Any idea what set her off?'

'Hard to say with Bertie. Could be the weather, could be a dream, could be the ghost of Christmas bloody past.' Shaun's expression darkened. 'I was told by one nurse she was on about visitors again this morning, though.'

'Visitors?'

'Keeps insisting people have been sniffing around, asking about her. Says there was a woman last week, a man before that. Very specific about them asking after Patrick and the old days.'

Declan's pulse quickened.

'Have you actually seen anyone?'

'That's what's got me twitchy – our log shows no visitors for Bertie except you and the social worker. But she describes them down to their bloody shoe leather. What they wore, what they asked, how they smelled.' Shaun ran a hand through what remained of his hair. 'Either her mind's creating detailed fiction, or someone's been very careful not to sign the book.'

'Someone who knows how shelters work, perhaps?'

'Exactly. Which if I'm being honest isn't that hard. I sneaked into them enough while I was on the streets. I can see others doing it too.'

Declan followed him through the dayroom; past residents hunched over paperbacks that had seen better decades and volunteers dispensing pills from a trolley that rattled like a mobile pharmacy.

In the garden Burlington Bertie stood among the winter vegetables, wearing her standard uniform of oversized tweed and men's clothing, looking like a scarecrow that had been left in charge of the place.

'About bloody time, Walsh,' she announced as they approached. 'The man came back.'

'The man?'

'The one who asks me about you,' Bertie replied.

'You mean my father?'

Bertie went to snap back, but then stopped, her eyes widening, as Declan realised the truth.

She thought he was Patrick.

Then as quickly as it came, it went, and she was back to her usual biting self.

'Listen, sunshine, I may be losing my marbles a handful at a time, but I've been watching faces for forty years. That's muscle memory,' Bertie replied. 'He came with the woman, too. She's been coming round, asking questions about Patrick and the old days.'

'When did you see her asking about my father?'

Bertie's eyes went distant, struggling with memories that seemed to slip like smoke through her fingers.

'After his funeral, maybe. Or before? Time's got all twisted up these days.'

'Bertie, I was in Hurley that day. You weren't at his funeral.'

'Of course I wasn't,' Bertie snapped. 'But I understand calendars, don't I? I knew the date – I said she came by after the funeral, asking questions.'

'What kind of questions?'

'About Patrick's work. The cases... the secrets he didn't talk about,' her voice dropped to a whisper. 'Said she was family, doing some genealogy bollocks. But I kept my promises. Patrick made me swear – some secrets stay buried until the grave opens.'

'What secrets, Bertie?'

Burlington Bertie glanced around the garden as if enemy agents might be hiding behind the Brussels sprouts.

'The kind that got people killed back then. The kind that could get people killed now, if the wrong person worked out the connections.'

'But you recognised the man?'

'He's a Gardner,' Bertie spat. 'Has the eyes of a Gardner. Probably Elizabeth's son, he's the right age.'

Declan glanced at Shaun.

'Bertie, from what we can find, Elizabeth Gardner went to prison after the Shadwell Foundry incident,' he said softly. 'And that was thirty years ago.'

'Then he *had* to be her son,' Bertie nodded, deciding this actually validated her claim.

'Bertie, Elizabeth was in her fifties,' Declan continued. 'She had a daughter, Linda, caught in the disaster. If this man was a brother, he'd be in his fifties too.'

'No, he was younger,' Bertie shook her head. 'Twenties, thirties, maybe.'

Declan leant closer.

'Bertie, when I was last here, you mentioned "poor Linda",' he started. 'You said she knew about the supports, tried to get them out. But they wouldn't listen. Do you remember?'

Bertie stared at Declan uncomprehendingly; the clarity was sliding away, and Declan could see her mind retreating into the maze of broken memories.

'Linda,' he continued. 'Did you mean Linda Gardner? Did you know her? Was she trying to save people? It's important you try to remember, please try?'

'Important?' She looked at him blankly. 'What's important?'

And just like that, she was gone again, wandering across the garden, drifting back towards the shelter like a ship that had lost its anchor.

'She'll be like this for a while,' Shaun said quietly. 'The clear moments are getting rarer, shorter.'

'How long has she been on about someone asking questions?'

'Honestly, I've got no idea. Only heard a lot of this earlier today. Nurses said it started a month or so back,' Shaun's expression grew troubled. 'Actually, now you mention it, I did notice a woman hanging about outside a couple of weeks back. Well-dressed, expensive coat, looked like she was waiting for someone. When I asked if she needed help, she said she was admiring the architecture.'

'Architecture? Of a homeless shelter?'

'My thoughts exactly. The building's made from Victorian workhouse brick with all the charm of a prison. Not exactly architectural porn.'

'I need to get back to the office,' Declan told Shaun. 'But call me the second Bertie has another clear spell. And if anyone else comes sniffing around – anyone at all – you call me first. Don't let them near her.'

Following Bertie back into the shelter but turning instead towards the entrance, Declan wondered for a moment how things would have been if his father had lived. Would this case have even happened if Ilse Muller hadn't killed him?

No. You can't dwell on the past, he thought to himself as he headed out to the car park and his Audi. *Bertie's a prime example of what happens then.*

ACROSS LONDON, MONROE AND ANJLI SAT ACROSS FROM ALEX Chen and Gary Webb in a glass-walled conference room that looked like it had been designed by someone who thought transparency was a corporate virtue rather than a legal obligation. Outside the windows, London's financial district hummed with the kind of purposeful energy that usually preceded someone losing money.

Alex Chen couldn't keep still, fidgeting with his phone, setting it down, picking it up again, checking the screen for messages that apparently weren't arriving fast enough.

Beside him, Gary Webb maintained the carefully neutral

expression that corporate lawyers perfected around the time they learned to bill by the quarter-hour.

'Thank you for finally making time,' Monroe began, settling into his chair. 'I know you're both very busy avoiding us.'

'We've had genuine scheduling conflicts,' Gary replied, though his tone suggested even he didn't entirely believe it. 'End of quarter pressures, you understand.'

'Course you have,' Monroe nodded with mock sympathy. 'That quarter that ends a month from now. Utterly understood. Can't be helped, laddie. But now we've got two dead players instead of one, and that rather changes priorities, doesn't it?'

Alex's phone buzzed, and he glanced at it reflexively before forcing himself to set it face down on the polished table.

'I'm not sure what our game has to do with these murders. We keep telling you, it's just water pistols and playing cards.'

'Is it, though?' Anjli asked, opening her notebook and clicking her pen in a way that somehow managed to sound ominous. 'Because from what we understand, the game changed significantly in recent years. Why don't we talk about these forfeits for eliminated players?'

The atmosphere in the room shifted like the pressure drop before a storm. Alex's restless energy stilled, and Gary's neutral expression became more carefully maintained.

'The forfeit system was implemented by group vote,' Gary said carefully. 'Everyone agreed to the enhanced rules.'

'Enhanced rules,' Monroe repeated, rolling the phrase around like he was tasting something unpleasant. 'What kind of enhancements are we talking about?'

'Initially, the forfeits were harmless,' Alex replied defensively. 'Embarrassing social media posts, silly public dares. University-level pranks, really.'

'But they developed?' Anjli pressed on, pen poised over her notebook.

Gary and Alex exchanged a glance that lasted a fraction too long – the kind of silent communication that suggested years of friendship and shared secrets. *Bad* secrets.

'The game became more psychologically sophisticated as we matured,' Gary said finally, choosing his words with lawyer-like care. 'More intellectually challenging.'

'Psychologically sophisticated,' Monroe's Scottish accent seemed to thicken slightly, which Anjli recognised as a warning sign. 'Care to elaborate on what that means in practical terms?'

Alex shifted in his chair, reaching for his phone again before catching himself.

'Well, after a while, simple pranks seemed... juvenile. We wanted something that engaged with real stakes, real consequences.'

'The forfeits began targeting what people actually cared about,' Gary added, warming to his explanation despite the obvious discomfort. 'Career ambitions, relationship concerns, personal insecurities. It elevated the game from children's play to genuine psychological chess.'

'Genuine psychological chess,' Monroe repeated slowly, as if he were memorising the phrase for future use.

'Sure. Before that, if you got killed in the game, there was no actual risk, so people didn't care if they died. Now, when you get killed in the game—'

'You actually get killed in the bloody game,' Monroe

finished the sentence for him. 'And whose brilliant idea was this evolution from harmless fun to psychological warfare?'

Another glance between them, this one more loaded with meaning.

Alex's phone buzzed insistently, and this time he ignored it completely.

'It emerged from group discussions,' he said carefully. 'Strategy sessions where we'd analyse the game's potential and explore ways to make it more engaging for adults.'

'Strategy sessions,' Anjli noted, her pen moving across the page. 'How often did these occur, and who participated?'

'Couple of times a year, mainly as we built up to November,' Gary replied, but his carefully modulated lawyer's voice had developed a slight edge of nervousness. 'Most players would attend – depending on personal commitments, obviously. Families, jobs, locations, all that. The game altered organically through collective input.'

'Nothing organic about systematic psychological manipulation,' Monroe observed darkly. 'But let's get specific, shall we? Daniel Foster's forfeit – what exactly was planned for our deceased barrister when you wee pranksters decided to out him to his employers?'

The temperature in the room seemed to drop several degrees. Alex reached for his phone reflexively, then caught himself and pulled his hand back as if the device had become suddenly radioactive.

'Daniel's forfeit was designed to address his professional anxieties,' Gary said with the kind of careful phrasing that suggested he'd rehearsed this explanation. 'To encourage authenticity in his career development.'

'Professional anxieties?' Anjli looked up with the expression of someone who'd just heard a particularly inventive excuse. 'Is that your professional legal term for threatening to out a gay man to his traditional chambers?'

'It wasn't meant to be threatening,' Alex's discomfort was rising by the second. 'The concept was therapeutic, actually. Helping him confront his fears about being authentic in his professional environment.'

'Authentic in his professional environment. Encourage authenticity in his career development. Christ, man, can you hear what you're both saying?' Monroe's voice was softening, anger building. 'By destroying his career if he didn't voluntarily come out to a chambers known for its conservative attitudes?'

'We never would have actually implemented—' Alex began, then stopped abruptly, as if realising he was about to admit something damaging.

'Go on,' Anjli prompted, pen poised again.

'We'd never have followed through with the consequences,' Gary finished smoothly, though he shot Alex a warning look that suggested his colleague had been about to venture into dangerous territory. 'The forfeits were psychological pressure designed to encourage personal growth, make the players consider their worldview, not actual punishment.'

'But Daniel didn't know that, did he?' Monroe leant forward slightly, his instincts sensing weakness. 'As far as he was concerned, losing the game meant professional and personal destruction. That's rather more than a forfeit, wouldn't you say?'

'Everyone understood the rules when they agreed to participate,' Alex said defensively, but it sounded rehearsed now, like a mantra he'd been repeating to himself.

'Did they? Did everyone truly understand they were

agreeing to have their deepest vulnerabilities targeted by professional-grade psychological manipulation?' Monroe was half rising with anger now. 'Because that's what you're describing, laddies. Systematic psychological blackmail disguised as adult entertainment.'

'I think you're fundamentally mis-characterising our activities, Detective Superintendent. This was consensual participation in a game with agreed-upon rules.'

'Then help me understand the correct characterisation,' Monroe replied with the kind of smile that wasn't entirely friendly. 'Whose idea was Daniel's specific forfeit? Because threatening to destroy someone's career seems rather more sophisticated than your average university graduate might devise.'

The silence stretched until it became genuinely uncomfortable. Alex picked up his phone, looked at the screen, set it down again, then looked at Gary with an expression that suggested he was drowning and desperately hoping for rescue.

'And who the bloody hell are you waiting for?' Monroe snapped. 'Leave the bloody phone alone, laddie! This is a murder investigation we're talking about! A real one, not your silly sodding games!'

There was a moment of awkward silence.

'The ideas came from various sources during our strategy sessions,' Gary said finally, each word carefully weighed. 'It was collaborative development.'

'Various sources,' Anjli repeated. 'Such as?'

'Which other players specifically?' Monroe asked. 'Surely you remember who suggested targeting Daniel's sexuality as a weapon?'

Another pause. Another meaningful glance between them.

'Victoria Lang was particularly insightful about psychological vulnerabilities,' Gary admitted reluctantly, as if the words were being extracted under duress. 'She brought professional expertise to our discussions about effective motivation techniques.'

'Professional expertise?' Anjli looked up sharply. 'You mean her psychology background?'

'Victoria has an intuitive understanding of personality types and psychological pressure points,' Alex said, seeming to gain confidence as he shifted responsibility elsewhere. 'She could identify what would be most motivating for specific individuals. She always has, ever since university.'

'Motivating,' Monroe repeated with obvious distaste. 'All the fancy phrases and bollocks about "effective motivation techniques" you can spout off isn't worth a crap right now. You're aware of this, right? And according to my wife, who's a Doctor of note, a psychology background does not make you a "people" psychologist – you need postdoc training for a few extra years. Did she have that? We can't find that in the notes.'

The question hung in the air.

Alex's phone buzzed insistently, and this time, with a sigh and a nod from Monroe, he answered it with obvious relief.

'I need to take this,' he said, rising from his chair with unseemly haste. 'It's about a technical emergency we had at the Liverpool office.'

He stepped outside the glass room, phone pressed to his ear, leaving Gary alone with two detectives who clearly weren't finished with their questions.

'It's been an extremely stressful week,' Gary replied,

adjusting his glasses with the movements of someone buying thinking time. 'Two members of our group are dead. We're all struggling to process what's happening. Forgive us if we're on edge.'

'Are you struggling to process? Or are you more worried about what else we might discover about your psychological experiments?'

Gary's carefully neutral expression flickered.

'I'm not sure what you're implying.'

'I'm implying,' Monroe leant forward again, his voice dropping once more to a more intimate register, 'that while your wee buddy out there's been staring at his phone as if it's going to kill him, you've been adjusting your tie, your glasses, checking the time. You're genuinely frightened about something beyond just these questions. What is it you're not telling us about your fellow players?

If Gary had been pale before, he went positively ashen now. His hand moved unconsciously to his throat, adjusting his tie with nervous fingers, doing exactly what Monroe had commented on.

'Dirk's been missing for a couple of days.'

'Missing or hiding?' Anjli asked quietly.

'Missing,' Gary said with forced firmness. 'He hasn't answered calls, hasn't been to work, hasn't contacted any mutual friends. It's completely unlike him.'

'When did you last see him?'

Gary considered this carefully, as if the timeline might be legally significant.

'Two weeks ago, perhaps three. There was an informal gathering at a pub in Liverpool Street. Sean organised it. Several of the game players attended.'

'Strategy meeting?'

'No,' Gary shook his head. 'More a misplaced attempt by Sean to get us to play nice and make up with Victoria. Didn't work.'

'How did he seem during this gathering?'

'Agitated,' Gary admitted after a moment's hesitation. 'Dirk had been asking strange questions about his father, about old legal cases. He seemed angry about something he'd discovered, but he wouldn't discuss details.'

'What kind of questions about his father?'

'Historical matters. Something about testimony his dad had given years ago. Dirk seemed to believe his father hadn't told him the complete truth about what had transpired. Anyway, the get-together fell apart when Vickie became a bitch as ever, Rachel stormed off, and we did an Irish goodbye and got the hell out.'

Gary sighs now, taking a moment to stare around the office, as if collecting his thoughts.

'I didn't contact anyone, but then a few days later Daryl said he'd gone to see Dirk but his boss said he was sick, and there was no answer from the house.'

He paused as Alex returned to the room, sliding his phone into his pocket with hands that Anjli noticed were trembling slightly.

'Sorry about that. Crisis averted, thankfully.'

'We were discussing Dirk VanMeerten,' Monroe said without missing a beat. 'Your colleague here was explaining Dirk's recent interest in his father's legal history.'

Alex sat down heavily, the careful composure he'd maintained earlier now completely absent.

'Dirk's been obsessed with that for months. Ever since he

discovered some documents among his father's personal effects.'

'What kind of documents?'

'Legal papers, witness statements, court transcripts – that sort of material. His dad was involved in some nineties case. Dirk seemed convinced his father had committed perjury, but this was because Dirk was a bloody armchair lawyer.'

'And this discovery upset him significantly?'

'More than upset,' Gary interjected. 'He was genuinely angry. Said his father had betrayed people, helped destroy innocent lives. He spoke about justice being perverted and truth being buried. Nobody asked him what he was talking about, as he was always a bit of a martyr. Socialist upbringing.'

Monroe raised an eyebrow at the comment.

'He'd been asking detailed questions about our families, our professional backgrounds, our personal histories. Almost like he was conducting research.'

'Research for what purpose?'

'We believe ...' Gary paused, exchanged another glance with Alex, then continued with obvious reluctance. 'We thought he was writing a book about us or something, but as it went on, we believed he held us, or perhaps our families responsible for something connected to whatever his father was involved in.'

Monroe sat back in his chair, processing this information.

'You think Dirk VanMeerten might be responsible for Sean and Rachel's murders?'

'We don't want to believe it,' Alex said quickly. 'But the timing is highly suspicious. He disappears just before the killings begin. He has military training inherited from his father – weapons handling, tactical awareness, all that "Action Man" shit. And his behaviour had become increasingly paranoid and vindictive.'

'Military training?'

'His dad served in the British Army for several years,' Gary explained. 'He always went on about it to Dirk during his childhood – took him out in the woods to stealth camp and do survival challenges. Probably why Dirk loved the game. It was certainly enough knowledge to be dangerous if misapplied.'

'So, you believe Dirk is hiding not because he's afraid, but because he's guilty?'

'It's a possibility we can't ignore,' Alex said. 'We've been genuinely worried he might target us next. The way he was researching our backgrounds, asking about our vulnerabilities... it felt like preparation for something sinister. Maybe he killed Daniel, and we never realised?'

Monroe exchanged a meaningful glance with Anjli. If Alex and Gary were correct in their assessment, their missing person case had just transformed into a manhunt for a suspect with military training and a decades-old grudge against his university friends.

'Is there anything else you haven't shared with us?' Monroe asked. 'Any other details about the game's evolution, about Daniel's death, about Dirk's increasingly troubling behaviour?'

Another pause, another exchange of uncertain looks between the two men.

'Chris has been asking questions as well,' Gary said finally, as if admitting to a minor indiscretion. 'About why Oliver Drake was recruited to replace Daniel. He seems convinced there's more to his selection than simple availability.'

'Is there?'

'Oliver was chosen because he was willing and available when we needed a replacement,' Alex said, but his tone suggested there might be additional factors he wasn't prepared to discuss.

'Available and willing for what, exactly?'

'To participate in the final round,' Gary said. 'To take Daniel's place in what we'd planned as our concluding game. I mean, he's Belinda's sidepiece, so I think he just wanted to be with her ...'

'Sidepiece?'

'Oh, we're all sure they're shagging when she's not at sodding recitals for her daughter, and good for her. Her partner's a prick. But as Gary said, Chris has been asking a lot of questions recently,' Alex added. 'About why he was specifically chosen. And Oliver's been questioning us too, mainly about our families, our backgrounds.'

'What kind of questions about families?'

Gary adjusted his glasses.

He seemed particularly interested in what our parents did in the early nineties. Asked about property development, legal work, government connections. Said he was fascinated by Dirk, and what he was looking into.'

'He was fascinated by Dirk?'

'I think it was more a case of "his new girlfriend's weird friends" and all that, but yeah,' Gary replied. 'It was almost like a psychiatrist looking at a patient, though. Like he was trying to understand it. Even offered to help Dirk here and there with research. We started to wonder if he was sleeping with Dirk too.'

It was said as a joke, but something in his expression suggested that Oliver taking Daniel's place and looking into their pasts might involve considerably more than simply playing with water pistols, sleeping with another player and collecting playing cards.

'Well, looks like he's a keeper,' Monroe replied.

11

TIMELINES

Arriving back at Temple Inn, Declan found the briefing room occupied by Billy and Doctor Marcos, Billy's laptop connected to the plasma screen and Doctor Marcos standing in front of it, scanning the now-gigantic forensic reports with her usual precision, moving through a selection of zoomed-in crime scene photos and timeline data, while waiting for the team to reconvene. He'd obviously arrived moments after Anjli, as she was still wearing her overcoat as he walked in.

'How did it go?'

'Like trying to nail jelly to a wall,' she replied, pulling off her overcoat and hanging it on the rack by the stairs to the kitchen. 'Corporate lawyers protecting corporate tech princes. Lots of careful words and strategic memory lapses. But we got some interesting admissions; Victoria Lang was much more involved in the forfeit system than she let on. And they're genuinely worried about Dirk VanMeerten. Oh, and they joked that Oliver might be shagging him and Belinda, but I think it's only Belinda.'

'Where's Monroe?' Declan asked, noting the absence of any white-haired Scotsmen.

'Stepped out when we arrived back here,' Anjli replied. 'Said he was following up on an old contact. Didn't elaborate, but he had that look he gets when he's onto something.'

'Okay then, I'm sure we'll find out at some point what he's up to,' Declan sighed as Anjli entered the briefing room, notebook in hand. 'Define "worried about VanMeerten".'

'Basically just that,' Anjli sat at her desk. 'As I said, lots of careful words and strategic memory lapses.'

Declan nodded, looking over at Billy in the briefing room.

'Anything more on the murders?' he called out.

'Our killer's been obsessively careful about digital traces – no CCTV, no phone signals, no electronic breadcrumbs. But they've made one mistake.' Billy glanced up from his laptop. 'Well, not exactly a mistake, but they couldn't avoid physics entirely.'

Doctor Marcos looked back from the plasma screen and her reports.

'The water samples match bottled alkaline water. Something like *ActiPH*, which you buy in posh health food shops, but we're talking more basic. Distinctive mineral profile.'

'So, our killer uses posh water?'

'Either drinks it regularly or chose it deliberately. Not something you'd waste on a ritual unless you had bottles lying around, but it's not one I can find, as none of the ones I've bought and tested match it exactly. It's unpurified.'

'Which means?'

Doctor Marcos considered the question.

'Which means our killer literally dug it out of the ground to squirt it on people,' she said. 'That, Declan, in the business is called a *clue*.'

In Interview Room Two, Bullman sat across from Victoria Lang, both women appearing comfortable despite the rather formal setting. Victoria's posture was perfect, her dark hair neat, her expression concerned but composed. Bullman had started by explaining this was just a chat, and as such, the conversation wasn't being recorded, just noted by Bullman – although she'd gained the distinct impression Victoria wouldn't have cared if it was.

'Doctor Lang, you mentioned that the forfeit system became increasingly sophisticated over time,' Bullman said. 'Can you elaborate on how that development occurred?'

Victoria paused thoughtfully, while still calm.

'The forfeits strengthened organically from group discussions about making the game more psychologically engaging,' she said. 'Alex and Gary were enthusiastic about exploring behavioural modification techniques, but they lacked the theoretical framework to implement them effectively.'

'So, you provided that framework?'

'I offered some insights from my professional training, yes. But I became uncomfortable when the forfeits began targeting genuine vulnerabilities rather than harmless embarrassments.'

'You mean Daniel Foster?'

'I mean many of their ideas. Not just Daniel.'

'Is that why you left the game?'

'Partially. If I'm being brutally honest about the whole thing, after seventeen-odd years, the group dynamics had become quite toxic. What started as innocent fun between old friends had grown into something much darker. We did it to keep in touch, but the only thing we did when we did reconnect—'

'Was try to kill each other with squirt guns,' Bullman finished as she consulted her notes. 'Tell me about Dirk VanMeerten's behaviour in recent months.'

At the name, Victoria's expression grew more serious.

'Dirk had been asking very intrusive questions about everyone's family backgrounds. Specifically about their parents' professional activities during the nineties. It felt like research rather than casual conversation. Too specific. Too intrusive.'

'Research for what purpose?'

'I wasn't certain at the time, but given recent events, I wonder if he was building profiles of potential targets,' Victoria waved a lazy hand, as if the act of showing the police's involvement was enough here. 'He seemed particularly interested in whose parents had been involved in property development or legal proceedings back then.'

'Did he mention any specific cases or incidents?'

'Actually, yes. He kept referring to something called the *Collective*. Said his father had been involved in some kind of court case years ago, and he'd discovered documents that suggested his father hadn't told him the whole truth.'

'How did the other players react to these questions?'

'Most found it uncomfortable. Nathan became quite defensive when Dirk asked about his father's business interests. Diane actually walked out of one gathering when Dirk started pressing her about her family's connections to the case.'

Bullman noted it down.

'Your relationship with Dirk?'

'Fine. He didn't really bother me. I mean he'd tried a

drunken fumble in finals, but once he realised I wasn't interested, then he wasn't interested. And my family wasn't part of whatever rubbish he was investigating, so he didn't bother me there. Lucky, really, if he's the killer.'

Bullman looked up at the comment.

'In your professional opinion, Doctor Lang, what type of person would be capable of the murders we're investigating?'

Victoria considered this carefully.

'Someone with intimate knowledge of the victims' routines and psychology. The staging suggests both personal motivation and professional competence. This isn't random violence – it's methodical elimination of specific targets.'

'Could one of the game players be responsible?'

'It's possible. The group dynamics had become quite strained over the years. Several members harboured resentments about past game results, annoyed that it awarded more physical players—'

'How so?'

'Look at Sean,' Victoria shrugged. 'He kept himself fit like he was Tom Cruise waiting for his next *Mission Impossible* movie. Spent eleven months of the year prepping for one month of game playing – and half the time it was over in a week. People like me, Chris, Diane, Rachel maybe? We didn't really go in with both feet. Sure, it was a thrill, but going too far ...'

She paused, chuckling.

'Something funny?'

'About ten years back, Justin really wanted to win,' Victoria explained. 'He'd been first out three times in a row and was taking crap from Sean. So he went "full player". Took out Diane in her place of work as she was leaving for lunch, forgetting she was an analyst in a bank, and pulling out a gun, no matter what colour it was... well.'

'What happened?'

'Taken down by security, smacked about a bit for being an idiot, let go with a warning.'

She sighed, her seriousness returning.

'Those were the fun games,' she said. 'Not the games that had these treatments, particularly regarding the forfeit system.'

'Which you created.'

'No,' Victoria waved her hands. 'I gave advice. I thought it was for when we got down to the last couple, and I sure as hell didn't think they'd go as far as they did on people.'

'Of the other players, who else had issues?'

'Oh, we all had issues,' Victoria smiled. 'We tried to kill each other once a year. That's "issues" right there. But for candidates for this? Dirk was the most obviously angry. He seemed to view the game as symptomatic of larger injustices. Said we were all products of privilege who'd never faced real consequences for our actions. But for all that, he idolised Sean. Even bought a stupid bloody bodycam when he did, although thankfully he decided not to wear it.'

'What about Daniel Foster's death? You mentioned to my colleague he'd become paranoid about the forfeit system?'

Victoria's expression grew sad.

'Daniel was convinced that Alex and Gary were deliberately targeting his vulnerabilities. He felt trapped between his professional obligations and his personal authenticity. The forfeit designed for him would have destroyed everything he'd worked for.'

'Did you try to help him?'

'I offered professional guidance, offered to speak on his

behalf, but Daniel was beyond the point where therapy could address his immediate crisis. He was terrified of exposure, but equally terrified of living a lie.'

'Do you think his suicide was genuine?'

Victoria hesitated.

'At the time, yes. But given what's happened since, I wonder if someone took advantage of his vulnerable state. If you wanted to eliminate Daniel and make it look like suicide, his existing mental health struggles would provide perfect cover.'

Bullman closed her notebook.

'I think that covers everything for now, Doctor Lang. Thank you for your cooperation.'

'Of course. I hope it helps.' Victoria gathered her handbag, then paused as if struck by a thought. 'Actually, Detective Chief Superintendent, there's something else that might be relevant. About Rachel specifically.'

'What about her?'

'I've been thinking about her behaviour in recent years. She was always troubled about her adoption, but it had become quite obsessive lately,' Victoria continued. 'She kept referring to her adoptive parents as her "fake parents" – very bitter language.'

Bullman reopened the notebook, writing this down.

'She was adopted?'

'Oh yes, though she didn't talk about it openly. Very sensitive subject. She mentioned feeling abandoned by her birth mother, said she'd spent years wondering why she wasn't wanted.' Victoria's expression grew concerned. 'I always thought she had abandonment issues from childhood trauma.'

'Did she ever mention trying to find her biological family?'

'She'd made some attempts but kept hitting dead ends. The adoption records were sealed, apparently. It was eating away at her – the not knowing.' Victoria leant forward slightly, resting her elbows on the table. 'You don't think Rachel's background could be connected to these murders, do you?'

'We're exploring all possibilities.'

'Of course. It's just... if someone was targeting the children of people involved in old cases, Rachel would fit that profile perfectly. She always said she felt like she was living someone else's life.'

Bullman made notes.

'Listen, I might be overstepping, but I have helped the police several times over the years,' Victoria added. 'I've been thinking about the staging of the murders, the psychological elements. If I could see the crime scenes themselves, I might be able to identify patterns that aren't obvious from descriptions alone.'

'That's not standard procedure,' Bullman said, but her tone suggested she was considering it.

'I understand. But as a psychologist, I can read crime scenes in ways that might not be obvious to investigators. The killer's choice of locations, the staging – it all reveals psychological patterns. Especially if this is connected to Rachel's adoption and family history.'

Bullman straightened, putting her notebook away.

'Alright. We'll start with the Harrington Finance building. It's closest, and the scene's still sealed.'

'Perfect. I'd be happy to take a look.'

As they left the Interview Room together, Victoria allowed herself the smallest of smiles.

THE *BLACKFRIAR* PUB HAD THE KIND OF VICTORIAN SOLIDITY that made London's glass towers look temporary. Built in 1875 on the site of a Dominican priory, it had survived The Blitz, several recessions, and countless attempts by developers to turn it into something more profitable. The art nouveau bronze friezes of monks adorning its wedge-shaped exterior had watched over this corner of the City for nearly a century and a half, outlasting most of the businesses that had sprung up around it. And Monroe tipped an imaginary cap to them as he pushed through the heavy doors, spotting his contact immediately in the corner booth – a man who looked like he'd been personally carved by forty years of London weather.

'Gordon McKinnon,' Monroe said, extending his hand to the grey-haired man nursing a pint. 'Appreciate you meeting me on short notice.'

'Alex bloody Monroe,' McKinnon replied with a grin that showed too many years of police canteen coffee and regular smoke breaks. 'Heard you'd made Detective Superintendent. Always knew you'd either end up running the show... or in prison.'

'Jury's still out on that,' Monroe replied, settling into the booth and signalling the barman. 'Pint of whatever he's having.'

McKinnon studied him.

'So, what's this about? Your message mentioned Emmy Clarke. That's a name I haven't heard in twenty years.'

Monroe rose, picked up his pint and returned to the table.

'And for you?' McKinnon asked.

Sighing, Monroe walked back to the bar and bought a second pint before returning and sitting.

'Emmy Clarke?' McKinnon reminded him.

'Aye. She's turned up at a homeless shelter, calling herself "Burlington Bertie", which was apparently a code name back then. Early dementia, but she's been talking about Patrick Walsh and old cases.'

'Christ,' McKinnon took a long pull of his pint. 'I was going to ask how is the mad old bird, but that ...'

'Aye,' Monroe sipped at the pint, wincing. 'Good Christ, Gordon, what is this shite?'

'Enjoy,' McKinnon grinned. 'So, what about her?'

'Well, she claims someone's been asking questions about Patrick's work. Specifically, the Garden Collective investigation and the Shadwell disaster, which was before my time at Tottenham. But you were desk officer in the early nineties, with Tom Keating?'

McKinnon's expression shifted.

'That's ancient history, Alex. Why drag it up now?'

'Because I've got two dead City workers with playing cards pinned to their chests, and Emmy's ramblings might be connected.'

'Bollocks.'

'Maybe. But Emmy knew things that weren't in any official files, and in her lucid moments, we're getting some scary coincidences. If someone's been pumping her for information ...'

McKinnon was quiet for a moment, considering. When he spoke, his voice had dropped to the conspiratorial whisper that coppers used when discussing things that shouldn't be discussed.

'Emmy Clarke was Patrick's best source, no question. Sharp as a razor, never got a detail wrong. But she had *baggage*.'

'What sort of baggage?'

'Personal stuff. Family complications that someone above Patrick's pay grade had to manage.'

'I don't follow.' Monroe leant forward.

McKinnon glanced around the pub, checking for eavesdroppers.

'Emmy had a daughter. Young girl, maybe seven or eight back then. Bright kid, but Emmy was terrified someone would use the girl to get to her. Maybe even then there were issues – I've got a cousin, yeah? acts just like Emmy did, diagnosed as bipolar. Remember, these were the early nineties, Alex. People classed mental illness as "being a bit odd".'

He shifted in his seat.

'The Shadwell case was getting political attention, and Assistant Commissioner Willis – I think he might have been before your time and moved across to Serious Crime a couple of years after – he arranged for the daughter to be placed with a good family, new identity, proper education.'

'That's not usual for this sort of thing.'

'Yeah, but then there was that shit with the people dying and the floor giving way. Westminster was pissed; the press were having a field day. Some Tory bigwig called Shipman sent his pet enforcer to fix it.'

'Christ,' Monroe half rose. 'Norman bloody Shipman sorted this with Bruno Field?'

'Maybe. Sounds familiar. You remember it then?'

'I remember them,' Monroe replied. 'Shipman and Field

appeared very heavily in a case we ran a couple of years back involving some teenage crime solvers in the early nineties called the *Magpies*.'

He leant back in his chair, shaking his head.

'Jesus. Patrick never mentioned any of this.'

'Course not. That's why it worked.' McKinnon finished his pint. 'But Emmy never got over it. Used to talk about her daughter constantly, wonder what she was doing, whether she was safe. Patrick would ask Willis, and he'd promised they'd be reunited whenever Emmy wanted to step down.'

'Were they reunited?'

'Willis made sure they weren't. When the Garden Collective case got shut down, Willis took orders from Shipman, who decided it was safer to keep them separated permanently. Emmy went into the woodwork; daughter grew up thinking she'd been abandoned. Willis died about ten years ago, took the secret with him. No idea about Shipman.'

'He's still an MP, still surviving somehow,' Monroe said, deciding not to mention that the last time he'd heard, Norman Shipman was still the de facto head of a secret cabal known as the *Star Chamber*, which was significantly worse than any Government department. 'This daughter – any idea what happened to her?'

'Adopted by a professional family. Patrick kept tabs for a few years, made sure she was settling in well. Clever girl, did well at school, went to university.'

'University where?'

McKinnon shrugged. 'Couldn't say. I think it was one of the big ones, though. Oxford, perhaps?'

Monroe was already rising from his seat.

'This daughter – did Patrick ever mention anything specific about her? Any details Emmy shared?'

McKinnon frowned, searching decades-old memories.

'Emmy used to call her "my little Queen of Clubs".'

'Queen of Clubs?' Monroe repeated, his blood running cold.

'Aye. Sweet really, the way Emmy talked about her. Said she was going to teach her proper card games when they were reunited. But that never happened, did it?'

Monroe's phone was already in his hand as he typed an urgent message to Declan. The pieces weren't just falling into place – they were crashing together.

'Gordon, I need to go. But this conversation never happened, understood?'

'Course not. But Alex ...'

'What?'

'If this girl's involved in whatever's happening now, be careful. Growing up separated from your mother, thinking she abandoned you... that kind of trauma can twist people in ways you don't see coming.'

Back at Temple Inn, De'Geer appeared in the doorway of the briefing room, his massive frame nearly filling it.

'Guv, got an update on the VanMeerten search,' he said. 'Still no sign of him, but we've tracked his movements up to Tuesday afternoon.'

'Where was he?' Declan asked.

'Kingston Library, of all places. Staff remember him because he spent hours in the local history section, requesting specific archives about court cases. Left with photocopies of what looked like legal documents.'

'Legal documents about what?'

'Staff weren't sure, but he was particularly interested in cases involving environmental protest groups. Asked specifically about witness testimony and perjury proceedings.'

'In Kingston?'

'Apparently so, Guv. They said he came in often, so I reckon he has a connection there.'

Anjli glanced at Declan.

'That fits with what Chen and Gary told us. Dirk's been obsessed with something his father testified about years ago.'

She paused as her phone buzzed.

'Bullman,' she said, reading it. 'According to Victoria Lang, Rachel Peterson was adopted, never knew her mother. Unsure if it's important.'

'Surely she would have if she was seven?' Declan frowned.

'Maybe the mother wasn't around?' Anjli shrugged. 'Just going on what I have here.'

Billy, who'd been working on the laptop while nobody needed images on the plasma screen suddenly looked up, his face pale.

'Guv, I've found something disturbing on Sean Acker's phone,' he said. 'Messages from Dirk VanMeerten.'

'What kind of messages?'

Billy pulled up the message thread on his screen and mirrored it on the plasma screen so everyone could see what he was talking about, as images of Victoria Lang started to appear.

'Dirk was sending Sean photos of Victoria Lang. Outside her office, at coffee shops, near her flat. Time-stamped over the past three weeks.'

'He was stalking her?' Doctor Marcos asked.

'Looks like it,' Billy confirmed, scrolling through the

messages. 'Sean's responses show he was confused and worried.'

On the screen, the messages appeared, all from Sean to Dirk.

> Why are you following Victoria? This is creepy, mate.

> What's wrong with you? Stop sending me these photos.

Declan moved closer to the screen.

'Any explanation from Dirk?'

'Just cryptic stuff. "You don't understand what's happening" and "She's involved somehow". Sean kept telling him to stop, said he was going to report it if Dirk didn't leave Victoria alone. Then there's a single text to Victoria, the day before his death, telling her to be wary of Dirk, because he's seen Dirk's "crime wall" and there's a lot they need to talk about.'

'Crime Wall?'

'Apparently.'

'When were these sent?' Anjli asked.

'The last batch from Sean and Dirk came Tuesday afternoon,' Billy replied. 'Hours before Sean was murdered.'

'Same day Dirk VanMeerten was in Kingston,' Doctor Marcos commented.

Declan's phone buzzed. Monroe's message appeared on the screen.

> Emmy Clarke had a daughter. Possibly went to Oxford University. Patrick arranged separation for safety in 1992. Emmy called her "Queen of Clubs." Rachel Peterson's card.

Declan read the message aloud, and the room went quiet.

'So, Rachel Peterson doesn't know her mother, and Burlington Bertie had a hidden daughter,' Anjli said slowly. 'Could this explain the Queen of Clubs connection?'

'This could mean someone's targeting the children of Garden Collective informants,' Doctor Marcos added.

'And Dirk VanMeerten has been stalking Victoria Lang for weeks,' Billy said, still staring at the photos on his screen. 'If he's our killer ...'

'Victoria's his next target,' Declan finished. 'We need to get Victoria Lang to safety immediately. Contact Bullman now. Tell her to keep Victoria in the interview room until we can arrange protection—'

He paused as he saw De'Geer's expression change.

'I saw her as I was coming here,' he said. 'Bullman signed out with Miss Lang about ten minutes ago. Said she was taking her to look at crime scene evidence.'

'What evidence? Where?'

'She didn't specify, sir. Just signed the log and left.'

'Her phone's going straight to voicemail,' Anjli said, looking at Billy. 'Tell me you have a tracker on her.'

Billy reddened, his habit of tracking colleagues most likely stemming from abandonment issues.

'She said she'd break my legs if I tracked her,' he shook his head. 'At best I can use ANPR.'

'Then do that,' Declan replied, looking up at the images of Victoria Lang on the plasma screen. 'And work out whether there's any connection with Victoria Lang to this bloody Bell Foundry disaster.'

He was about to continue when the office door swung open, and Alex Chen stumbled in, looking like he'd aged a decade in the last hour, PC Cooper trying desperately to slow him down. His bespoke suit hung from his frame like borrowed clothes. Dark circles carved shadows beneath bloodshot eyes.

'Sorry Guv,' Cooper said, pulling at him. 'He wouldn't be stopped.'

'DCI Walsh, DI Kapoor,' Alex croaked, ignoring her. 'I need to talk to you about Dirk.'

Declan caught the edge in Alex's voice and glanced at Anjli.

'Did you forget something?' she asked softly. 'Maybe something you couldn't say at the office?'

Alex stared around wide-eyed and then nodded.

'I think something's happened to Dirk,' he blurted finally. 'And Christ, I think I might be responsible.'

12

SELF STORAGE

ONCE THE DOOR CLICKED SHUT, ALEX PACED THE SMALL interview room like a caged animal, five steps each way before turning. The fluorescent light buzzed overhead, casting sickly shadows across his face.

'Sit,' Declan commanded, gesturing to one of the two chairs on the other side of the desk. 'Start from the beginning.'

Alex collapsed into the chair as if his strings had been cut. He dragged his hands through his hair, leaving it sticking up in odd directions.

'Dirk called me Tuesday,' his voice cracked. 'Said he'd found something in his father's old files about the Garden Collective – something about testimonies and the Shadwell Bell Foundry.'

'What specifically?'

'He wouldn't say, not properly.' Alex leant forward, elbows on knees. 'Bloody fool was always too paranoid for phone calls. But he kept saying mad stuff like "Someone in the game is connected" and "it's all been a lie". Proper psycho shit. Kept going on about how we'd never properly asked about each other's families, about histories, about what our parents did back then, like it bloody mattered! We all came from different places; the only reason we knew each other was the game.'

'Did you meet him? After the call?'

Alex's laugh was hollow, brittle.

'That's the thing, isn't it? I bloody well laughed him off,' he stared at his hands. 'Dirk's always been… intense. Conspiracy theories, hidden agendas, shadowy cabals. When Sean used to go on about Royal Marines, Dirk would counter with black ops stories, the two of them constantly trying to one-up each other, and out "spy gadgets" each other. We all stopped listening years ago.'

Alex pulled out his phone, hands trembling slightly.

'He left a voicemail. Listen.'

He navigated to the message and set the phone on the table between them. After a couple of seconds, Dirk VanMeerten's voice filled the small room, tight with tension.

'Alex, it's Dirk. I've found something about the testimony and the Bell Foundry case. Someone in the game is connected to it all! I bloody knew it! I'm going to confront them, but I wanted someone to know in case—'

The message cut off with a sharp click.

'That's all he said,' Alex added. 'I assumed he was in a bad signal area. But now …'

'Did he mention where he was going?' Declan leant forward. 'Who he planned to confront?'

'No. That's it. The whole bloody message.' Alex snatched back his phone. 'I tried calling back, but it went straight to voicemail. Left it, didn't I? Thought he was being Dirk – dramatic, paranoid, making mountains out of conspiracy molehills.'

'And you're only bringing this to us now?' Declan's voice darkened. 'We've spoken to you twice now, and neither time did you even insinuate this was an issue.'

Alex's face flushed.

'Look, I didn't connect it to the murders until today, alright? Gary and I were talking after you left, and we realised – nobody's heard from Dirk since before Sean died,' he swallowed hard. 'There's something else. Dirk has a storage unit in Kingston. Not many people know about it.'

'Storage unit?'

'Kingston Self Storage on Richmond Road. Unit thirty-seven or thirty-eight, I can't remember exactly.' Alex's fingers drummed an anxious rhythm on his thigh. 'He keeps his father's stuff there – military memorabilia, papers, records. He took me once a few months back. Had this entire wall covered in conspiracy stuff, all based in the early nineties, but hidden behind a moveable pinboard. Felt like I was at a spy movie. His dad testified at some trial, and Dirk was obsessed with it. I'd contacted them, asking if he still had it. I was waiting for the callback when I was talking to your colleagues. Had to pretend it was a work thing so Gary didn't know I'd done it.'

'Gary would have been unhappy?' Declan texted De'Geer the information, including the last known phone message from Dirk VanMeerten as Alex continued.

'Yes. No. I don't know any more.'

'Is there anything else you can tell me? Any recent behaviour that seemed out of character?'

Alex's gaze drifted to the wall.

'Dirk changed these past few months. Started digging into everyone's backgrounds, family histories, like he was building dossiers on all of us. We just thought he was taking a leaf out of Sean's book and really leaning into the game, especially as it's the last one, but as we said in the interview, he'd somehow convinced Oliver to start believing his bullshit. The two of them spent more time together, so much even Sean started to get jealous.'

He hesitated before continuing.

'About two weeks ago, I went to meet Dirk for lunch and saw him talking to this odd woman in Covent Garden. Dressed in men's clothes – tweed jacket, tie, the lot. Looked completely out of place. They seemed... intense. When I asked him about it later, he brushed it off. Said she was a source for his "research project".'

'Did he mention her name?' Declan asked, but he didn't really need an answer here.

Burlington Bertie was being busy, it seemed.

'No,' Alex shook his head. 'But he seemed rattled afterward. Said something about how "the past never stays buried for long". Pure Dirk dramatics, I thought at the time.'

'Did he ever mention Victoria Lang specifically?'

Alex hesitated, his expression shifting subtly.

'Not directly. But he asked weird questions about Victoria leaving the game, even though he was there when she threw her shit-fit and left and started quizzing us about Daniel before his death. Asked if I'd noticed anything off about them, any strange behaviour.'

Declan's phone buzzed. A message from De'Geer.

> On our way to storage unit now – have taken Cooper. ETA 20 mins.

'Alright, Alex.' Declan rose. 'I need you to stay put. We may have more questions.'

'Am I a suspect?' Alex looked up, suddenly smaller in the harsh light.

'Honestly? Based on what we've seen so far, I'd say everyone connected to the game is of interest right now,' Declan replied, the diplomatic non-answer coming automatically. 'But your cooperation is noted—'

The door opened before he could continue, and a uniformed officer stood there, flushed, with an older man, black slicked-back hair, suited and with a briefcase behind her.

'Mister Chen's solicitor is here,' they explained as the man pushed past.

'Mister Webb?' Alex now rose. 'I didn't call—'

'No, Gary did,' the solicitor, apparently Gary Webb's father or uncle replied. 'Said you'd start digging holes. Is he under arrest?'

'No,' Declan replied. 'He came here on his own cognisance.'

'Then he'll leave here on his own cognisance,' Mister Webb said, waving Alex to follow. 'He's done here.'

And with that, Alex Chen, giving Declan an apologetic glance, left the interview room.

'What the bloody hell was that?' Declan shook his head in astonishment.

Kingston Self Storage squatted on the outskirts of the borough like a concrete bunker – a two-storey labyrinth of metal doors and numbered units surrounded by a chain-link fence topped with razor wire. De'Geer's hulking frame made the unmarked police car look like a child's toy as he and Cooper pulled into the visitor parking space at the front.

'Still don't see why we couldn't have taken the bike,' he muttered.

'Because I'd rather sit in comfort,' Esme replied calmly, an answer she'd given many times.

'You can be comfortable on a police bike,' De'Geer argued as they walked up to the main entrance, hammering on the door.

'Yes, you can,' Esme smiled sweetly. 'If you're behind a rider of human size. Not a giant who takes up most of the seat and the pillion.'

De'Geer reddened at this.

'Sorry,' he said as the door opened behind him.

The manager – balding, paunchy, and with the suspicious eyes of someone who'd seen too many storage units cleared out after missed payments – required both warrant cards and a phone call to his supervisor before reluctantly leading them to Unit 37.

'Haven't seen the gentleman who rents this in ages,' he muttered, fumbling with a ring of master keys that would have made a Victorian jailer proud. 'Sure you've got authority for this?'

'Of course we're sure,' De'Geer's accent deepened when annoyed. 'Just open it, please.'

Cooper, checking her messages, showed him one that had just arrived from Declan.

Check behind pinboard

She placed the phone away as the lock clicked, and the manager heaved up the metal door. The smell hit them instantly – that unmistakable, sickly sweet odour of human decomposition that no police officer ever forgot.

'Jesus Christ!' The manager staggered backwards, hand clamped over his mouth. Cooper, however, was already pulling on latex gloves, her face grim as she reached for her radio.

'Control, it's Cooper. We need forensics and Doctor Marcos at Kingston Self Storage, Unit thirty-seven. Suspected homicide scene. Sergeant De'Geer and I securing the location now.'

The unit was approximately four metres by three, and inside it every surface was crammed with military memorabilia, filing boxes, and the kind of organised chaos that suggested a mind constantly connecting invisible dots. Filing cabinets lined one wall, a corkboard the other.

In the centre of the concrete floor, partially hidden behind stacked boxes, lay a body covered with a military-issue tarpaulin.

De'Geer approached with the caution of experience, using a pen to lift one corner of the covering. Beneath it, Dirk VanMeerten's body lay in early decomposition, his face frozen in an expression of surprise. A single stab wound to the chest had penetrated between his ribs, and pinned to his chest with a metal spike was a black and silver playing card – the King of Hearts – his game identity.

'Looks like he was killed a couple of days ago, maybe longer,' De'Geer murmured, examining the body without disturbing anything. 'If he was contacting people on Tuesday, then this could have been shortly before Sean Acker.'

'First victim, not third,' Cooper agreed. 'Changes the whole timeline.'

She paused as she noticed something partially hidden

beneath a stack of papers – a small wooden box with an aged brass plate on the lid.

SHADWELL BELL FOUNDRY – 1894.

'Morten,' she gestured towards it, stepping back as De'Geer pulled out his phone and photographed it carefully before opening it with a gloved hand. Inside, nestled in faded velvet, were four decorative metal finials; what looked to be ornate Victorian craftsmanship with distinctive scrollwork.

'These look interesting,' De'Geer said, taking photos from several angles. 'Not sure what they are, but they're definitely antiques. Leave them where they are, I think Doctor Marcos will want to see this.'

Cooper, meanwhile had found a receipt half-hidden beneath the box. Carefully, she pulled it out.

'Architectural Salvage Auction, Lot 47 – Four Victorian Finials, ex-Shadwell Bell Foundry,' she read. 'Purchased two years ago. Cash payment but signed by D. VanMeerten. Wonder why he was interested in these?'

She straightened and glanced around the location, eventually pausing at the back wall.

'Look – a pinboard.'

She walked to the pinboard wall and, after a moment's checking, slid it to the side, revealing the hidden chaos behind it.

Photographs of each player in the game had been pinned in a semicircle with what looked to be notes about their family backgrounds, occupations, and personal details. Victoria Lang's photo had several notes beside it, including "Medical records don't match?" and "Birth certificate inconsistencies".

'Dirk wasn't just playing the game,' De'Geer observed, phone already at his ear, the call to Declan connecting. 'He was investigating the players. Looking for connections. Guv, we've found Dirk. Been dead since shortly before Sean Acker, I believe. Playing card pinned to his chest, same MO.'

He paused, listening to Declan's response.

'There's more. Found some decorative finials from the Bell Foundry that might be worth looking at. And Dirk was investigating Victoria Lang – his notes say there are inconsistencies in her medical records and birth certificate.'

As he ended the call, Cooper had walked over to a side table and was looking back with an expression of horror.

'Morten, is this what I think it is?' she asked quietly, indicating an open, carbon fibre black box on the table. De'Geer walked over and stared into it, noting both the dark grey foam and the gun shaped hole.

'Looks like a gun case,' he whispered. 'Without a gun.'

'Sean Acker was killed with a 9mm,' Cooper added. 'Have we just found where the murder weapon came from? And if so, why did Dirk have it?'

'More importantly, there's no silencer here,' De'Geer looked around. 'If Sean was killed by this gun, and there's no space in the case for one, where the hell did they get it?'

At Temple Inn, Billy stared at his father's latest message without opening it. Three more had arrived in the last hour, each with increasingly urgent subject lines. The latest simply gave three words, all in capitals.

CALL ME NOW.

He set his phone face-down on the desk and returned to the database search he'd been running on Victoria Lang; the tension headache that had been building since his father's first call that morning was now a full-blown migraine.

'You look like you're contemplating either murder or an extremely expensive whisky,' came a familiar voice from the doorway. 'Perhaps both.'

Billy looked up to find his great-uncle Chivalry Fitzwarren standing there, resplendent in his customary Harris tweed and corduroy trousers. At what had to be approaching seventy, Chivalry still carried himself with the straight-backed arrogance of the aristocracy, though his beard had more white than brown these days. He also seemed to be able to come and go as he pleased, probably because of bribery and banter with the desk sergeants.

'Uncle Chivalry,' Billy said, genuinely surprised. 'What are you doing here?'

'The mountain wasn't calling Mohammed, so I thought I'd save us all time and make the journey myself,' Chivalry glanced around the office with polite interest. 'Is there somewhere we might talk privately? I suspect what I have to say isn't for the ears of your colleagues.'

Billy checked his watch – Cooper and De'Geer wouldn't be back from Kingston for at least another twenty minutes, and Declan was with Monroe reviewing case notes.

'The canteen should be empty this time of day,' he said, rising from his desk. 'But I've only got a few minutes. We're in the middle of a multiple homicide investigation.'

'You're *always* in the middle of a multiple homicide investigation,' Chivalry smiled widely, falling into step beside Billy. 'A few minutes will suffice, family business rarely requires more.'

True to Billy's prediction, the canteen area was deserted, and he steered his great-uncle to a table by the coffee machine, making himself one as he did so.

'I assume this is about Father's message?' he asked, not bothering with small talk.

Chivalry smiled, but there was no humour to it.

'Yes, it's about your father's sudden desire to abdicate his responsibilities. Or more accurately, it's about the trap he's setting for you.'

Billy's eyebrows rose.

'Trap?'

'Your father is many things, William, but he's never been a fool,' Chivalry said, his voice low despite the emptiness of the room. 'This entire charade – the supposed scandal, the immediate abdication – it's all designed to force your hand.'

'To what end? He knows I want nothing to do with the title or the estate. And the family pretty much disowned me en masse when I had Uncle Bryan arrested.'

'Pish and tosh, Bryan deserved everything he got,' Chivalry muttered. 'But you are right, he's counting on your refusal. He wants you to hate the idea so much, you'll use the significant sway the whole family believes you have with Charles Baker to have the whole thing removed.'

Billy's eyes narrowed.

'You mean the scandal?'

'Manufactured,' Chivalry said dismissively. 'A convenient fiction – or at least a half-conceived one that if revealed will cause him embarrassment and likely force him off the company board for a year or two, but nothing more.'

'Christ,' Billy muttered. 'So, this whole panic attack I've been having since I heard about his abdication has all been for nothing?'

'Not for nothing,' Chivalry corrected. 'It's given you valuable insight into the family's machinations. Your father is clever, but predictable as ever. He expects you to run from your heritage as you always have, finding a way to fix everything so he keeps his seat on the board – and his not insubstantial yearly bonus.'

'He could have just bloody well asked me for help,' Billy grumbled.

'But would you have?' Chivalry raised an eyebrow. 'Also, would he have swallowed his pride to do so? Of course he bloody wouldn't have. And likely, neither would you.'

'So, you're suggesting what, exactly? That I should embrace becoming Viscount bloody Fitzwarren and tell him to be damned with it?'

'I'm suggesting,' Chivalry said, leaning forward, 'that you call his bluff. Accept the title, take control of the whole damned thing. It would give you resources beyond anything you've imagined, William. Resources you could use far more ethically than your father ever has.'

Billy stared at his great-uncle, processing the implications.

'The family never wanted me to be a police officer,' he said softly and slowly, thinking through the situation as he spoke. 'But I don't know if this is the way to do it.'

'There are always alternatives,' Chivalry acknowledged with a slight smile. 'But I merely wanted to ensure you understood the true nature of the game before making any hasty decisions.'

Billy downed the coffee he made and instantly began making a fresh one.

'I need to get back downstairs,' he said. 'It's a weird one.'

'Weird enough for me to help?'

'Well, if you like murders involving water pistols—'

'I think I'll leave this one to you,' Chivalry grinned wolfishly as he rose smoothly. 'Guns? Exciting. Squirt guns? Not so much. Still, murder waits for no man, not even a viscount-in-waiting. I'll see myself out.'

'Wait,' Billy said, something occurring to him. 'You've been on the board of the Historical Buildings Trust for decades, right?'

'Well, there's being on the board and actually *being* on the board,' Chivalry frowned. 'I've only been on it in name for the last ten years or so.'

'But you were on it in the nineties?'

'I believe so. Why?'

'Did you ever have dealings with a group called the Garden Collective?'

Chivalry's expression changed subtly.

'Now that,' he said carefully, 'is a name I haven't heard in quite some time. Why do you ask?'

'It's connected to our case. Multiple murders linked to an old activist group.'

'I remember them,' Chivalry nodded slowly. 'Passionate but misguided. Their methods became... extreme. Actually, I believe I still have the old notes from back then, I might have some materials that could prove useful.'

Billy nodded, already heading for the stairs.

'I'll hold you to that,' he said. 'Sooner the better.'

'THE TIMING FITS,' MONROE SAID, RUBBING HIS JAW. 'DIRK discovers something, leaves an ominous message, then disappears right before Sean is killed.'

'And now De'Geer's found his body,' Declan added grimly. 'With the same signature – playing card pinned to the chest.'

They were standing behind Billy as he worked at his monitors, having wisely kept out of the way until Chivalry Fitzwarren left the main office. Now, they read the information flashing up on the screen as Billy hunted through old rental agreements for the Kingston lockup.

'The pattern's changing,' Billy commented without looking up from his screen. 'Hypothetically, we have Daniel as the first murder – if you class him as such – maybe made to look like suicide. Then Dirk, hidden away in his own storage unit, stabbed, and a gun found there.'

'Why didn't the killer use the gun there?' Declan wondered.

'Maybe they didn't have the silencer yet,' Monroe suggested. 'Loud bang, small room, brings attention.'

He waved for Billy to continue.

'Then Sean – public murder with the same gun, and a suppressor that's been possibly picked up elsewhere,' Billy tapped the screen. 'Now Rachel – same signature but similar method to Dirk; a stabbing.'

'The killer's getting bolder,' Monroe agreed. 'More theatrical.'

'Or it's different killers,' Declan suggested.

'Multiple killers?' Monroe raised an eyebrow.

'Think about it – Daniel's "suicide" is different from the others. Maybe someone killed him, then a second killer started targeting people connected to Daniel's death. Maybe Dirk discovered this and became the next target. Maybe Rachel was stabbed because there were security in the building and the gunshot would have echoed in the stairwell.'

'But the gun had a silencer,' Billy replied, looking around. 'You wouldn't have heard it.'

'Unless the gun was elsewhere, which could prove the "two killers" idea,' Declan continued his theory. 'Or, if the gun wasn't on the killer, this could have been a spur of the moment attack.'

'Aye, it's possible,' Monroe conceded. 'But if you're right on the first count, that would mean both killers are connected to the game *and* the Garden Collective. Bit of a coincidence, no?'

'I don't believe in coincidences,' Declan replied. 'But I do believe in patterns.'

Monroe nodded, his expression grim.

'Let's see what Rosanna finds. If Dirk was investigating the connections between these players and the Garden Collective, his research might give us the missing pieces.'

'And Burlington Bertie,' Declan added. 'If Rachel was adopted in 1992 at age seven, she matches the timeline for Emmy Clarke's daughter. We need to confirm that connection.'

The office door opened, and Bullman entered with Victoria Lang. Victoria looked composed as ever in her tailored suit, observing the suddenly quiet room with a psychologist's neutrality.

'Quite the war room you've assembled,' she commented, nodding towards the evidence spread across the desks. 'Any breakthroughs?'

Monroe glanced at Bullman, but she gave nothing back, simply walking over to the desks, checking some of the paperwork there.

'A few promising leads,' Declan replied, carefully gathering the papers. 'Thank you for your help at the crime scene. I understand you provided some valuable insights.'

'I hope so,' Victoria said. 'The positioning of Rachel's body in that stairwell suggested someone with knowledge of liminal spaces – psychological thresholds. It's fascinating from an academic perspective.'

Declan frowned.

'The body was gone by the time you arrived.'

'I could see where it fell by the layout of the tape,' Victoria explained.

There was an uncomfortable moment as Declan kept eye contact with Victoria, who stared back, quite relaxed.

'Speaking of academic perspectives,' Monroe said, keeping his tone conversational as he changed the subject, 'our boss here mentioned you've studied identity formation in separated children. Given what we now know about Rachel's adoption, do you think that could be relevant to why she was targeted?'

Victoria's expression remained neutral, though Declan thought he detected the slightest pause before she answered.

'It's possible. Adopted children often struggle with identity issues well into adulthood. Rachel had mentioned searching for her birth mother in recent years. Perhaps she uncovered something that put her at risk.'

'Had she made any progress in that search?' Declan asked.

'Not that she shared with me,' Victoria replied. 'Though we weren't particularly close in recent years. The game had become rather intense, which is partly why I stepped back.'

'Thank you for your insight, Victoria, but would you excuse us for a moment?' Declan said. 'Guv, perhaps you could show Doctor Lang to the canteen? We need to confirm some sensitive items that have just come to light before we bring her onto the case.'

Bullman frowned but knew he wouldn't ask her to do something this menial without a reason, and so nodded, motioning for Victoria Lang to follow.

Once they'd left, Declan turned to Monroe.

'Something's off,' he said quietly. 'I can't see how she could know positioning without a photo.'

'Could have been an educated guess,' Billy suggested. 'Psychologists do that sort of thing.'

'Not crime-scene layouts,' Declan's eyes followed Victoria's retreating figure. 'There's something about her ...'

'She's helping with the investigation, Declan,' Monroe reminded him. 'Let's not start seeing killers in every shadow until there are *actual* killers in every shadow. And you know the police rule about keeping friends close ...'

'And suspects closer,' Declan nodded, the nagging feeling persisting. 'Let's hope we work it out before those killers arrive. Let me know when Anjli's back.'

'She said she had something personal to do,' Billy replied.

At this, Declan frowned.

'What sort of personal thing?'

'Are you sure you want to pry, laddie?' Monroe asked quietly, but Billy had already turned around.

'Something in Westminster—'

'Ah, Christ,' Declan was already heading to his office and grabbing his coat. 'She's gone to pick a fight with Tamara Banks.'

13

THE WESTMINSTER CONNECTION

RAIN PELTED ANJLI'S UMBRELLA AS SHE MARCHED UP Whitehall, heels striking the wet pavement with an almost military precision. She'd spent the journey down the Strand mentally rehearsing what she'd say to Tamara Banks, and none of it was remotely diplomatic. Three emails, two voicemails, and now a text bordering on threatening – all insisting she and Banks "align their mutual interests" before what Banks felt was an almost inevitable leadership transition. The latest message, sent from that pinstripe-suited weasel Craig half an hour earlier had snapped her patience.

> Your future career trajectory requires this conversation. Further delays will be noted.

Turning a corner before the bridge, she reached Portcullis House, the modern glass and steel structure that housed parliamentary offices, its modernist architecture a deliberate contrast to the Gothic grandeur across the street. The security guard at the entrance nodded in recognition – Anjli had been here often enough during various investigations to be a familiar face, but they still had to do the dance, no matter what.

'DI Kapoor, City of London Police,' she said, flashing her warrant card, the guard's expression bland as they continued the ritual. 'Here to see the Defence Secretary.'

'Do you have an appointment?'

'No, but she's been hassling me for weeks to come by, so I decided to do just that.'

The guard walked off, made a phone call, nodded, and then returned.

'Sign in, please,' he said, pushing a tablet towards her. 'Her office is in the main building, fourth floor, west corridor.'

'I know where it is,' Anjli replied, scrawling her signature on the digital screen and handing over her shoulder bag, watching as it passed through the X-ray. Parliament security had tightened considerably since the Westminster Bridge attack, and nobody got a free pass any more, not even police.

'All clear,' the guard nodded, returning her bag.

She navigated the maze of corridors that connected Portcullis House to the main Parliament buildings, passing harried-looking researchers and parliamentary assistants clutching folders and tablets – although it was now well into the evening, the people here slept less than Anjli and her team, it seemed. The underground walkway tunnelled beneath Bridge Street, its fluorescent lighting and modern design a stark contrast to the historic buildings it connected. Even here, beneath the road, she could hear the muffled rumble of traffic and the distant patter of rain from the drains above.

As she crossed into the Palace of Westminster proper, the atmosphere changed – modern practicality giving way to

Gothic splendour and ancient tradition. The air felt different here, heavy with the weight of history and the peculiar mix of polish and dust that permeated buildings where decisions had been made for centuries. She'd never tired of the building and had lectured Declan many times over the years about the Palace's history.

Anjli was even sure he remembered some of it.

She rounded the corner to find Tamara Banks's office – all glass and chrome furnishings jarring against the historic surroundings. Craig Ellison, who'd cornered her at dinner weeks ago and had sent the most recent text message, glanced up from his desk. This surprised her – she hadn't expected him to be a PA, more a special advisor, a temporary civil servant, distinct from the permanent, politically impartial civil service.

It seemed, however, that Banks kept her advisors very close.

'DI Kapoor? The Defence Secretary is just finishing a call—'

'Not bothered,' Anjli cut him off, already pushing towards the inner office door.

'I really must insist—'

'And I really don't give a toss,' Anjli shouldered past him. 'And if you send me a text like that again, I'll break your legs off and feed them to you.'

Tamara Banks sat behind an imposing and likely very expensive desk, phone at her ear. In her mid-to-late forties, the Defence Secretary blended ruthless ambition with meticulous image cultivation – her steel-grey power suit and geometric bob projecting authority in exactly the way her focus groups had recommended. With her Prada outfit and calculated poise, she was Thatcher, but with sharper teeth.

Many in Westminster whispered she was the bastard daughter of Cruella De Vil and Heinrich Himmler – a comparison Tamara Banks would likely consider a compliment rather than an insult.

'I'll call you back,' Tamara said, eyes narrowing as she set down the phone. 'Detective Inspector Kapoor. How unexpected.'

'Is it? After three weeks of your office hounding me?'

Tamara's smile never reached her eyes.

'Hounding? Just persistent encouragement. I do hope Craig hasn't overstepped his bounds. Please, sit.'

'I'll stand,' Anjli positioned herself by the door. 'I'm here to make one thing crystal clear. I am not, nor will I ever be, "your version of Declan Walsh". I don't belong to politicians.'

'Ah. Rumours and misunderstandings. Context gets so easily lost.'

'There's no context where claiming to "own" a police officer works,' Anjli snapped. 'Or suggesting I'd provide whatever "services" you imagine Walsh performed for Baker.'

'Your directness is refreshing, Detective Inspector. And precisely why I've been eager to speak with you.' Tamara leant back in her chair. 'What I actually said was that you represent the same potential for solving delicate matters with discretion and competence that Walsh demonstrated for Charles. Hardly claiming ownership.'

'Not what I heard. Either way, I'm not interested in being anyone's tame detective.'

'Such melodrama,' Tamara laughed softly. 'I'm offering a mutually beneficial professional relationship. Nothing more, nothing less.'

'And I'm declining. Nothing more, nothing less.'

'Let's be frank, Detective Inspector,' Tamara leant

forward, dropping the political veneer. 'You're ambitious. Smart. Career-focused. I respect that. But in today's policing landscape, advancement requires more than just solving cases—'

'It requires political patronage,' Anjli finished. 'Thanks, but I'll take my chances with merit.'

'Merit?' Banks's laugh was genuine this time. 'How charmingly naïve. Ask DCI Walsh how far merit got him before Charles Baker took an interest. He and his boss – your boss too – were almost out of the door before Baker started pardoning people. You think he gained his DCI status by merit? That Monroe wasn't fired by merit? Of course not. The system rewards those who understand its true nature.'

'And what nature is that?'

'Symbiotic. We help each other. Simple as that,' Banks rearranged some papers on her desk. 'I have certain matters that occasionally require a detective with... flexibility. Discretion. Someone who sees the bigger picture.'

'And one my colour helps, yeah?' Anjli snapped. 'I know your history, Miss Banks. I know about your National Front membership, the hen night at the Eagles Nest, the dressing as Eva Braun at parties, the copy of *Mein Kampf*. You might look like Thatcher, but I see a lot of Enoch Powell and Oswald Moseley in front of me.'

If Tamara Banks was surprised at this, she didn't show it, as she leaned back in the chair and considered this.

'I sued the *Daily Mail* when they printed those lies,' she said. 'Nobody could substantiate these rumours. It was nothing more than a smear campaign.'

'Your Nationial Front membership isn't a rumour.'

'No, but it was the product of an abusive relationship while I was a student, with a racist boyfriend who both groomed and gaslit me into his way of thinking,' Tamara replied coldly. 'Both he, and the opinion, are long gone.'

Anjli acknowledged the comment with a nod.

'Either way, I'm not interested.'

'You haven't even heard what I'm asking.'

'I don't need to.' Anjli moved to leave. 'My answer is no.'

The door opened behind Anjli, and she turned to find Declan standing there, his face giving nothing away. He looked flushed, and Anjli realised he'd probably run all the way from Temple Inn to get here.

'DI Kapoor,' he said, tone professionally bland. 'I've been looking for you.'

'DCI Walsh,' Tamara smiled broadly now, genuine pleasure clear in her voice. The newly appointed Defence Secretary seemed almost relieved by the interruption. 'What an unexpected pleasure. Please, join us.'

'I'm afraid we need to go, Defence Secretary,' Declan replied calmly and cooly. 'Active murder investigation.'

'Of course, of course,' Banks waved a hand dismissively. 'Though you should know, Walsh, your colleague here seems to have some rather dramatic misunderstandings about—'

'About exactly how the police maintain independence from political influence?' Declan suggested mildly. 'I'm sure it's all a misunderstanding. Ready, Anjli?'

Anjli nodded, though her eyes never left Tamara.

'I don't think Charles Baker believes that,' the Defence Secretary added softly.

'Frankly, Miss Banks, I don't give a toss about what Baker believes, and if we're being honest here, I don't think you do either,' Declan looked to his side. 'We done here?'

'Yeah, we're done here,' Anjli said, her eyes fixed on

Tamara. 'Thank you for your time, Defence Secretary. Don't fall down any stairs, Craig.'

'We'll continue this conversation another time, Detective Inspector,' Tamara replied cordially, the warmth in her voice at odds with the steel in her gaze.

'I doubt that,' Anjli replied as she turned to leave. 'But live in hope, yeah?'

OUTSIDE IN THE CORRIDOR, DECLAN WAITED UNTIL THEY WERE safely out of earshot before speaking.

'Want to explain why you're picking a fight with possibly the next Prime Minister?'

'I was just clarifying boundaries,' Anjli replied. 'We both know she's been pushing for a meeting for weeks.'

'And you thought storming her office was the diplomatic approach?'

'Diplomacy's overrated.'

'Anjli,' Declan stopped. 'What exactly did she say that's got you ready to torch your career?'

'You told me what Shaun Donnal said – that Banks has been telling people I'm "her version of you" – that she "owns" me the way Charles Baker supposedly owned you,' Anjli snapped, showing Declan the message she'd received from Craig. 'And then I got this tonight. I'm not letting this arrogance and belief I'd simply roll over stand.'

'And your solution was to confront her directly? Without backup?'

'I don't need—'

'Yes, you bloody well do,' Declan cut her off. 'Come on, Anjli, you know better. You can't let your anger take control here! These people play the long game. They don't forget slights, and they have very long memories.'

'So, what, I should just ignore it? Let her think she can manipulate me?'

'No. You gather evidence, build allies, and strike when you have leverage,' Declan sighed. 'Politics is a chess game, not a boxing match.'

'Maybe I prefer boxing,' Anjli muttered.

'Well, in this case, the referee would have already disqualified you,' Declan replied.

'You do it.'

'Yes and I'm one step from being fired constantly, while you're the one with the promising future,' Declan retaliated. 'You need to think of your future.'

They were about to head towards the exit when a voice called from down the corridor.

'Walsh!'

They turned to see Norman Shipman striding towards them; hawkish features fixed in a politician's smile. Despite being well into his seventies, the skeleton-thin backbencher moved with surprising energy.

'Mister Shipman,' Declan nodded, maintaining a neutral expression. 'It's been a while.'

'Indeed,' Shipman replied, extending a hand that Declan took after a brief hesitation. 'Hopefully I'm not the subject of today's visit?'

'No, sir.'

Shipman turned to Anjli, offering his hand again.

'Detective Inspector Kapoor. Still keeping our friend Walsh here out of trouble, I see.'

'Trying to,' Anjli replied, her tone carefully neutral as she shook the MP's hand.

'Perhaps you two might join me for a moment?' Shipman gestured down the corridor. 'I believe we share a mutual interest in Emily Clarke.'

Declan and Anjli exchanged a glance.

'How did you—'

'My office,' Shipman cut him off, already walking away with the absolute certainty they would follow.

14

CROSSING THE RUBICON

Unlike Banks's ministerial suite, Shipman's backbencher office was cramped and functional: standard-issue furniture that hadn't been updated in decades, filing cabinets with faded labels, walls covered with constituency photos. The desk was buried under paperwork, a small window offering a dismal view of an interior courtyard.

'Scotch?' he offered, moving to a battered side table.

'We're on duty,' Declan replied. 'You mentioned Emmy Clarke?'

Shipman settled behind his desk, the chair creaking.

'I understand you've been speaking with her. And that she's been sharing stories about the Garden Collective.'

'How do you know this?' Declan asked.

'Information is currency in Westminster,' Shipman steepled his fingers. 'Especially when it involves cases that were carefully managed thirty years ago.'

'Like the true story of the Shadwell Bell Foundry collapse?' Declan asked.

'Among others,' Shipman nodded.

'Could you give us more on it?' Anjli opened her notebook.

Shipman saw this and sighed.

'Off the record, or at least not from me, right? The case had too many connections to powerful people,' he continued. 'Property developers, councillors, MPs with investment interests. There was a Lord, Harold Hargreaves who was particularly, well, *cooperative* during the investigation.'

'Cooperative how?' Declan asked.

'His investment trust had significant interests in the redevelopment area. When the Bell Foundry collapsed, Harold's consortium gained the site at a remarkably low price. Had planning permissions, architectural drawings, contractor agreements – all ready within weeks of the incident. Almost as if they'd been expecting the building to become available.'

Anjli looked up from her notes.

'Are you suggesting Harold Hargreaves knew the building would collapse?'

'I'm suggesting Harold Hargreaves was a pragmatic businessman who recognised opportunities when they arose,' Shipman replied carefully. 'Unfortunately for Harold, what appeared to be an opportunity became a very expensive mistake.'

'How so?'

Shipman's smile was thin.

'There was an underground tributary running under Shadwell and the foundry, which had already weakened the foundations, and which meant when the terrible accident happened, the entire floor caved in. After this, listed building status was retroactively applied, heritage groups intervened, legal challenges mounted. Harold's consortium found themselves owning a site they couldn't develop and couldn't sell. Sometimes advance preparation can backfire spectacularly.'

'And even you couldn't help,' Declan commented.

'All I could do was assist with keeping the collateral damage low,' Shipman replied irritably. 'Three dead, over a dozen injured – one critical – and both an activist group and developer who pointed fingers publicly at each other? It was a PR nightmare, especially with Hargreaves being a Tory donor. Your father understood the necessity. Emmy Clarke, however, became... problematic.'

'Problematic how?'

'Believe it or not, she turned up during our selection process for the *Magpies* back in the day,' Shipman said, tone shifting. 'Her child was too young to be considered, but Emmy herself had an interesting background. Petty theft, minor fraud, radical activism – enough to make her unemployable in conventional circles.'

'So, you exploited her criminal record to force her cooperation,' Declan concluded.

'I prefer to think of it as offering an opportunity for rehabilitation. We promised to expunge her record if she helped us infiltrate certain groups. The Garden Collective had caught our attention due to their increasing radicalism, and high-level connections.'

'Blackmail by any other name,' Anjli muttered.

'Politics, Detective Inspector,' Shipman corrected. 'Emmy was naturally gifted at infiltration. But she was also in the early stages of what we'd now recognise as bipolar disorder.'

'Undiagnosed, I assume?' Declan asked.

'Back then, such conditions were often overlooked,' Shipman replied. 'Her manic phases made her extraordinarily persuasive, perfect for the role. But they also made her volatile. She went deeper into the Collective than we'd anticipated, became genuinely invested in their cause. Then the Bell Foundry incident happened.'

'Was that you?'

'Christ, no. By then Willis, the Assistant Commissioner, was involved. No, that was the higher ups in the Collective, deciding martyrs worked better than protests. They thought a massive disaster would gain sympathy. All it did was make people run from them.'

'And her daughter?' Anjli asked. 'I'm guessing removing the child wasn't for protection?'

'Emmy had become increasingly erratic. There were... incidents. The decision was made to remove the daughter while Emmy stabilised.'

'Stabilised? You mean treatment?' Declan's voice had a dangerous edge.

'Psychiatric evaluation, mostly outpatient. After her initial recovery, Emmy continued working as an informant for your father. She was too valuable to sideline completely.'

'But you still took her daughter away,' Anjli pressed.

'A temporary arrangement that became permanent,' Shipman acknowledged. 'Emmy's condition made her unpredictable, dangerous even, around the child.'

'And the daughter? Where did she end up?'

'With a carefully selected family in Oxford. I wasn't involved in this, plausible deniability and all that, but the people who do such things gave her the identity of a child who had died a few years earlier – standard practice back then for creating clean documentation.'

'You stole a dead child's identity for her,' Anjli said, disgust visible.

'They created a new life for her,' Shipman corrected. 'The

goal was eventual reunification once Emmy stabilised. Unfortunately, that never happened.'

'And my father's role in all this?' Declan asked.

'I never dealt with him personally, but I heard things. Then-DS Walsh was a practical man. He understood that certain compromises were necessary. He helped manage Emmy, kept her focused on specific targets rather than the broader operation.'

'He used her,' Declan said flatly.

'They used each other,' Shipman corrected. 'Patrick got his arrests and his promotion to DI and then DCI, Emmy got her revenge against specific Collective members.'

'Why revenge?'

'Emmy tried to stop the collapse,' Shipman explained placidly. 'But they stopped her first. It could have been worse – if they hadn't had any warning, they would likely all have died. That said and done, they didn't, but Emmy blamed herself for not doing more.'

'Hence revenge.'

'Exactly, and we kept out of this, because it meant certain sensitive matters remained contained.'

'Except Emmy's daughter,' Anjli pointed out.

'Why are you telling us this now?' Declan asked. 'You would have been informed the moment we arrived, so you finding us wasn't a coincidence.'

'Because Emmy has become active again. Sharing stories, making connections, becoming a bloody pain,' Shipman leant forward. 'And because three people loosely connected to the Garden Collective case are now dead.'

'You're worried about bad publicity?' Anjli asked incredulously.

Shipman didn't reply.

'We actually believe one of the victims was Emmy's daughter,' Declan said, watching Shipman's reaction. 'Rachel Peterson. The timing fits.'

'Rachel Peterson? No, impossible,' Shipman's expression flickered with genuine surprise.

'You seem certain for someone who claimed not to know the daughter's identity.'

'I don't know who she became,' Shipman clarified. 'But I do know it wasn't Rachel Peterson. When I saw the bodies piling this morning, I looked into your department's files—'

'How?'

Shipman smiled.

'Let's just say I did it off the books.'

'The bloody Star Chamber.'

'Perhaps. Either way, Rachel Peterson was adopted. Emmy's daughter was given a fake identity. The two are completely different.'

'Convenient,' Declan remarked.

'Prudent,' Shipman corrected. 'Though I can check the records if it would assist your investigation.'

'Do you know the daughter's original name?'

'Jane,' Shipman smiled. 'I remember it because of the *Magpies* connection – what with Jane being a member.'

Declan bit back the comment that there were *two* Janes – Shipman would know this; he'd simply decided to keep to the false narrative that had risen up.

'We need to go,' he said, rising. 'Other aspects of the case need attention. If you think of anything else ...'

'Of course,' Shipman nodded. 'Though I'd appreciate updates on your progress.'

'We'll be in touch,' Declan replied non-committally.

In the corridor, Anjli waited until they were well clear before speaking.

'Do you believe him? About Emmy being an intelligence asset?'

'Parts of it,' Declan replied. 'But remember the last time we dealt with him? He flip-flopped from Labour to Conservative, kept secrets for decades and still kept his seat when it all came out. Shipman's always selective with the truth. The question is why is he telling us now.'

'He's afraid,' Anjli concluded. 'The daughter might have discovered the truth.'

'And Bruno Field is probably already monitoring the situation,' Anjli added. 'Or, rather Sebastian Klinger, now he's gone back to the name.'

'Almost certainly,' Declan confirmed. 'He's probably been watching since the first body dropped. Welcome to another round of patrician politics.'

Nathan Hargreaves drummed his fingers on the scarred wooden table at the Bell Tavern, his half-empty pint glass leaving wet rings on the surface. He checked his watch again.

Daryl was late.

The medication blister pack in his jacket pocket felt heavy, but not by weight. He hadn't taken today's dose; he needed to stay sharp, feel the edges of things, and recently the medication had made him fuzzy.

The door swung open and Daryl Collins stepped in,

shaking raindrops from his coat. He spotted Nathan and approached cautiously.

'Didn't expect to hear from you,' he said, dropping into the opposite seat. 'Not after everything.'

'You got my message,' Nathan said, voice tightly controlled. 'About Gary.'

'Yeah, but what d'you expect me to do? The game's over, Nathan. Sean's dead, Rachel's dead. Dirk's vanished, although Alex reckons they found a body as he was let go. Time for *us* to let it go, mate.'

'Let it go?' Nathan's voice dropped dangerously. 'Gary is restarting the game. After everything. After Daniel.'

'Look, I know you and Daniel were close—'

'You don't know *anything*,' Nathan hissed. 'None of you knew. Gary and Alex destroyed him with that forfeit, and now they're doing it again.'

'What are you on about?' Daryl frowned, accepting his pint from the server. 'There's no new game. Nobody's contacted me.'

'I got a message today,' Nathan snapped, pulling out his phone and showing it.

> The game continues. New targets assigned.
> Check your inbox.

'And you believed it?' Daryl shook his head. 'After Sean and Rachel? Someone's winding you up.'

'Or someone's cleaning house,' Nathan leant forward. 'Dirk knew too much about the Garden Collective. He'd been digging into *his* father's testimony against my own father, talking to that old woman at the shelter. Then Sean started poking around too, following Dirk's leads. You know how they wound each other up.'

'What old woman?'

'The one who worked for the police.' Nathan's eyes burned with intensity. 'The one who knows what really happened back then. Dirk found her weeks ago. It's the same trail Daniel was following before he died two years back. History repeating itself.'

Daryl studied him over his glass.

'You're not taking your meds, are you?'

'Don't patronise me.' Nathan's jaw tightened.

'I'm not. But you're not making sense. Garden Collective? Old women in shelters?'

'It's all connected,' Nathan insisted. 'Sean, Rachel, Dirk. The cards. The water. It's about what happened thirty years ago. What our parents did.'

'My parents didn't—'

'Thomas Collins!' Nathan snapped. 'Helped launder money from the property deals, cleaning up the dirty, tainted costs! He was as much to blame for what happened as my father was!'

Daryl stared long and hard at Nathan, taking a deep breath before letting it go.

'The game is dead, Nathan. Walk away.'

'Doesn't work like that,' Nathan's hand trembled. 'The game doesn't end until someone wins. Those are the rules.'

'Rules?' Daryl laughed harshly. 'People are dying. This isn't about rules any more.'

'It's always been about rules,' Nathan's eyes narrowed. 'And consequences for breaking them.'

'What the hell does that mean?'

Nathan drained his glass and set it down.

'Have you spoken to Victoria?'

'Victoria?' Daryl frowned. 'Why would I? She left a couple of years back.'

'She's been helping the police. Getting close. Learning what they know.'

'How would you know that?'

'I have sources,' Nathan said cryptically. 'She's playing a different game. Always has been.'

'You need help, mate. This paranoia – it's not healthy.'

'Paranoia?' Nathan barked a hollow laugh. 'Three friends dead or missing, and I'm paranoid?'

'You're not thinking clearly,' Daryl said as he reached across the table. 'Let me call someone—'

'Don't *touch* me,' Nathan jerked away. 'You're all the same. None of you believed Daniel either, until it was too late. Daniel knew what was happening. Found the connections, the old records. That's why they targeted him. He knew too much.'

'Who's "they"?' Daryl asked carefully.

'Gary. Alex,' Nathan's eyes darted around the pub. 'Victoria. Maybe others. The children of the Garden Collective. They're all connected – their parents were all part of it. Even Oliver.'

'Oliver? He's like twelve! And what about *your* father?' Daryl asked. 'Harold Hargreaves invested in half those development projects the Collective fought. He was on the other side.'

Nathan's face darkened.

'Like your father.'

'My father wasn't protected like yours,' Daryl said coldly. 'He did his time in court, almost lost his livelihood. Your father was strangely absent that day.'

'My father was protected, but for different reasons from the others,' Nathan struggled to explain, feeling the lack of medication start to catch hold now. 'Dirk and Daniel's parents testified against the Collective, but my father funded the developments. All of them together, with your father too, no matter how much you want to spin it, buried the truth about the Foundry.'

'I'm leaving,' Daryl pushed his pint aside. 'Seek help.'

'No!' Nathan grabbed Daryl's wrist. 'You can't go. You need to understand. They're coming for us next. All of us who knew Daniel. All who might work it out.'

'That's enough.' Daryl pulled away from the grasp, but as he did so Nathan lunged across the table at him.

'Listen to me!'

'Get off me!' Daryl shoved him back.

'You're one of them, aren't you? You've been compromised!' Nathan's face contorted.

'Listen to yourself,' Daryl shook his head. 'You sound mental.'

'I'm trying to save your life, you ungrateful prick!'

Daryl, now backed against the wall pulled out a switchblade, the blade snapping open with a click.

'Stay back,' he warned. 'I don't want to use this.'

Nathan froze.

'Where'd you get that?'

'Been carrying protection since Sean died,' Daryl said. 'Back off.'

But the Rubicon had been crossed. Nathan grabbed the barstool he'd been sitting on and swung it. Daryl ducked, the stool glancing his shoulder, and he stumbled backwards, knife extended.

'He's got a knife!' someone shouted, and chaos erupted.

Nathan charged again. Daryl slashed reflexively, the blade catching Nathan's forearm, drawing blood.

'Police!' a voice bellowed from the doorway. Two uniformed officers, likely passing and called in by people rushing out pushed through, X-75 tasers ready. 'Drop the weapon!'

Daryl immediately dropped the knife, hands rising.

'He attacked me. Self-defence.'

Nathan stood frozen, blood trickling down his arm.

'He's part of it,' he said quietly. 'They all are.'

The officers moved swiftly, one securing the knife while the other checked Nathan's wound. Within minutes, both men were cuffed, being led to separate patrol cars, and pulling away, blue lights cutting through the darkness.

Neither Nathan nor Daryl noticed the shadowed and hooded figure watching from across the street, who turned and walked away, phone already at ear.

'It's done,' they said simply. 'By the time anyone connects the dots, everything will be in place.'

15

MORNING REVELATION

'Thanks for the nod on this,' Declan said, accepting two visitor passes from the desk sergeant at Bishopsgate.

DS Finlay, a balding man with the look of someone who'd been wrestling paperwork all night rather than actual criminals, offered a weary smile.

'Figured it connected to your playing-card murders. Wasn't about to turn down Last Chance Saloon taking this one off our plate. Got enough bloody domestics to keep us going till Christmas.'

'Public knife fight seems below our threshold,' Anjli commented, clipping her pass to her jacket.

'Knife fight involving two members of the same social circle where two others have turned up dead with cards pinned to their chests?' Finlay snorted. 'Not a coincidence in my book. Both of them had to go to hospital to be stitched up before coming back, and the bearded one wouldn't shut up about conspiracies. Proper nutter.'

'Did he specify what sort of conspiracies?' Declan asked, exchanging a glance with Anjli.

'Something about people being picked off one by one. Usual paranoid bollocks. Doctor had to sedate him in the end – he's more coherent now, but I still wouldn't leave any sharp objects lying about.'

'We'll split them up,' Declan decided. 'Anjli, you take Collins. I'll handle Hargreaves.'

A uniformed constable led Declan to Interview Room One, where Nathan Hargreaves sat nursing a paper cup of what the station laughably called tea. The transformation was remarkable. Gone was the wild-eyed man Finley had described, and the reports from the pub altercation had detailed. Instead, Nathan looked alert but controlled, the slight tremor in his hands the only evidence of whatever storm raged beneath.

'DCI Walsh,' he acknowledged as Declan entered. 'I expected you'd be called in.'

Declan took the seat opposite. 'How's the arm?'

'Six stitches.' Nathan gestured vaguely towards his bandaged forearm. 'Self-defence, technically. Though I might have provoked it.'

'How are you feeling this morning?'

'Clearer. The medication helps.' Nathan tapped his temple. 'Quiets things down up here.'

'PC Cooper mentioned your prescription. Lamotrigine?'

'And Risperidone,' Nathan nodded. 'Usually keeps me stable when I take it properly.'

'Which you hadn't been doing.'

'I thought I needed clarity, needed to see connections

others were missing.' Nathan sighed. 'Ironic how that worked out.'

Declan considered this.

'Who else knows of your condition?'

'Oh, pretty much everyone knows, it's hard to hide over decades, but only a few really know. I find the ones who take the piss are worse than the ones who look at me different when they hear I'm incredibly bipolar. Of late, Oliver's been supportive about my condition. He's one of the few people who doesn't treat me differently because of the medication.'

'How does he know about your medication?'

'Victoria told him. Said it would help him understand if I had any episodes during the game, but also because he works for the same company, he could be someone I could contact if I had an episode. Oliver was very understanding about it, actually – said his own family had experience with mental health issues.'

'What kind of experience?'

'He mentioned his mother died young, said it affected his father's mental state for years. Made him sympathetic to people struggling with... similar issues.'

Sensing Nathan was starting to close up now, Declan changed the subject.

'Tell me about last night.'

'I overreacted. Daryl and I have known each other for twenty years. I needed him to understand what was happening, but ...' he trailed off, shaking his head. 'Off the meds, I see threats everywhere.'

'And now? With the medication?'

'I can separate fact from fear.' Nathan straightened in his chair. 'Sean and Rachel are dead. Dirk's missing. Someone's targeting our group.'

'Let's talk about the message you showed Daryl,' Declan said. 'The one supposedly from Gary.'

'I received it yesterday,' Nathan confirmed. 'Said the game was continuing, new targets assigned.'

'You believed it was genuine?'

'Initially, yes. It came from an anonymous webpage, but that's how Gary always communicated – adds to the game's mystique. But later I started thinking about the tone, the phrasing ...'

'Yet you used it to get Daryl to meet you.'

'I needed to warn him. Everyone who knew what Dirk was investigating has become a target.'

'And what exactly was Dirk investigating?'

Nathan hesitated, clearly weighing his words.

'Why ask?' He stared at the table. 'You probably know it all by now.'

'Indulge me.'

'The Garden Collective. His father testified against members during the trials after the Bell Foundry collapse.'

'We're familiar with the Collective,' Declan said. 'How does it connect to your current situation?'

'My father invested in projects the Collective opposed,' Nathan replied. 'Several others in our group had peripheral connections through their parents.'

'Including Daniel Foster?'

A flicker of pain crossed Nathan's face.

'Daniel was investigating the same thing before his death. He learned somehow his dad had been the solicitor who covered up the deaths.'

'His father worked with your father?'

'No, he worked for the Government,' Nathan shook his

head. 'But I think they were working with my dad so who knows.'

'Your relationship with Daniel – that was more than friendship, wasn't it?'

Nathan met his gaze directly.

'We were involved. Kept it quiet. His chambers were traditional, and my bank ...' He shrugged. 'Neither place appreciates diversity, shall we say.'

'I'm sorry,' Declan said. 'That must have been difficult.'

'Worst day of my life,' Nathan mumbled. 'After Daniel died, Dirk picked up his research – started asking the same questions. Now Dirk's gone too. He's dead, isn't he?'

'Yes,' Declan replied. 'I'm sorry. Do you have any of Daniel's research? Anything concrete that connects these deaths to the Garden Collective?'

Nathan hesitated.

'I kept some of his notes. They're in a safe at my apartment. Most of it is fragmented: newspaper clippings, court transcripts, lists of names. Daniel was convinced someone was systematically eliminating people connected to the old case, or at least warning them off.'

'People like who?'

'Children of witnesses, investigators, even peripheral figures. There was a solicitor who'd worked on the prosecutions – his son died in a hit-and-run three years ago. A journalist who'd covered the Bell Foundry collapse – her daughter almost drowned on a solo sailing trip, no explanation. All ruled accidents or misadventure.'

'That could be coincidence,' Declan pointed out.

'Twelve deaths – or almost deaths, enough to scare someone off – in three decades, all connected to the same case?' Nathan shook his head. 'Daniel didn't believe in coincidences of that magnitude. Neither do I.'

'On that subject, let's talk about coincidences,' Declan paced as he spoke. 'Your father, Lord Hargreaves, bought the foundry before the collapse. He was also the person who the Garden Collective seemed to target. You've just mentioned that Daniel was the son of a solicitor working with him through the Government. Dirk's father? A whistleblower.'

'And the rest.' Nathan's composure cracked slightly. 'Daniel's father worked for Gary Webb's father. They helped cover up and silence people after the event. Daryl's dad laundered the money.'

'That's five out of twelve,' Declan paused. 'And you don't think this is a coincidence?'

'Of course I don't,' Nathan sighed. 'But how the hell do I explain it? The only thing we had in common was that we were at Oxford! We didn't seek each other out!'

'Nobody forced you together?'

'No!' Nathan was getting agitated now. 'Look, people always assume the worst about developers. My father helped rebuild the area after the tragedy, provided jobs, housing. He stepped in when others wouldn't.'

'Very quickly, from what we understand.'

'That's good business – being prepared to help communities when they need it most,' Nathan said defensively. 'Someone had to take responsibility for the area, especially after the water underneath started leaking through.'

He was fidgeting now, so Declan took it back a notch.

'You mentioned being in crisis management lockdown at your bank all day Tuesday. Is that correct?'

'Yes. Trading floor, from two until after eleven. Multiple witnesses, security logs.'

'We're verifying that,' Declan said. 'What about Victoria Lang? What's her role in all this?'

Nathan's expression sharpened.

'What has she told you?'

'She's been assisting with our investigation. Providing insights into the killer's psychology.'

'Of course she bloody has,' Nathan murmured. 'She would position herself that way.'

'Meaning?'

'Victoria's always been several steps ahead of everyone else. It's what made her such a formidable player. Her leaving the game never sat right with some of us.'

'Beyond the ethical concerns about the forfeit system?'

'That was her official reason, but she helped create it. She didn't just know psychology – she weaponised it.'

'She said Gary and Alex bastardised her suggestions.'

'Did she mention how she created the game in the first place?' Nathan looked up now. 'Her, Gary, Alex – they were the architects.'

Declan made a note, keeping his expression neutral despite the surge of interest.

'The playing cards – they're important to whoever's doing this. The cards left on Sean and Rachel weren't standard issue, were they?'

'Special deck. Black background, silver and gold ink. We commissioned them for the tenth anniversary of the game. Only twelve sets were made – one for each player.'

'So, the killer would need access to that specific deck.'

'Yes, but we all have them. Hard to narrow it down that way, unless you check each deck for missing cards.'

'What about the metal spikes used to pin the cards?'

'Not part of the game,' Nathan said, frowning.

Declan leant back in his chair.

'Dirk,' he said, changing tack. 'Did he ever mention owning a gun?'

'No, but his father had one,' Nathan replied. 'Military-issue Glock, I think. He showed it to me once, years ago, while mansplaining how water pistols were inaccurate compared to real firearms.'

Declan nodded.

'And a silencer?'

'Wouldn't know what it looked like even if you showed one to me,' Nathan shrugged. 'Only ever seen them in movies.'

'We'll be investigating your alibi, Mister Hargreaves. In the meantime, you'll be released pending further inquiries.'

'You don't believe me,' Nathan said flatly.

'I believe something happened to Sean, Rachel, and Dirk,' Declan replied. 'Beyond that, I'm reserving judgment until the evidence speaks for itself.'

As Declan gathered his notes, Nathan leant forward.

'Be careful with Victoria. Whatever she's telling you about the case – about me – it's calculated.'

'For what purpose?'

'That's what Dirk was trying to figure out when he disappeared.'

IN INTERVIEW ROOM THREE, ANJLI WAS MAKING HER OWN progress with Daryl Collins.

'It was self-defence,' Daryl insisted, touching the bandage on his shoulder. 'He came at me with a barstool. What would you have done?'

'Not brought a flick knife to a pub,' Anjli suggested dryly.

'After what happened to Sean and Rachel?' Daryl shook his head. 'We're all on edge. Nathan more than most.'

'Tell me about his behaviour recently.'

Daryl sighed.

'He hasn't been himself since Daniel died. They were together – not officially, but anyone with eyes could see it. When Daniel died, Nathan fell apart. Started missing his medication, seeing conspiracies everywhere. Weirdly, it made him better at work; I suppose the jumpy nervousness works on the trading floor or something.'

'And last night?'

'He showed me some text he claimed was from Gary – about the game continuing despite everything.' Daryl shook his head. 'When he texted to meet I thought he was having another episode, so I agreed, thinking I could talk sense into him.'

'That worked well,' Anjli observed.

'He was worse than I expected. Kept going on about the Garden Collective, about how we were all being hunted. When I tried to leave, he grabbed me. I pulled the knife, he grabbed a stool, and... well, you know the rest.'

'What specifically did he say about the Garden Collective?'

'Something about Dirk investigating connections between our families and this activist group. Said Dirk disappeared because he was getting too close to the truth.'

'And what truth would that be?'

'That someone's targeting the children of those involved in some old case.' Daryl shrugged. 'It's nonsense. My parents were accountants in Bristol – no connection to any activists.'

Anjli watched his face as he spoke.

He's lying.

'Tell me about Dirk VanMeerten,' Anjli said. 'When did you last see him?'

Daryl frowned, thinking.

'Three, maybe four weeks ago? He'd become... intense. We had drinks near Liverpool Street, and he spent the whole time showing me newspaper clippings about this protest group.'

'Did he mention why he was so interested?'

'He'd found his father's testimony from the Bell Foundry trials. Apparently, his dad had lied under oath to protect some bigwig involved in the development project.' Daryl shook his head. 'Dirk was obsessed with uncovering the "real story" as he called it.'

'What about Daniel Foster? Was he interested in the same thing?'

'Maybe. Daniel was... complicated. Brilliant mind, but private. If he was investigating the Collective, he kept it to himself,' Daryl said before he hesitated. 'Though there was that strange conversation at Nathan's Christmas party.'

'What conversation?'

'Before he died. Daniel had been drinking which was unusual for him. He cornered me by the bar, asked if I'd ever wondered why our group had stayed together for so long. Said something about how "games have architects" and we were all playing roles we didn't understand.'

'Did he mention Victoria Lang?'

Daryl rubbed his beard.

'Not directly. But when she left the game the year before he died, Daniel was the only one who didn't seem surprised. Almost like he'd been expecting it.'

'Did Nathan mention her last night?'

'He said something about her "playing a longer game" than any of us realised. I assumed it was the paranoia talking.'

Anjli paused as her phone buzzed – a message from Declan.

'Where were you on Tuesday afternoon?' Anjli asked, having read it.

'Meeting with Henderson Capital from three until nearly seven, then drinks with the team afterwards. Why?'

'Just establishing timelines,' Anjli replied, waving the phone. 'Nathan claims he was in crisis management lockdown at his bank all day Tuesday. Does that sound right?'

Daryl frowned.

'I wouldn't know directly, but ...'

'But?'

'I ran into Brad Walters yesterday – he works with Nathan and Oliver. Said something odd about Nathan asking him to "cover" for him if anyone asked about Tuesday afternoon. Brad thought it was about some woman Nathan was seeing, but Nathan doesn't play for *that* team.'

'When was this conversation?'

'Yesterday morning, at *Pret*. Didn't think anything of it at the time,' Daryl's expression grew troubled. 'You don't think Nathan had something to do with Sean's death, do you?'

'We're exploring all possibilities,' Anjli replied. 'Has Nathan always been on medication?'

'Since university, I think. Though it was never a big deal until Daniel died. He managed it well – most of the group didn't even know. Well, if they did, they never said anything.'

'Who, in your opinion, did know?'

'Daniel, obviously. Me. Victoria, because she helped him

find the right psychiatrist after an unpleasant episode in our final year. That's how they became close initially.'

'Victoria helped with his treatment?' Anjli made a note.

'She wasn't a proper doctor then, just a trainee psychiatrist or something. But she recognised the symptoms, got him proper help.' Daryl shifted in his chair. 'Look, Nathan's unwell, but he's not violent. At least, he wasn't before last night.'

Anjli nodded, finishing her notes.

'You'll be released pending further inquiries, Mister Collins. I'd suggest staying away from Nathan Hargreaves for the time being.'

'Don't worry,' Daryl said grimly. 'That friendship's dead and buried.'

DECLAN WAS WAITING IN THE CORRIDOR WHEN ANJLI EMERGED.

'Learn anything?' he asked quietly.

'Nathan asked a colleague to cover for his absence during his supposed lockdown on Tuesday,' she replied. 'And apparently Victoria Lang helped Nathan with his bipolar diagnosis back at university – that's how they became close. You?'

'Nathan claims Daniel found a list of deaths and people warned off that were connected; all people related to the Garden Collective case.'

'That's quite a pattern,' Anjli frowned. 'Did he have any proof?'

'Says he has Daniel's research inside a safe in his apartment. Worth checking out—' Declan paused as his phone buzzed.

'Go ahead, Billy,' he said, putting the call on speaker.

'You're going to want to hear this,' Billy's voice came through, excited. 'I've been looking into Victoria Lang's background. University records, professional certifications, the works. There are inconsistencies everywhere – gaps, mismatched dates, records that don't quite line up.'

'Anything specific?' Declan asked.

'Her birth certificate, for starters. Or rather, birth certificates, plural. There's one in the official system, all standard. But I found a second one – same name, different date – in a sealed archive from 1984. That one's for a Victoria Marianne Lang who died at eight months.'

'Someone's using a dead child's identity,' Anjli murmured. 'And that's not the first time we've heard this story.'

'Gets better,' Billy continued. 'Doctor Marcos called about the water samples from both victims. It's not high-class drinking water as she thought – it has a specific alkaline mineral profile matching a spring near Clerkenwell. Apparently, it runs beneath the old Bell Foundry site into the Thames near Whitechapel but needs purifying to be drinkable. The water on the bodies isn't treated.'

'You're saying it's raw water from beneath the Foundry site?'

'Exactly. And the only people who'd have access to that source would be maintenance workers, the foundry's management team or someone with access to the current building's systems.'

'Any connection to Victoria?'

'Actually yes. Her practice asked to buy some a year back for "hydration therapy" with patients but then claimed it didn't fulfil the requirements,' Billy replied.

'So, Victoria had access to the water,' Declan muttered.

'Yes, but Victoria was at a conference on Tuesday,' Billy replied. 'All day. On stage too, doing two panels and a network session in the evening. Her alibi is rock solid.'

'Which means she couldn't have killed Dirk or Sean ...' Anjli sighed. 'Damn.'

'Nathan claims he was locked down at work all day,' Billy added. 'So, I've requested their security logs. But here's where it gets interesting – I checked CCTV around the bank. There's a service exit on the east side of the building, not covered by their key security system. At three in the afternoon on Tuesday, someone looking very similar to Nathan left through that door.'

'Can you confirm it was him?' Declan asked.

'Face wasn't clear – he kept his head down. But height, build, clothing all match what Nathan was wearing earlier when he entered the main entrance.'

'Keep digging,' Declan instructed. 'And check if you can trace his movements after he left the building.'

'Already on it. If he took public transport, we'll find him,' Billy paused. 'Oh, and Shaun Donnal called. Burlington Bertie's extremely agitated again. Keeps insisting she knows where her daughter is.'

'We'll head over there,' Declan decided. 'And Billy, keep this between us for now. If Victoria's helping with the investigation—'

'Already ahead of you. I've isolated anything related to her in a secure folder.'

'Anything else?'

'Just a heads-up – Victoria called Monroe while you were out. Says she has new information about the case. She's coming in at noon.'

'Perfect timing,' Declan said. 'We'll be back before then.

Oh, and as well as looking at all the "Royal Court", check their parents, specifically the Bell Foundry disaster. I think they're all more connected than we, and even they, realise.'

As they headed for the car, Anjli glanced at Declan.

'So, Victoria Lang might not be Victoria Lang,' he mused.

'If she's using a dead child's identity, Shipman's story about Emmy Clarke's daughter gains credibility,' Anjli suggested. 'But until we're a hundred per cent sure, we still don't know who Victoria really is, or why she's targeting these specific players.'

'Burlington Bertie might be our best lead,' Declan replied, sliding behind the wheel. 'Let's hope she's having a lucid day.'

As they pulled away from Bishopsgate, Anjli glanced at Declan.

'So, Nathan Hargreaves slips out his office's back door on Tuesday afternoon. Hours later the same day, both Dirk VanMeerten and Sean Acker are dead.'

'Coincidence?' Declan asked.

'You know how I feel about coincidences,' Anjli replied. 'But if Nathan killed them both, why is he drawing attention to the Garden Collective? Why point us towards Victoria?'

'Either he's cleverly misdirecting us,' Declan said, 'or there's a bigger game being played than we realised.'

'With Victoria Lang as the Gamesmaster?'

'Let's see what Burlington Bertie has to say,' Declan replied as they headed towards St. Benedict's shelter. 'Maybe she can finally tell us exactly who Victoria Lang really is.'

16

THE FRAME

BERTIE WAS PACING WHEN THEY ARRIVED, AGITATED HANDS working at the edge of her tweed jacket like a pianist rehearsing scales. The St. Benedict's day room had been cleared of other residents – a kindness from Shaun Donnal that Declan silently appreciated.

'She's been like this since eight,' Shaun told them, his voice low. 'Keeps saying she knows where her daughter is, that she needs to warn her about something.'

Declan watched Bertie move, noticing how her movements held a strange precision despite her apparent distress. The lucidity was there, just beneath the surface chaos, like a radio signal fighting through interference.

'Bertie,' Declan called gently. 'It's Declan Walsh. I've brought DI Kapoor with me.'

Bertie stopped mid-stride, her head snapping towards them with sudden focus.

'Walsh Junior,' she acknowledged, the cloud in her eyes briefly clearing. 'Did you bring it?'

Declan exchanged a confused glance with Anjli.

'Bring what?'

'The photograph. Her photograph,' Bertie tutted impatiently. 'My daughter. I need to see her face.'

There was a moment of confusion as Declan looked over at Anjli for help.

'This woman?' Anjli pulled out her phone, bringing up a photo of Victoria Lang, before turning it to show Bertie, who approached cautiously, eyes narrowing as she studied the image.

For a long moment, she said nothing, her weathered fingers hovering just above the screen as if reluctant to make contact.

'That's her,' she finally whispered. 'My little Queen of Clubs. She'd steal it from the deck whenever we played. Patrick started calling her it.'

'Patrick Walsh?' Declan asked. 'My father?'

Bertie's face softened.

'She thought he was her father, too. Used to call him "Daddy Pat" when she was little. So proud to be a policeman's daughter.'

Declan felt a chill that had nothing to do with the shelter's inadequate heating.

'Are you saying Victoria Lang is your daughter? And that she believed my father was her father? That would make her ...'

He paused, the implication hanging in the air.

'Bertie, are you suggesting Victoria could be my *half-sister?*'

'Is that what you hope? Or what you fear?' Bertie's eyes narrowed, studying his face before shaking her head firmly. 'No. Patrick wasn't her father... we never... he just let her believe it. Easier that way, he said. Gave her stability.'

'Bertie—'

'Emmy,' Bertie corrected absently. 'My name is Emmy. Emmy Clarke.'

Her eyes refocused, suddenly sharp as cut glass.

'They took her from me in ninety-two. Said it was temporary, just until I got better. Patrick promised she'd be safe, that one day we'd be together again.'

She began pacing again, muttering under her breath.

'But they lied to her, told her I'd abandoned her. What would you do, Detective, if someone stole your child and told them you never wanted them?'

Declan thought of Jessica, and of the fierce protectiveness that defined their relationship despite the years living apart.

'I'd move heaven and earth to find them.'

Bertie – *Emmy* – stopped, regarding him.

'That's what she's doing. Moving heaven and earth. Only heaven doesn't want to be moved, does it?'

She abruptly turned, crossing to a small shelf of belongings. From beneath a tattered paperback, she extracted an old envelope, its edges softened with age and handling.

'Keep this safe,' she said, pressing it into Declan's hand. 'It's the only one I have of my little girl.'

Inside was a faded photograph – a young girl, perhaps seven, with dark hair and solemn eyes, standing between Emmy and a younger Patrick Walsh. The girl was holding a playing card – the Queen of Clubs.

'When did you last see her?' Anjli asked gently.

'She started visiting after Patrick died. Never during regular hours. She'd come at night, slip past the front desk. Not here, at the old place. We'd talk about old times, about what happened,' Bertie's face clouded. 'When she found out Patrick wasn't her father, that he'd kept us apart all those years, that there was more behind the collapse, and how Whitehall had pushed to hide it, something broke in her. Not on the outside where you could see. Deep inside, where it matters.'

As she spoke, Anjli had picked up the playing deck, rifling through them casually.

'And the Garden Collective?' Declan prompted. 'How does that connect?'

Emmy's eyes darted to the windows, checking for eavesdroppers.

'I was their informant. The police needed someone inside, and I had... a history that made me useful. Victoria... no, that's not her name... but I suppose it is now. Anyway, she found my old journals a couple of years back. The names, the cases, everything Patrick and I did.'

'What exactly did you and my father do?'

'Necessary things,' Emmy replied, a hardness entering her voice. 'People died at the Foundry because the Collective wanted martyrs. It couldn't go unpunished. The Gardners needed to pay for what they did.'

'How so?'

Bertie said nothing, looking away.

'Bertie?'

'People couldn't leave,' Bertie replied sadly. 'I had to keep them there.'

'Christ, are you telling me you kept everyone inside the Shadwell Bell Foundry, knowing it was set to collapse?'

'No! Of course not!' Bertie shook her head vigorously, but then stopped, her eyes widening. 'But there was someone... they helped ...'

She shook her head again, this time as if shaking away a bad memory.

'Can't recall.'

'And Victoria knows all this now?'

Bertie nodded slowly.

'She said she understood, that she forgave me, when she read the truth. But there was something in her eyes ...' She trailed off, and Declan could see her momentary clarity was beginning to slip. 'You need to help her, Patrick. Before she finishes what she's started.'

'What has she started, Emmy?' Anjli asked, noticing the mistaken name.

But any semblance of Emmy Clarke was gone, as Burlington Bertie shuffled back to her chair, muttering about tea and biscuits and a game of patience. The moment of connection had passed like a shooting star, brief but illuminating.

'Sorry, Declan,' Shaun said sadly.

'She mentioned the "old place",' Declan asked. 'Do we know where that was?'

'I can check, but she was in and out of a dozen such places over the last couple of years,' Sean replied. 'And knowing records the way I do, the chances are half of them didn't even have her registered, didn't know she was there.'

'But someone did,' Declan nodded, and was about to leave when he paused.

'Shaun, when did you become an MP?' he asked.

'Ninety-seven, when Blair won,' Shaun frowned. 'Why?'

'Did you deal with Norman Shipman?'

Shaun visibly shuddered as he remembered the name.

'Luckily, no,' he replied. 'He jumped sides before the election, but they kept him out of the way for a few years. It was known he was up to some dodgy shit in the Tories with

Leonard Banks, though, and jumped before he was pushed. Why?'

'Just curious,' Declan smiled. 'Nothing more.'

OUTSIDE, DECLAN AND ANJLI PAUSED ON THE SHELTER'S steps.

'I checked the cards,' Anjli began. 'You said there was one missing. Guess what it was.'

'Queen of Clubs,' Declan guessed correctly.

'If Victoria Lang is Emmy Clarke's daughter ...' Anjli continued

'Then she has more than just a professional interest in our case,' Declan finished. 'And if she grew up believing my father was her father—'

'Only to discover he was the one who separated her from her mother?' Anjli shook her head. 'That's the kind of betrayal that breaks people. Question is, did it break her enough to start *killing* people?'

NATHAN HARGREAVES'S APARTMENT BREATHED MONEY – tasteful minimalism that required a fortune to achieve, and the deliberately sparse elegance that disguised the cost of each carefully chosen item. De'Geer felt like a bull in a particularly expensive china shop as he followed Nathan through the sleek living room towards what appeared to be a home office.

'Daniel kept physical copies of everything,' Nathan was explaining, his movements edged with a nervous energy.

'Said he didn't trust digital storage for the really sensitive stuff. Too many ways to manipulate data.'

'Smart man,' De'Geer commented, ducking slightly to avoid a hanging light fixture.

'He was,' Nathan's voice caught. 'The smartest person I've ever known.'

The home office was as meticulously arranged as the rest of the apartment – a glass desk with a single MacBook, bookshelves filled with economic texts and financial histories, and a small wall safe concealed behind a framed print of Turner's *Rain, Steam and Speed.*

'Daniel gave me copies of his research right before he died,' Nathan said, removing the artwork to reveal the safe. 'And a message that arrived after his death said if anything happened to him, I should wait a year before doing anything with it.'

'Why a year?'

'He didn't explain. Just made me promise.' Nathan punched in a code, his fingers steady despite the tremor De'Geer had noticed in his hands earlier. 'After his death, I honoured that promise. Then when the year was up, I started looking through what he'd collected.'

'How did he tell you after he died?'

'Deadman's switch,' Nathan pulled at the safe door as it swung open. 'You know, you can set up an email to come out at a set time, and you keep pushing it back. When you don't ...'

'It sends the email,' De'Geer understood. 'Not many people go that far, though.'

'You do if you're involved with the type of people who play the bloody game—' Nathan froze, his body going rigid.

Inside, nestled on a shelf, sat a handgun – a Glock 17,

gleaming black in the office's recessed lighting. Beside it, arranged in a neat row, was a black silencer, five metal spikes identical to those used on the victims, and at the back of the safe, were both a black, bloodied bodycam and a manila folder labelled 'Daniel – Research' in neat block letters, visible to all.

'This isn't right,' Nathan whispered, his face draining of colour. 'That's not my gun. Those aren't mine.'

De'Geer tensed, instantly alert.

'Step back from the safe, please, Mister Hargreaves.'

'You don't understand,' Nathan's voice rose with panic. 'Someone's been in here. That gun – those spikes – they're not mine!'

'Sir, I need you to step back and remain calm.' De'Geer's hand moved subtly towards his taser. 'Is that Sean Acker's bodycam?'

Nathan's eyes darted from the safe to De'Geer, then to the door. In one quick motion, he lunged forward, grabbing the gun from the safe.

'Nathan—' De'Geer warned, reaching for his taser.

'I'm not going to prison for something I didn't do!' Nathan brandished the weapon, his hand shaking. 'Someone's setting me up. Don't you see? Just like they did to Daniel!'

'Put the gun down,' De'Geer said evenly, his voice calm despite the rapid calculations running through his mind. 'We can sort this out.'

'No one sorted it out for Daniel,' Nathan's eyes were wild now. 'They let him die and called it suicide. I won't let that happen to me.'

With the gun still aimed at De'Geer, Nathan backed towards the door.

'I'm going to find who's really behind this. Tell Walsh –

tell him to look harder at Victoria Lang. She knows more than she's saying.'

Before De'Geer could respond, Nathan bolted from the room. By the time De'Geer reached the apartment door, Nathan had disappeared down the building's service stairs, having exited from a dozen different possible doors.

'Bollocks!' De'Geer cried out. Hargreaves knew the area, knew the short cuts – he'd be picked up on CTTV, but right now a foot chase was out of the question, with the starting direction unknown.

All De'Geer could do now was call it in.

'So, Nathan Hargreaves is now armed and on the run,' Monroe summarised, pacing the length of the briefing room. 'With a gun that potentially matches the one used to kill Sean Acker, with Sean Acker's camera and a handful of metal spikes identical to those used on both victims found in his safe?' Monroe shook his head. 'I should have sent more officers.'

Following De'Geer's close call with the business end of a Glock, the team had assembled at Temple Inn, the evidence from Nathan's apartment laid out on the briefing room table before them. The spikes, held in an evidence bag gleamed under the fluorescent lighting. The SD card from the bodycam was currently being reviewed by Billy.

'It's too convenient,' Declan said, studying the folder De'Geer had grabbed from Nathan's safe. 'Everything we need to close the case, neatly packaged in one place.'

'Gift-wrapped with a bow,' Anjli agreed. 'And Nathan's

reaction – grabbing the gun and running – just completes the picture.'

'Panic response,' Bullman suggested from her usual position at the door. 'Fight or flight. He chose flight.'

'Or he knew he was caught,' Monroe countered.

Doctor Marcos, who'd been examining one spike with a jeweller's loupe, looked up.

'These are fascinating. Handcrafted, not machine-produced. Made from a copper-tin alloy with traces of lead – consistent with Victorian-era decorative metalwork.'

'Like those finials from Dirk's storage unit?' Declan asked.

'Exactly like them,' Marcos confirmed. 'I'm not a hundred per cent sure, but they're the same composition, same casting techniques. Someone literally melted down historical artefacts to create murder weapons.'

'But how?' Monroe asked. 'Dirk VanMeerten's finials matched the receipt, and none had been taken.'

'Any news on the silencer?'

'It's definitely the one that killed Sean Acker,' Doctor Marcos straightened. 'Ballistics match the markings. But there's no record of Dirk's father owning one.'

'Could Hargreaves have bought it?'

'Not without a firearm certificate,' Billy said, 'And from what I can see, there's no such thing in his name. He'd have to pick it up illegally. But on the subject of the storage unit, I've been looking more closely at the invoice.'

He tapped at his laptop, sending an image to the plasma screen.

'Look at the bottom corner, near the lot number.'

The team turned to see a magnified section of the auction receipt. Billy adjusted the contrast, revealing a faint, partially erased marking.

'There,' he pointed. 'It's been altered. I can up the contrast and play around with the image curves, and we can see here that originally, it said "x2" – indicating two identical lots purchased, not one.'

'You're saying Dirk bought two sets of these finials?' Anjli leant closer to the screen.

'Exactly. I've emailed the auction house to confirm, but if I'm correct, then Dirk purchased two identical boxes of Bell Foundry finials two years ago, but we only found one box in his storage unit.'

'So, there's another set out there,' Declan mused. 'Which explains how the killer had the same material to make spikes before Dirk was killed.'

'And suggests whoever killed Dirk had access to his possessions long before his death,' Monroe added. 'Someone close enough to take one set without him noticing.'

'Or with his blessing,' Declan suggested.

The main office doors opened, and Cooper escorted Victoria Lang into the office, leading her to the glass-walled briefing room. She looked immaculate as always – tailored suit, hair perfectly styled, the picture of professional composure. She carried a leather portfolio under one arm, her expression concerned but controlled.

'I came as soon as I could,' she said, taking in the serious faces around the table. 'I understand Nathan Hargreaves has fled custody?'

'Not custody,' Declan corrected. 'He was assisting with inquiries when he discovered incriminating evidence in his own safe. Evidence he claims was planted.'

Victoria raised an eyebrow.

'Planted? That's convenient.'

'Please, sit down, Doctor Lang.' Bullman gestured to an empty chair. 'We'd appreciate your insights.'

Victoria settled into the offered seat, placing her portfolio on the table.

'Of course. Nathan's behaviour doesn't surprise me, unfortunately. He's been increasingly unstable since Daniel's death. The paranoia, the conspiracy theories – classic manifestations of unprocessed grief complicated by his underlying condition.'

'You knew about his diagnosis?' Anjli asked.

'Since university,' Victoria nodded. 'I recognised the symptoms during a particularly severe episode in our final year.'

'Severe episode?'

'He tried to kill himself,' Victoria tapped her wrist. 'Luckily he tried to cut across, not down.'

Anjli nodded at this.

'He claimed it was a carpal tunnel treatment scar, but it's there,' she admitted. 'Cooper and I saw it the first time we spoke.'

'He has *Bipolar I with psychotic or aggressive features*,' Victoria continued. 'I helped him find proper treatment, and he's been medicated ever since, but after Daniel died, he became inconsistent with his medication regimen.'

'And that's when he began fixating on you?' Declan prompted.

Victoria hesitated, then opened her portfolio.

'Yes. At first, I thought he was just grieving, but then ...'

She extracted several photographs, laying them on the table.

'These are from my private investigator. Nathan, outside my office. Outside my home. Following me in public places.'

The images showed Nathan in various locations, clearly surveilling Victoria. The timestamps spanned the past year.

'He blamed me for not preventing Daniel's suicide,' Victoria continued. 'Said that as a psychologist, I should have seen the signs, intervened somehow. The surveillance escalated over time.'

'Why didn't you report this?' Monroe asked.

'Professional courtesy, initially. I thought I could help him process his grief. And when I heard he was hanging around with Dirk, who I've already said had a fixation on me, well... when Sean and Rachel were killed, I began to wonder if his fixation had become something more dangerous.'

She extracted another photograph – a grainy image showing Nathan near Stationers' Hall.

'My investigator took this the night Sean was killed. Nathan, in the vicinity just before the estimated time of death.'

She placed another image beside it.

'And this shows him entering the Harrington Finance building on the afternoon Rachel died.'

'Why are you bringing these to us now?' Declan asked, keeping his tone neutral. 'Why not earlier?'

'Because I believe in doctor-patient confidentiality, even if he's following me, and even if Nathan is responsible for these deaths,' Victoria said firmly. 'His obsession with the Garden Collective, his deteriorating mental state, his fixation on me – it all fits. When Dirk began investigating the same connections, Nathan eliminated him too. I felt it was my duty to bring these to light.'

'What about Oliver Drake?' Anjli asked suddenly. 'Why was he brought into the game to replace Daniel?'

Victoria's expression flickered – surprise, quickly masked.

'Belinda insisted on Oliver. Said something about his energy being similar to Daniel's ...' she paused. 'It seemed strange to me at the time – Oliver works in Nathan's building. I'd seen him around. The coincidence felt... forced. And there was the fact Belinda always sided with Nathan – their families knew each other from before Uni. Whenever Belinda gives an idea, you know Nathan came up with it.'

Throughout Victoria's explanation, Bullman had remained silent, watching her with the stillness of a predator assessing its prey. Now, she straightened beside the doorframe.

'You've made a compelling case against Nathan Hargreaves, Doctor Lang,' she said. 'Very thorough. Very professional.'

'Thank you. I try.'

Bullman leant forward slightly.

'Now, let's make an equally compelling case against *you*.'

Victoria froze. 'I'm sorry?'

'We spoke with Emmy Clarke this morning,' Declan said quietly, placing the childhood photograph on the table between them. 'She gave us this.'

Victoria stared at the image, her professional mask slipping for just a moment – enough to reveal raw emotion beneath before she regained control.

'Where did you get that?' Her voice had lost its clinical detachment, dropping to a near-whisper.

'From your mother,' Bullman replied. 'Who remembers you calling Patrick Walsh "Daddy Pat" when you were little.'

Declan and Bullman exchanged a look, and Declan nodded slightly.

My turn.

'The steward at the Reform Club recognised your photo

an hour ago,' Declan added. 'Confirmed you tried to access my father's files, claiming to be my sister. I can only guess this was to confirm whatever stories your mother had given you, but I could be wrong.'

'And then you conveniently offered your "help" with our investigation,' Bullman continued, 'once you knew we had those same files.'

'We also know,' Declan added softly, 'that you grew up believing Patrick was your father. That you only learned the truth after his death – and that you'd been separated from Emmy when you were seven years old and given a new identity.'

Victoria looked around the room, her eyes moving from face to face, seeing the unified knowledge there. When she finally spoke, her voice was low, controlled, but with an unmistakable edge.

'Do you have any idea what it's like to discover your entire life is a lie?' she asked. 'To learn that the man you thought was your father – the man you *idolised* – was the one who stole you from your mother?'

She stood slowly, her dignity intact despite the revelation.

'Yes, Emily Clarke was-*is* my mother. Yes, I was taken from her when I was a child and given a new identity. Yes, I believed Patrick Walsh was my father for thirty years, although I could never get confirmation on that.'

She lifted her chin as her gaze fixed on Declan.

'Your father, the MP Norman Shipman, and Assistant Commissioner Bernard Willis took everything from me, Detective Chief Inspector Walsh. My mother, my identity, my history. Everything. But if you think that makes me a murderer, you're going to need more than a childhood photograph to prove it.'

Her eyes swept around the room.

'Besides, if someone is targeting the original families, you have it backwards. *I* was the original Queen of Clubs in our game, not Rachel. If the killer is following the card identities, Rachel's death was a mistake – and *I* should be next.'

Declan went to reply, but saw Cooper in the main office, on the phone – she looked up at him, waving him over.

'Hold that thought,' he said, walking out to speak to the officer. A moment later, he returned, his eyes cold.

'You might be telling the truth there,' he said. 'We just had a call from Belgravia police – apparently someone just tried to set fire to your house.'

17

BASEMENTS

ANJLI AND VICTORIA LANG HAD LEFT PRETTY MUCH immediately with Cooper offering to drive, and as they did so, Monroe glanced over at Bullman.

'You could have told me you were playing her,' he muttered. 'I genuinely thought you believed her.'

'That was the point, Alex. I'm not some wet behind the ears rookie,' Bullman shrugged. 'I knew something was wrong. But she was good. Kept me going. Even then, there was something off. She thought she was playing me, so I went along with it to see how far she'd go.'

'And?'

'For a supposed expert in crime scenes, she was rubbish at the procedures, even if she worked out where Rachel had fallen.'

She paused Declan from speaking with a finger.

'And before you talk about "positioning of the body" there was a bloody great smear of dried blood on the floor. Even you could have worked it out.'

The jibe was good natured but interrupted by Billy.

'Look,' he said, moving the video from his laptop screen to the plasma screen on the wall. On it, they watched from Sean Acker's perspective as he died.

He was in an alley – likely the one he was found in, but the darkness and lack of lighting didn't help. Sean spun around a corner, his gun aimed up, but then pausing as a figure no more than a few feet away stared at him.

Nathan Hargreaves.

'Oh, for God's sake,' Sean muttered, lowering the gun. *'Didn't you listen to the rules? When approaching another player you're supposed to—'*

Phut.

Nathan fired his own Glock, the silencer on the end, and the perspective changed as Sean sagged to his knees. Nathan now unscrewed the silencer and placed their gun away, pulling out a blue water pistol and aiming at Sean's face.

'Why?'

The camera tilted, likely as Sean slumped to the side, and a water pistol squirted him, the water hitting the camera of the bodycam.

At a side angle now, Nathan placed the water pistol away, leaning down, and with latex-gloved hands, reached into Sean's pockets, pulling out the two playing cards. Then, sticking them in their own pocket, he pulled out the black and silver King of Spades, before unclipping Sean's bodycam and turning it off.

There was a moment of silence.

'Pretty damning,' Monroe said.

'No wonder he wanted to keep it hidden,' Declan frowned. 'But am I the only one thinking it's too convenient?

Billy looked up from his laptop.

'The dialogue doesn't fit.'

'How so?' Monroe asked.

'Sean tells Nathan they don't know the rules about approaching another player. But Nathan's played this game for twenty years.'

'Stress makes people say stupid things,' Bullman suggested.

'Maybe,' Declan replied. 'But it's not the first time we've dealt with doctored footage. Billy? I want you to analyse the footage properly.'

'Give me an hour and I'll tell you if someone's been messing about with the evidence,' Billy nodded. 'I can't do much with the printed photos of Nathan Victoria gave us, but if I saw the originals, I could check those too.'

As he went to reply, Declan's phone rang. Anthony Farringdon's name appeared on the screen, and with a frown, he glanced at Monroe before accepting the call.

'Declan, my boy,' Farringdon's voice spoke through the speaker. 'I've been digging into that Garden Collective business. Found some rather unsettling information that needs immediate attention.'

'Can you meet?' Monroe asked, checking his watch. 'National Liberal Club in an hour?'

'Ah, Alex. Hello. No, not there. Too exposed.' Farringdon's voice dropped to a whisper. 'Westminster. There are things I need to show you that can't leave the building. Meet me at the Carriage Gates in twenty minutes. Only you and Monroe, Declan.'

The line went dead.

'Curiouser and curiouser,' muttered Bullman. 'I'll check with Guildhall, see if there's anything else I can find.'

'Right,' Declan said, grabbing his coat. 'Monroe and I are off to see what's got Anthony spooked.'

'And if I find someone's playing games with us?' Billy asked.

Monroe's grin held no warmth.

'Then we'll play games right back. But better.'

WESTMINSTER ON A FRIDAY AFTERNOON MEANT SECURITY guards who'd seen everything twice and still looked bored. The police who would usually check them over stepped to the side as instead a Doorkeeper, wearing his black long-tailed coat, white bow tie, and a silver-gilt waist badge of office named Campbell led them through corridors that got less fancy the further they went, until they reached a lift that needed his special card.

As they did so, Declan observed the man. The Doorkeepers of the Houses of Parliament had served for centuries, their origins tracing back to the days when armed guards stood watch to protect Members from royal interference – and sometimes from each other. By the Nineteenth Century, their role had formalised into one of order and ceremony, drawn largely from the ranks of former soldiers. In black tailcoats and silver-gilt chains, they managed access to the chambers, enforced protocol, and kept quiet watch over the business of democracy – rarely noticed, but always present, and each with a book that showed names and faces of all six hundred and fifty members of Parliament.

And, up to a few years ago, all of them had worked under Anthony Farringdon.

'Down we go,' Campbell said, like he was announcing the weather.

The lift kept going. And going. Declan lost count of the floors.

'Christ on a bike,' Monroe muttered. 'We heading for Australia?'

'Just the archives, sir.'

The doors opened onto a corridor that looked like something from a Cold War film. Reinforced doors led to dim lighting and the smell of old secrets and older paper.

Campbell stopped at door 847. There was no nameplate, no window, just a number. Inside, Anthony Farringdon looked up with a smile.

'Took your time,' he said.

'Traffic,' Monroe lied smoothly. 'What've you got that's so bloody urgent?'

'Sit down. Both of you,' Farringdon gestured to chairs that had seen better decades. 'What I'm about to show you changes everything you thought you knew about the Garden Collective.'

He opened a folder marked with more classification stamps than a passport office.

'The Bell Foundry wasn't an accident. It was a hit job. It wasn't Government-sanctioned, but it was planned as an elimination of people who'd found out things they shouldn't have.'

'Such as?' Declan asked.

'Property fraud. Planning corruption. Ministers taking kickbacks.' Farringdon spread out documents like he was dealing cards. 'Your Nathan's dad, Harold Hargreaves, was buying buildings before the Collective even knew they existed. Someone was feeding him information.'

'Inside job?' Monroe leant forward.

'The Collective was riddled with informants from day

one. Everything they planned, someone else knew about first.'

Farringdon opened another folder. Crime scene photos, surveillance shots, intelligence reports.

'Three people died in the collapse, but it was like it was cursed, as twelve more died over the next three decades. All of them connected to the Collective. All of them ruled natural causes or accidents.'

He laid out photographs methodically.

'Michael and Sarah Thornton – that's Rachel's mother and father – they were activists and two of the people who died that night. David Chen, Alex's uncle, apparent suicide after talking to journalists. Thomas Collins, Daryl's father, hit and run after finding God and deciding to come clean a decade later.'

More photos joined the pile.

'Jennifer Taylor-Knight, connected to Diane's family, planning committee. Drug overdose. Peter Morris, Belinda's biological father, building regulations. Sailing accident. And Linda Gardner, who tried to warn people before the collapse, maybe even realised it was happening before it did? Died in hospital from childbirth two years later.'

'Childbirth?' Monroe frowned. 'That's surely not connected—'

'Complications connected to internal injuries she gained in the accident,' Farringdon paused at Linda's photo. 'Linda had a child. No idea if it's a son or daughter, records are sealed. Her partner, the father, took them after she died, but the trail goes cold and we don't have details – the people doing this weren't the police, after all. And the moment anyone started asking, questions about why they were asking would begin.'

'A literal ouroboros,' Monroe muttered.

'Exactly, eating its own tail. Meanwhile, the people who helped cover it up got rich.'

Farringdon opened a different folder.

'George VanMeerten, Dirk's dad, gave false testimony that avoided mentioning government involvement, perjuring himself in the process. Promoted within months. Jonathan Foster, Daniel's father, handled the legal cover-up. Made QC within five years.'

'What about the others?' Monroe asked.

'Robert Wilson, Christopher's father, false security testimony. His firm got government contracts worth millions. James Kelly, Justin's father, communications suppression. Ended up heading a major PR firm. Gary Webb's father worked the financial law side with Hargreaves, now runs a massive law firm in the City. Sean Acker's father provided security clearances, most likely for the night before the accident, and controlled by Westminster.'

'Every single Royal Court family,' Declan said.

'Children of perjured activists and those who benefited from that perjury. All brought together while at university by someone who knew exactly who they were.'

'And who was running this show?' Monroe asked.

Farringdon opened the final folder.

'Norman Shipman. MP with sway then, backbench survivor now. We all know how he'd been playing the back rooms with his Magpies plans. This was his next *magnum opus*, but he took it too far. Needed to end things.'

'How?'

'Elizabeth Gardner.' Farringdon held up pieces of paper, various notes, replacing them one after the other, showing the wealth of documentation here. 'Her daughter Linda was arrested on a protest after she used a Molotov cocktail on a police car—'

'That doesn't sound peaceful,' Monroe commented.

'At what point did I ever say these people were peaceful?' Farringdon placed his hands on the table 'She was going to prison for it – an example to be made. So, Elizabeth wasn't stupid, and called Shipman, begged for leniency. Shipman said the Collective needed to end and end big.'

He shook his head.

'Of course, never tell a radical anarchist to "end big". And never send someone like Emmy Clarke in to plan it out.'

'Christ, *she* set up the foundry accident. Linda must have found out, tried to stop it, got caught in the collapse.'

'Exactly.' Farringdon now pulled out an authorisation memo. 'Shipman knew he'd screwed up. He'd aimed his pet lawyer Bruno Field at them, but Field had gone too far. Now everyone was looking at this. Eyes from every country, and Shipman was in the headlights. So, in the aftermath of the 1992 incident, he moved quickly to contain the fallout. A DSMA Notice, still known informally as a D-Notice at the time, was issued to all major media outlets, advising editors not to report on the event or its location. Though not legally binding, the press complied, as was typical when national security was invoked. His department invoked the Official Secrets Act to silence civil servants, emergency responders, and anyone else with direct knowledge. Those briefed were reminded of their legal obligations – some signed fresh undertakings under threat of prosecution.'

'He tried to smother it,' Declan muttered.

'Almost succeeded too, but the court case was still going ahead,' Farringdon continued. 'In court, where related matters arose, Public Interest Immunity was claimed to prevent disclosure of evidence that could, some argued, endanger national security or undermine trust in government institutions. Documents were withheld. Witnesses were gagged. And for most of the public, the event simply never happened. And it was all signed by Assistant Commissioner Willis, the Home Secretary – either Kenneth Clarke or Kenneth Baker, I'm not sure which one as it's just signed "Kenneth" – and Leonard Banks.'

'Leonard Banks?' Declan read the signature. 'Shaun Donnal said during his time in the Labour Party, his dealings with Shipman were small, but that it was known he was up to some dodgy shit in the Tories with Leonard Banks, and jumped before he was pushed.'

'Junior Minister for Planning. Also Tamara Banks's dear old father.'

'The Defence Secretary's father was in on this?' Monroe whistled.

'Made a fortune from inside information while little Tamara was still in pigtails. He also ran the Star Chamber, which we all know does whatever the hell they want.'

Declan nodded at this. The Star Chamber had effectively killed Kendis Taylor years earlier and tried to frame him as not only a terrorist handler, but public enemy number one.

'So, they handled the wet work... we're not just looking at historical murders,' Declan said. 'We're looking at a government conspiracy that's still running. And someone's decided payback time has arrived.'

'Why didn't you tell anyone?' Monroe asked.

'I never read these until now,' Farringdon replied, as if it was the simplest thing in the world. 'Remember it was before my time, when I was starting here. I had no need to check into this.'

He smiled.

'Now, of course, I do. The question is, Declan – your father was closed down when he went off books against the government. What are *you* going to do when they try to close *you* down?'

Billy stared at his screens and felt that familiar itch that meant something was seriously wrong. The bodycam footage looked right, sounded right, but it wasn't right.

He pulled up the audio analysis first. Sean's voice checked out – stress patterns, accent, all normal, and at first glance everything looked correct but the metadata was buggered. Creation timestamps didn't match the recording sequence, and there were upload times that came before download times. Basic errors that professional software wouldn't make.

Then there were the lighting inconsistencies. The shadows were wrong on Nathan's face. Not by much, and again it would have been shrugged off by the average viewer. But Billy wasn't the average viewer, and he could see the colour temperature jumped around like someone had been mixing footage from different sources.

Billy dove deeper into the technical analysis. The "Nathan" in the footage was wrong in ways that were hard to spot but impossible to ignore once you knew what to look for. Facial recognition threw up anomalies. Gait analysis didn't match. Even the micro-expressions were off.

The door to the main office opened and Doctor Marcos walked in, carrying evidence bags with the playing cards in, and looking pleased with herself.

'Billy, perfect. I've got something about those playing

cards that'll interest you,' she said as she set the bags on his desk, holding up one of them. 'Rachel's Queen of Clubs is original. Ten years old, aged ink, wear patterns from being handled. But look at these.'

She held up two more bags.

'Sean's King of Spades and Dirk's King of Hearts are reprints. Fresh cardstock, new ink, crisp edges.'

'Different printing?'

'Exactly. Rachel's death was rushed – someone had to use their own card. The others were planned in advance, with fresh cards prepared.'

'So, Rachel found out something that made her an immediate threat.'

'That's my assessment.'

Billy turned back to his screens.

'I think she wasn't the only one being removed as a threat. This bodycam footage is fake. Complete digital fabrication.'

'Then who is the killer?' Doctor Marcos leant closer to the screen, examining it.

'We'll find out soon,' Billy smiled. 'They may have painted over the real face, but I'm a master restorer.'

VICTORIA'S HOUSE LOOKED EXACTLY LIKE IT HAD WHEN ANJLI visited before – posh, perfect, and mostly undamaged by any fire, although a fire engine was outside, the firefighters replacing the hoses. Victoria had her keys ready, but paused as she realised the front door had been smashed open, likely by the same firefighters.

'I need to check my study,' Victoria said, entering. 'See

what's been damaged. Give me a minute to assess the situation.'

Before Anjli could stop her, however, one of the firefighters stepped in their way.

'You get called in too?' he asked when he saw Cooper's uniform. 'Nothing more than a small fire in the hallway Minimal fire damage, probably more water damage now we've been here. I think they were trying for the ground floor, but one of the neighbours called it in before it could take effect.'

'This is bollocks,' Cooper whispered. 'The man who called said it was a major fire.'

'Did he say what department he was from?'

Cooper went to reply, stopped herself and frowned.

'Actually, no,' she said. 'Just passing information.'

'We need to get eyes on Victoria,' Anjli said as she looked back the way Victoria had disappeared. As if by magic, Victoria's voice called from somewhere deeper in the house

'Not as bad as I thought, just some paper damage. Need a few minutes to sort through what's salvageable.'

Anjli's phone rang. Billy.

'What've you got?' she answered.

'I need those playing cards Victoria showed you,' he said. 'Doctor Marcos needs them for comparison with the evidence.'

'We're at her house now. I'll find them.'

'Good. And Anjli? That bodycam footage is complete bollocks. Professional-grade fake.'

'Understood.' Anjli hung up and nodded to Cooper. 'Keep an eye on the front. I'm going to find Lang and those cards, and get a proper bloody answer from her.'

She headed down the corridor, past rooms that showed

no sign of fire damage. The study door was open, but the room was empty. Papers scattered on the desk, but they looked arranged rather than damaged.

'Victoria?'

No answer.

The last time Anjli had been here, Victoria had walked over to a desk drawer at the side, unlocked it and removed a playing card, placing it on the coffee table. The Queen of Hearts with black background and silver ink.

Walking over to it now, Anjli saw the desk was unlocked, and the desk drawer where Victoria had kept the card was empty.

'Victoria?' Louder this time.

She moved through the house, checking rooms. The back door was open, cold air streaming in. Beyond it, a small garden led to a mews where she could hear a car engine fading into the distance.

Anjli ran to the entrance to the mews and saw fresh tyre marks on wet pavement. There was, however, no Victoria.

She pulled out her phone, calling Monroe.

'Guv, we've got a problem. Victoria's gone. The fire was fake, and she's done a runner with the evidence.'

'Bollocks. How long?'

'Minutes. She could be anywhere.'

'Get back here now. If Victoria Lang is who we think she is, Nathan's walking into a thirty-year trap.'

Anjli looked around the perfect house. Everything was wrong – the staged photos, the unread books, the props that passed for personal items. Victoria Lang's entire life had been a performance.

Was this even her house?

'Cooper!' she called. 'We're leaving. Now.'

As they drove away, Anjli was furious at herself for letting the firefighter distract her. Victoria had needed something from the house – the cards that could prove her involvement, perhaps. The fake fire had been her excuse to get a police escort, then slip away once she'd secured what she needed.

So who set the fire?

Somewhere in London, Victoria Lang was loose with a thirty-year plan reaching its endgame, a yet-unknown accomplice beside her... and they were already several moves behind.

18

THE OUTCAST

NATHAN HARGREAVES PRESSED HIMSELF INTO THE DOORWAY OF the closed newsagent, collar up against the November rain that had started an hour earlier.

Nine hours.

That's how long it had been since he'd fled the Viking-looking police sergeant's shocked face in his own apartment, since he'd seen the planted gun and metal spikes that would destroy his life.

Nine hours of running through London streets with no destination, no plan, just the desperate need to stay moving.

Nine hours of phone calls from a pay as you go phone he'd bought, syncing his contacts list to it before moving on, with calls that went unanswered, messages that were ignored, the gradual understanding that everyone he'd considered a friend now believed he was a killer.

Nine. Hours.

The Glock sat heavy in his jacket pocket. He should have left it behind, should have let the police take it as evidence. But panic had taken over, the fight-or-flight response that had served him well in trading floors useless now. Taking the gun had only made him look more guilty, but it was too late to go back.

His hands trembled as he pulled out his phone again. Seventeen missed calls to various members of the bloody game. Seventeen attempts to reach someone, anyone, who might listen to his side of the story.

But the silence was deafening.

The last response had come from Gary three hours ago.

> Nathan, turn yourself in. Get help. We can't be involved.

That was it. Twenty years of friendship, dismissed in a single text message.

Nathan scrolled through his synced contacts again, his thumb hovering over Belinda's name. She was the most logical of the group, the one who approached problems with spreadsheet precision rather than emotional reactions. If anyone would listen to reason, it would be her.

The rain intensified, running off the shopfront above him in steady streams. Across the road, Belinda and her family's upper-floor, Victorian-conversion apartment sat under amber streetlights, its windows glowing warm against the November darkness. He'd been watching for twenty minutes, trying to work up the courage to approach; every time he started to cross the street, the enormity of his situation hit him again.

He was a fugitive. A man with a history of mental illness, one he'd covered up for decades, carrying a murder weapon.

Even if Belinda believed his story about being framed, what could she do? Call the police? They'd arrest him on sight. Help him hide? She'd become an accessory.

But he was running out of options.

The medication Victoria had been prescribing him ever since he begged her to help after Daniel's death, when he realised his company wouldn't understand, was leaving his system and with it, the fog that had clouded his thinking for years. Fragments of memories were surfacing – conversations with Victoria where she'd suggested things he couldn't quite remember agreeing to, times when he'd woken up with no clear recollection of the previous evening, gaps in his timeline that had worried him but which she'd explained away as part of his condition.

'You've been diagnosed with Bipolar I Disorder. Specifically, the form that includes psychotic features, rapid cycling, and mixed episodes. It's one of the most severe classifications, and what that means is, you may experience mania and depression at the same time, and there are instances where you could lose touch with reality; hallucinations, delusions, that kind of thing. The cycling between episodes happens frequently and unpredictably. It's a condition that often requires long-term medication, mood stabilisers and antipsychotics and in some cases, hospitalisation. Statistically, the suicide risk associated with this diagnosis is significantly elevated. We'll need to monitor you closely. But we can fix this, Nathan.'

What if there was no condition? What if Victoria had been creating the very symptoms she claimed to be treating?

Nathan's phone buzzed. A text from an unknown number, but the name given to it froze him.

FROM: DANIEL

Getting cold out there. Time to come inside.

He looked around, scanning the street for any sign of

surveillance. Nothing. Just empty pavements and the occasional car pushing through puddles.

But someone was watching him. Someone who knew exactly where he was.

Someone who wanted him to believe Daniel was alive.

Who are you?

A moment later, a reply.

You know who I am, Nathan. Did I mean that little to you?

Nathan bit back a whimper. Daniel was dead. This was nothing more than a sick game.

Another text appeared on the screen.

Belinda's expecting you. Don't keep her waiting.

The blood drained from Nathan's face.

Someone was in Belinda's apartment. Someone was using her as bait.

Before he could think it through properly, Nathan was crossing the road, rain hammering his shoulders. The building's front door was solid Victorian timber with modern security additions that looked oddly out of place as he pressed the intercom doorbell.

'Hello?' Belinda's voice came through the speaker, tinny and distorted.

'Belinda, it's Nathan. I need to talk to you.'

Silence stretched long enough that he thought she'd hung up. Then she continued.

'Nathan, I don't think that's wise right now.'

'Please,' he said, leaning closer to the speaker. 'I know how this looks, but someone's setting me up. You've known me for twenty years – do you really think I'm capable of murder?'

'I don't know what to think any more,' she replied, her voice small and uncertain. 'The police were here earlier, asking questions. They showed me photos of evidence they found in your apartment. A gun, Nathan. Sean's bodycam. And those metal spikes ...'

'They were planted,' Nathan said desperately. 'Someone broke into my apartment and left them to frame me. I've never seen them before in my life.'

Another pause. Then, softer, 'Come up. But Nathan... if you try anything, if you make me feel threatened in any way, I'm calling the police immediately.'

'I understand.'

The door buzzed open with a harsh electronic sound that echoed off the brick walls. Nathan climbed the narrow staircase, his wet shoes squeaking on carpet that had seen better decades. Each step upwards felt like walking deeper into a trap, but he had nowhere else to go.

By the time he reached the third floor, his heart was hammering against his ribs. Not from the physical exertion, but from the growing certainty that this was exactly where someone wanted him to be.

Belinda's door was ajar, held by the security chain. Her eye appeared in the gap, taking in his dishevelled appearance with obvious concern.

'You look terrible,' she said.

'Feel worse,' Nathan replied, pushing his wet fringe back from his forehead. 'Can I come in?'

She studied his face for a long moment, then closed the

door to unhook the chain. When it opened again, she stepped back quickly, keeping distance between them.

'Keep your hands where I can see them,' she said.

Nathan nodded, holding his hands slightly away from his body as he entered the apartment. Belinda Morris had always been the most practical member of their group – an accountant who solved problems with logic rather than emotion. Her apartment reflected this personality: clean lines, neutral colours, everything organised carefully. The living room served multiple functions – dining area, workspace, entertainment centre – but nothing was out of place.

What caught Nathan's attention immediately was the man sitting on Belinda's sofa, wineglass in hand, looking entirely at ease in her space.

Oliver Drake.

'Nathan,' Oliver said with what appeared to be genuine concern. 'I didn't expect to see you here. Are you alright?'

Nathan stared at him, something nagging at the edge of his consciousness. There was something about Oliver's seated posture, his tone, the way he held himself. Like an actor who'd studied his role carefully but wasn't quite comfortable in the character's skin.

'What are you doing here?' Nathan asked, his voice sharper than he'd intended as he looked back to her. 'Where's James and Emma?'

'Visiting his mother for a few days,' Belinda replied, and Nathan caught a hint of resentment in the tone. 'With the deaths and the police, we thought it was best if they weren't around me right now.'

Nathan winced at this – the words felt like an attack.

'And him?' Nathan looked back at Oliver. 'I mean, Christ,

Bel, we knew you two were hooking up, but in your own apartment? With the bed barely cold?'

'I was worried about Belinda,' Oliver replied smoothly, ignoring the accusation. 'With everything that's happened – Sean and Rachel's murders – I thought she might need some company. Some protection.'

'Protection from what?'

'From whoever's been killing members of our group,' Oliver said, his gaze steady and concerned. 'The police seem to think it's someone connected to the game, someone who knows our routines and vulnerabilities.'

The implication hung in the air between them. Nathan felt heat building in his chest.

'You think it's me.'

'I didn't say that,' Oliver replied carefully. 'But you have to admit, the timing of your... episode... is concerning, and you do seem to have a gun, apparently. Do you still have it?'

'Episode?' Nathan's voice rose slightly. 'Is that what we're calling it?'

'Nathan, please sit down,' Belinda said, offering him a towel from the kitchen. 'You're dripping all over my carpet.'

But Nathan remained standing, his attention fixed on Oliver. Something about the man's presence here felt wrong, calculated.

Too convenient.

'How long have you been here?' Nathan asked.

'About an hour,' Oliver replied. 'We were just talking about the old days, trying to make sense of what's been happening to the group.'

'The old days?' Nathan's voice sharpened with suspicion. 'You've only known us for a year and change, Oliver. You've only worked with me for eighteen months. What old days would those be?'

Oliver's smile flickered almost imperceptibly.

'I meant... well, Belinda was telling me about the group's history. How close you all were at university, how the game kept you connected over the years.'

'Were,' Nathan repeated, catching the past tense. 'Very observant of you.'

Oliver leant forward slightly, his expression growing more concerned.

'Nathan, you seem agitated. When did you last take your medication?'

The question hit Nathan like a physical blow. He'd heard it so many times over the years, always from Victoria, always when he started asking questions or expressing doubts about his treatment.

'My medication,' Nathan said slowly. 'Right. The medication that's been keeping me compliant for years.'

'Nathan ...' Belinda started, but he cut her off.

'Tell me something, Oliver. What do you know about the Garden Collective?'

The reaction was subtle – just a slight pause, a barely perceptible tightening around Oliver's eyes – but it was there. Nathan caught it, filed it away.

'I'm not sure what you mean,' Oliver said carefully.

'Environmental protest group. They were involved in a building collapse at the Shadwell Bell Foundry.'

Oliver's expression remained neutral, but Nathan was watching closely now, looking for any crack.

'No idea what you're talking about. Before my time. Why do you ask?'

'How can you know it's before your time when you also

claim you don't know about it?' Nathan asked, his voice gaining strength as the pieces began clicking together in his mind. 'You would have heard of it when you helped Dirk. Did he tell you about it? Or did *you* tell *him?*'

'Nathan, you're starting to frighten me,' Belinda said, her voice tight with growing alarm.

'We're all connected to that case through our families,' Nathan continued, ignoring her concern. 'All of us. My father was a property developer who profited from sites the Collective targeted. Dirk's father testified against them in court. Daniel's father was involved in the legal proceedings. Even Sean's family had security contracts that benefited from the aftermath.'

He turned his full attention to Oliver, studying the man's face with new intensity.

'And you, Oliver. You're about thirty, thirty-one years old? Born in the early nineties, right around the time of the Bell Foundry collapse?'

'I don't see what my age has to do with anything,' Oliver replied, but there was a subtle shift in his posture, a slight stiffening that Nathan caught.

'Don't you?' Nathan stepped closer, his voice dropping to a more intimate register. 'Tell me about your family, Oliver. Your real family. Not the vague stories you told me when I interviewed you for the Junior Analyst role.'

For just a moment – only a heartbeat – Oliver's mask slipped. His eyes went cold, calculating, before the concerned expression returned.

'Nathan, I think you need help,' Oliver said, his tone carefully modulated. 'These conspiracy theories, this paranoid thinking – they're symptoms of your condition getting worse.'

'My condition,' Nathan repeated, and laughed bitterly.

'The condition that conveniently makes me look insane whenever I start asking the right questions.'

He pulled the blister pack of medication from his pocket, holding it up so both Belinda and Oliver could see it clearly.

'Risperidone,' he said. 'Heavy-duty antipsychotic medication. But here's the thing – I don't have psychosis. I never have. This stuff has been keeping me docile, confused, dependent on Victoria for guidance and support.'

'Nathan, that's paranoid thinking—' Oliver started.

'Is it?' Nathan interrupted. 'Because I'm remembering things differently now. Things that don't match what Victoria told me about my episodes, my blackouts, my supposedly dangerous behaviour.'

He stepped closer to Oliver, who remained perfectly still on the sofa.

'I think Victoria's been working with someone. Someone who needed a patsy, someone who could be easily manipulated and controlled. Someone whose father was connected to the Garden Collective case in a way that made him a perfect target for revenge.'

'That's enough,' Belinda said firmly, reaching for her phone. 'Nathan, I think you should leave. You're clearly unwell.'

But Nathan was beyond listening now, replaced by a clarity that felt almost painful in its intensity.

'You know what I think?' he said to Oliver, his voice steady despite the adrenaline coursing through his veins. 'I think you've been planning this for a very long time. Getting close to our group, learning our weaknesses, figuring out how to destroy us one by one.'

Oliver's expression remained concerned, but Nathan

caught something else now – something akin to interest, or calculation.

'You're working with Victoria, aren't you?' Nathan pressed. 'She provided the psychological profiles, helped you understand how to manipulate each of us. Christ, she's the one who brought us all together, all those years back! She kept me medicated and confused so I'd make the perfect scapegoat when the time came to kill people.'

'Nathan, please,' Belinda whispered, backing towards the door.

'The timing was perfect,' Nathan continued, his voice growing stronger as the connections became clearer. 'Victoria calls me, tells me my medication needs adjusting, arranges to meet me. Next thing I know, I'm waking up with gaps in my memory and Daniel is dead.'

Oliver's mask of concern slipped.

'That's a very serious accusation,' he breathed. 'Victoria Lang is a respected psychologist. Why would she risk her career to help someone commit murder?'

'Because she has her own reasons for wanting us dead,' Nathan replied. 'Something connected to the Garden Collective, something that goes back thirty years.'

'And what's that?'

'I don't know what it is!' Nathan yelled in anger. 'If I did, I wouldn't be here!'

The room fell silent except for the sound of rain against the windows and Belinda's increasingly rapid breathing.

'Oh... you're very good at this,' Nathan said finally, his gaze locked on Oliver's face. 'Very calm, very reasonable. But you made one mistake.'

Oliver stood slowly, his movements controlled and deliberate. For the first time since Nathan had entered the flat, he looked genuinely uncomfortable.

'I think that's enough excitement for one evening,' he said, moving towards the door. 'Belinda, you should call the police. Nathan clearly needs professional help.'

'Don't worry,' Nathan called after him, his voice carrying a note of dark satisfaction. 'I'll make sure they know exactly who to look for when they investigate further.'

Oliver paused at the door, turning back to look at Nathan with a look that could have been pity or contempt – it was impossible to tell which.

'Good luck with that,' he said quietly, his tone suggesting he knew something Nathan didn't. Then he was gone, leaving behind only the echo of his footsteps on the stairs.

Belinda was dialling 999, her hands shaking as she spoke into the phone.

'Police? Yes, I need help. Nathan Hargreaves is in my flat. He's got a gun and he's been making threats and wild accusations. Please hurry.'

Nathan stood in the middle of the room, rain still dripping from his clothes onto Belinda's pristine carpet, understanding with perfect clarity that he'd walked directly into a trap. In minutes, the police would arrive. They'd find him exactly where someone wanted him – cornered, desperate, carrying evidence that would condemn him.

His phone buzzed in his pocket. A text message from the same unknown number. From "Daniel" once more.

> You're exactly where you need to be. Game over.

Nathan stared at the message, his mind racing. Someone had orchestrated this entire evening. Someone who knew he'd try to contact Belinda, who knew Oliver would be here, who wanted this confrontation to happen exactly as it had.

But there was something else, something that gave him a sliver of hope. Oliver had reacted when Nathan mentioned the Garden Collective. Just for a moment, his composure had cracked, revealing something cold and calculating underneath the concerned expression. Which meant Nathan was on the right track, even if he couldn't prove it yet.

'I'm sorry,' he said to Belinda, who was huddled by the door, phone pressed to her ear. 'I'm sorry you got dragged into this. But I need you to remember what happened here tonight. Really remember. Because I have a feeling the truth is going to matter more than anyone realises.'

He moved to the window, looking down at the roof below that descended into the narrow alley behind the building. A jump of two floors wasn't impossible, even in the rain.

'Nathan, don't,' Belinda pleaded. 'Please. Just wait for the police. Let them help you.'

'They're not coming to help me,' Nathan replied, already opening the window. 'They're coming to arrest me for murders I didn't commit. But maybe, just maybe, I still have time to find the actual killer before it's too late.'

The rain hit his face as he climbed out onto the ledge, the brick cold and slick under his hands. Behind him, he could hear Belinda crying, speaking frantically into the phone. Below, the alley stretched dark and empty, offering at least a temporary escape.

Hanging down and dropping to the garage rooftop below, Nathan Hargreaves disappeared into the London night, leaving behind only wet footprints, unanswered questions, and the growing certainty that the game he'd been playing for twenty years was far deadlier than any of them had realised.

Outside, in the shadow of a doorway across the street, a figure watched the police cars arrive, their blue lights cutting through the rain-soaked darkness.

Oliver Drake pulled out his phone and typed a brief message.

Phase complete. Target isolated and discredited.

Then he walked away into the night, his expression unreadable in the November rain, satisfied that everything was proceeding exactly according to plan.

19

OLD SCHOOL TIE

NATHAN HARGREAVES DUCKED INTO THE DOORWAY OF A convenience store, closed for the night but offering a sliver of shadow between street lights. Three hours since Belinda's apartment, three hours of sprinting through London's back streets like a rat in a maze, and the walls were closing in.

His phone no longer buzzed – the burner he'd used had joined his original phone; he'd thrown it into the Thames as he'd crossed onto the Southbank. He knew the police could track him with it, and that was the last thing he wanted. Besides, the messages from "Daniel" had given him panic attacks – much better now they were gone. The police thought he was a killer – armed, dangerous, a man whose bipolar disorder had finally snapped him into violence. The story wrote itself, neat as a headline.

He couldn't fault it; he would have believed it himself.

Nathan forced himself to move again, sticking to the railway arches of Southwark where the Victorian brickwork swallowed sound and the CCTV cameras had blind spots. Every police car made him freeze, and every helicopter sound sent him scrambling for cover. But his head was clearing with each step; somewhere out there, the real killer was watching this manhunt and smiling.

Billy Fitzwarren had been staring at his monitors for hours now, surviving on coffee and the kind of focused obsession that made him excellent at his job and terrible at relationships.

Shit. That reminds me. I should message Sam—

Oh shit. I was supposed to have dinner with Sam.

Taking a moment to text his boyfriend, apologising, but once more blaming the job, he returned to the screen. Sam would understand – he'd even worked with the team before, so he saw how it all worked.

He might not like it, but he saw.

The analysis results sprawled across three screens like a digital crime scene, each connection more damning than the last.

'Bloody hell,' he muttered to himself, cross-referencing university admission records with financial transaction logs. 'She actually did it.'

'Did what?' Bullman asked from Monroe's office door – she'd requisitioned it again but had been loitering with intent over the last hour, as if looking for something to do, and was currently talking to Declan, who now walked over to the screens to look.

'Victoria Lang didn't stumble across the Royal Court at Oxford,' Billy looked over to them. 'She manufactured them, piece by carefully orchestrated piece. I've traced the paper trail backwards through scholarship applications, student society formations, even dormitory room assignments – every single element influenced by strategic recommendations, anonymous donations, and what could only be described as social engineering on a professional scale.'

'She did this as a teenager?'

'I think she had help, but I can't see who from,' Billy muttered. 'Someone with sway had to be behind this. The scholarship committees are the smoking gun. Victoria managed to find someone connected to three different panels during her second year of A Levels, always with voting rights on applications from students whose parents had connections to the Garden Collective case. She'd identified her targets before they'd even applied to university.'

Billy pulled up Daniel Foster's application.

'Full scholarship, despite his family's wealth. Nathan Hargreaves had a partial scholarship for "innovative financial analysis techniques". Sean Acker had a military history bursary that had been created specifically for his application, as he'd technically "served" with the Royal Marines.'

'One by one, she gathered them like chess pieces,' Bullman said, reading the documents. 'Positioning them exactly where she wanted them.'

And it wasn't just the Universities. The evidence was overwhelming once Billy understood the pattern. Rachel Peterson hadn't developed her interest in pharmaceutical research naturally – she'd been steered towards it through a series of "coincidental" internship opportunities, all at companies where Victoria had professional connections somehow. Nathan's medical records painted an even darker picture; years of carefully calibrated medication adjustments that enhanced his bipolar symptoms whilst creating a complete dependency on Victoria's guidance. Billy cross-referenced prescription dates with significant events in Nathan's life – every promotion, every relationship milestone, every moment when Nathan might have started asking uncomfortable questions, there was a corresponding medication change, including dosage increases that coincided with the anniversary of Daniel's death, and new prescriptions that appeared whenever Nathan started questioning his memory gaps or expressing doubts about his treatment.

'Jesus,' Billy whispered, reading through years of systematic psychological manipulation. 'She's been running a human experiment.'

'But how?' Declan, asked. 'Someone would have had to connect to a dozen different companies and agencies, all ...'

He stopped.

'Good God, it's Emmy Clarke, not Victoria Lang.'

Billy glanced around, confused, and Declan recalled what had been said when he spoke to Anthony Farringdon about her.

'Fearless little thing. Could slip into places others couldn't – board meetings, private clubs, property developers' offices. Gathered intelligence that seemed impossible to obtain, used contacts and favours nobody realised she was owed.'

'She had debts owed across London to her,' he said. 'What if Emmy – Bertie – whatever she called herself here, was pulling the strings? She still helped Shipman, and in return ...'

'He helped her,' Billy nodded as he read through more notes. 'The others have been controlled through different methods but with the same precision. Alex Chen's technology expertise was cultivated and directed towards projects that served Victoria's agenda – including ...'

Billy's eyes widened.

'Including facial recognition software, that could have been used to doctor the bodycam footage. Even their social relationships were orchestrated. I've traced bank transfers, cross-referenced social media posts, mapped out twenty years of "coincidental" encounters and chance meetings. The Royal Court game itself? It's Victoria's masterpiece – a tradition that kept the group connected over twenty years whilst providing her with detailed psychological profiles, personal vulnerabilities, and operational intelligence.'

'But why the forfeits?' Declan asked. 'She could have let things go.'

'She needed an excuse to leave,' Bullman replied. 'And maybe she wanted to see what happened?'

'Did anything Farringdon gave us help?' Declan asked.

'I've got phone intercepts going back years, which I've been able to compare to notes my great uncle gave me, showing what's bollocks and what's not. Email monitoring through compromised accounts.' Billy rattled off a list now, counting off his fingers. 'Location tracking via social media posts and financial transactions. Twenty bloody years of watching, planning, and preparing.'

'Anything on the video yet?'

'No, but I have something else.' Billy pulled up another screen. 'The silencer was bought with a card in the name of Nathan Hargreaves.'

'How? I thought this was impossible without a licence?'

'Grey area store,' Billy leant back. 'Countries like the Czech Republic, Slovakia, or parts of the Baltics have laxer rules on gun parts. A suppressor, or a silencer, can be bought without a firearms licence in some of those countries and shipped as a "metal tube" or "machined part". These are sometimes advertised as solvent traps, barrel extensions or replica props.'

'So, Nathan bought it from one of these?'

Billy nodded.

'I checked with Interpol, found other suppressors linked to the same supplier, and used in European shootings,' he explained. 'Once I had the supplier, I could reverse the details. They were happy to provide details for the "airsoft replica" they sent. Nathan apparently bought it with a pay-as-you-go Visa card, topped up with cash, and had it sent to his office.'

He pulled up a scanned receipt. On it was a signature.

'This is Nathan's proof of acceptance.' Billy pointed at the image. 'But that's not his signature.'

'So, someone could have set him up,' Bullman mused. 'That or he was just covering his tracks.'

'We'll know in the next hour as I'm checking CCTV of when it was bought,' Billy replied, but stopped as his phone buzzed, rising as he saw the message. 'Enough time to fix this other thorn in my side.'

'Your father?'

'My father.' Billy grabbed his coat and left the office.

'You know, he seems to be taking his family issues fairly well,' Bullman commented, before walking back into her office.

The Reform Club after hours felt like a mausoleum of power – all marble and shadows and the weight of centuries pressing down on anyone who didn't belong. Billy climbed the grand staircase, nodding to members who recognised him but couldn't quite place the context.

Third floor. Library. Where deals were made and legacies decided.

Edward Fitzwarren sat in a leather armchair that had probably hosted Prime Ministers, reading legal documents with the focused attention of a man running out of options. Billy's father looked every inch the aristocrat – silver hair perfectly styled, Savile Row suit immaculate even at this hour, brandy snifter held like a sceptre.

'William,' he glanced up as Billy approached. 'I wondered if you'd come.'

'After seventeen missed calls? Couldn't ignore the royal summons forever.'

Edward gestured to the opposite chair.

'Sit. We need to discuss your future.'

Billy remained standing.

'My future, or your problems?'

'Both, as it happens,' Edward's tone held that particular upper-class chill which could freeze champagne. 'The situation with the board has become... complex.'

'The scandal you manufactured to force my hand, you mean?'

Edward's eyebrows rose fractionally, and a moment of surprise was replaced by irritation.

'Chivalry.'

'Uncle Chivalry only confirmed what I'd already worked out. You want me to use my supposed influence with Charles Baker to clean up whatever mess you've actually made.'

'And will you?'

Billy looked around the library – mahogany shelves, oil

paintings of dead politicians, the accumulated weight of tradition and compromise.

Then he smiled.

'No.'

The word carried clearly through the library's hushed atmosphere. Several members looked up from their newspapers, recognising the tone if not the content of a family drama unfolding.

'I won't help you manipulate the system,' Billy continued, his voice gaining strength. 'I won't be your political fixer. And I certainly won't be blackmailed into preserving your comfortable retirement.'

'William, lower your voice—'

'Why?' Billy turned to address the room. 'Embarrassed by your son's lack of breeding? Worried about what the other members might think?'

'Sir, please—' A club steward approached nervously.

'It's fine,' Billy said cheerfully. 'Just a family discussion about hereditary responsibility. You must have them here all the time – *noblesse oblige* and all that.'

Edward's face had gone very still.

'Sit down. Now.'

'I'll stand, thanks.' Billy's grin widened. 'Better acoustics for what I'm about to say.'

The library had gone quiet now, thirty-odd members pretending to read whilst listening to every word.

'You see, Father, I've decided about the inheritance. The title, the estates, the responsibilities you've been so eager to escape – I'll take them. *All* of them.'

Edward leant forward.

'William, you don't understand what that means—'

'I understand perfectly,' Billy's voice carried to every

corner of the room now. 'It means taking responsibility instead of avoiding it. Managing estates properly instead of bleeding them dry. Using the position to help people instead of hiding behind it.'

'The financial obligations alone—'

'Are about to become manageable by someone who actually manages them.' Billy pulled out his phone, displaying spreadsheets. 'I've reviewed the publicly available records. You've been treating the estate like your personal bank account for years.'

A murmur ran through the assembled members. Financial impropriety was the kind of scandal that transcended party lines, and everyone there now wanted to know more.

'Sir, if you could please—' the steward tried again.

'Oh, I'm nearly finished.' Billy pocketed his phone. 'Just explaining to my father that *Detective Sergeant The Lord William Fitzwarren, Viscount Fitzwarren* has different priorities than his predecessor.'

The title hung in the air like a challenge. Edward's composed face cracked slightly.

'You can't be serious.'

'Dead serious. Just like you've wanted me to be for years, right? Next week I'll be a police officer who holds a hereditary title. With all the resources that title provides and none of the traditional obligations to protect family reputation above justice.'

Billy turned towards the door, then paused for maximum effect.

'Oh and, Father? Your scandal – manufactured or real – is your problem to solve. The Fitzwarren name is no longer available for purchase.'

He walked out to absolute silence, leaving Edward alone

with thirty witnesses to his son's very public rejection of everything the Reform Club represented.

The quiet stretched until someone cleared their throat.

'Well,' a voice said from the corner. 'That was refreshing.'

Another member chuckled. 'About time someone told the truth in here.'

Edward Fitzwarren sat alone, staring at legal documents that had suddenly become irrelevant. Around him, the club's members returned to their newspapers and brandy, but the atmosphere had shifted. His son's performance had been theatrical, deliberate, and utterly devastating.

After a long moment, Edward began to laugh. Quietly at first, then building to genuine amusement that drew stares from across the room.

'Sir?' The steward approached cautiously.

'It's fine,' Edward said, wiping his eyes. 'Just... proud of my son, actually. He's got more spine than I gave him credit for.'

BILLY EMERGED FROM THE REFORM CLUB FEELING LIKE HE'D shed twenty-seven years of accumulated expectations. The November air cut through his shirt, sharp and clean after the stifling atmosphere of inherited privilege and gentlemen's agreements.

Detective Sergeant The Lord William Fitzwarren, Viscount Fitzwarren.

He'd definitely need new business cards. Probably have to get them printed on proper paper stock now.

He was looking for a taxi to take him back to Temple Inn

when a figure stepped from the shadows between streetlights.

'DS Fitzwarren... Billy ...?'

Billy's hand moved instinctively towards his extendable baton before recognition stopped him cold. Nathan Hargreaves looked like London had chewed him up and spat him back out: expensive suit torn and filthy, hair matted against his skull, eyes wild with the particular desperation of a hunted animal. But beneath the panic, there was something else. A clarity that Billy hadn't seen in any of their previous interactions – although these had been years ago and at events Rufus had organised.

'Nathan. God, man, you look terrible.'

'Feel worse.' Nathan stepped closer, hands clearly visible and movements careful, non-threatening. 'But I need your help.'

'And why would I help?'

'You knew Rufus before he died. He always talked about the old school networks. How they protected each other, covered things up, made problems disappear,' Nathan's voice was hoarse from hours of running and hiding, but his words came with startling precision. 'I'm hoping you still have access to that world. Because I'm about to be arrested for murders I didn't commit, and someone's been planning this for years.'

Three hours ago, Billy would have called for backup immediately. Nathan was wanted for multiple homicides, armed and dangerous according to the police bulletins. But three hours ago, Billy hadn't known about Victoria's systematic psychological manipulation.

'The medication,' Billy said quietly. 'Victoria was controlling you through your treatment.'

Nathan's face crumpled with relief so profound it was painful to watch.

'You know. Thank God, you actually know.'

'I've been analysing the case, tracking financial connections, mapping communication patterns.' Billy glanced around, checking for police presence. 'Victoria's been orchestrating this since university. The entire Royal Court formation, your psychological treatment, probably the murders themselves.'

'She's working with someone,' Nathan said urgently, his voice gaining strength as he realised he was finally being believed. 'Oliver Drake. He's not who he claims to be. There's something about his background, his family connections to the old cases—'

Billy's phone buzzed insistently.

FACIAL RECOGNITION COMPLETE

He pulled up the attached file, glanced at the screen, and nodded to himself.

'Nathan,' his voice was carefully controlled, the tone he used when delivering news that would change everything. 'The bodycam footage from Sean's murder – the one in your safe? It showed footage of you killing Sean.'

'I didn't do it,' Nathan almost whined. 'I didn't take the bodycam.'

'I know,' Billy gave a small smile, softening his voice. 'I've been running digital forensic analysis on it.'

Nathan froze as Billy held up his phone, showing the analysis results in stark technical detail.

'It's fake. Professional-grade facial replacement technology. Sophisticated enough to fool the average person, but not quite good enough to fool someone who knows what to look for.'

'Then who—' Nathan's voice caught, hope and terror warring in his expression.

Billy played the revised footage, and the two of them, standing outside the Reform Club, watched on Billy's screen as Sean Acker was shot, the real killer moving into shot.

Billy paused the image.

'Oliver Drake,' Nathan said coldly. 'He did this.'

'He killed Sean Acker, then used advanced deepfake technology to superimpose your face over his own in the footage,' Billy said. 'Even though you ran, this and the Victoria connection? It shows you're a patsy. And we can help.'

Nathan staggered slightly, gripping a nearby car for support, as the weight of vindication and horror crashed over him simultaneously.

'I knew it. I bloody well knew someone was setting me up, but I couldn't prove it. Every time I tried to think clearly, the medication would kick in and I'd start doubting myself.'

'That was the point.' Billy pocketed his phone, decision made. 'Victoria's been running a long-term psychological manipulation programme. You were the perfect patsy – someone with a documented mental health condition who could be controlled through medication and made to look guilty when the time came. We need to get to Temple Inn – convince the team, show them the evidence.'

'They'll arrest me the moment I walk through the door.'

'Not if I'm with you.' Billy straightened his shoulders, feeling the weight of his new title and the responsibilities it carried. '*Detective Sergeant The Lord William Fitzwarren, Viscount Fitzwarren* has certain advantages when it comes to being believed by superior officers. Amazing how a hereditary title opens doors, even in modern policing.'

'Wait, your name is what?' Nathan managed a weak smile despite everything. 'That's the most pretentious thing I've ever heard.'

'Just wait until I start wearing the family signet ring.' Billy headed towards an approaching cab, waving his hand to stop it. 'By the way, though – how did you know I'd be here?'

Nathan gave a weak smile.

'I've been following you since you left Temple Inn,' he said. 'Waiting for the right moment.'

'Well it's a good job you did,' Billy grinned. 'Come on. Time to crash a very exclusive party, although I suspect Victoria Lang has been waiting for us to make exactly this move.'

20

WALK IN

THE DESK SERGEANT AT TEMPLE INN LOOKED UP FROM HIS crossword as Billy Fitzwarren walked through the front doors, and then nearly choked on his tea when he saw who was following behind.

'Bloody hell, Billy,' Sergeant Mastakin muttered. 'That's Nathan Hargreaves.'

'It is indeed,' Billy replied calmly. 'And he's here voluntarily to assist with inquiries.'

'He's wanted for—'

'Multiple murders, yes.' Billy's tone carried unusual authority. 'But I've got evidence he's been framed. Digital forensics that'll blow the case wide open.'

Mastakin stared at Nathan, who stood with his hands clearly visible and an expression of exhausted resignation, then at Billy, who looked like he'd just inherited something significant and was deciding what to do with it.

'Your funeral,' Mastakin said finally, reaching for the phone to buzz them through. 'But when this goes tits up, I never saw either of you.'

As they climbed the stairs towards the main office, Nathan finally spoke.

'Are we going to talk about *Detective Sergeant The Lord William Fitzwarren, Viscount Fitzwarren*?'

'Don't start,' Billy warned. 'I'm still getting used to it myself.'

'How exactly does that work? Practically, I mean.'

'No idea. But hopefully right now it opens doors and makes people listen when they might otherwise shoot first and ask questions later.'

The main office of the Last Chance Saloon was lit like a war room, with everyone now in, aside from Declan who was visibly absent from the proceedings. Monroe looked up from a spread of documents as they entered, his expression shifting from surprise to calculation as he saw Nathan.

'Where's Declan, Guv?' Billy asked, noting the DCI's absence.

'Gone to have a word with an "old friend",' Monroe replied curtly. 'He'll catch up with us later. Christ, Billy. What have you done?'

'Brought you the one person who can prove Victoria Lang is behind everything,' Billy replied, guiding Nathan towards the briefing room. 'And the evidence to back it up.'

De'Geer was already reaching for a phone to call for backup, but Billy held up a hand.

'Don't, please. Let's hear what we have to say first.'

'He's wanted for—'

'Multiple murders he didn't commit, I know,' Billy finished. 'I've got digital forensic proof that the bodycam footage was manipulated. Professional-grade deepfake technology used to superimpose Nathan's face over the actual killer.'

The office went quiet. Anjli looked up from her desk, Doctor Marcos paused in her examination of evidence bags, even Bullman said nothing from the office doorway.

'Show me,' Monroe said. 'Everyone. Briefing room. Now.'

'What about Declan?' Anjli asked.

'We'll fill him in later,' Monroe decided. 'Until then, Mister Hargreaves can pretend to be him.'

Billy connected his laptop to the main plasma screen as the team gathered – Anjli from her desk, Doctor Marcos with her paperwork, De'Geer taking a call but apparently on hold, Cooper from the canteen, a fresh coffee in hand, and Monroe and Bullman beside the door.

Billy brought up the bodycam footage, playing it through once at normal speed.

'This is what we found in Nathan's safe,' Billy explained. 'Watch Nathan's face. It's him, right? Dead to rights. Lock him up, throw away the key, do not pass Go, do not collect two hundred pounds.'

He played it again, this time with his analysis overlays showing facial recognition data, biometric inconsistencies, digital artefacts.

'Now watch this,' Billy clicked to a new window. 'The real killer.'

On screen, the footage played again, but this time Oliver Drake's face was clearly visible as he shot Sean Acker, squirted the water pistol and unclipped the bodycam, as Nathan sat heavily on one of the briefing room chairs, looking like a man who'd been carrying the weight of the world and finally found somewhere to set it down.

'I've been trying to tell someone this,' he whispered. 'But every time I tried to think clearly, the medication would kick in, and I'd start doubting myself.'

'The medication Victoria prescribed,' Anjli said, understanding dawning in her voice.

'Carefully calibrated to enhance my bipolar symptoms whilst creating dependency on her guidance,' Nathan nodded. 'She's been controlling me for years, since before Daniel died.'

'Something else.' Billy opened up another folder, showing a shop CCTV. On it was a man, facing away from the camera as he bought something from the counter. It was hard to work out who it was, but the one thing that was obvious was that it wasn't Nathan Hargreaves. 'This is "Nathan" putting money on the card he bought the silencer on. A silencer that arrived at his office a week later.'

'And was signed for by someone who intercepted it, who likely worked at the office.' Monroe pulled up a chair across from Nathan, his expression serious but no longer hostile. The evidence on the screen was compelling, and Nathan's lucidity was a stark contrast to the paranoid, medicated man they'd interviewed before. 'Tell us about Oliver Drake. How long have you known him?'

'About eighteen months. He started working at Carrington-Howe as a junior analyst, seemed keen. I even interviewed him for the job and he asked good questions. When we needed someone to replace Daniel in the game, Belinda suggested him.'

'Belinda's idea?'

'So she claimed. But looking back ...' Nathan rubbed his face with both hands. 'Victoria and Belinda had been spending time together. Coffee meetings, shopping trips. I assumed it was innocent friendship, but now I'm wondering if Victoria was manipulating her too. God, she probably told him how to act in the interview, giving the answers she knew I'd look for.'

Monroe glanced back at the screen, his expression growing darker by the minute.

'This is sophisticated work. The kind of video manipulation that requires professional equipment and expertise. Where would Oliver get access to this technology?'

'Justin Kelly's company,' Billy replied, bringing up another screen showing corporate connections and financial flows. 'I've been tracing the links. Victoria most likely steered Justin towards developing facial recognition software years ago. His company has all the tools needed for this kind of manipulation.'

'So, Justin is involved too?'

'Unwittingly, I think. Victoria's been playing a very long game, positioning people like chess pieces. Twenty years of careful manipulation, steering careers, creating dependencies, building the perfect setup for revenge.'

'For what? Being children of people connected?' Monroe frowned. 'No, laddie, I don't see that. There has to be more.'

'If it comes out, then everything comes out,' Billy replied. 'The whole conspiracy. Maybe she wants to take down the whole establishment?'

'But why now?'

'Maybe she was building to a particular point but this being the last year forced her hand?' Billy offered. 'Or maybe something happened with Emmy Clarke that pushed the deadline forward?'

Doctor Marcos looked up from her paperwork now.

'The playing cards found on the victims. There were special decks made for the group's anniversary?'

'Ten years ago. Black cardstock with silver and gold ink,' Billy nodded.

'The cards on Sean and Dirk were fresh reprints,' Doctor Marcos continued. 'But Rachel's Queen of Clubs was original – aged ink, wear patterns from being handled over years. Someone had to use their own card for Rachel, as the killing wasn't planned in advance like the others.'

Monroe was studying the timeline displayed on Billy's screens, tracing connections between events.

'Rachel worked in pharmaceuticals. She would have recognised the signs of medication manipulation if she'd seen Nathan's prescription history.'

'She did more than recognise it,' Nathan mumbled. 'Two weeks ago, she suggested I talk to Victoria about trying newer medications. Said the pharmaceutical industry was developing better treatments for bipolar disorder. I mentioned it to Victoria during our next session.'

'And Victoria realised Rachel was getting too close,' Anjli said.

'So, she eliminated the threat using her own playing card,' Doctor Marcos added. 'Then tried to create a fire to take out her office and remove the evidence.'

'Which the fire brigade stopped too early,' Anjli replied. 'All designed to frame the perfect patsy.'

'The patsy's you,' Monroe smiled at Nathan.

'There's something else,' Nathan said. 'The night Daniel died. I was supposed to meet him, but Victoria called and said my medication needed adjusting. She wanted to see me immediately for an emergency session. I took what she gave me but woke up the next morning with no clear memory of the evening. I woke up to a ton of messages – Daniel was dead.'

'You think she killed him too?'

'I think she pushed him over the edge. Used her psychological training to manipulate him into suicide. Daniel was already struggling with the forfeit, with being outed, likely suggestions by her to get him into this state of mind. Victoria would have known exactly what to say, how to make him feel like he had no other choice.'

Monroe stood, pacing to the window overlooking Temple Inn's courtyard. The car park below was empty except for patrol cars and the occasional late-night pedestrian. London at its most peaceful, unaware of the conspiracy that had been festering in its heart for decades.

'The question now is what Victoria and Oliver are planning next. They've successfully framed you, eliminated the people most likely to expose them and positioned themselves as helpful witnesses assisting with the investigation.'

'They think they've won,' Anjli said.

'Which gives us an advantage, lassie,' Monroe added with a predatory smile. 'They don't know we've figured it out.'

Billy was already pulling up current surveillance data, monitoring systems he'd been running in the background throughout the investigation.

'I've been tracking communications, financial movements, social media activity. There's been a spike in encrypted messaging between several Royal Court members in the last few hours.'

'Can you access the messages?' Monroe asked.

'The encryption's too strong, but ...' Billy paused, looking at Nathan. 'You're still in the WhatsApp group, aren't you?'

Nathan's face fell.

'I threw my phone in the Thames hours ago. I thought the police were tracking me.'

Billy thought for a moment, then pulled out his own phone.

'I can access the group through the web interface if I have your login details.'

'I can't remember my password.'

'I don't need it, just your permission,' Billy was already typing as he grinned back.

'Fine, yes, I give permission.'

Billy continued typing, and within moments accessed Nathan's WhatsApp web interface on his laptop, projecting it onto the main screen.

'Victoria's been messaging everyone. Says she's heard from DCI Walsh, who wants to meet at Shadwell Foundry. Says "the police have new evidence on Nathan's plot, need to show it personally and keep us together".'

'How many responses?' Monroe asked.

'Four confirmations so far. Belinda, Gary, Alex, Daryl. They're all heading there now.'

'Right then,' Monroe said after a moment. 'Looks like we're going on a trip. Billy, what else can you find on Oliver?'

Billy was already typing, pulling up deeper records, cross-referencing databases that required elevated access permissions.

'I've been focusing on his employment history, family records, birth certificates... Oliver Drake, born 1994... but there's something odd here. His ID shows his father as Michael Drake, but there's a surname change record for both Michael and Oliver from when Oliver was eighteen months old.'

'A surname change?' Nathan leant forward. 'What's the original name?'

Billy kept reading as the records populated his screen.

'I had to unseal records. These had been hidden deep, and honestly? Anyone else would have missed them.'

'Aye, we all know you're a wee bloody genius, laddie. What does it say?'

'It says his name was Oliver Thompson. His biological father is listed as Michael Thompson. Mother... Linda Gardner.'

The room went dead quiet.

'Gardner,' Monroe said slowly. 'Michael Thompson was Linda Gardner's partner – the woman who was critically injured in the Bell Foundry collapse and died two years later from complications during childbirth.'

Nathan sat back in his chair as if he'd been physically struck.

'That's why he joined the game. That's why he got close to us all. He's not just working with Victoria – this is personal revenge for his mother's death.'

Billy was still typing, pulling up more records, tracing connections that had been hidden for thirty years behind sealed files and changed names.

'Michael changed his surname to Drake a couple of years later, probably found enemies of the Collective targeting him. Moved to Scotland with the baby, raised Oliver away from London and everything connected to the Garden Collective. But look at this – Oliver applied to transfer to London when he turned eighteen. Specifically requested work placements in the financial sector.'

'He's been planning this since he was a teenager,' Monroe realised.

'Likely from when Victoria found him,' Nathan added. 'Or he found her. Two people with their own reasons for wanting revenge on the families connected to the Garden Collective case.'

Billy pulled up more records, his expression growing increasingly grim.

'Michael Drake died two years ago. Cancer. That's when Oliver moved back to London permanently, got the job at Carrington-Howe through a series of very convenient recommendations. The timing matches exactly with when Victoria started speeding up her surveillance of the Royal Court members.'

'Two years to plan, to infiltrate, to gain our trust,' Nathan shook his head. 'And I helped him do it. I vouched for him, brought him into the building, gave him access to everything he needed to destroy us all.'

Doctor Marcos looked up from her evidence bags.

'The finials from Dirk's storage unit – if Oliver needed metal from the Bell Foundry for the murder weapons, he would have known Dirk had them. Easy enough to steal one set when Dirk trusted him.'

'Poetic justice,' Monroe said grimly. 'Using the foundry's own metal to kill the children of the people he blamed for his mother's death. But with no proof ...'

De'Geer, finishing his call and hearing this, waved to grab everyone's attention from the other office.

'We might have that, Guv,' he said. 'Kingston forensics have been going over everything they found in Dirk's lockup – apparently they just found a bodycam high in a corner. Same make as Sean's, been left on for days and filming like a security camera.'

'How quick can they get it to us?'

'I think they want to examine it themselves,' De'Geer's expression showed he wasn't a fan of this. 'I'm going to pop over and show them the errors of their ways.'

'Aye, do that and then pass it to Billy.' Monroe looked over to Billy, but he wasn't even paying attention, cross-referencing communication patterns, financial records, and digital footprints spanning years.

'They've been in contact for at least three years,' Billy said, stunned. 'Encrypted communications, financial transfers, shared resources. It'll take me weeks to decrypt it all, but I can tell you just by skimming, that this isn't just revenge – it's been a coordinated campaign with multiple phases and contingency plans.'

'But why now?' Anjli asked. 'Why wait twenty years and then strike so quickly?'

Monroe was studying the timeline on Billy's screens, pieces falling into place.

'Patrick's death. When Victoria found out he wasn't her real father, that he'd kept her from Emmy all those years, it broke something in her. She'd idolised him. And Emmy,' Monroe added thoughtfully. 'If she's got dementia now, she might have started forgetting what she'd set in motion. Started talking to us about her own plan without realising it. And Nathan was the perfect patsy,' Monroe added. 'Someone with a documented mental health condition, access to all the potential victims and a dependency relationship with Victoria that made him easy to control and manipulate.'

Billy pulled up a blueprint of the Shadwell Bell Foundry, held empty for decades.

'If Oliver's spent years planning this, he won't have overlooked security measures or escape routes,' he said. 'And if

Victoria's been manipulating people for decades, she'll have contingency plans for every possible scenario.'

'Except the scenario where a handsome Scot and his team of misfit toys crash their revenge party,' Monroe smiled.

'Why, do you know a handsome Scot who could do that?' Doctor Marcos smiled sweetly at her husband.

'Armed response?' Anjli asked.

'Nathan has a gun,' De'Geer pointed out.

Monroe glanced at the evidence laid out on the tables, particularly at Sean's custom water pistol in its evidence bag, and smiled.

'Aye,' he nodded. 'And so he does. Let's go remind Victoria Lang and Oliver Drake that revenge is a game two can play. And we've had more practice.'

Norman Shipman emerged from the Houses of Parliament, deep in conversation with two backbench MPs about committee assignments and constituency matters, the kind of mundane political business that kept Westminster functioning whilst larger conspiracies played out in its shadows.

He spotted Declan Walsh immediately – a figure waiting by the Thames Embankment, hands in his coat pockets, watching the building.

'Gentlemen,' Shipman said to his colleagues. 'I'll catch up with you later. Something's come up.'

The MPs nodded and continued towards their cars, leaving Shipman alone with whatever reckoning Declan Walsh represented. He walked slowly towards the detective, each step deliberate.

'We need to talk about Emmy Clarke,' Declan said without preamble as Shipman approached.

'I wondered when you'd work it out,' Shipman replied quietly. 'Though I'd hoped it would take longer.'

'You never controlled Emmy Clarke, did you? She controlled you.'

Shipman's laugh was hollow, bitter.

'Controlled? That's putting it mildly. Emmy Clarke's been pulling strings in Westminster for thirty years, and I've been dancing to her tune like a bloody marionette.'

'The Garden Collective case. The cover-up. The separation from her daughter.'

'All Emmy's idea. She wanted revenge on Elizabeth Gardner for manipulating her daughter Linda into the foundry bombing – took that death personally, as Emmy had passed doctored intelligence that caused the collapse. Said the best way to hurt Elizabeth was to make sure her followers paid the price whilst the real architects walked free.'

He sighed.

'But the problem was, Emmy didn't remember that she was the one who did this, and over the years created a different narrative, one based around the Collective doing this, and screwing over Elizabeth.'

Declan felt pieces clicking into place; a conspiracy far more complex than anyone had imagined.

'She's been in contact with Victoria all along, hasn't she? Her daughter. Patrick never knew.'

'Patrick thought he was protecting them both by keeping them apart. Noble bastard never realised Emmy had found ways around his surveillance within months of the separation.' Shipman pulled out a hip flask. 'Emmy fed Victoria information about how the families had screwed over the

Gardners, even though it'd been her, guided her education, helped her get into a position to take revenge on the families connected to the case, even provided all the assistance – with my reluctant help, of course – to aim the children of every target she could find at the same University.'

'Twenty years of planning.'

'Thirty,' Shipman corrected. 'Emmy's been building this since Linda Gardner died. Patient as death itself, that woman. And twice as dangerous.'

'What does she have on you?'

Shipman's smile was grim.

'Everything. Financial irregularities, planning corruptions, sexual indiscretions, political manipulations spanning three decades. Enough to destroy not just my career but my entire legacy. She's been collecting evidence since we first brought her in, and I've been her grateful servant ever since.'

Declan stared in horror at Shipman.

'And your career was worth these deaths?' he snarled. 'Worth keeping secret all these years?'

'Don't be so bloody naïve!' Shipman shouted back. 'What choice did I have? Resign? I'd lose the safety I have here! I'd be eaten by wolves! If I wasn't of any use to her, I'd be dead by the end of the month!'

'And now?'

'Now she's losing her mind and cashing in her chips. Victoria's finishing what Emmy started, and I'm powerless to stop it.'

Declan studied the older man, seeing not the manipulative politician he'd expected, but a broken figure trapped by decades of willing, and brutal compromise.

'Not powerless. Complicit. You've been helping them all along.'

'I've been surviving,' Shipman corrected. 'Something you'll understand when Emmy Clarke decides you know too much. You know how people thought she was manic, bipolar? Well, we had someone do a full psych report on her a few years back. She didn't know.'

'And?'

'She's not bipolar. She has Frontotemporal Dementia.'

'That doesn't sound like one of the nice things to get.'

'It's not. It's rare, but can definitely hit in your thirties, especially the behavioural variant, that's the one where personality and emotional control break down first. It's not like Alzheimer's, where memory goes. With this, people often start getting really impulsive, aggressive, or socially inappropriate, and everyone thinks it's some kind of breakdown or bipolar episode at first,' Shipman explained. 'In fact, a lot of younger patients get misdiagnosed for years – they're told it's depression, bipolar, borderline personality, or even substance abuse. But it's actually their brain changing. The damage hits the frontal and temporal lobes, the parts that control decision-making, empathy, inhibition – so you can get someone who was totally calm and responsible suddenly becoming reckless, angry, or even dangerous. You know, when you become someone in the family who just "went off the rails" and was never the same.'

'So, instead of being bipolar, she was some kind of borderline psychotic? And you just let her do what she wanted for years?'

'What could I do?' Shipman shrugged. 'There was even a point where she realised the Tories were on the way out and she still needed me in power. She was the one that made me swap sides!'

'And you never told my father?'

'Never.'

Declan stared at Shipman, forcing back the urge to punch him in the teeth.

'You escaped justice with the *Magpies* case,' he hissed. 'But now your debts are being called in. Time to accept what you owe and help us stop this.'

'And then what?'

Declan didn't answer. He didn't need to.

21

WHOM THE BELL TOLLS

THE UPPER FLOOR OF THE OLD BELL FOUNDRY HAD BEEN rebuilt in the late nineties, steel beams and modern concrete replacing the Victorian ironwork that had given way thirty years earlier. But the walls still held their secrets – brick and mortar that had witnessed three deaths and a conspiracy that had shaped decades of lies.

Victoria Lang stood at the centre of the restored floor, her composure perfect despite the circumstances that had brought them all here. Around her, the surviving members of the Royal Court sat in a rough circle on mismatched chairs someone had dragged up from the ground floor. The atmosphere was thick with tension and unspoken questions.

'I know this feels dramatic,' Victoria said, her voice carrying the authority of someone accustomed to being listened to. 'But after everything that's happened – Sean, Rachel, Dirk – we needed somewhere private to talk.'

Belinda Morris shifted uncomfortably in her chair, glancing towards the windows that looked out over London's industrial landscape.

'Why here, though? This place gives me the creeps.'

'Because it's where it all started,' Victoria replied simply. 'The Garden Collective. The connections between our families. Everything that's been happening traces back to this building.'

Gary Webb adjusted his glasses, his lawyer's mind already working through implications.

'What connections? My family had nothing to do with any environmental protesters.'

'Didn't they?' Victoria's smile was patient, almost maternal. 'Your father worked on the financial law side with Harold Hargreaves. Helped structure the legal frameworks that allowed certain people to profit from the tragedy.'

'That's his job. That's what solicitors do.'

'Including the solicitors that followed the collapse of this building,' Victoria continued. 'Three people died here, Gary. Your father made sure the right people were blamed and the wrong people walked free.'

The silence that followed was broken only by the sound of wind through the building's broken windows. Alex Chen, who'd been quiet since arriving, finally spoke up.

'You're saying our parents were *all* connected to what happened here?'

'More than connected,' Victoria replied. 'They were instrumental. The collapse wasn't an accident – it was sabotage by radical elements within the Garden Collective who wanted martyrs for their cause. But the aftermath, the cover-up, the people who profited from the tragedy – that involved all your families.'

Oliver Drake, who'd been sitting slightly apart from the others, leant forward with the expression of concerned interest he'd perfected over the years. 'That's a serious accusation, Victoria, and I hear a lot of "your" in it, and not "our". Do you have proof?'

'I have thirty years of research,' Victoria replied, pulling a folder from her bag. 'Documents, witness statements, financial records. The Garden Collective was infiltrated from the beginning by government informants. The collapse was allowed to happen because certain people stood to profit from it.'

She opened the folder, spreading papers across the wooden floor.

'Wait,' Belinda interrupted, looking confused. 'Where are the police? You said they were coming, that we needed protection—'

'They're positioned outside,' Victoria replied smoothly. 'But they need concrete evidence before they can act. That's why we're here – to identify the killer amongst us so they can make an arrest that will stick in court.'

'Bullshit,' Gary muttered. 'None of this is admissible without the presence of the police. And besides, Nathan's the killer.'

'He's the prime suspect. We need to make sure they're correct,' Victoria replied calmly. 'Harold Hargreaves – Nathan's father – had planning applications ready before the building even fell. Thomas Collins – that's Daryl's family – handled the financial arrangements that cleaned up the money afterwards. The Webbs, the Chens, the Kellys – all your families played their parts.'

Daryl Collins, who'd been staring at the floor, looked up sharply.

'My father was an accountant. He didn't kill anyone.'

'He didn't need to. Money laundering after the fact was just as valuable to the conspiracy,' Victoria's voice remained calm, professional. 'Three people died in this room, and within months, your families were all richer for it.'

'The building couldn't be sold,' Gary replied. 'I remember this place. It was given some kind of Grade listing that stopped it being built on, so where did the money come from?'

'The government, and hush money,' Victoria's eyes were wide now as she spewed out the words. 'The Government paid Hargreaves, and helped him build his business. They knew the truth, and they knew he could destroy them.'

'Bullshit,' Gary repeated.

Christopher Wilson, tall and awkward in his chair, raised a trembling hand like a schoolboy.

'My dad was building security. How does that connect to any of this?'

'Security reports, Christopher. False testimonies about structural integrity, access logs that were altered or destroyed. Your father helped cover up the evidence of sabotage.'

Justin Kelly had gone very pale.

'This is insane. You're talking about a conspiracy involving dozens of people.'

'Not dozens,' Victoria corrected. 'A very select group who knew exactly what they were doing and exactly how much they stood to gain.'

The folder contained photocopied documents, newspaper clippings, what appeared to be official government papers with significant sections redacted. Victoria spread them out methodically, building her case like the psychologist she was.

'The woman who was caught in, and died after the collapse – Linda Gardner – she'd tried to warn people. She knew the building had been sabotaged, tried to evacuate others before the floor gave way. She was critically injured saving lives and died in hospital from internal complications during childbirth two years later. As you can see, the pain and death didn't just end that night. Technically, she was the fourth – it just took a while.'

Oliver's expression remained concerned, sympathetic, but something flickered behind his eyes.

'That's tragic. But what does a thirty-year-old conspiracy have to do with Sean and Rachel being murdered?'

'Because Nathan's been hunting the children of the people responsible,' Victoria replied. 'Systematic elimination of the next generation. Daniel Foster wasn't a suicide – Nathan pushed him over the edge using his knowledge of Daniel's psychological vulnerabilities. Sean and Rachel were killed by Nathan, who had intimate knowledge of their routines, their fears, their weaknesses. He stole items from Dirk and left him for dead in his lockup in Kingston.'

She paused, letting the implication sink in.

'Nathan's been planning this for years. He had access to all of us, understood our group dynamics, could manipulate us into trusting him even as his mental state deteriorated.'

The accusation hung in the air like smoke. Each member of the group looked towards the windows, as if expecting Nathan to appear at any moment.

'Why?' Gary spoke now. 'His father made the most, so why does he want this revenge?'

'He doesn't want revenge.' Victoria shook her head. 'He wants to clean up all loose ends.'

'You think Nathan's coming for us,' Belinda whispered.

'I know he is,' Victoria replied. 'And I think we all know I'm right. The killer had to be someone with access to all of us, someone who knew our routines, our vulnerabilities. Someone who's been unstable for years.'

She paused, letting the implication settle.

'Nathan's been deteriorating since Daniel's death. His medication compliance has been erratic, his paranoia increasing. The gun – Dirk's *father's* gun – they found in his apartment, the bodycam footage, it all points to someone who's lost touch with reality. But is he working alone?'

Gary leant back in his chair, working through the evidence.

'The cards were from our special anniversary deck. Only twelve sets were ever made.'

'Exactly. Nathan had his own set, and access to ours through the game. He's been using our own tradition against us.'

The silence was deafening, and the rebuilt floor beneath them seemed to creak with the weight of secrets.

Oliver cleared his throat.

'If that's true, shouldn't we call the police? This is too dangerous for us to handle alone.'

'I've already been working with them,' Victoria replied. 'DCI Walsh and his team know about the Garden Collective connections. But they need proof, evidence that will stand up in court. That's why we're here – to force the killer into making a mistake.'

'You're using us as bait,' Alex said, his tech entrepreneur's mind grasping the strategy immediately.

'I'm giving Nathan a chance to confess,' Victoria corrected. 'To explain why years of guilt and mental deterioration culminated in murdering his friends. To tell us if anyone here has been helping him. That's why we're here – in the place where it all started, where his father's greed began this cycle of violence.'

'I can't buy this,' Gary shook his head, pacing now. 'We've known Nathan for over twenty years.'

'Gary, you never know truly—'

'And what about you, Victoria?' Gary snapped back, cutting her off. 'You've not mentioned any connection here. Why are you involved? What did your parents do that night?'

The wind through the broken windows seemed to grow stronger, carrying with it the distant sounds of London traffic and the Thames, and the upper floor felt isolated from the world.

Victoria stood, moving to the windows that looked out over the Thames.

'I don't have a connection,' she muttered. 'I'm here by sheer dumb luck. Nathan's guilt about his father's role in the conspiracy has pushed him over the edge. He's been planning this systematically, using our routines and vulnerabilities to pick us off one by one.'

Oliver shifted in his chair, his concerned expression deepening.

'Victoria, this is terrifying, but we can't just sit here and wait for something to happen. If one of us is dangerous—'

'Then we need to be very careful about what we do next,' Victoria finished. 'Because the killer is getting desperate. Nathan's disappearance has disrupted their timeline, forced them to accelerate their plans. If anyone else here dies, then we need to make sure we're all on the same page, that Nathan's the killer—'

The sound of footsteps on the ground floor made everyone freeze. Heavy boots, moving through the building below. Victoria held up a hand for silence, listening intently.

'Police?' Gary whispered.

Victoria shook her head, but her expression had changed – concern replacing her professional composure. The footsteps were wrong, too deliberate, too focused. The sound of someone climbing the stairs echoed through the building, each step deliberate and measured. The group instinctively drew closer together, united by fear and shared history.

'Whatever happens,' Victoria said quietly, 'remember that we've known each other for twenty years. We've been through everything together. Don't let suspicion destroy what we've built.'

The footsteps reached the top of the stairs and a shadow appeared in the doorway, backlit by the failing daylight from the stairwell. For a moment, the figure was unidentifiable, a dark silhouette against the grey afternoon.

Then Nathan Hargreaves stepped into the room, and the collective intake of breath echoed off the concrete walls.

He looked terrible – clothes torn and filthy, hair matted against his skull, eyes wild with the particular desperation of a hunted animal. But more terrifying than his appearance was what he held in his right hand, as the Glock pistol caught the light from the windows.

'Did you really think I wouldn't find you?' Nathan's voice was hoarse, cracked with exhaustion and something that might have been madness. 'Did you think you could hide from me in the place where it all started? Which one of you is sending me texts as Daniel? Because it was "Daniel" who told me to come here.'

Victoria stepped forward, hands raised in a calming gesture.

'Nathan, you're not well. Daniel's dead. You need help—'

'Help?' Nathan's laugh was sharp, brittle. 'Like the help

you've been giving me for years? The medication that's been keeping me compliant, confused, dependent on your professional guidance?'

He moved into the room properly now, and the others could see the full extent of his deterioration. But beneath the surface of chaos, there was something else – a clarity.

'I know what you've all done,' Nathan continued, his voice gaining strength as he spoke. 'I know about the Garden Collective, about the Bell Foundry collapse, about how our families profited from murder.'

'Nathan, please,' Belinda whispered. 'You're scaring us.'

'Good!' Nathan snapped. 'You should be scared! Do you know where you are? This exact floor collapsed thirty years ago. Right here, where you're sitting so comfortably, three people died because of greed and conspiracy.'

He gestured wildly with the gun, and several people flinched.

'No. *Four*. Linda Gardner was one of them. A young woman who tried to save lives and died for it. Her blood is literally in the foundations of this place.'

Oliver had gone still, his concerned expression frozen in place.

'She had a child,' Nathan continued, his ranting taking on a more focused intensity. 'A baby boy who grew up never knowing his mother was on an internal-injuries countdown, all because she was trying to prevent a massacre. Never knowing that the people responsible went on to get rich and powerful whilst his family was destroyed.'

'Nathan—' Oliver started to speak, but Nathan cut him off.

'Shut up!' The gun swung towards Oliver, and the young man pressed back into his chair. 'You don't get to speak.

None of you get to speak until you understand what you've done.'

Nathan began pacing, his movements erratic but purposeful, like a lecturer delivering a mad sermon.

'For twenty years, we've been playing our little game. Water pistols and playing cards, hunting each other like it was all just innocent fun. But it was never innocent, was it? It was training. Preparation. Learning each other's weaknesses, mapping each other's lives, building the perfect foundation for revenge.'

Victoria tried again to reach him.

'Nathan, your medication—'

'My medication was keeping me docile!' Nathan screamed, spittle flying from his lips. 'You've been controlling me for years, feeding me chemicals that enhanced my symptoms whilst making me depend on you for guidance. But I'm not taking them any more, and I can see clearly now.'

He turned his attention to Oliver, who was sitting unnaturally still.

'Do you know what the worst part is?' Nathan asked, his voice dropping to a whisper that was somehow more terrifying than his screaming. 'The worst part is that I trusted you. I brought you into our group. I vouched for you at work. I gave you access to everything you needed to destroy us all.'

Oliver's mask of concern was beginning to crack, something colder showing underneath.

'I don't know what you mean,' Oliver said carefully.

'Don't you?' Nathan laughed again, the sound echoing off the concrete walls. 'Oliver Drake. Such an unimportant name for someone who needed to hide his real identity. But I know who you really are.'

The room had gone completely silent except for the

sound of wind and Nathan's laboured breathing. Victoria had given up trying to stop it, and was now watching the exchange with professional fascination, as if observing a psychological experiment in progress.

'Your mother was injured in this building,' Nathan continued, his voice gaining certainty and power. 'Linda Gardner. She was trying to evacuate people when the floor collapsed. She died two years later from injuries she sustained right here, right where we're sitting.'

Oliver's expression had changed completely now. The concerned, helpful expression was dissolving, replaced by something cold and calculating and filled with thirty years of rage.

'Don't,' Oliver whispered. 'Don't you dare speak her name.'

'*Linda Gardner!*' Nathan shouted, the gun now pointed directly at Oliver's chest. 'Your mother! The woman who died because of their parents' greed and conspiracy!'

Oliver stood slowly, his movements controlled and deliberate. The helpful, nervous young man was gone, replaced by someone who looked capable of calculated violence.

'She wasn't just trying to evacuate people,' Oliver said, his voice steady despite the gun pointed at him. 'She knew exactly what was going to happen. She'd discovered the sabotage, tried to warn everyone, but they wouldn't listen. They were too busy on their various crusades to care about collateral damage. She was trying to get help.'

The admission hung in the air like a confession. Victoria watched the exchange with the slightest of smiles, her plan coming together exactly as she'd orchestrated.

Nathan was trembling now, whether from exhaustion, medication withdrawal, or the weight of revelation. 'You killed them. Sean and Dirk. You've been systematically murdering our friends.'

Nathan's finger tightened on the trigger. Oliver tensed, preparing to move. Victoria opened her mouth to say something that might prevent bloodshed.

And then, cutting through the tension like a blade, came the sound of slow, measured footsteps on the stairs. Not the hurried steps of police or the desperate flight of another fugitive, but the calm, deliberate pace of someone who was exactly where they intended to be.

The footsteps reached the top of the stairs and paused. In the doorway, backlit by the grey afternoon light, appeared the silhouette of someone new.

He surveyed the scene – the terrified survivors, Nathan with his gun, Oliver's revealed malevolence, Victoria's eager expression – and smiled.

'Right then,' Declan said calmly, his voice cutting through the chaos like authority made manifest. 'I think it's time we ended this properly.'

22

DENOUEMENT

Declan Walsh stepped through the doorway and surveyed the chaos before him. Nathan with a gun, Oliver finally showing his true colours, Victoria's mask slipping, and seven terrified people who'd just realised their twenty-year friendship had been a lie.

Nathan's Glock was shaking badly, his whole body trembling with exhaustion and pharmaceutical withdrawal.

'DCI Walsh... it's not what it looks like – these bastards have been – I can't think straight any more—'

'I know,' Declan said simply. 'But let's start with the murders first, eh? Three dead bodies tend to focus the mind.'

He moved into the room, hands buried in his coat pockets, as casual as if he were discussing the evening news rather than multiple homicides. The remaining Royal Court members pressed themselves against the walls, suddenly aware they were witnesses to something far beyond their comprehension.

'Three deaths in three days,' Declan continued, his gaze

settling on Oliver. 'Dirk VanMeerten, Sean Acker, Rachel Peterson. All killed by people they trusted implicitly.'

'Yes,' Oliver replied, pointing at Nathan. 'Him!'

Declan paused, turned and faced Oliver, and cocked his head.

'I think the time for false witness has passed,' he said. 'No more lies.'

'He had Sean's bodycam in his safe!' Oliver argued, looking around. 'Did you watch it? Did you see Nathan on it?'

'Interesting thing about bodycams,' Declan ignored the question. 'Did you know there were two bought? Dirk got one at the same time. But it wasn't found on him. Know why?'

Oliver had dropped his helpful newcomer act entirely. The nervous energy was gone, replaced by cold calculation and steady nerves.

'No.'

'Because he wasn't wearing it for the game,' Declan replied. 'He wanted it for his own safety. Kingston police found it an hour or so ago in his lockup in Kingston, angled like a security camera. Man never wore it, but he used it. From what they could see, it'd been recording for days, left alone.'

He waited for the implication to set in.

'Can you imagine what we'll find once we go through the SD card?'

Declan knew Oliver didn't have to imagine – the chances were it'd show, in HD quality, the death of Dirk VanMeerten.

'We also have the original, unedited cam footage of Sean's death, and CCTV of the cash top-up of the burner credit card that paid for the silencer used in the murder,' Declan added. 'Not looking good, I'll be honest.'

Sighing, Oliver straightened, stretching out his back, as if awaking from a long sleep.

'You want the truth?'

'It'd be nice.'

Oliver chuckled at this.

'Are you sure?' he mocked. 'Truth? It's like poetry. And most people, when they hear it? *Really* hate poetry.'

Declan didn't reply, simply waiting. After a moment, Oliver gave a loud theatrical sigh and continued.

'Dirk was getting too close to the truth,' he said simply, to a gasp across the room from Belinda.

'Which truth would that be?'

'He'd found his father's testimony from the Garden Collective trials. Realised George VanMeerten had committed perjury, lied under oath to protect certain people. Dirk wouldn't let sleeping dogs lie, especially when the conspiracy nut found he was part of one.'

Nathan swung the gun towards Oliver now.

'Dirk was my friend! He was just trying to help figure out what our bloody parents did!'

'That's exactly why he had to die,' Oliver said with chilling matter-of-factness. 'I'd spent months helping with his research, gaining his complete trust. We'd go through documents together, and I was feeding everything back to Victoria—'

'Now wait a moment—' Victoria started but stopped as Oliver held up a hand to pause her.

'Give up, it's over,' he said, turning his attention back to Declan. 'When I suggested examining his father's army items, he was eager to show me.'

'Including the service revolver Glock you later used to kill Sean, which Nathan here now has,' Declan observed.

'Yeah, the one you don't seem to be worried about!' Daryl shouted.

'Why should I?' Declan shrugged. 'I haven't hurt Nathan. I'm not someone who screwed him over. I'm fine.'

He looked back at Oliver.

'But Dirk himself – that was a knife, wasn't it?'

'Yes. Quieter in the storage unit. Quick, clean, professional. I didn't have the silencer on me; I'd left it at work after I signed for it. Dirk never saw it coming.'

Gary Webb, pressed against the far wall, found his voice.

'You sick bastard. He thought you were his friend.'

Oliver's expression didn't change.

'Friendship was never part of the plan here. I had a job to do.'

'Which brings us to Sean,' Declan said, keeping the interrogation moving forward. 'Same night, completely different approach. Poor Sean seemed to have a massive victim attitude, but this time his paranoia of the world being against him was entirely justified.'

'Sean was more complicated,' Oliver admitted, shifting slightly but keeping his attention on Nathan's wavering gun. 'He'd been working with Dirk, the two of them feeding off each other's conspiracy theories. That bloody bodycam of his, set up to record his hunts like some kind of military operation. If he'd captured evidence of what was really happening ...'

'So, you used the game against him,' Declan said. 'Twenty years of trust, twenty years of following the same rules. Until you confronted and killed him.'

There was a moment of silence, and Declan could visibly see Oliver pivoting with the new information.

'Sean was paranoid about the game,' Oliver eventually said. 'He'd spotted someone following him, thought it was part of the hunt. When he saw me in that alley, he lowered his guard – recognised me as another player.'

Nathan's whole body was trembling now, whether from rage or the pharmaceutical fog lifting from his brain.

'You murdered him! He was just trying to play the bloody game!'

'He died exactly as he lived,' Oliver said coldly. 'Following rules someone else had made, trusting people who were manipulating him, never questioning why things worked the way they did. Just like the soldier he *never was*.'

'The King of Spades pinned to his chest with a metal spike,' Declan added. 'Made from those Victorian finials you melted down. Rather poetic.'

'I used metal from the original building,' Oliver smiled. 'Stole them from Dirk a couple of weeks earlier. It seemed appropriate at the time.'

'And then you used advanced facial recognition software to superimpose Nathan's face over yours in the bodycam footage. Make it look like Nathan was the killer.'

'That was Victoria's suggestion. She said we needed Nathan to look guilty when the time came to wrap everything up. She also suggested using a burner card in his name.'

Victoria went to respond but seemed to think better of it.

'Which brings us to Rachel,' Declan said, his attention shifting to Victoria. 'Different killer entirely, different motive altogether. She worked in pharmaceuticals – wanted to offer a new drug to help Nathan, but you needed to keep him on your regimen.'

Victoria said nothing now.

'She'd started asking questions about Nathan's medication,' Declan explained to the room. 'Recognising patterns that suggested systematic chemical manipulation rather than legitimate psychiatric treatment. Rachel worked with drug interactions every day – she knew what deliberate dependency looked like.'

Nathan stared between them with growing horror.

'You – both of you – working together to murder us—'

'I had to act quickly with Rachel,' Victoria continued, her clinical detachment at odds with the chaos surrounding them. 'A knife was quieter than a gun in that office stairwell, less likely to attract immediate attention from security or other tenants. But I still needed to maintain the pattern Oliver had established.'

'Using your own Queen of Clubs card,' Declan noted. 'The one piece of physical evidence that could tie you directly to the murders. Rachel's card was original, aged, from your personal anniversary set. Oliver's replicas for Sean and Dirk were perfect forgeries, but Rachel was eliminated in panic before proper preparation could be completed.'

'It was a calculated risk,' Victoria admitted.

'Not exactly,' Declan replied. 'Though it confirmed what we suspected about you both working together.'

Christopher Wilson, who'd been silent throughout the revelations, finally spoke up.

'You're both completely barking mad! Murdering people over something that happened decades ago!'

'That's where you're wrong,' Declan said, his tone shifting to something more serious. 'This isn't about something that happened decades ago. This is about something that's been happening your entire adult lives. A conspiracy that shaped every major decision you've made since you first met each other at Oxford.'

Oliver's jaw tightened.

'My mother tried to save lives. She knew the building had been sabotaged, tried to evacuate everyone before the floor gave way. She spent two years dying slowly because of what happened in this room.'

'She did die because of what happened here,' Declan agreed. 'But not for the reasons you've spent three decades believing. You see, the Garden Collective wasn't infiltrated by government informants – it was infiltrated and influenced by *one* from the very beginning.'

Nathan's gun wavered as confusion replaced rage.

'What the bloody hell are you on about?'

'Emmy Clarke,' Declan said simply. 'I know her as Burlington Bertie. The harmless old woman with dementia who's been living in a homeless shelter, telling stories about the good old days.'

Victoria glared at him as he continued.

'Spoke to an MP named Norman Shipman tonight, the man who sent Emmy into the Collective. Not Patrick Walsh, as people thought. My father was on the side, doing his own thing, but Shipman was the architect,' Declan explained patiently. 'But what he didn't tell anyone was that Emmy had been diagnosed in her early thirties with Frontotemporal Dementia – specifically the behavioural variant. Not bipolar disorder, as she was initially misdiagnosed by doctors who didn't understand the condition, but actual progressive brain damage affecting her frontal and temporal lobes.'

Victoria had stopped, her psychological training understanding the implications before anyone else.

'The frontal and temporal lobes control decision-making, empathy, social inhibition,' Declan continued. 'When they're damaged by this particular type of dementia, especially at such an early stage, people become impulsive, manipulative, capable of extraordinary deception whilst appearing completely normal to casual observers. Emmy's condition made her the perfect undercover operative, so Shipman kept her in, unaware of the ticking time bomb he created.'

'But that means she was never really stable,' Gary said, his legal mind working through the implications.

'It means Emmy Clarke was the most dangerous person in the entire Garden Collective operation,' Declan said bluntly. 'When Elizabeth Gardner's daughter Linda started asking inconvenient questions about the protest here, Emmy saw an opportunity to solve multiple problems simultaneously.'

Oliver's face had gone pale.

'What are you saying exactly?'

'Emmy convinced Elizabeth Gardner that the only way to save the Garden Collective's reputation was to create martyrs for the cause,' Declan said, his words falling into the silence like stones into still water. 'Frame the property developers by making it appear they were willing to kill protesters to protect their investments. Elizabeth trusted Emmy completely – she'd become like an older sister to Linda, offering the guidance and stability that Elizabeth's own chaotic activist lifestyle couldn't provide.'

'No,' Oliver whispered.

'Linda discovered the sabotage the night of the collapse,' Declan continued relentlessly. 'She tried to evacuate everyone, tried to stop what was about to happen. But Emmy had planned too thoroughly, prepared too carefully. I'm not too sure of the full details, but I'd guess she stopped Linda somehow, and the supports gave way whilst Linda was still inside, trying to save lives that Emmy had deliberately put at risk for her own purposes.'

Declan's voice carried genuine sympathy, but his words remained unyielding.

'Your mother gained mortal injuries and eventually died trying to prevent what Emmy Clarke had orchestrated. For thirty years, since birth, even your father's been feeding you his believed truth – lies given by Emmy, his partner's "sister". Because of this, you've been planning revenge against the families who profited from the aftermath, never realising that the person truly responsible was the one who'd been guiding your quest for justice from the very beginning.'

The silence stretched like a wire under tension. When Oliver finally spoke, his voice was hollow, broken.

'Victoria. Did she tell you this? Did you know?'

Victoria's carefully constructed mask finally shattered completely.

'Oliver, you don't understand the complexity of the situation—'

'You knew!' Oliver's voice rose to a scream that echoed off the concrete walls. 'You knew your mother killed mine, and you used me to murder innocent people! You gave me the water from under this same bloody building to soak them with! You turned me into a weapon against the very families your *own mother* destroyed!'

'It's not just you, Oliver – you've all been part of a thirty-year psychological experiment,' Declan said, his voice cutting through Oliver's rage. 'Victoria's been in contact with Emmy since childhood, despite my father's belief that he was protecting them both by keeping them separated. Emmy's condition made her paranoid about official channels, so she developed alternative methods of communication.'

He gestured to encompass the remaining Royal Court members.

'The university placements weren't coincidental. The scholarships that brought you all together, the social connections that seemed so natural, even the formation of your precious game – all of it was orchestrated by Victoria under Emmy's long-term guidance, using Shipman to grease the wheels.'

'Over twenty years of profiling,' Alex Chen said, his voice barely above a whisper.

'A complete psychological experiment with twelve unwitting test subjects,' Declan confirmed. 'Victoria needed detailed profiles of each of you – your vulnerabilities, your pressure points, your breaking thresholds. The forfeit system wasn't about making the game more engaging for adults – it was about gathering operational intelligence once she started her endgame. Maybe to find ways to destroy your careers, but then brought forward by Oliver's arrival, fear of being found out, and the fact this was the last ever game.'

'But why now?' Diane now spoke.

'Everything had to be perfect,' Victoria said, her voice taking on the desperate edge of someone watching decades of careful planning collapse in real time. 'The evidence trails, the digital manipulation, the psychological conditioning. Nathan was the ideal scapegoat – someone with documented mental health vulnerabilities who could be chemically controlled and positioned to take responsibility when the operation reached its predetermined conclusion.'

He nodded downwards, as if looking through the floor.

'So you know, that conclusion was a ton of construction

explosive attached to the base supports. The plan was likely to claim she was going to "get the police", with Oliver going with her for support... and then remote control detonate once far enough away.'

He looked at Oliver now.

'We had the bomb squad remove the detonator,' he continued calmly. 'No boom tonight. But I wonder whose fingerprints will be found on it? Yours? Victoria's? Or Nathan?'

Nathan's face twisted with rage and betrayal.

'All those bloody drugs! All those sessions where you systematically undermined my confidence, made me doubt everything I remembered!'

He looked around the room.

'I was stressed on Tuesday,' he explained. 'More than usual. Singapore markets, other issues, I asked Vickie for advice. She said she had a nootropic I could take, hush-hush shit that would fix things, but I had to sneak out to get it. Of course, it was the same time as Oliver killed Dirk and Sean. Of course it made me a suspect. I needed a friend, and she needed a scapegoat. Then the following day, she had me meet her but never turned up. At the very same time Rachel died.'

'You were becoming inconveniently stable,' Victoria replied with clinical detachment. 'Your natural recovery from Daniel's death threatened the operational timeline. Chemical management was necessary to maintain your usefulness whilst preventing unwanted clarity about what was really happening.'

'But Daniel's death wasn't suicide, was it?' Declan said quietly. 'You manipulated him into killing himself because he was getting too close to the truth about the family connections.'

'Daniel was investigating the same historical patterns that eventually consumed Dirk,' Victoria admitted. 'His legal background gave him access to sealed records, and he was piecing together the actual relationships between our families and the Garden Collective case. I used his psychological vulnerabilities against him – his fear of exposure, his career anxieties, his relationship with Nathan.'

'You pushed him over the edge,' Nathan said, his voice cracking.

'I provided the psychological pressure necessary to achieve the desired outcome,' Victoria corrected with chilling professionalism.

'The irony,' Declan said, 'is that Emmy's dementia made her forget about you, didn't she? She started talking to us, describing the strange man and woman who'd been visiting her, asking about 1992. She thought she was reporting suspicious activity – she was actually describing you two. Emmy brought us into this case herself, not realising she was exposing her own daughter's plans – plans *she herself* had brought into action.'

Oliver's control finally snapped. With a howl of rage, he lunged at Nathan, grappling for the gun and snatching the weapon, pointing it directly at Victoria's chest.

'Oliver, don't!' Declan shouted.

Suddenly, the stairwell echoed with heavy footsteps – and Monroe's distinctive Scottish voice calling out orders – as they approached.

'Thirty bloody years!' Oliver screamed at Victoria; the gun pointed directly at her chest. 'All my life I've been planning this revenge, and you *knew*! You *knew* it was all built on lies!'

'At least you had your father! I spent my life believing he was my brother!' Victoria shouted back – throwing an accusatory finger at Declan. 'That I was a secret daughter, an embarrassment, always listening to my mother, always staying away so I didn't cause a scene and rock the boat! Only when Patrick Walsh died and I demanded to attend the funeral did she tell me the truth – I resulted from some random hookup she never knew the name of!'

Oliver stared at Victoria.

Victoria stared at Oliver.

The sound of footsteps came closer.

Tears streaming down his face, Oliver shook his head and squeezed the trigger.

Pfft.

Water sprayed across Victoria's face and chest, soaking her hair and expensive suit.

'Well now,' Monroe said, appearing in the doorway with Anjli behind him. 'I believe that technically qualifies as attempted murder. Bit damp for a proper execution, though.'

Oliver stared at the water pistol, laughing brokenly.

'Even this. Even this final moment was part of your manipulation.'

Nathan stepped forward, his entire demeanour shifting as the performance fell away.

'Actually, no,' he said. 'This part was *my* manipulation. Playing the part purely for you to think you were in control.'

He looked at Victoria who, surprisingly, started to chuckle gently – as if the realisation that all of this had been for nothing had become nothing more than some kind of cosmic joke.

'You know what the truly beautiful thing is? All those years you convinced me I was losing my mind. All those medication adjustments, all those therapy sessions where you systematically undermined my confidence in my own perceptions,' he gestured at the dripping weapon. 'But I wasn't going mad – I was getting better. When I finally figured out what you were doing, I had one advantage you didn't account for. Twenty years playing this ridiculous game. I know every rule, every tradition, every psychological manipulation you've used.'

Victoria's eyes widened with realisation.

'Never trust the person who's been controlling your mind,' Nathan finished. 'That's Sean's water pistol. The carbon fibre Glock replica he was oh, so proud of. I just used a black sharpie on the orange bit.'

As handcuffs clicked around Oliver's wrists and then Victoria's while a remote detonator was removed from Oliver's pocket, the surviving Royal Court members stood in stunned silence.

Twenty years of friendship, all revealed as an elaborate psychological experimentation.

'What happens to us now?' Belinda asked quietly.

Declan looked around the room – at Nathan, finally free from chemical manipulation, at Oliver broken by betrayal, at Victoria's sociopathy exposed, at friends trying to process decades of lies.

'Now the game ends,' he said simply. 'All of it. The lies, the manipulation, the thirty-year cycle of revenge built on fundamental misunderstandings. Emmy's dementia destroyed her own plans. Victoria's manipulation was undone by her mother's failing memory. Oliver's quest for revenge served his *true* enemy.'

As they led the prisoners away into the November night, Declan thought about games and their consequences. Some weren't meant to be played by ordinary people –the stakes were too high, the rules too complex, the price of losing too permanent.

But this one was finally over.

The rain had started again as they reached the street; London washing itself clean again.

EPILOGUE

Billy hadn't expected to be called to the Reform Club so quickly, but within days of his very public acceptance of his new role, his father, after going silent on the matter, had called him in.

And so, once more, Billy now stood in the Reform Club's reading room as his father, Edward Fitzwarren sat in the same leather armchair he had the previous time they met.

'William,' he said, sitting back in his chair and staring at his son. 'You're probably wondering why I called you here today.'

'Not particularly,' Billy replied. 'You have to remember, Father, I'm a detective. I can use my incredible detective brain to deduct what bullshit's happening today.'

Edward raised an eyebrow, as if surprised that his son would say such a thing. Billy glanced around the Reform Club, seeing the same tired faces watching, hoping for some kind of entertainment.

'You've decided that I'm not up to the task,' he went on. 'Probably realised you've made a mistake about abdicating the viscountcy. Do we call it viscountcy? I'm not sure. But you've reluctantly been forced to accept the role once more, rather than give it to your wayward, lackaday son. How am I doing so far?'

His father said nothing.

Billy shrugged, carrying on.

'You decided that whatever problems you had, the ones you thought I would fix for you that I *haven't* fixed, are not worth the loss you'll make if I actually called your bluff and took on the mantle of Viscount,' Billy looked around once more, noting the increased interest that had gathered in the conversation. 'I can't blame you, Dad. It's what I would've done if I needed somebody to clean up my shit. But that's the difference between us, isn't it?'

'And what would that be?' Edward Fitzwarren asked darkly.

'I don't need people to clean up my shit,' Billy muttered.

'Are you sure about that?' Edward rose from the chair now, facing his son. 'I heard about the affair with the Colombian consulate. I heard that you're now shacking up with some kind of art forger. You've always been a disappointment to me, William.'

'You know what, Father?' Billy had tired of the conversation now. 'If we're going to talk about people being unimpressed with others or disappointing others, you're top of my list. When I had Uncle Bryan arrested, it was because he broke the law in multiple places, and all you wanted to do was to have me turn a blind eye because he was one of us. He was never one of us. You were never one of us. And if you think that the two of you together were, then *I* was never one of us.'

'You know what, William, I think that's the first correct

thing you've said all day.' Edward returned to his seat, whatever confrontation he was going to have with his son decided against for the moment. 'It will be made public that I have decided against allowing you to take over. People will ask why. I won't say anything.'

'Oh, I'm sure you won't,' Billy interrupted, 'but I'm pretty bloody sure you'll hint strongly that I wasn't up to the task. Well, let me explain something to you, Father. The moment I see *anything* stating that I wasn't up to it, I will reply with everything that I've learned about your little scandal publicly in the press. You won't be able to prove it was me. I'm very good at hiding my tracks. And the fact I've told you in front of witnesses still won't stand, as you always told me, "What happens within these hallowed walls stays within these hallowed walls" – Chatham House rules and all that.'

He winked at an old man getting a little too close, smiling as he scuttled back to his seat.

'But know this, Father. I took down my uncle's Ponzi scheme when I was still just learning what I could do. The last few years, I've worked with Monroe and Temple Inn and I've moved forward in leaps and bounds. There aren't many people on this planet that are better than I am at my job. And the best bit about that, is one of the people who could make me look like an amateur without even trying? She's a friend. And trust me, Father. If you test me, insult me, go against me, stop me from seeing my family? I will call on *her* to do the things I cannot do.'

He took a breath, allowing the words to sink in as he stared at his father.

'And believe me, the things I *can* do would destroy you and my family. Do not think for one second I wouldn't do it.

You've made it very clear for the last three years that I am not a member of this family, so perhaps it's time for me to become just that.'

Billy nodded, his rant almost over.

'Say hi to Mum for me,' he said, and Edward stared, dumbfounded, as Billy turned and stiffly walked out of the Reform Club.

'Oh,' he shouted as he paused in the entranceway, 'and my membership here can go to hell as well. I wouldn't be a member of any club that would accept my father.'

IF TAMARA BANKS HAD EXPECTED ANJLI TO APPEAR AT HER Westminster office door unannounced, she managed to hide it well as her eyes widened.

'Miss Kapoor,' she said, forcing her voice into a semblance of calm. 'I don't believe we had an appointment today.'

'Sorry, Ma'am,' Craig said, leaning from behind Anjli. 'She didn't take no for an answer.'

'She never has done,' Tamara muttered, rising and walking around her desk, approaching Anjli so they could face each other more clearly. 'Have you come back to accept my offer?'

'Actually, I've come back to tell you no,' Anjli replied. 'I've had a think, solved a case – you know how it goes – and at the end I decided that it really isn't worth my time to bid on a horse that's not going to win.'

Tamara's eyes widened slightly at a comment she hadn't expected to hear.

'You don't think I'll beat Charles Baker?'

'I don't think it'll happen,' Anjli shrugged. 'Charles still has his friends in Parliament and... well, I don't think your star is as high-flying as you think it is.'

'You haven't been looking at my numbers,' Tamara replied.

'But that's the problem,' Anjli said. '*You've* been looking at your numbers. In fact, you've probably been staring at nothing more than your numbers all day long, when what you should've been looking at are other figures, other people's *reputations* – your father's, for example.'

At her father's mention, Tamara's eyes narrowed.

'Be very careful what you say, Detective Inspector.'

'Don't worry, I'm not here to say much,' Anjli said. 'We've just solved a case, you see – one that leads back to the Shadwell Bell Foundry disaster of 1992. You might have heard of it; your father definitely did. His name's on several documents I found, passed to us by Norman Shipman.'

She smiled.

'You know Norman – you've been on the same Star Chamber together for years now.'

Tamara said nothing, and Anjli could see from her eyes that she was quickly trying to work out what was going on here.

'My father and Norman Shipman worked on many things,' she said carefully. 'He placed his name on many items.'

'He placed his name on items that showed a conspiracy to cover up three deaths when the Bell Foundry's floor collapsed,' Anjli said. 'We have the documentation. It's come from beneath this very building. You know, the little basement room where you hide your dirty secrets. We have it all, Tamara.'

'Norman Shipman will—'

'Norman Shipman is currently writing his resignation letter, as we speak,' Anjli continued. 'We didn't get him when we solved the *Magpies* case, but this one *really* left him in a place where he couldn't get out. And because of that, your help, your mentor figure, is now gone. Your father's many sins while in office could appear at any time. And do you honestly think you can get past that?'

Tamara straightened her expression, turning to one of arrogance.

'Yes,' she said simply. 'I got past everything that was said about me – the *Daily Mail* gossip, the Nazi accusations, even my National Front membership. Why do you think something my *father* did is going to affect me?'

'Because it affected the public,' Anjli explained. 'A disaster where people died –where *protesters* died – well, it's just bad optics. And when the murder, and what happened there are revealed to everyone, and the lords and the high-powered donors that've been funding for all this time learn that Norman, who worked with your father, had been controlled by a mentally ill woman, doing her bidding to save his and likely Leonard Banks's jobs, causing at least twelve deaths over the years... well, it's not going to look good for you. Especially if it comes out at the same time you start your leadership bout.'

'You wouldn't dare,' Tamara whispered.

'Try me,' Anjli replied. 'I don't like you. I don't like what you think, and what you stand for. I don't like Charles Baker much, but he's the better of the two of you. So, listen closely.

If you ever step out of line, if you ever try to gain one up on me or my colleagues, this information will leak and your chances at high-level politics will die. And if you do go for the leadership, and if by some miracle you do win, be aware that you'll be a Prime Minister who's owned by me. Because again, the moment this comes out and you're in Number Ten, you're writing your "I want to spend more time at home with my family" speech within an hour.'

'Bullshit,' Tamara shook her head. 'You don't have that power.'

'Ask Michelle Rose that,' Anjli smiled. 'And remember how long she lasted as Prime Minister when she went against us.'

She looked back at Craig.

'I don't expect to see you interrupting my dinners any more. In fact, I don't expect to see either of you unless we're working together.'

She smiled as she looked back at Tamara.

'So, continue making your fur coat out of Dalmatians or whatever it is you're doing right now. And forget about me becoming your pet detective. In fact, forget about anybody becoming your pet detective. Because if you play this shit anywhere else? Well, you already know what I'm going to do. I don't need to belabour the point. Do we understand each other?'

'Oh, we understand each other very well,' Tamara said coldly.

'Good,' Anjli nodded. 'Oh, and if you think about doing something off the books, remember that I'm friends with Johnny Lucas, and he wrote the *book* on how to work off the books. This isn't checkmate, Tamara. We're still giving you a chance to do what you want to do but be aware that we will not be your patsies. Good luck in your leadership battle.'

Her point made and her message passed, Anjli Kapoor turned and left the offices of Westminster.

SHE DIDN'T LEAVE FULLY, HOWEVER, PAUSING IN THE GREAT Hall, waiting ten more minutes until Declan appeared.

His face was emotionless, but she knew that he'd gone through a similar conversation with Norman Shipman.

'How did it go?' she asked.

'He's writing his resignation letter,' he said. 'But before that, he's using his position as the de facto head of the Star Chamber to remove Tamara Banks. They'll put somebody else in.'

'Do you know who?'

Declan shrugged.

'Probably Jennifer bloody Farnsworth-Ewing,' he said. 'But again, it's somebody we can control, so I'm okay with that. As long as Tamara Banks loses her power, that's all I care about.'

'You know, this will just make Charles Baker even more convinced that you're his buddy,' Anjli smiled.

'Yeah, well,' Declan said, 'it'll give more budget to Shaun and his outreach programme, so I can live with that for a while.'

'How does that work?' Anjli asked. 'Baker's not gonna think Donnal helped him.'

'He will when I explain that it was through Shaun that his prime ministership was saved,' Declan said. 'Which in a way is quite ironic, considering how much they hate each other.'

He looked at his watch.

'Talking of which, I need to see Burlington Bertie. Do you want to come with me?'

'Are you sure you want to do this?'

Declan nodded.

'Shaun contacted me this morning, said she's deteriorating quickly. I think this might be the last chance I ever get.'

Anjli nodded, patting Declan on the arm.

'I'm going back to the office,' she said. 'See how Billy's doing. I think he spoke to his father today.'

'Seems to be a day for hard conversations,' Declan replied, giving a small smile. 'Let's hope it's the only day we have that.'

It was late in the day by the time Declan reached St Benedict's, probably for the last time. Entering through the main entrance, he saw Shaun Donnal standing nervously beside the day room.

'Everything okay?' he asked.

In response, Shaun shook his head.

'She's getting worse,' he said, inviting Declan to follow him. Instead of walking out into the garden or even into the dayroom, this time they walked towards the bedrooms where, at the third door on the left, Declan entered to see Burlington Bertie.

Bertie – or rather Emmy Clark – was in bed, sitting up. No longer was she wearing the tweed suit or tie. No longer did she look like a little woman dressing like a man.

Now she wore pyjamas and a dressing gown, playing cards on a table that was positioned over the bed.

She looked up as she saw him enter.

'Hello,' she said, a voice calm and pleasant and completely devoid of any recognition of Declan. 'Have you come to play cards?'

Declan glanced at Shaun, who shrugged and stepped back through the doorway.

'I'll leave you two alone for a while,' he said.

Declan walked over slowly and sat down in the chair beside the bed.

'I could play if you wanted,' he said. 'It looks like you're playing solitaire, though.'

Emmy Clark – as this was very much Emmy rather than any form of Burlington Bertie – looked at him, smiled, and then frowned.

'You look familiar,' she said. 'Have we met?'

'We have,' Declan replied, and wondered whether he should explain the full details. But then, before he could speak, her eyes widened, and she dropped the cards, reaching across and hugging him tight.

'I knew you'd come back, Walsh,' she said. 'I knew it. You've got to get me out of here. They don't trust me.'

'What do you mean they don't trust you?' Declan pulled away as Emmy straightened.

'They know things,' she whispered. 'Things about us.'

'What do you mean "us"?' Declan asked, wondering now where this was going. They'd agreed not to prosecute Emmy for what she'd done over the years, mainly as she no longer remembered it, and would likely deteriorate completely before any court case, but this felt like Emmy was trying to escape.

Emmy glanced around and Declan wondered if Burlington Bertie was returning after all.

'They want to take Victoria from me,' she said. 'Shipman, the MP. He says he'll keep her safe. You'll do that, won't you? You'll keep her safe, Paddy?'

At the name, Declan felt a sliver of ice slide down his spine.

She's not talking to me. She's talking to my father.

'Of course I will, Emmy,' he said softly. 'I always promised you I would, didn't I?'

Emmy looked away, staring back at the door.

'You've got a son, haven't you?'

'Yes,' Declan said.

'He around the same age?'

'A couple of years older.'

Emmy was nodding.

'Maybe you could take Victoria in. Declan could have a sister.'

'I don't think that's a good idea, do you?'

'No, probably not,' Emmy said, looking back at the cards. 'My little Queen of Clubs. You'll find her somewhere, though, right? Somewhere good, with people who love her?'

'Of course I will,' Declan said gently, resisting the urge to scream at this small frail woman – who'd caused so much pain, death and misery, and yet would remember none of it. 'You don't need to worry about her any more.'

Emmy looked up at Declan, staring deep into his eyes.

'You know I've loved you,' she said, 'ever since I met you. I'm sorry that she's not yours.'

Declan felt a shiver. This conversation wasn't going the way he wanted, and now he started to think that Emmy's earlier conversation, when she was still Burlington Bertie – where she'd said that she *hadn't* slept with his father – might have been a simple fallacy to give Declan peace of mind.

'You don't need to think about that,' Declan said, and wondered if he was saying this more to himself than to the frail old woman in front of him.

Emmy nodded, as if accepting the order.

'I killed them, didn't I?' she said, the subject suddenly taking a dark turn. 'When they all fell, that was me.'

'No, no,' Declan said, patting her shoulder. 'It was an accident. It wasn't your fault...'

He paused.

No.

'Actually, Emmy, it *was* you,' he said. 'You won't remember this in a minute, I'm sure, but know that your actions led to all of this. You did kill them. And you spent decades getting Whitehall to hide it, working to your whim like a mad puppeteer. And you'll never be sentenced or charged with anything. But I wasn't going to let you forget, even if it's for one moment.'

Emmy stared at Declan, her eyes wide and tear-filled, and then nodded, swallowing hard as she picked up her cards and dealt again...

then paused on the third card, looking back at Declan.

'Oh, hello,' she said. 'I didn't see you there. Have you come to play cards?'

'No, Emmy,' Declan said, rising. 'Just wanted to check in on you one last time.'

'Oh, that's nice.' Emmy smiled. 'Do you work for St Benedict's? Or do you have somebody here?'

Declan said nothing, forcing himself to smile, patting Emmy on the hand and walking away.

As he reached the door, he looked back and Emmy, forgetting he was even in the room, was playing cards once more.

He glanced across the corridor at Shaun, who nodded.

'You're not to blame for any sins your father gained,' he said. 'Believe me, the sins of our past do not make us – and I'm speaking from experience.'

'Just keep me updated, yeah?' Declan replied, and with that, he turned and walked out of St Benedict's, climbing into his Audi and driving back to Temple Inn.

As he did so, he dialled a number, the speaker on the car now beeping with the phone's ring.

'Dad?' the voice of Jess Walsh answered. 'You're okay?'

'Sure,' he said. 'Why wouldn't I be?'

'Because you're phoning me in the middle of a weekday,' Jess replied. 'Is there a case? Do you need my help?'

'No,' Declan smiled as he drove down the roads back to Central London. 'I just wanted to check in on you – make sure you were doing okay. You know... parent stuff.'

THE CALL HAD COME AS A SURPRISE TO MONROE.

It had been very cloak and dagger in how Ellie Reckless had spoken, with Monroe asked not to bring anyone else; an urgent discussion connected to Johnny Lucas and Monroe's past.

There were too many parts of the conversation that raised alarm bells in Monroe's mind, but at the same time, Ellie Reckless was his onetime protégé, now apparently some kind of arbitrator for London gangs, and had helped him as many times as he had helped her over the years.

There was also a name that had come up in the conversation.

Danny Martin.

Monroe wasn't sure why he'd been mentioned; after all, the last time Monroe even spoke to him, it had been after Moses Delcourt's badly timed attempt to take over North London.

But Ellie sounded urgent, and that was enough for Monroe to go.

She met him down a side road beside St Bride Church, a likely midpoint between Temple Inn and her swanky Farringdon offices. However, as he approached, Monroe saw she was stepping from foot to foot, nervous, something he hadn't seen before.

'Are you okay?' he asked.

Ellie looked up at him.

'Alex,' she murmured, 'I'm sorry.'

I'm sorry.

Two words with so much meaning behind them.

As Monroe went to ask what she was sorry about, he suddenly realised that Ellie's hand, which had been in her pocket as he arrived, now came out holding what looked to be an automatic pistol.

'Lassie, this had better be a bloody game you're playing here.'

Once more, Ellie Reckless looked apologetic.

'I'm afraid I have to do this,' she whispered. 'If I don't, Tinker's going down for murder.'

And with that, she waved the gun towards a car waiting – a black BMW with tinted windows. In it sat a man whose face he didn't recognise.

'If you go down this route ...' he started.

'Alex, I've been walking this route for a very long time,' Ellie replied. 'And unfortunately, my debts now must be paid.'

Without another word, Monroe climbed into the black BMW. Ellie Reckless, gun still trained on him, sat beside him, and the car drove off into the London evening.

Want to know what happens to Monroe? Then check out TAKE THE KING, the sixth Ellie Reckless book, out in September!

Want the next Declan Walsh novel? CLICK HERE, or turn the page...

DCI Walsh and the team of the *Last Chance Saloon* will return in their next thriller

HIS DEAD MAN'S HAND

Order Now at Amazon:

www.mybook.to/hisdeadmanshand

ABOUT THE AUTHOR

Jack Gatland is the pen name of *#1 New York Times Bestselling Author* Tony Lee, who has been writing in all media for thirty-five years, including comics, graphic novels, middle grade books, audio drama, TV and film for *DC Comics, Marvel, BBC, ITV, Random House, Penguin USA, Hachette* and a ton of other publishers and broadcasters.

These have included licences such as ***Doctor Who, Spider Man, X-Men, Star Trek, Battlestar Galactica, MacGyver,*** BBC's ***Doctors, Wallace and Gromit*** and ***Shrek***, as well as work created with musicians such as ***Ozzy Osbourne, Joe Satriani, Beartooth, Pantera, Megadeth, Iron Maiden*** and ***Bruce Dickinson.***

As Tony, he's toured the world talking to reluctant readers with his 'Change The Channel' school tours, and lectures on screenwriting, story craft and comic scripting for festivals and conferences such as *Raindance* in London and *Author Nation, The Global Publishing Summit* and *20Books* globally.

An introvert West Londoner by heart, he lives with his wife Tracy, just outside London.

Feel free to follow Jack / Tony on all his social media by clicking on the links below, to engage, discuss Declan and put the world to rights.

www.jackgatland.com
www.hoodemanmedia.com

Visit Jack and Tony's Reader's Group Page
(Mainly for fans to discuss his books):
https://www.facebook.com/groups/jackgatland

Subscribe to Jack's Readers List:
https://bit.ly/jackgatlandVIP

www.facebook.com/jackgatlandbooks
www.twitter.com/jackgatlandbook
ww.instagram.com/jackgatland

Want more books by Jack Gatland? Turn the page...

Printed in Dunstable, United Kingdom

66268257R00214